Dear Reader,

No matter how busy your day, there'll *always* be time for romance. TAKE 5 is a new way to indulge in love, passion and adventure—and still be on time to pick up the kids! Each TAKE 5 volume offers five condensed stories by top Harlequin and Silhouette authors. Now you can have the enjoyment and satisfaction of a full-length novel, but in less time—perfect for those days when it's difficult to squeeze a longer read into your hectic schedule.

This volume of TAKE 5 features five love stories of suspense and adventure...five *riveting* escapes! *New York Times* bestselling author Linda Lael Miller entices with an enemies-to-lovers story in *Part of the Bargain*. Harlequin Intrigue bestselling author Rebecca York offers her trademark murder and mayhem in *Bayou Moon* and *Trial by Fire*. And *USA Today* bestselling author Jasmine Cresswell turns up the suspense in *Free Fall* and *Undercover*.

Why not indulge in all four volumes of TAKE 5 available now—tender romance, sizzling passion, riveting adventure and heartwarming family love? No matter what mood you're in, you'll have the perfect escape!

Happy reading,

Marsha Zinberg
Senior Editor and Editorial Coordinator, TAKE 5

D0957878

New York Times bestselling author **Linda Lael Miller** started writing at age ten and has made a name for herself in both contemporary and historical romance. Her bold and innovative style has made her a favorite among readers. Named by *Romantic Times* "The Most Outstanding Writer of Sensual Romance," Linda Lael Miller never disappoints.

Jasmine Cresswell is a multitalented author of over forty novels. Her efforts have gained her numerous awards, including the RWA's Golden Rose Award and the Colorado Author's League Award for the best original paperback novel. Born in Wales and educated in England, Jasmine met her husband while working at the British Embassy in Rio de Janerio. She has lived in Australia, Canada and six cities in the United States. Jasmine and her husband now make their home in Sarasota, Florida.

Rebecca York is the pseudonym of Ruth Glick and Eileen Buckholtz, who started Harlequin Intrigue's popular 43 LIGHT STREET series together. Recently, Ruth has been writing the series on her own as Rebecca York. Her book *Shattered Vows* was honored as Intrigue's 500th book. *Nowhere Man* was honored by *Romantic Times* as the Best Intrigue of 1998, and by *Affaire de Coeur* as Best Contemporary novel. Eileen Buckholtz is a master computer scientist and Internet consultant. Taking a break from writing fiction, she fulfilled a lifelong dream to work on Capitol Hill, published a bestselling business e-book and developed several popular worldwide community service Web sites.

TAKE 5

Quick Reads. Great Escapes.

NEW YORK TIMES
BESTSELLING AUTHOR

Linda Lael Miller

Jasmine Cresswell

Rebecca York

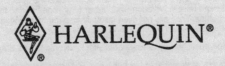

HARLEQUIN®

TORONTO • NEW YORK • LONDON
AMSTERDAM • PARIS • SYDNEY • HAMBURG
STOCKHOLM • ATHENS • TOKYO • MILAN • MADRID
PRAGUE • WARSAW • BUDAPEST • AUCKLAND

ISBN 0-373-83504-3

TAKE 5, VOLUME 8

Copyright © 2002 by Harlequin Books S.A.

The publisher acknowledges the copyright holders of the individual titles as follows:

PART OF THE BARGAIN
Copyright © 1985 by Linda Lael Miller

UNDERCOVER
Copyright © 1986 by Jasmine Cresswell

FREE FALL
Copyright © 1989 by Jasmine Cresswell

BAYOU MOON
Copyright © 1992 by Ruth Glick and Eileen Buckholtz

TRIAL BY FIRE
Copyright © 1992 by Ruth Glick and Eileen Buckholtz

Printed in U.S.A.

CONTENTS

PART OF THE BARGAIN

Linda Lael Miller

The landing gear made an unsettling *ka-thump* sound as it snapped back into place under the small private airplane. Libby Kincaid swallowed her misgivings and tried not to look at the stony, impassive face of the pilot. If he didn't say anything, she wouldn't have to say anything either, and they might get through the short flight to the Circle Bar B ranch without engaging in one of their world-class shouting matches.

It was a pity, Libby thought, that at the ages of thirty-one and thirty-three respectively, she and Jess still could not communicate on an adult level.

"New York was all right," she said, in the most noninflammatory tone she could manage. *Except that Jonathan died,* chided a tiny, ruthless voice in her mind. *Except for that nasty divorce from Aaron.* "Nothing to write home about," she added aloud, realizing her blunder too late.

"So," he said suddenly, gruffly, "New York wasn't all the two-hour TV movies make it out to be."

The mirrored sunglasses glinted in the sun as Jess Barlowe turned to look at Libby Kincaid. His powerful shoulders were taut beneath the blue cotton fabric of his workshirt.

"Leave Cathy and Stace alone, Libby," he warned with blunt savagery. "Their marriage has had problems lately, and if you make the situation worse, I'll see that you regret it."

Libby would have done almost anything to escape his scrutiny just then, short of thrusting open the door of that small four-passenger Cessna and jumping out, but her choices were undeniably limited. With a sigh, she faced the fact that there was every chance a lot of people would believe she had been involved with Jess's brother, Stacey Barlowe. There had, after all, been that exchange of letters, and Stace had even visited her a few times in New York, in the thick of her traumatic divorce, though in actuality he had been in the city on business. Although how anyone could believe she'd ever hurt Cathy in any way she didn't know.

To her relief and surprise, Jess turned his concentration on piloting the plane. The timbered land below began to give way to occasional patches of prairie-cattle country. Soon they would be landing on the small airstrip serving the prosperous 150,000-acre Circle Bar B, owned by Jess's father and overseen, for the most part, by Libby's.

Libby had grown up on the Circle Bar B, just as Jess had, and her mother, like his, was buried there. Even though she couldn't call the ranch home in the legal sense of the word, it was *still* home to her, and she had every right to go there—especially now, when she needed its beauty and peace and practical routines so desperately.

The wheels of the plane screeched and grabbed as they made contact with the asphalt. When the Cessna came to a full stop, Libby wrenched at her seat belt, anxious to put as much distance as possible between herself and Jess Barlowe. But his hand closed over her wrist in a steel-hard grasp. "Remember, Lib—these people aren't the sophisticated if-it-feels-good-do-it types you're used to. No games."

Hot color surged into Libby's face. "Let go of me, you bastard!" she breathed.

He flung Libby's wrist from his hand and turned away to push open the door on his side and leap nimbly to the ground.

Libby was still tugging impotently at the handle on her own door when her father strode over, climbed deftly onto the wing and opened it for her. She felt such a surge of love and relief that she flung herself into his arms, nearly sending both of them tumbling to the hard ground.

Once they were clear of the plane, Ken Kincaid held his daughter at arm's length and grinned. "Rough trip?"

Libby's throat tightened unaccountably. "You know that it's always rough going where Jess and I are concerned," she said.

Her father's brows lifted speculatively as Jess flung Libby's luggage into the back of the mud-speckled station wagon and sped away in it without so much as a curt nod or a halfhearted so-long.

Libby felt some of the tension drain from her as her father opened the door on the passenger side of his truck and helped her inside. Ken climbed behind the wheel and started the powerful engine. The truck was moving now, jolting and rattling over the rough ranch roads with a pleasantly familiar vigor.

Ken swept off his old felt cowboy hat and ran a practiced arm across his forehead. "Been reading your comic strip in the funny papers."

Libby smiled. Her career as a syndicated cartoonist was certainly safe conversational ground. Her character, Liberated Lizzie, a cave-girl with modern ideas, had created something of a sensation.

She would have to work hard to fulfill her obligations—there was the weekly cartoon strip to do, of course, and the panels for a projected book had to be sketched in. She hoped that between these tasks and the endless allure of the Circle Bar B, she might be able to turn her thoughts from the mess she'd made of her personal life.

"Career-wise, I'm doing fine," Libby said aloud, as much to herself as to her father. "I don't suppose I could use the sunporch for a studio?"

Ken laughed. "Cathy's been working for a month to get it ready, and I had some of the boys put in a skylight. All you've got to do is set up your gear."

Impulsively Libby leaned over and kissed her father's beard-stubbled cheek. "I love you!"

"Good," he retorted. "A husband you can dump—a daddy you're pretty well stuck with."

The truck lurched a little as Ken brought it to a stop in the gravel driveway. Cathy Barlowe, Libby's cousin and cherished friend, was dashing down the driveway.

After an energetic hug had been exchanged, Cathy lifted a graceful hand to sign the words: "I've missed you!"

"And I've missed you," Libby signed back.

Cathy's green eyes sparkled. "You haven't forgotten how to sign!" she enthused, bringing both hands into play now. She had been deaf since childhood, but she communicated so skillfully that Libby often forgot that they weren't conversing verbally. "Have you been practicing?"

She had. Signing had been a game for her and her stepson, Jonathan, to play during the long, difficult hours she'd spent at his hospital bedside. Libby nodded and tears of love and pride gathered in her dark eyes.

"I'll be back later," Ken said quietly, signing the words.

The interior of the house was cool and airy, and Libby followed along behind Cathy to the glassed-in sunporch that overlooked the pond.

Libby drew in a swift, delighted breath. The old wicker furniture that had been stored in the attic for as long as Libby could remember had been painted a dazzling white and bedecked with gay floral-print cushions. Small rugs had been scattered about, and there was a shelving unit built into the wall behind a new art table.

"Wow!" cried Libby, her arms spread wide. "Cathy, you missed your calling! You should have been an interior decorator."

Though Libby hadn't signed the words, her cousin had read them from her lips. Cathy's green eyes shifted quickly from Libby's face, and she lowered her head. "Instead of what?" she motioned sadly. "Instead of Stacey's wife?"

Libby felt as though she'd been slapped.

One tear slid down Cathy's cheek. "He went to see you in New York," she challenged, her hands moving angrily. "You wrote him letters!"

"Cathy, it wasn't what you think—"

"Wasn't it?"

Cathy turned and hurried out of the sunporch-turned-studio and a moment later the back door slammed. Libby ducked her head and bit her lower lip to keep the tears back. That, too, was something she had learned during Jonathan's final confinement in a children's hospital.

Just then, Jess Barlowe filled the studio doorway. He set down her suitcases and drawing board with an unsympathetic thump. "I see you're spreading joy and good cheer as usual," he drawled in acid tones. "What, pray tell, was *that* all about?"

Libby glared at him. "As if you didn't know! How could you be so mean...so—"

"Did you think your affair with my brother was a secret?"

"We didn't *have* an affair!"

"That isn't what Stacey says," replied Jess with impervious savagery.

Libby's knees weakened and she groped blindly for the stool at her art table and then sank onto it. "My God..."

Jess crossed the room and caught her wrists in a furious grasp. Then he whirled away from her, his broad back taut, one powerful hand running through his obsidian hair in a typical gesture of frustration. "Damn you for ever coming back here," he said.

"No problem," Libby said with effort. "I'll leave."

Jess turned toward her again. "It's too late," he said, his voice low. "He'd follow."

Just then Ken strode into the room and demanded, "What the hell's going on in here! I just found Cathy running up the road in tears!"

Libby could bear no more. She flung herself bodily at Jess Barlowe, just as she had in her childhood, fists flying. She would have attacked him gladly if her father hadn't caught hold of her around the waist and forcibly restrained her.

Jess raked her with one last contemptuous look and moved calmly in the direction of the door.

LIBBY SAT on the dock, shoulders slumped, her gaze fixed on the pond. She'd yearned for the quiet sanity of this place almost from the moment of leaving it. On the other hand, she wasn't certain that she'd been wise to come back...to face this gossip about being involved with Stace Barlowe. Stace was a warm, outgoing person and he had been a tender and steadfast friend. But Libby wasn't in love with Stace.

Jess Barlowe, standing in the shade, studied her in silence, feeling things that were at wide variance with his personal opinion of her. He was certain that he hated Libby, but something inside him wanted to touch her, to comfort her, to know the scent and texture of her skin. He caught his skittering thoughts, marshaling them back into stern order.

In an instant they were loose again. Jess suddenly imagined Libby naked, free and welcoming. But the man in this mental scenario was not himself—it was Stacey. The thought lay sour in Jess's mind.

"Did you come to apologize, by any chance?"

Jess lifted his hands to his hips at the sound of her voice and stood fast against whatever it was that was pulling him toward her. He didn't understand this tug of attraction he'd always had for Libby that inevitably caused them to argue and distress each other. There probably is, he mused, a fine line between wanting, loving and hating, even despising. What see-saw were they on now? *I want to make love to you,* he thought, and the truth of that ground in his spirit as well as in his loins. "I'm not here to apologize," he said coldly.

"Then why?" she asked with chiming sweetness.

He wondered if she knew what that shoulderless blouse of hers was doing to him. Damn. Before Jess could stop himself, he was striding along that small wharf, sinking down to sit beside Libby and dangle his booted feet over the sparkling water. He'd never be entirely certain what sorcery made him ask what he did next.

"What happened to your marriage, Libby?"

Pain leapt in her eyes and then faded. "Are you trying to start another fight?"

"No," he answered quietly. "I really want to know." On an impulse, Jess touched her mouth with the tip of one index finger. He saw the shadow of a nameless, shifting ache inside her.

Incredibly, she fell against him, wept into the shoulder of his blue cotton workshirt. And it was not a delicate, calculating sort of weeping—it was a noisy grief.

"I'm sorry," he said hoarsely.

Libby trembled beneath his arm and wailed like a wounded calf. The sound solidified into a word usually reserved for stubborn horses and income-tax audits.

Jess laughed and, without understanding why, kissed her forehead. "I love it when you flatter me," he teased.

Miraculously, Libby laughed too. But when she tilted her head back to look up at him, and he saw the tear streaks on her beautiful, defiant face, something within him, something that had always been disjointed, was wrenched painfully back into place.

He bent his head and touched his lips to hers, gently, uncertainly. He expected her to stiffen, to thrust him away with some indignant—and no doubt colorful—outburst. Instead, Libby gave a soft, lusty cry, shuddered and caught her hands in his hair, drawing him closer.

"This is me," he reminded her gruffly. "Jess."

"I know," she whispered. Her words were halting. "What's happening to us? We h-hate each other."

Jess laughed and began kissing his way softly down over her rib cage. The sound of car doors slamming broke the spell. Color surged into Libby's face and she bolted upright.

"Lib!" yelled a jovial masculine voice, approaching fast. "Libby?"

Sudden fierce anger surged, white-hot, through Jess's aching, bedazzled system. Standing up, he glared at Libby and rasped, "I guess reinforcements have arrived."

She gave a primitive cry and shot to her feet, her ink-blue eyes flashing with anger and hurt. Before Jess could brace himself, her hands came to his chest like battering rams and pushed him easily off the end of the dock.

When he surfaced, Jess's hair hung in dripping ebony strands, and his eyes were jade-green flares. Silently and effortlessly, he hoisted himself back onto the dock. "We'll finish our...discussion later," he said, with a smile that was at once tender and evil. And then, without so much as a word to his brother, he walked away.

"What the hell did he mean by that?" barked Stacey.

The look Libby gave the man beside her was hardly friendly. "You've got some tall explaining to do, Stacey Barlowe," she said. "You've been lying about me!"

"I haven't been lying!" he protested.

"You have! You've been telling everyone that I...that we..."

"That we've been doing what you and my brother were doing a few minutes ago?"

Libby was thrown by his accusation, but if Stacey had shoved her into the water, she couldn't have been more shocked by what he said next: "I love you, Libby."

"You love *Cathy!* Oh, Stacey, don't do this..." Libby retreated a step, stunned. "Stacey, I need to be here. Please...don't force me to leave."

Stacey smiled. "If you do, I'll be right behind you."

She shivered. "You've lost your mind!" She wanted to race into the house, but he was barring her way. "Stay away from me, Stacey," she said as he advanced toward her.

"I can't, Libby. Don't look at me like that—I'm not crazy."

She lifted her chin. "Let me be, Stacey." She was sick with the knowledge that he meant to pursue her.

"You needed me in New York, Libby, and now I need you."

"Let her pass, Stacey."

Libby looked up quickly to see Jess, unlikely rescuer that he was. His hair was towel-rumpled and his jeans clung to muscular thighs—thighs that only minutes ago had pressed against her own in a demand as old as time.

Stacey shrugged affably and walked past his brother without a word of argument.

"You were right," she muttered miserably to Jess. "You were *right.*"

The whole world seemed to be tilting and swirling. Too much, it was all too much. Jonathan's death, the ugly divorce, the trouble that Stacey had caused with his misplaced affections—all of those things weighed on her, but none were so crushing as the new feelings exposed by Jess's kiss. It was apparent to Libby now that the lovemaking they had almost shared, so new and beautiful to her, was all caught up in their families' entwined history and the still raw anguish she'd brought back from New York.

His face was grim, but Jess lifted Libby into his arms and carried her up the little hill toward the house.

She didn't remember reaching the back door.

*

"WHAT THE DEVIL happened on that dock today, Jess?" Cleave Barlowe demanded of his son. "Ken's mad as hell, and I don't blame him—that girl of his was shattered!" The senator swore roundly. "You were harassing Libby about these blasted rumors your brother has been spreading, weren't you?"

Jess sighed, set aside the drink he had yet to take a sip from, and faced his angry father. "Yes," he said.

"Mulehead," Cleave muttered furiously. "Ken Kincaid's the best foreman I've ever had and if he gets riled and quits because of you, Jess, you and I are going to come to time!"

Jess almost smiled. Not too many years before, the phrase "come to time," had presaged a session in the woodshed. He wondered what it meant now that he was thirty-three years old, a member of the Montana State Bar Association, and a full partner in the family corporation. "What was I supposed to do—stand by and watch Libby and Stace grind Cathy up into emotional hamburger?"

Cleave gave a heavy sigh and sank into the richly upholstered swivel chair behind his desk. "I love Cathy too," he said at length, "but Stacey's behind this whole mess, not Libby. Dammit, that woman has been through hell from what Ken says—she was married to a man who slept in every bed but his own, and she had to watch her nine-year-old stepson die by inches from leukemia. Now she comes home looking for a little peace, and what does she get? Trouble!"

Jess lowered his head, turned away—ostensibly to take up his glass of Scotch. He'd known about the bad marriage—often enough Ken had cussed the day Aaron Strand was born—but he hadn't ever asked about the little boy.

The Scotch was in his hand now. The taste was reminiscent of scorched rubber, but since the liquor seemed to quiet the raging demons in his mind, he finished the drink and poured another.

He fully intended to get drunk. Maybe he would stop hardening every time he thought of Libby, stop craving her, stop being angry with her. His emotional turmoil shocked him and he didn't want to remain sober any longer than necessary.

LIBBY OPENED her eyes. She tossed back the covers on the bed she had once shared with Cathy and sleepily made her way into the bathroom.

As she took off her short cotton nightshirt, she remembered the raging sensations Jess Barlowe had ignited in her the day before. Even though she had made a fool of herself, many of Libby's doubts about herself as a woman had been eased, if not routed. She was not as useless and undesirable as Aaron had made her feel. She had caused Jess Barlowe to want her, hadn't she?

Big deal, she told the image in her mirror as she brushed her teeth. *How do you know Jess wasn't out to prove that his original opinion of you was on target?*

Not surprisingly, the kitchen was empty by the time she went downstairs. Ken had probably left the house before dawn, but there was coffee on the stove and fruit in the refrigerator.

The telephone rang just as she was finishing her second cup of coffee.

"Hello?"

"Ms. Kincaid?" asked a cheerful feminine voice. "This is Marion Bradshaw, and I'm calling for Mrs. Barlowe. She'd like you to meet her at the main house for riding and a swim."

Libby looked down at her jeans and boots and smiled. In one way, at least, she and Cathy were still on the same wavelength. "I'll be there as soon as I can," she told the senator's housekeeper.

Libby started out, striding along the winding tree-lined road. The sun was high and it was warm for spring.

Finally the main house came into view, and she made her way around the side to the stables. Cathy was leading two horses out— a dancing palomino gelding and the considerably less prepossessing pinto mare that had always been Libby's to ride. The look in Cathy's eyes was cool. Distant.

As if to break the spell, Cathy lifted one foot to the stirrup of the palomino's saddle and swung onto its back. Though she gave no sign of greeting, her eyes bade Libby to follow suit. A moment later they were off across the open pastureland. Cathy rode faster and faster, stopping only when she reached the trees that trimmed the base of a wooded hill. There she turned in the saddle and flung a look at Libby.

"You're out of practice," she said clearly, though her voice had the slurred meter of those who had not heard another person speak in years. Cathy had learned to talk before the childhood illness that had made her deaf, and when she could be certain that

no one else would overhear, she often spoke. It was a secret the
two women kept.

"Thanks a lot!" snapped Libby as she jumped from the pinto's
back. "Were you trying to get me killed?"

Watching Libby's lips, Cathy grinned. "Killed? You're my
cousin. That's important. It implies a certain loyalty, don't you
think?"

Libby braced herself. She'd known this confrontation was coming.

"Are you having an affair with my husband?"

"No!"

"Do you want to?"

"What the hell kind of person do you think I am, Cathy?"
shouted Libby.

"I'm trying to find that out," said Cathy, her eyes on Libby's
mouth.

"You already know," retorted her cousin.

For the first time, Cathy looked ashamed. But there was uncer-
tainty in her expression, too. "What about all his visits to New
York?"

Libby's shoulders slumped. "You knew about the divorce, and
about Jonathan. Stacey was only trying to help me through—we
weren't lovers."

The lush grass moved as Cathy got down from her horse. "I'm
sorry about your little boy," she said. A lonely, haunted look rose
in her eyes. "Stacey wanted us to have a baby," she confided.

"Why didn't you?"

Sudden color stained Cathy's cheeks. "I'm deaf! I wouldn't
know when it cried!"

Libby spoke slowly. "Cathy, there are solutions for that sort of
problem. There are trained dogs, electronic devices—"

"Trained dogs!" scoffed Cathy, but there was more anguish in
her face than anger. "What kind of woman needs a dog to help
her raise her own baby?"

"You could hire a nurse."

"No!"

Cathy was back in the palomino's saddle before Libby could
even rise from the ground.

After that, they rode without communicating at all. Libby hoped
that Cathy would realize that the bonds of their friendship and
love were as strong as ever and that Libby could never have set
out to hurt Cathy. Time would help to heal the breach caused by

Stace's ridiculous thoughts. Cathy must feel as mixed up as Libby did—fixing up the porch and inviting her to ride and then confide about a baby but still be scared of the truth behind the rumors.

Back at the stables, Libby surrendered her horse to a ranch hand with relief. Already the muscles in her thighs were aching dully from the ride.

Cathy looked breezy and refreshed, and from her manner no one would have suspected that she harbored any ill feelings toward Libby. "Let's take a swim," she signed.

Inside the gigantic, elegantly tiled room that housed the swimming pool and the spacious hot tub, Libby eyed the latter with longing. Thus, it was a moment before she realized that the pool was already occupied.

Jess was doing a furious racing crawl from one side of the deep end to the other, his tanned, muscular arms cutting through the blue water with a force that said he was trying to work out some fierce inner conflict. Watching him admiringly from the poolside, her slender legs dangling into the water, was a pretty dark-haired woman.

The woman greeted Cathy with an easy gesture of her hands, though her eyes were fixed on Libby.

"I'm Monica Summers," she said.

Monica Summers. The name was familiar to Libby. Of course. Monica was Senator Barlowe's chief assistant.

"Hello," Libby said. "I'm—"

"I know," Monica broke in smoothly. "You're Libby Kincaid. I enjoy your cartoons."

Monica's subtle emphasis on the word "cartoons" made Libby feel defensive. Monica smiled and turned away to take up her adoring-spectator position again.

Was Jess more than friendly with Monica Summers? Libby moved over to the hot tub and slid in.

The heat and motion of the water were welcome balm to Libby's muscles, if not to her spirit. She tilted her head back, eyes closed. She was sexually attracted to Jess Barlowe. But it would pass. All she had to do to accelerate the process was to remember how demeaning Aaron's lovemaking had been.

Libby's skin prickled as she recalled the way Aaron would ignore her for long weeks and then pounce on her with a vicious and alarming sort of determination.

In retrospect, Libby realized that Aaron must have been trying to prove something to himself concerning his identity as a man, but at the time she had known only that sex, much touted in books and movies, was to be feared.

Not once had Libby achieved any sort of satisfaction with Aaron—she had only endured. After she had caught her husband with the first of his lovers, she had moved out of his bedroom permanently, remaining only because Jonathan had needed her so much.

The knowledge that so many people thought she had been carrying on a torrid affair with Stacey brought a wry smile to her lips. If only they knew.

"What are you smiling about?"

The voice jolted Libby back to the here and now. Libby looked wildly around for Cathy and the elegant Ms. Summers.

"They went in to have lunch," Jess informed her. Beads of water sparkled in the dark brown hair that matted his chest. Smelling pleasantly of chlorine, he came nearer.

Jess seemed to read the question in her face, and it made him laugh. The sound was soft—sensuously, wholly male. Overhead, spring thunder crashed. And then he was beside her in the hot tub, so near that she could feel the hard length of his thighs against her own. "I intend to finish what we started yesterday beside the pond."

Libby gasped as his moist lips came down to taste hers. She tried to twist away from him, but his kiss deepened and he lifted her legs, draping them around his rock-hard hips. And suddenly, Libby realized, she wasn't trying to twist away anymore.

*

WHEN JESS drew back from his soft conquering of her mouth, his hands rose gently to draw down the modest top of her swimsuit. She was transfixed, caught up in primal responses that had no relation to sanity. She let her head fall back and saw through the transparent ceiling that gray clouds had darkened the sky, promising a storm that couldn't begin to rival the one brewing inside Libby herself.

A soft moan escaped her, and she tilted her head even farther back, so that her breasts were still more vulnerable to the plundering of his mouth.

Inside Libby's swirling mind, a steady voice chanted a litany of logic. Jess didn't really care for her, he was only trying to prove that he could conquer her. Or prove her lack of morals. And, though her reason argued against him, it had no effect on her rising need to join herself with this man.

With an unerring hand, Jess found the crux of her passion.

Jess left her breast to nibble at her earlobe, chuckled hoarsely when the tender invasion of his fingers elicited a throaty cry of welcome.

"Go with it, Libby," he whispered. "Let it carry you high... higher..."

Libby was already soaring, sightless, mindless, conscious only of the strange force inside her that was building toward something she had only imagined before.

A savage trembling began deep within Libby, causing her breath to quicken to a soft, lusty whine.

The thunder in the distant skies covered her final cry of release.

Gradually Libby's reason returned. Forcing wide eyes to Jess's face, she saw no demand there, no mockery or revulsion. Instead, he was grinning at her.

Wild embarrassment surged through Libby. She tried to avert her face, but Jess caught her chin in his hand and made her look at him.

"Don't," he said gruffly. "Don't look that way. It wasn't wrong, Libby."

"I suppose you think...I suppose you want..."

"I think I've been thinking all the wrong things." Jess spared her having to search any further for the words. "You've a certain air of innocence. You've never been with any man besides your husband, have you, Libby? And as for what you just experienced, I'd say it was the first time.... Don't worry, princess. I'll court you if that's what you want. But I'll have you, too. And thoroughly." Having made this incredible vow, he calmly walked out of the room.

WITH CAREFULLY maintained dignity, Jess Barlowe strode into the shower room adjoining the pool. As he stepped under the biting, sleetlike spray, he gritted his teeth. Good God, if he didn't have Libby Kincaid soon, he was going to die of pneumonia. A man could stand only so many plunges into icy ponds, only so many cold showers.

He donned fresh clothes quickly and left. Jess was not surprised to find that Libby wasn't with Cathy and Monica in the kitchen. Mostly to avoid speculation in Monica's eyes, Jess glanced toward the windows. They were sheeted with rain. He glanced at Cathy, saw an impish light dancing in her eyes.

"You can catch her if you hurry," she signed.

Jess bolted out of the house. The old station wagon, an eyesore among the other cars parked in front of the house, almost refused to start, and his aggravation grew. Finally he found Libby near the mailboxes, slogging despondently along.

"Get in!" he barked.

Libby told him to do something that was anatomically impossible.

"If you don't get your backside into the car *right* now," he bellowed. "I'll *throw* you in!"

An evil smile curved Libby's lips and she stalked toward the automobile, purposely stepping in every mud puddle along the way. "Home, James," she said smugly, grinding her mud-caked boots into the floor carpeting.

When they didn't take the road Libby expected, the smug look faded from her face and she stared at Jess with wide, wary eyes. "Where are we going?"

"My place," he answered, still angry. "It's the classic situation, isn't it? I'll insist that you get out of those wet clothes, then I'll toss you one of my bathrobes and pour brandy for us. After that, lady, I'll make love to you."

"Suppose I tell you that I won't give in to you until the first Tuesday after doomsday?"

"The way you didn't give in in the hot tub?" he gibed.

Libby blushed. "That was different! You...you *cornered* me, that's how."

His next words were out of his mouth before he could call them back. "I know about your ex-husband, Libby. About the women."

The high color drained from Libby's face. "I don't want to talk about this," she said after an interval long enough to bring them to Jess's driveway.

One tear rolled over her face. "Why do you want to talk about Aaron?" she said in low, ragged tones. "So you can feel superior?"

"You know better." Jess's hands tightened on the steering wheel. It took great effort to reach down and shut off the engine. "We're both wet. Let's go inside."

"You won't take me home?" Her voice was small.

He sighed. "Do you want me to?"

Libby considered, lowered her head. "No," she said.

*

IF LIBBY were honest with herself—and she tried to be, always—
she had to admit that the chances were good that she had loved
Jess for a very long time.

She was wrapped in his blue-and-white bathrobe, the belt securely tied, and cuddled under a knitted afghan by the time Jess
joined her in the living room, looking reprehensibly handsome in
an old terry robe. His hair, like her own, was still damp, and there
was a smile in his eyes, probably inspired by the way she was
trying to burrow deeper into her corner of the couch.

"There isn't any brandy," he said with a helpless gesture of
his hands. "Will you settle for chicken soup?"

Libby nodded and tried to concentrate on the leaping flames in
the fireplace, but she could hear the soft thump of cupboard doors,
the running of tapwater, the singular whir of a microwave oven.
The sharp *ting* of the appliance's timer bell made her flinch.

Too soon, Jess returned, carrying two mugs full of steaming
soup.

Libby's cheekbones burned. She lowered her eyes and watched
the noodles colliding in her soup.

"I'm sorry," Jess said softly.

She swallowed hard and met his eyes. He did look contrite.
Because of that, Libby dared to ask, "Do you really mean to...to
make love to me?"

"You must know that I wouldn't force you, Libby."

Sooner or later, she was going to have to accept the fact that
all men didn't behave in the callous and hurtful way that Aaron
had. "Do you think I'm a fool, Jess? I mean...well...because
Aaron was...he..."

"He was with other women," supplied Jess quietly.

Libby nodded, managed to look up.

"And you stayed with him." He was crouched before her, and
took the cup from her hands to set it aside. "And there was your
stepson."

"I just thought..."

"What?" prodded Jess when her sentence fell away.

Tears clogged her throat. "I couldn't be very desirable if my o-own husband couldn't...wouldn't..."

Jess gave a ragged sigh. "My God, you don't think Aaron was unfaithful because of some lack in you?"

That was exactly what she'd thought, on a subliminal level at least. "Just how terrific could I be?" she erupted suddenly, in the anguish that would be hidden no longer. "Just how desirable? My husband needed other women because he couldn't bring himself to make love to me!"

Jess drew her close, held her as the sobs she had restrained at last broke free. "That wasn't your fault, Libby," he breathed, his hand in her hair now, soothing.

"Of course it was!" she wailed into his robe. "If I'd been better...if I'd known how..."

"Shhh. Baby, don't. Don't do this to yourself."

Once freed, Libby's emotions seemed impossible to check. They ran as deep and wild as any river, swirling in senseless currents and eddies, causing her pride to founder.

Jess caught her trembling hands in his, squeezed them reassuringly. "Listen to me, princess," he said. "You are desirable." He paused, searched her face with tender, reproving eyes. "I can swear to that."

Libby still felt broken, and she hadn't forgotten the terrible things Aaron had said to her during their marriage—that she was cold and unresponsive, that he'd never been impotent before marrying her. Time and time again he had held up Jonathan as proof that he had been virile with his first wife, taken cruel pleasure in pointing out that none of his many girlfriends found him wanting.

Wrenching herself back to the less traumatic present, Libby blurted out, "Make love to me, Jess."

And Jess came to her, lifted her easily into his arms. Without a word, he carried her up the stairs, across the storm-shadowed loft room to the bed. After pulling back the covers with one hand, he lowered her to the sheets.

It took all of Libby's courage to say the words again. "Make love to me, Jess."

His eyes searched her face. "Are we going to be making love, Libby, or just proving that you can go the whole route and respond accordingly?"

When she didn't answer Jess sighed heavily, but his hands were already sliding up Libby's back, gently kneading the firm flesh there. Libby closed her eyes. The motion of his hands on her back was hypnotic. She should tell him that she loved him, that maybe, despite outward appearances, she'd always loved him, but she didn't dare. This was a man who had thought the worst of her at every turn, who had never missed a chance to get under her skin. Allowing him inside the fortress where her innermost emotions were stored could prove disastrous.

His hands came slowly around from her back to the arching roundness of her breasts. "Answer me, Libby," he drawled, his voice a sleepy rumble.

She was dazed; his fingers came to play a searing symphony at her nipples, plying them, drawing at them. "I...I want you. I'm not trying to p-prove anything."

"Open your eyes," he commanded in a hoarse rumble. "Look at me, Libby. Tell me," he insisted raggedly, "that you're not seeing Stacey or your misguided ex-husband. Tell me that you see *me*, Libby."

"I do, Jess."

His mouth came down on hers, harshly demanding.

"Touch me, Libby," Jess said, and Libby moved her hands down over his rib cage to the sides of his waist, up his warm, granite-muscled back. *I love you,* she thought, and then she bit her lower lip lest she actually say the words.

Presently he caught her shoulders in his hands and held her at arm's length, boldly admiring her bare breasts. "Beautiful," he rasped. "So beautiful."

Libby had long been ashamed of her body, thinking it inadequate. Now, in this moment of storm and fury, she was proud of every curve and hollow.

His hands moved over every part of her—her breasts, her shoulders, her flat, smooth stomach, the insides of her trembling thighs. Libby's back arched and a spasm of delight racked her. The storm came inside the room and swept her up, up, up, beyond the splitting skies.

When she came back inside herself, Jess was beside her on the bed, soothing her with soft words, stroking away the tears that had somehow gathered on her face.

When at last Jess poised himself above her, strong and fully a man, his face reflected the flashing lightning that seemed to seek them both.

"I'm Jess," he warned again in a husky whisper.

Libby drew him to her with quick, fevered hands. "I know," she gasped, and then she repeated his name like some crazy litany, whispering it first, sobbing it when he thrust his searing magnificence inside her.

He moved slowly at first, and the finely sculptured planes of his face showed the cost of his restraint, the conflicting force of his need. "Libby," he pleaded, "Oh, God...Libby..."

As his pace accelerated, Libby moved in rhythm with him, one with him, his. The tumult flung them high, tore them asunder, fused them together again. Libby cried out and heard an answering cry from Jess.

She was flushed, reckless in her triumph. "I did it," she exalted, her hands moving on Jess's back. "I responded..."

Jess's head shot up from its resting place in the curve where her neck and shoulder met. He was wrenching himself away from her, searching for his clothes, pulling them on. "Congratulations!"

Libby sat up, confused, wildly afraid. "Jess, wait!" she pleaded.

"For what, Libby?" he snapped from the top of the stairs. "Is there something else you want to prove?"

"Jess!"

But he was storming down the stairs, silent in his rage.

"Jess!" Libby cried out again.

The only answer was the slamming of the front door.

KEN WAS ABOUT to shut off the lamp in the front room when he saw headlights swing into the driveway. Seconds later, there was an anxious knock at the door.

"Jess?" Ken marveled, staring at the haggard, rain-drenched man. "What the hell...?" In silence Ken led the way into the kitchen, poured a dose of straight whiskey into a mug, added strong coffee.

"You look like you've been dragged backward through a knothole," he observed when Jess was settled at the table.

Jess closed his hands around the mug. "I'm in love with your daughter," he said after a long time.

Ken sat down, allowed himself a cautious grin. "If you drove over here in this rain just to tell me that, friend, you got wet for nothing."

"You knew?" Jess seemed honestly surprised.

Jess downed the coffee and the potent whiskey. There was a struggle going on in his face, as though he might be fighting hard to hold himself together. Ken rose to put more coffee into Jess's mug, along with a lot more whiskey. If ever a man needed a drink, this one did.

Ken sat back in his chair and waited. When Jess was ready to talk, he would. There was, Ken had learned, no sense in pushing before that point was reached.

"Libby's beautiful, you know," Jess remarked presently, as he started on his third drink.

Ken smiled. "Yeah. I've noticed."

Simple and ordinary though they were, the words triggered some kind of emotional reaction in Jess. He began to talk, brokenly at first, and then with stone-cold reason.

Ken didn't react openly to anything he said; much of what Jess told him about Libby's marriage to Aaron Strand came as no real surprise. The level of whiskey in Ken's bottle went down as the hour grew later. Finally, when Jess was so drunk that his words started getting all tangled up with each other, Ken half led, half carried him up the stairs to Libby's room.

Libby in Jess's room; Jess in hers. Each invading the other's world in their absence.

Not for the first time, Ken Kincaid felt a profound desire to get them both by the hair and knock their heads together.

*

LIBBY CRIED until far into the night and then, exhausted, she slept. When she awakened, her face felt achy and swollen.

Downstairs in Jess's house, Libby stood staring at the telephone, willing herself to call her father and confess that she needed a ride home. Pride wouldn't allow that, however, and she had made up her mind to walk the distance, when she heard an engine outside, then the slam of a door.

Jess was back, she thought wildly. But when Libby opened the front door, she saw her father, not Jess, striding up the walk. Embarrassment stained her cheeks.

"Ride home?" he said.

Unable to speak, Libby only nodded and followed him back to his truck.

"Pretty bad night?" he ventured in his concise way when they were driving away.

"Dismal," replied Libby, fixing her eyes on the red Hereford cattle grazing in the green, rain-washed distance.

"Jess isn't in very good shape either."

Libby's eyes were instantly trained on her father's profile. "You've seen him?"

"Seen him?" Ken laughed gruffly. "I poured him into bed at three this morning."

"He was drunk?" Libby was amazed.

Ken glanced at her, turned his eyes back to the rutted, winding country road ahead. "Jess is hurting," he said, and there was a finality in his tone that kept Libby from asking so much as one more question.

Presently the truck came to a stop in front of the big Victorian house that had been "home" to Libby for as long as she could remember. Ken made no move to shut off the engine, and she got out without saying goodbye. She felt estranged from him now, subdued.

Libby went into the studio Cathy and her father had improvised for her. Even during the worst days in New York, she had been able to find solace in the mechanics of drawing her cartoon strip.

Today was different.

Even if she had been able to get the drawings right, she couldn't have come up with a funny thought for the life of her.

Libby paced the studio, haunted by thoughts of the night before. *I did it,* she'd crowed. God, how could she have been so stupid? So insensitive? And then, stifling her sobs in her palms, she cried.

Small, strong hands were suddenly pulling Libby's own hands away from her face. Gently Cathy hugged her. For a moment they were two motherless little girls again, clinging to each other.

The embrace was comforting, and after a minute or two Libby recovered enough to step back and offer Cathy a shaky smile. "I've missed you so much, Cathy," she said.

"Don't get sloppy," teased Cathy. She tilted her head to one side. "Did you really stay with Jess last night?" she asked with swift hands.

"Aren't we blunt today?" Libby shot back. "Who told you?"

"Nobody had to," Cathy answered aloud. "You're not going to work?" she signed.

Libby confessed, "I couldn't keep my mind on it."

"After a night with Jess Barlowe, who could?"

Libby suddenly felt challenged, defensive. "What do you know about spending the night with Jess?"

Cathy rolled her beautiful green eyes. "Nothing," she signed emphatically. "For better or worse, I'm married to Jess's brother—remember?"

Libby swallowed, feeling foolish. "Where is Stacey, anyway?"

The question brought a shadow of sadness to Cathy's face. "He's away on one of his business trips."

Libby sat down on her art stool, folded her hands. "Maybe you should have gone with him, Cathy. You used to do that. Maybe if you two could talk...really talk, the way you do with me."

"No. I sound like a record playing on the wrong speed."

Libby frowned. "Stacey knew you were deaf before he married you, for heaven's sake. He loves you but you're so independent."

"You're the independent one! You have a career...you can hear—"

"Will you stop feeling sorry for yourself, dammit, and fight for the man you love!"

Cathy went to the windows and stared out at the pond, her chin high. Finally she sniffed and turned back to offer a shaky smile. "I didn't come over here to fight with you," she said slowly, but surprisingly clear. "I'm going to Kalispell, and I wanted to know if you would like to come with me."

Libby agreed readily.

BY THE TIME Cathy and Libby had spent the day shopping they had reestablished their old, easy relationship.

Cathy was guiding the powerful car off the highway and onto the road that led to the heart of the ranch. Looking off into the sweeping, endless blue sky, Libby saw a small airplane making a graceful descent toward the Circle Bar B landing strip.

"Who do you suppose that is?" Libby asked, catching Cathy's attention with a touch on her arm.

The question was a mistake. "Why don't we find out?" Cathy asked, and suddenly the Ferrari was bumping and jostling off the road to the landing strip as the plane came to a smooth stop.

"Oh, God," said Libby, sinking into the car seat. She would have kept her face hidden in her hand forever, probably, if it hadn't been for the crisp, insistent tap at her window.

Having no other choice, she rolled the glass down and squinted into Jess Barlowe's unreadable, hard-lined face. "Come with me," he said flatly.

Before she had a chance to respond, Libby heard a gasp beside her and turned just as Cathy flung open the door and sprang from the car. Then, looking through the windshield, Libby saw Stacey and watched as Cathy sternly approached him, then stopped abruptly, leaving a disturbing distance between them. Cathy was glaring into Stacey's face, and Stacey was casting determined looks in Libby's direction.

"They need some time alone," Jess said, his eyes linking fiercely with Libby's.

After a moment she broke her gaze away and noticed that Jess's station wagon was parked close by. Without looking back at Stacey and Cathy, Libby got out of the Ferrari and followed Jess to his wagon. Sliding gratefully into the dusty front seat, she closed her eyes. Not until the car was moving did she open them, staring at Jess's rock-hard profile. She could read there how heavy his lingering suspicion still weighed.

"I didn't know Stacey was going to be on that plane," she said.

"Sure," he drawled, a muscle pulsing at the base of his jaw.

"It was Cathy's idea to meet the plane!"

"Right."

Libby swallowed miserably. "Cathy told me there was a fight at the stables this morning," she dared after a long silence. "What happened?"

A shrug preceded his reply. "One of Ken's men said something I didn't like. Like didn't it bother me to sleep with my brother's mistress?"

Libby couldn't hold back her tears. She turned her head as far away from Jess as she could, but the effort was useless.

Jess stopped the station wagon at the side of the road, turned Libby easily toward him. Through a blur, she saw the Ferrari race past.

"Let go of me!"

Jess not only didn't let go, he pulled her close. "I'm sorry," he muttered into her hair. "God, Libby, I don't know what comes over me, to say things to hurt you."

"Garden-variety hatred!" sniffled Libby.

"No. I couldn't ever hate you, Libby."

She looked up at him, confused and hopeful. Before she could think of anything to say, however, there was a loud *pop* from beneath the hood of the station wagon, followed by a sizzle and clouds of steam.

"Goddammit!" rasped Jess.

Libby laughed. "This crate doesn't exactly fit your image, you know," she taunted. "Why don't you get yourself a decent car?"

He turned from glowering through the windshield at the hood of the station wagon to smile down into her face. "It is time I got a new car," he conceded with an evil light glistening in his jade eyes. "Will you come to Kalispell and help me pick it out, Libby?"

A thrill skittered through Libby's body and flamed in her face. "I was just there," she protested, clutching at straws.

"It shouldn't—" Jess bent, nipped at the side of her neck with gentle teeth "—take long. A couple of days at the most."

"A couple of days!"

"And nights." Jess's lips were scorching their way across the tender hollow of her throat. "Think about it, Lib. Just you and me. No Stacey. No Cathy. No problems."

*

THE INSIDE of the Barlowe condominium in Kalispell was amazingly like Jess's house on the ranch. There was a loft, for instance, this one accessible by both stairs and, of all things, a built-in ladder. The general layout of the rooms was also much the same, except the floors were carpeted rather than bare oak, and the entire roof was made of heavy glass.

"I don't know what I'm doing here," she said pensively as she and Jess cleared the dinner table and started toward the kitchen with the aftermath of a delicious take-out meal. "I must be out of my mind."

Jess dropped Chinese food cartons and crumpled napkins into the trash compactor. "Thanks a lot," he said.

He drew her to him; his fingertips were butterfly-light on the small of her back. His hands pulled her blouse up and out of her slacks, made slow-moving, sensuous circles on her bare back. His head and shoulders blocked out the light of the stars. "I came here to—"

"Buy a car?" broke in Libby.

He nuzzled his face between her warm, welcoming breasts. "My God," he said, "what an innocent you are, Libby Kincaid!" One of his hands came down, gentle and mischievous, to squeeze her bottom. "Nice upholstery."

Libby gasped and arched her back as his mouth slid over the rounding of her breast to claim its peak. "Not much mileage," she choked out.

Jess laughed against the nipple he was tormenting so methodically. "A definite plus." His breath quickened at Libby's immediate response. "Starts easily," he muttered.

WHEN MORNING CAME, casting bright sunlight through the expanse of the glass ceiling overhead, she was alone in the tousled bed.

Grinning mischievously, Libby rose from the bed to rummage through her suitcase until she found the T-shirt she had bought for Jess the day before, when she'd come to Kalispell with Cathy. She pulled the garment on over her head and, in a flash of daring, swung over the loft to climb down the ladder.

Her reward was a low, appreciative whistle.

"Now I know why that ladder was built," Jess said. "The view from down here is great."

Reaching the floor, she whirled, her face crimson, to glare at him.

Jess read the legend printed on the front of the T-shirt and laughed explosively. "'If it feels good, do it'?"

Libby's glare simply would not stay in place. Her mouth twitched and then she was laughing as hard as Jess was.

His next words came as a shock.

"Libby, will you marry me?"

She stared at him, bewildered, afraid to hope. "I...what...?"

"I thought you only talked in broken sentences at the height of passion. Are you really as surprised as all that?"

"Yes!" croaked Libby after a struggle.

His broad shoulders moved in a shrug. "It seemed like a good solution to our problems," Jess said airily. Persuasively. "Stacey couldn't very well hassle you anymore. And you could stay on the ranch. We're good in bed," he offered.

"It takes more than that!"

"Does it?" He looked exactly like what he was: a trained, skillful attorney pleading a weak case. "You want children, don't you? And I know you like living on the ranch."

Libby broke in coldly. "I guess I meet all the qualifications. So why don't you just hog-tie me and brand me a Barlowe?"

Every muscle in Jess's body seemed to tense. He looked at her with unreadable eyes.

Libby looked into Jess's face and was thunderstruck by how much she cared for him, needed him. "I don't understand any of this."

Jess took one of her hands into both of his. "Do you want to marry me or not?"

She did love Jess, there was absolutely no doubt of that, and she wanted, above all things, to be his wife. Dammit, why couldn't he say he loved her?

"Would you be faithful to me, Jess?"

He touched her cheek. "I would never betray you."

Libby felt her resolve weakening and chided herself silently. *Fool, fool! Don't you ever learn, Libby Kincaid? Don't you ever learn?* Then quieting the voice in her mind, she lifted her chin. Life was short, and unpredictable in the bargain. Maybe Jess would learn to love her the way she loved him.

"I'll marry you," she said.

SITTING INDIAN-STYLE on the living-room sofa, Libby twisted the telephone cord between her fingers and waited for her father's response to her announcement.

It was a soft chuckle.

"You aren't the least bit surprised!" Libby accused.

"I figured anybody that fought and jawed as much as you two did had to end up hitched," replied Ken Kincaid in his colorful way.

Libby swallowed hard, gave Jess a warning glare as he moved to slide an exploring hand inside the top of her bathrobe. "Aren't you going to say that we're rushing into this? Some people will think it's too soon—"

"It was damned near too late," quipped Ken. "What time is the ceremony again?"

There were tears in Libby's eyes, though she had never been happier. "Two o'clock Friday, at the Kalispell courthouse."

"I'll be there, dumplin'. Be happy."

The whole room was distorted into a joyous blur. "I will, Dad. I love you," said Libby, sniffling as she gently replaced the receiver.

Jess chuckled, touched her chin. "Tears? I'm insulted."

Libby made a face and shoved the telephone into his lap. "Call your father," she said.

Jess settled back in the sofa as he dialed the number of the senator's house. While he tried to talk to his father in normal tones, Libby ran impudent fingertips over his bare chest. Jess caught the errant hand in a desperate hold, only to be immediately assaulted by the other. Mischief flashed in his jade eyes, followed by an I'll-get-you-for-this look. "See you then," he finally said to his father, his voice a little deeper than usual. There was a pause, and then he added, "Oh, don't worry, I will. In about five minutes, I'm going to lay Libby on the coffee table and kiss her in all the best places. Yes, sir, by the time I get through with her, she'll be—"

Libby snatched the receiver out of Jess's hand and pressed it to her ear. The line was, of course, dead.

Libby moved to struggle off his lap, but Jess's hands were strong on her upper arms, holding her in place. "Oh, no you don't, princess. You let this horse out of the barn, lady. Now you're going to ride it."

Libby gasped as Jess reached out and untied her bathrobe. He took wicked delight in Libby's capture and began guiding her soft, trim hips. All the while, he used soft words to lead her.

When her vision cleared, Libby saw that Jess had been caught in his own treachery. She watched in love and wonder as he gave himself up to raging sensation—his head fell back, his throat worked, his eyes were sightless. She accelerated the motion of her hips until he shuddered violently beneath her, stiffened and growled her name.

When he didn't have to drag air into his lungs, he caressed her with his eyes. The effect was almost as though he'd said he loved her.

Libby was still incredibly moved by the sweet spectacle she had seen played out in his face as he submitted to her, and she understood then why he so loved to watch her respond while pleasuring her.

Jess reached up, touched away the tear that tickled her cheek.

It would have been a perfect time for those three special words she so wanted to hear, but he did not say them.

*

THE NEXT AFTERNOON, when he returned to the condominium from a secret outing, the glee in Jess's eyes made Libby's heart twist in a spasm of tenderness. "Presents await. Come on," he said as he dragged her across the living room.

Jess opened the front door and pulled her outside. There, beside his new maroon Land Rover, sat a sleek yellow Corvette with a huge rosette of silver ribbon affixed to its windshield.

Libby gaped at the car, her eyes wide.

"Like it?" Jess asked softly, his mouth close to her ear.

"Like it?" Libby bounded toward the car, heedless of her bare feet. "I love it!"

Jess followed and opened the door on the driver's side so that Libby could slide behind the wheel. When she did, she got a second surprise. Taped to the gearshift knob was a ring of white gold with a diamond setting that formed the Circle Bar B brand.

"I'll hog-tie you later," Jess said.

Libby's hand trembled as she reached for the ring. It blurred and shifted before her eyes as she looked at it.

"Listen, if you hate it..."

Ripping away the tape, Libby slid the ring onto her finger. "Hate it? It's the most beautiful thing I've ever seen."

RAIN PATTERED and danced on the glass ceiling, a dismal heralding of what promised to be the happiest day of Libby Kincaid's life.

She heard the door open, heard Senator Barlowe's deep laugh and exuberant greeting. When Libby went downstairs, she was delighted to see that Cathy was with the senator.

"Where's Dad?" Libby asked when hugs and kisses had been exchanged.

"He'll be here in time for the ceremony," Jess's father said. "When we left the ranch, he was heading out with that bear patrol of his."

Libby frowned, feeling uneasy.

"We've lost a few calves to a rogue grizzly," Cleave went on easily, as though such a thing were an everyday occurrence.

Cathy, sitting at her father-in-law's elbow, seemed to sense her cousin's apprehension and signed that she wanted a better look at Libby's ring. The tactic worked, but as Libby offered her hand, she looked into Cathy's face and saw dark smudges under the green eyes.

"Are you all right?" she signed.

Cathy's responding smile was real, if wan. She lifted her hands. "I want to see your wedding dress."

When the two women went up to look at the new burgundy dress, the haunted look was back in Cathy's eyes. "Stacey's living at the main house now," she confessed. "Libby, he says he wants a divorce."

"Cathy. If only you would talk to him. Stacey loves you. I know he does."

"How can you be so sure?" whispered Cathy. "How, Libby? Marriages end every day of the week."

"No one knows that better than I do. But some things are a matter of instinct, and mine tells me that Stacey is doing this to make you notice him, Cathy. And maybe because you won't risk having a baby."

"Having a baby would be pretty stupid now, wouldn't it? Even if I wanted to—my husband moved out of our house!"

"I'm not saying that you should get yourself pregnant, Cathy. But couldn't you just talk to Stacey, the way you talk to me?"

"I told you—I'd be embarrassed!"

"Embarrassed! You are married to the man, Cathy—you share his bed! I'm amazed you've been able to keep silent all this time. When Stace finds out, he could be hurt. He loves you, I know it. You've got to stop being so afraid that someone is going to think you're silly, dammit! So what if they do? What do you suppose people thought about me when I stayed with a man who had girl-friends?"

Cathy's mouth fell open. "Girlfriends?"

"Yes," snapped Libby, stung by the memory. "I'm sorry if I was harsh with you," Libby answered. "I just want you to be happy, Cathy—that's all. Will you promise me that you'll talk to Stacey? Please?"

"I...I'll try."

Libby hugged her cousin and then rose from her seat on the bed, taking up the pretty burgundy dress to hang it in the closet.

When that was done, the two women went downstairs together. By this time Jess and his father were embroiled in one of their famous political arguments.

Feeling uneasy again, Libby went to the telephone with as much nonchalance as she could muster and dialed Ken's number. There was no answer—she had been almost certain that there wouldn't be—but the effort itself comforted her a little.

LIBBY STOOD at a window overlooking the courthouse parking lot, peering through the gray drizzle, anxiously scanning each vehicle that pulled in.

"He'll be here," Cathy assured her.

Libby sighed and reached out for her bridal bouquet. When she went back to the window, she spotted a familiar truck racing into the parking lot, lurching to a stop. Two men in rain slickers got out and hurried toward the building. Ken had arrived. At last Libby was prepared to join Jess in Judge Henderson's office down the hall.

She saw that august room through a haze of happiness. Everyone seemed to move in slow motion. The judge took his place, and Jess, looking quietly magnificent in a tailored three-piece suit of dark blue, took his. His eyes caressed Libby, even from that distance, and drew her toward him.

Libby's sense of her father's presence was so strong that she did not need to look back and confirm it with her eyes. She tucked her arm through Jess's and the ceremony began.

When all the familiar words had been said, Jess bent toward Libby and kissed her tenderly. The haze lifted and the bride and groom turned, arm in arm.

Instead of congratulations, they met the pain-filled stares of two cowboys dressed in muddy jeans, sodden shirts and raincoats.

"The bear..." said one of them. "We got Mr. Kincaid to the hospital fast as we could."

Libby was too frightened and sick to speak from the moment she heard the words. Time started to blur. The trip to the hospital, made in the senator's limousine, seemed hellishly long.

Stacey was there, and Cathy ran to him. He embraced her without hesitation, crooning to her, smoothing her hair with one hand.

"He's in surgery," Stacey said and his gaze shifted to Libby. "It's bad."

Libby shuddered, more afraid than she'd ever been in her life.

An uncomfortable silence settled over the waiting room. The sounds and smells peculiar to a hospital were a torment to Libby. She had lost Jonathan in an institution like this one—would she lose Ken, too?

"I can't stand it," she whispered.

The words brought a startling cry of grief from Cathy, who had been watching from her chair. "I won't let him die!" she shrieked, to the openmouthed amazement of everyone except Libby.

Stacey stared down at her, his throat working. "Cathy?"

Because Cathy was not looking at him, could not see her name on his lips, she did not answer. Her hands flew to her face and she wept for the man who had loved her as his own child, raised her as his own, been her strength as well as Libby's.

Libby was sorry for Stacey, reading the pain in his face, the shock. Of course, it was a blow to him to realize that his own wife had kept such a secret.

"Cathy was afraid to talk to anyone but me," Libby explained quietly. "She is very self-conscious about the way her voice sounds to hearing people."

"That's ridiculous!" barked Stacey, looking pale. "For God's sake, I'm her husband!"

"Some of us had a few doubts about that," remarked Jess in an acid undertone.

Stacey whirled, full of fury, but the senator stepped between his two sons. "This is no time for arguments," he said evenly but firmly. "Libby and Cathy don't need it, and neither do I."

Both brothers receded, Stacey lowering his head a little, Jess averting a gaze that was still bright with anger.

More than two hours went by before a doctor appeared in the waiting-room doorway, still wearing a surgical cap, his mask hanging from his neck. "Mr. Kincaid was severely injured," the surgeon said, "but we think he'll be all right, if he rests."

Libby was all but convulsed by relief. "I'm his daughter," she managed to say finally. "Do you think I could see him, just for a few minutes?"

Three hours later, Ken Kincaid was moved from the recovery

room to a bed in the intensive-care unit, and Libby was allowed into his room.

Ken was unconscious, and there were tubes going into his nostrils. His chest and right shoulder were heavily bandaged, and there were stitches running from his right temple to his neck.

Libby went to the bedside. "I hear you beat up on a bear," she whispered.

There was no sign that Ken had heard her, of course, but she went on talking, berating him softly for cruelty to animals, informing him that the next time he wanted to waltz, he ought to choose a partner that didn't have fur.

Before an insistent nurse came to collect her, Libby planted tender kisses on his forehead. She returned to the waiting room.

"He's going to live," Libby said, and then the room danced and her knees buckled and everything went dark.

She awakened to find herself on a table in one of the hospital examining rooms, Jess holding her hand. "Some wedding day, huh, handsome?" Libby managed.

"That's the wild West for you. How do you feel, princess?"

"I'm okay," she insisted.

Jess smiled, kissed her forehead. "Cathy reacted a little differently to the good news than you did."

Libby frowned. "How do you mean?"

"She lit into Stacey like a whirlwind. It seems that my timid little sister-in-law is through being mute—once and for all."

Libby's eyes rounded. "You mean she was yelling at him?"

"Was she ever. When they left, he was yelling back."

Despite everything, Libby smiled. "In this case, I think a good loud argument might be just what the doctor ordered."

THE NEXT DAY they were assured that Ken was steadily gaining ground. When she and Jess were alone, Libby voiced another subject that had been bothering her. "You plan to go looking for that bear, don't you?"

A muscle in his cheek twitched. "Yes."

Libby swallowed the sickness and fear that roiled in her throat. God in heaven, wasn't it enough that she'd nearly lost her father to that vicious beast? Did she have to risk losing her husband too?

"I promise not to get killed," he said softly.

Libby stiffened in his arms, furious and full of terror. "That's comforting!"

He kissed the tip of her nose. "You can handle this alone, can't you? Going to the hospital, I mean?"

Libby bit her lower lip. Here was her chance. She could say that she needed Jess now, she could keep him from hunting that bear. But in the end, she couldn't use weakness to hold him close. "I can handle it."

An hour later, when Stacey and the senator left for the ranch, Jess went with them. Libby was now keeping two vigils instead of one.

*

THAT EVENING when Libby went to the hospital, Ken was awake. He managed a weak smile.

"Sorry about missin' the wedding," he said.

Libby dashed away the mist from her eyes. "You've seen one, cowboy, you've seen them all. Thanks for scaring me half to death," she said.

Ken tried to shrug, winced instead. "You must have known I was too mean to go under," he answered. "Libby, did they get the bear?"

Libby stiffened. "No," she said after several moments.

Ken sighed. He was pale and obviously tired. "Jess went after him, didn't he?"

Libby fought back tears. "Yes," she admitted.

"Jess will be all right, Libby."

"Like you were?" Libby retorted without thinking.

Ken studied her for a moment, managed a partial grin. "He's younger than I am. Tougher. No grizzly in his right mind would tangle with him."

"But this grizzly isn't in his right mind, is he?" Libby whispered, numb. "He's wounded, Dad."

"All the more reason to find him," Ken answered firmly.

DURING THE LONG drive to the Circle Bar B, Libby made excuses to herself. She wasn't going just to check on Jess—she needed her drawing board, her pens and inks, jeans and blouses. The fact that she could have bought any or all of these items in Kalispell was carefully ignored.

Libby drew the Corvette to a stop in the wide driveway of the main ranch house. She didn't find Jess. She found only Monica Summers sitting in the kitchen, sipping coffee and reading a weekly newsmagazine.

Even though Monica smiled, her dark gray eyes betrayed her malice. "Hello...Mrs. Barlowe. I was very sorry to hear about your father. Is he recovering?"

Libby sat down. "Yes, thank you, he is."

"Will you be staying here with us, or going back to Kalispell?"

There was something annoyingly proprietary in the way Monica said the word "us," as though Libby were somehow invading territory where she didn't belong. She lifted her chin and met the woman's stormy-sky gaze directly. "I'll be going back to Kalispell," she said.

"You must hate leaving Jess. Of course, I'll be happy to...look after him," sighed Monica, striking a flame to the fuse she had been uncoiling. "It's an old habit, you know."

Libby suppressed an unladylike urge to fly over the table, teeth bared, fists flying. "Sometimes old habits have to be broken," she said.

Monica arched one perfect eyebrow. "Do they?"

Libby leaned forward. "Oh, yes. You see, Ms. Summers, if you mess with my husband, I'll not only break the habit for you, I'll break a few of your bones..."

Monica paled, muttered something about country girls.

"I am not a girl," Libby pointed out. "I'm a woman, and you'd better remember it."

"Oh, I will," blustered Monica, recovering quickly. "But will Jess? That's the question, isn't it?"

"I don't see how he could possibly forget," she said and left the house, hoping for a glimpse of Jess.

He was nowhere in sight.

Libby drove the relatively short distance to her father's house to get the things she needed. She was just walking past the side of Ken's truck when she heard the sound—a sort of shifting rustle, followed by a low, ominous grunt.

Dear God, it couldn't be... She turned slowly, and the beast growled. On its flank was a blood-crusted, seeping wound.

In that moment, it was as though Libby became two people, one hysterically afraid, one calm and in control. Fortunately, it was this second Libby that took command. Slowly, ever so slowly, she eased her hand back behind her, to the door handle, opened it. Just as the bear lunged toward her, making a sound more horrifying than she could ever have imagined, she leapt inside the truck.

The raging beast shook the whole vehicle as it flung its great bulk against its side, and Libby allowed herself the luxury of one high-pitched scream before reaching for Ken's CB radio under the dashboard. She knew that the cowboys would be carrying receivers, in order to communicate with each other.

"Cujo!" she screamed into the CB radio. She closed her eyes, gasping. This is not a Stephen King movie, she reminded herself.

"Libby!" the radio squawked suddenly. "Come in!"

The voice was Jess's. "Th-the bear," she croaked.

"Where are you?"

Libby closed her eyes as the beast again threw itself against the truck. "My dad's house—in his truck."

"Hold on, baby, hold on. We're not far away."

"Hurry!" Libby cried, as the bear battered the windshield again.

WHEN THE PICKUP truck was in sight, Jess breathed, reaching for the rifle in his scabbard, drawing it out, cocking it. "Easy," said Jess, to himself more than the men around him.

He shot one time, then recocked and shot again.

Stacey and several of his men reached the fallen bear just as Jess wrenched open the door of Ken's truck. Libby scrambled out from under the steering wheel to fling herself, sobbing, into his arms. Jess buried his face in her neck.

"It's over, sweetheart," he said. "It's over."

When she was calmer, Jess caught her chin in his hand. "What the hell did you mean, yelling 'Cujo!'"

Libby sniffled. "There was this book about a mad dog..."

Jess lifted his eyebrows and grinned.

"Oh, never mind!" hissed Libby.

*

THE COMING DAYS were happy ones for Libby, if hectic. She visited her father morning and evening and worked on her cartoon strip and the panels for the book between times in the middle of the condo's living room.

Jess commuted between Kalispell and the ranch; many of Ken's duties had fallen to him. Instead of being exhausted by the crazy pace, however, he seemed to thrive on it, and his reports on the stormy reconciliation taking place between Cathy and Stacey were encouraging. It appeared that, with the help of the marriage counselor they were seeing, their problems might be worked out.

Libby's thoughts occupied her mind now as she sat waiting for Jess at a booth in a steak house that was part of the Barlowe's family-owned chain. Her dad was getting out of the hospital that afternoon.

Libby looked up suddenly and saw Stacey standing beside her. "What are you doing here?"

He laughed, turning his expensive silver-banded cowboy hat in both hands. "I own the place, remember?"

"Where's Cathy?"

Stacey slid into the bench seat beside Libby. "She's seeing the doctor," he said, and for all his smiling good manners, he seemed nervous.

Libby felt self-conscious with Stacey, though he'd long since stopped making advances and disturbing comments. "What's going on? Is Cathy sick?"

"She's just having a checkup. Libby..."

Libby braced herself inwardly and moved a little closer.

"I owe you an apology," he said, meeting her eyes. "I acted like a damned fool and I'm sorry."

Knowing that he was referring to the rumors he'd started about their friendship in New York, Libby chafed a little. "I accept your apology, Stacey, but I truly don't understand why you said what you did in the first place."

He sighed heavily. "I love Cathy very much, Libby," he said. "But we do have our problems. At that time, things were a lot worse, and I started thinking about the way you'd leaned on me when you were going through all that trouble in New York. I liked having somebody need me like that, and I worked the whole thing up into more than it was.''

Tentatively Libby touched his hand. "Cathy needs you, Stacey. Just be there for her, Stace. The way you were there for me when my whole life seemed to be falling apart. I don't think I could have gotten through those days without you.''

At that moment Jess walked in. "Now, that," he drawled acidly, "is really touching."

Libby stared at him, stunned by the angry set of his face. Then she realized that both she and Stacey were sitting together and knew that it gave an impression of intimacy. "Jess..."

He looked down at his watch, a muscle dancing furiously in his jaw. "Are you going to pick your father up at the hospital, or do you have more interesting things to do?"

Stacey was suddenly, angrily vocal. "Dammit, Jess, you're deliberately misunderstanding this!"

"Am I?"

"Yes!" Libby put in, on the verge of tears.

The long muscle in Jess's neck corded, and his lips were edged with white, but his voice was still low, still controlled. "Are you going to collect Ken?"

Stacey's jaw was rock-hard as he stood up to let a shaken Libby out of the booth. Taking a firm grip on Libby's arm, Jess propelled Libby into the Land Rover.

"Jess—damn you—will you *listen* to me?"

Jess started the engine, shifted it into reverse. "I'm afraid storytime will have to wait," he informed her. "We've got to go and get Ken, and I don't want him upset.''

"Do you think I do?"

Jess sliced one menacing look in her direction but said nothing. It took all her determination not to physically attack him. "Jess," she said evenly. "I'll pick Dad up myself, and we'll go back to his house—''

"Correction, Mrs. Barlowe. *He* will go to his house. You, my little vixen, will go to mine."

"I will not!"

"Oh, but you will. Despite your obvious attraction to my brother, you are still my wife.''

Libby was too shocked to protest. They drove in silence to the hospital. When they reached the hospital parking lot, the Land

Rover lurched to a stop. Jess smiled insolently and patted Libby's cheek in a way so patronizing that it made her screaming mad. "That's the spirit, Mrs. Barlowe. Walk in there and show your daddy what a pillar of morality you are."

Simply to get away from him, she did as he said. But going into that hospital and pretending that nothing was wrong was one of the hardest things Libby had ever had to do.

PREPARATIONS for Ken's return had obviously been going on for some time. His front lawn had been mowed and the truck had been repaired.

Ken, still not knowing the story of his daughter, his truck and the bear, paused after stepping out of Jess's Land Rover, his arm still in a sling. He looked his own vehicle over quizzically. "Looks different," he reflected.

Jess rose to the occasion promptly, smoothly. "The boys washed and waxed it," he said.

To say the very least, thought Libby, who would never forget, try though she might, how that truck had looked before the repair people had fixed and painted it.

The inside of the house had been cleaned by Mrs. Bradshaw and her band of elves. The refrigerator had been stocked and a supply of the paperback westerns Ken loved to read had been laid in.

As if all this wasn't enough to make Libby's services completely superfluous, it turned out that a nurse was there too. Libby's last hopes of drumming up an excuse to stay the night, at least, were dashed.

While Ken was getting settled in his room, Libby edged over to her husband. "I was telling the truth!"

Stubbornly, he refused her the satisfaction of any response at all, beyond an imperious glare, which she returned.

They said their goodbyes to Ken fondly.

"You overbearing bastard!" Libby hissed as her husband squired her out of the house and toward his Land Rover.

Jess opened the door, helped her inside, met her fiery blue gaze with one of molten green. Neither spoke, but the messages flashing between them were all too clear anyway.

Jess, considerate of Ken, did not gun the Land Rover's engine or back out at a speed that would fling gravel in every direction.

They passed his house, with its window walls, and started up a steep road leading into the foothills beyond.

"Where are we going?" she demanded.

He ground the Land Rover into a low gear and left the road, now little more than a cow path, for the rugged hillside. "On our honeymoon, Mrs. Barlowe."

Libby swallowed, unnerved by his quiet rage and the jostling, jolting ascent of the Land Rover itself. "If you take me in anger, Jess Barlowe, I'll never forgive you. Never."

He paled as he stopped the Land Rover with a lurch and wrenched on the emergency brake. "Goddammit, you *know* I wouldn't do anything like that!"

"Do I? You've been acting like a maniac all afternoon!"

Jess's face contorted and he raised his fists and brought them down hard on the steering wheel. "Dammit all to hell," he raged. "You drive me crazy! Why the devil do I love you so much when *you drive me crazy?*"

Libby stared at him, almost unable to believe what she had heard. Not even in their wildest moments of passion had he said he loved her.

"What did you say?"

Jess sighed, tilted his head back, closed his eyes. "That you drive me crazy."

"Before that."

"I said I loved you," he breathed, as though there was nothing out of the ordinary in that.

"Do you?"

"Hell, yes." The muscles in his sun-browned neck corded as he swallowed, his head still back, his eyes still closed. "Isn't that a joke?"

The words tore at Libby's heart. "A joke?"

"Yes." The word came, raw, from deep within him, like a sob.

"You idiot!" yelled Libby, struggling with the door, climbing out of the Land Rover to stalk up the steep hillside. At the top of the rise, she sat down on a huge log, her vision too blurred to take in the breathtaking view of mountains and prairies and an endless, sweeping sky.

She sensed Jess's approach, tried to ignore him.

"Why am I an idiot, Libby?"

Though the day was warm, Libby shivered. "You're too stupid

to know when a woman loves you, that's why!'' she blurted out, sobbing now. "Damn! You've had me every way but hanging from a chandelier, and you still don't know!''

Jess straddled the log, drew Libby into his arms and held her. Suddenly he laughed, and the sound was a shout of joy.

JESS'S ATTENTION was firmly fixed on the road home.

"Jess," Libby said, "before we made love that first time, when you said I was essentially innocent, you were right. Even the books I've read couldn't have prepared me for the things I feel when you love me.''

"It might interest you to know, Mrs. Barlowe, that my feelings toward you are quite similar. Before we made love, sex was just something my body demanded, like food or exercise. Now it's magic.''

She stretched to plant a noisy kiss on her husband's cheek. "Magic, is it? Well, you're something of a sorcerer yourself, Jess Barlowe. You cast spells over me and make me behave like a wanton.''

He gave an exaggerated evil chuckle. "I hope I can remember the hex.''

Libby moved the things that were between them into the back seat and slid closer, taking a mischievous nip at his earlobe. "I'm sure you can," she whispered.

Jess shuddered involuntarily and snapped, "Libby, I'm driving.''

She was exploring the sensitive place just beneath his ear with the tip of her tongue. "Umm. You like getting *me* into situations where I'm really vulnerable, don't you, Jess?'' she breathed, sliding one hand inside his shirt.

"Libby...''

"Revenge is sweet.''

And it was.

*

JESS WAS in the kitchen, staring out at the snow blanketing the hillside. Libby came up as close behind him as her stomach would allow.

"I've just had a pretty good tip on the Great Barlowe Baby Race," she said.

The muscles beneath his bulky sweater tightened, and he turned. "My God!" he yelled, and suddenly they were both caught up in a whirlwind of activity. Phone calls were made, suitcases were snatched from the coat-closet floor, and then they were driving over snowy roads to the airstrip. The Cessna had been brought out of the hangar.

"Jess, this is ridiculous!" she protested. "We have plenty of time to drive to the hospital."

Jess ignored her, and less than a minute later the plane was taxiing down the runway. Out of the corner of one eye Libby saw a flash of ice blue.

"Jess, wait!" she cried. "The Ferrari!"

The plane braked and Jess craned his neck. Stacey and Cathy had abandoned their car and were running toward them, if Cathy's peculiar gait could be called a run.

Stacey leapt up onto the wing. "Going our way?" he quipped, but his face was white.

"Get in," replied Jess. "The race is on."

Cathy was the first to deliver, streaking over the finish line with a healthy baby girl, but Libby produced twin sons soon after. Following much discussion, the Great Barlowe Baby Race was declared a draw.

UNDERCOVER

Jasmine Cresswell

At first Diana was aware only of the murmur of voices and the muted hum of traffic. Then she realized she was thirsty. When she moved restlessly on the narrow bed, sunshine touched her face. As she turned toward the light, pain exploded beneath her eyelids, and she felt the drag of an I.V. needle in her arm.

Immediately she remembered everything: the long drive from London to Salisbury; the winding, dusk-shadowed road leading to Raleton Manor; the oncoming Jaguar; the patch of oil, the skid and the crash.

A tall, slim man and a nurse stood by the window. Diana's gaze came to rest on the man. He wore a plain white shirt, a discreetly striped tie and a gray business suit. He had dark brown hair, and his skin was tanned, even though it was only May. A small triangular scar stood out against his left cheekbone. All in all, Diana thought, Matthew, Ninth Baron of Raleton, looked exactly like his photographs: aristocratic, self-possessed, subtly sensual—and dangerous.

Seeing that she was conscious, he moved swiftly to her side. "Diana," he murmured. "How are you feeling?"

She tried to answer him, but no words emerged from her parched throat. "Water," she finally managed to whisper hoarsely. "I need water."

The elderly nurse nodded her consent, and Matthew poured water into a glass on the nightstand, bending the straw for Diana.

"My head hurts," she said at last. Her fingers clutched at the bedclothes, as she realized that although she had seen videotapes and dozens of pictures of Matthew Raleton, she had never actually met him—so she ought to pretend not to recognize him. It disturbed her that this simple fact had only just occurred to her.

"Who are you?" she croaked. "How do you know my name?"

The nurse bustled forward. "This is Lord Matthew Raleton, my dear. He brought you here last night in the police car. This is Salisbury General Hospital."

"Salisbury!" Diana exclaimed. "What am I doing here?"

"It's the closest major hospital to where you had your accident, Mrs. Foxe."

"I'm not Mrs. Foxe!" she protested. "I'm Diana Mackenzie, and I've never seen this man before. I don't know anybody who's a lord! I'm an American!"

Matthew Raleton sat on the bed, brushing a heavy strand of hair out of Diana's eyes. "We didn't mean to confuse you. Of course you're an American, and your name is Diana Mackenzie."

"Then why did the nurse call me Mrs. Foxe?" She detected a gleam of sympathy in Matthew Raleton's gray eyes.

"Peter Foxe was my stepbrother, Diana. I've been abroad for the past few weeks, which is why you and I have never met." He hesitated. "You married Peter a couple of weeks ago, just before he died."

Diana allowed the silence to fill the small room before she covered her face. "Oh, my God!" she whispered. "Peter's dead."

Tears trickled through her fingers in a convincing imitation of grief. She could cry virtually on demand but this time she felt an unexpected surge of guilt as she exploited her skill. There was something deeply repugnant about pretending to be Peter Foxe's grieving widow. Poor, weak, *handsome* Peter.

"How could I have forgotten?" she murmured brokenly, taking care not to overdo the dramatics. Charlie Groves, her boss, was always telling her she'd missed her vocation: she was a natural ham who would have been right at home on Broadway. "We'd been married only a few days before...before he died."

"Yes, so you informed me when you phoned last week," he said softly. "I'm sorry, Diana. This must have been rough for you. I wish I'd been around to offer some help."

"There was nothing you could have done," she mumbled.

"Perhaps not, but I wish I'd known you and Peter were married. Why did you keep the wedding ceremony such a secret?"

What reason had she been told to give? For a terrifying moment, her mind went blank, as panic overwhelmed her. But she improvised quickly.

"I can't remember where we got married! I can't remember a thing about it! I'm going crazy!"

The nurse stepped forward. "I don't think this is the right moment for any more questions," she said to Matthew, and patted Diana's hand reassuringly. "Please don't worry, Mrs. Foxe. Some loss of memory is quite routine after an accident. You have a minor concussion, but your CAT scan shows no serious damage to the brain. Dr. Jennings said you might suffer from a bit of mental confusion, that's all."

That was a *very* fortunate remark of the doctor's, Diana thought. She wondered how long she could blame her concussion for any inconsistencies in her cover story.

"I don't want to talk about Peter," she said huskily. "I just want to go back to Chicago and my family."

"You must get a little stronger first," the nurse said.

Diana licked her dry lips. "How long have I been here?"

"Since early last night. It's Wednesday morning now."

"Wednesday?" Diana repeated with deliberate vagueness. "But what am I doing in this part of England?"

"You were coming to visit me," Matthew said. "The accident occurred only a mile from my home, and by a lucky coincidence we were virtually passing each other when your car went into a skid."

My foot, Diana thought. By his own admission, Matthew was expecting her, so why was he driving his Jaguar *away* from Raleton Manor at a speed close to fifty miles an hour? Unfortunately, she couldn't ask any probing questions without alerting him to her suspicions. He was less likely to view her as a threat if she pretended to be a little slow-witted.

She looked up at the nurse, alarmed at how easy it was to sound both silly and totally panic-stricken. "I don't want to stay here! I don't like hospitals. I want to go back to America!"

"I wouldn't make any important decisions until you've recovered from the bang on your forehead," Matthew said quietly.

His winter-cool eyes scrutinized her with a piercing intensity that belied his casual words. Diana tossed restlessly on the narrow bed, anxious to avoid his gaze. She had forgotten her injured ribs, and gasped as pain suddenly radiated through every pore. The room began to spin, and for a few minutes it required every ounce of her willpower not to be violently sick.

Matthew touched Diana lightly on the shoulder and smiled reassuringly. She blinked, disconcerted. Either the medication or the pain must be having a disastrous effect on her if she was beginning to think the Wicked Baron had honest eyes. The last thing she needed was to find redeeming qualities in her chief suspect.

"You should rest, Diana," he said. "We can talk some more this evening. I have to go now, but if you're good and do everything the doctors and nurses say, I'll bring you a present."

He sounded like an indulgent uncle and she watched him walk swiftly to the door. Her head ached abominably as she closed her eyes to shut out the pain.

When she opened them again, Dr. Jennings had come into the room, and Matthew Raleton, ninth-generation aristocrat and suspected first-generation crook, had gone.

"YOU'RE A LUCKY woman, Mrs. Foxe," the young doctor said as he probed her bruises. "I know you've been in England only a short time, but you should have realized that our winding country roads can be dangerous. If Raleton hadn't acted so promptly, risking his own life, you'd have been burned alive when your car exploded."

"My car...burned? He pulled me out?"

"Yes, I thought you knew. Fortunately, it didn't explode for a couple of minutes. By the time the police arrived, it was a mass of flaming metal."

Diana shuddered. "I don't remember anything after my car went into a skid," she said. "I must have blacked out."

"I expect you did." The doctor studied her charts for a moment in silence.

A niggling doubt at the edges of Diana's consciousness swam suddenly into sharp and troubling focus. If Matthew Raleton had set up the accident, why had he pulled her free? Why had he rushed her to the hospital? If he had left her wedged behind the steering wheel of her Toyota, nobody would have blamed him. He could even have claimed that he arrived on the scene after her car exploded.

Or if Matthew hadn't tried to kill her, who had? He undoubtedly had associates, and perhaps his fellow criminals were more violent than he. Could her "accident" have been arranged without his knowledge and approval? She wasn't sure whether that thought reassured her or not.

Dr. Jennings made a couple of quick notations on her chart. "Well, Mrs. Foxe, you've got a cracked rib, a minor concussion and a few dozen cuts and abrasions. Fortunately for you, there's no major injury." He crossed the room and lowered the window shades. "I can see that you're not feeling too comfortable," he said with masterly understatement. "But I'm afraid I can't give you a sedative. Painkilling drugs don't mix well with concussion. Try to relax, and don't worry too much. Sleep is about the best medicine you could have at the moment."

Diana promised that she would sleep all afternoon, but it wasn't easy. She seemed to have bruises wherever she didn't have cuts or aching muscles, and to top it all, she was dreading her next encounter with Matthew Raleton.

Back home in Washington, D.C., before she'd actually met him, it had seemed quite reasonable to agree to infiltrate his home and search for evidence of his role as a major dealer in stolen high technology. After all, Diana had five years' experience as an undercover agent with the U.S. Customs Service. But now...

When Charlie Groves had originally explained her task, it had seemed simple. A CIA agent had followed the Soviet commercial attaché into London's Hyde Park and photographed him talking to a man later identified as Peter Foxe. When the agent turned up the information that Peter's company, Business Art, frequently exported European antiques to the States and imported American office equipment, he informed a colleague in Customs. A routine search of the next Business Art shipment to England turned up half a dozen sophisticated electronic servomechanisms among the boxes of legally declared typewriters and desk calculators.

Customs experts estimated the value of the illegal shipment at slightly more than half a million dollars. After a quick conference, senior officials decided to repackage the crates and let the contraband go through. At the same time, an undercover operation was authorized to gather hard evidence as a legal basis to extradite Peter Foxe and his unknown associates for trial in the United States.

Charlie Groves summoned Diana to his office for a preliminary briefing and launched into one of his familiar diatribes.

"Those number-crunchers in the Budget Office have just discovered that while they've been cutting our funds, the other side has been running around buying up the American store," he said. "Illegal exports are flowing out of this country like water over the Hoover Dam." He sighed deeply. "Ah, well, at least we're getting the funds for a few in-depth investigations, and you'll be working on one of the most interesting. Get your tail over to the briefing section, honey, and ask for Kenneth Brown. He'll take you through the details."

Brown was tall, plump and conservatively dressed, his manner deceptively self-effacing.

"Good morning, Ms. Mackenzie," he said. "I hope you don't mind if I call you Diana, and you must call me Ken. We'll be seeing a lot of each other over the next couple of weeks.

"Please sit down," he continued without waiting for her to reply, "and watch these videotapes carefully while I fill you in on

Peter Foxe's background. We'd like to catch him red-handed, but even more we're anxious to find out who his associates are. We suspect that he is only a small cog in a very large operation.'' He flipped the light switch.

The film had been taken at a disco, but its quality was relatively good. ''This is Peter Foxe,'' Ken said, using a pointer to indicate a tall, dark and extremely handsome young man. ''He's thirty and a great success with the ladies. We think he changes girlfriends every two months or so.''

Ken pointed to the woman Peter was dancing with. ''This is his current lover, a twenty-two-year-old nitwit. Her name is Liz Fotheringay, but she isn't important, except that you will replace her.''

''You mean as Peter Foxe's girlfriend?'' Diana asked quickly.

''Yes. If Peter runs true to form, he should be ditching Liz in three or four weeks. We're short of time. We want to be sure you're right there when his gaze starts roving. He always goes for the same type, and you're perfect. You're almost a twin of Foxe's last two girlfriends, but with green eyes. He likes American women, too.''

The camera zoomed in and Diana stared incredulously at the woman she supposedly resembled. Some of Liz's straight blond hair hung loose down her back, but it had been shaved off over her ears, leaving a pointed patch of naked pink skin. Her front hair was cut short and spiked with gel. She had sequined eyelids, purple blush, and lipstick so dark it gleamed almost black.

Diana had spent two years working undercover on the Chicago police vice squad before Customs, so she knew about the dramatic transformations clothes and makeup could achieve. Even so, she could hardly imagine converting her neat, sensible self into a copy of the exotic creature dancing with Peter Foxe.

''Well, that woman is blond, and so am I,'' she said dryly. ''But frankly, Ken, I can't see any other similarity.''

''We have three weeks to work on you. That's time enough to achieve miracles. You're blond, green-eyed and five foot seven, which is just about made to order for our friend and, fortunately, you don't look your age.''

''I'm only thirty, for heaven's sake!''

''Peter likes his women young and flaky.''

''So maybe he should hitch himself up with a croissant.''

Diana muttered several rude remarks under her breath as the tape played out and Ken rapidly filled her in on Peter Foxe. On his twenty-fifth birthday, Peter had inherited a modest legacy left

in trust by his father. He had used it to set up Business Art. Peter
traveled all over Europe buying antiques and minor works of art—
mainly for American companies.

But Peter was better at spending money than managing a company. He was soon teetering on the verge of bankruptcy. KGB
agents could spot such businessmen; once their victim was tar-
geted, he was often drawn into some smuggling scheme before he
even realized it.

About three years earlier, Peter had suddenly started importing
the office equipment while continuing to ship antiques out. Customs' financial experts calculated that he was losing money on the
legitimate imports, so there seemed little doubt that Peter bought
those solely to cover up the shipment of illegal high-technology
items for resale in the Soviet Union.

As the videotape faded, Ken quickly switched on the light.
"This operation is vitally important to us for several reasons, Diana. For one thing, we have good reason to believe this is a very
big smuggling ring, and we're sure Foxe isn't running it alone.
He simply doesn't have the brains to organize something on this
scale."

"Who do you think is the master criminal pulling his strings?"

Ken switched the videotape recorder on to show several views
of a gracious country mansion. "This is Raleton Manor," he said.
"Home of Peter Foxe's stepbrother, Lord Matthew Raleton.
There's a two-hundred-year-old stone wall running all the way
around the property and an up-to-the-minute electric fence built
directly inside it. There are only two functioning gates, both op-
erated by electronic voice controls. All the other gates have been
welded shut. The only way to get inside Raleton Manor without
a search warrant is to have Matthew Raleton invite you in."

"Maybe he just values his privacy," Diana suggested.

"And maybe he has something to hide. Wait till you see the
next bit of film from Monte Carlo." The scene switched to a tall,
dark man in evening clothes, strolling through the casino. "That's
Matthew Raleton," Ken said.

Diana's stomach gave a weird little leap as the man gazed un-
knowingly into the videocamera. She had the impression that he
stared directly into her eyes, his expression cool, searching, and
utterly unnerving. His eyes, she noted, were the color of the North
Sea in winter.

The camera angle changed, and Diana quickly switched her attention to the red-haired woman walking at Matthew's side.

"Good grief!" she exclaimed, recognizing the star of last season's hottest movie. "That's Jessica Jeffries!"

"Yes, and look who's with him the next night." The screen flashed a new shot of Matthew Raleton smiling gallantly as he provided one of Europe's more notorious princesses with a stack of gaming chips.

"The baron must be very rich," Diana said. "Did he inherit a lot of money from his father?"

"Apart from Raleton Manor and its contents, nothing but debts. Matthew Raleton hasn't spent a day in gainful employment since he graduated from Oxford fifteen years ago."

"What about his income tax returns?"

"They've been checked twice and show a decent annual income from various stocks and bonds. About enough to pay for the upkeep of Raleton Manor, if he's careful. But we've been keeping tabs on his rate of expenditures, and he obviously has an undeclared source of income."

Diana's breath expelled in a swift sigh. "And you think it's Business Art's illegal shipments."

"Yes. We estimate that Business Art's sideline is netting about two million dollars a year."

"Are there shareholders?"

"Yes, and they're all family members. Peter Foxe owns most of the shares. His mother owns a few, and so do a couple of cousins. One, Roger Dauntry, has an overdraft at his bank and no sign of living high on the hog. Nevil Cranston is the other cousin. He's an antiques dealer with an excellent reputation. His lifestyle's on the luxurious side, but then, he made a tidy profit on his own business for years. Matthew Raleton is the only other shareholder, and a relatively minor one."

"Okay, so Raleton is our most likely suspect. What has your investigation of him turned up so far?"

"Basically, that he's a hell of a tough guy to investigate. Routine details, of course: his parents are both dead, but he has a stepmother called Janet Foxe. She married Matthew's father when she was about thirty-three and Peter was a boy of fourteen. Nowadays she divides her time between Raleton Manor and an apartment in London."

"Is she rich?"

"Comfortable. She got a hefty divorce settlement from Mr. Foxe, and the old baron left her a reasonable income. Peter is her only child. Oh, and Raleton has an elderly widowed aunt called the Honorable Emily Carruthers. The research department's briefing files will fill you in on anything I've missed."

"Good enough."

"And of course you'll have a contact in England. Bob Heinrichs, our senior undercover agent, has been working on the case from the beginning. He'll identify himself by its code name: Temptation. We're hoping Peter will find you a temptation that's impossible to resist. *And* as soon as you make friends with him, we want you to get yourself an invitation to Raleton Manor. Matthew Raleton is the primary focus of your investigation. Seducing Peter is simply a means to that end."

"Okay, Ken, but before I agree to take this on, there's something you should know. I don't mind having my hair shaved over my ears so that Peter Foxe will think I look cute. I don't mind wearing leather miniskirts and purple satin panties because he has kinky tastes. But I draw the line at a sexual relationship. I know there are other agents who have different feelings about this, but my personal moral code allows me to go only so far."

"Your feelings on this subject are on record," Ken said. "We're not happy about the situation, but we need your precise looks—and you think fast in emergencies, Diana. That's most important for this assignment. But you probably can't hold out much longer than a month without losing Foxe's interest."

"I can unearth quite a lot in four weeks."

"Yes, but remember that you must get yourself invited to Raleton Manor. Fortunately, Peter Foxe visits the place most weekends. And one last thing, Diana. We've concluded that Foxe is relatively harmless; but he's been playing way out of his league. I'm sure I don't have to remind you that the KGB doesn't retire its mistakes, it kills them. And its middlemen work the same way. If you slip up, we may not have time to pull you out. So...I'm required to remind you formally that your life may be placed at risk if you accept this assignment."

"Do I get promoted if I pull it off?" Diana asked with an attempt at lightness.

"Sure. You'll be a GS 12 almost before you know it."

"Then I accept, seeing as how I could use a raise."

"That's great news!" Ken smiled. "We're going to nail those bastards."

Diana grimaced ruefully. "If they don't nail me first."

THE SHEETS BURNED against Diana's skin, yet she felt icy cold inside and acutely vulnerable.

She was glad when a nurse came in to offer her a glass of chilled apple juice.

"Do you feel well enough to talk to somebody who's been waiting to see you, Mrs. Foxe?"

"Matthew Raleton?" Diana asked.

"No, it's a detective from the local police force. He wants to take a statement from you about the accident."

THE DETECTIVE, a man in his middle thirties, radiated health and vitality as he strode into the drab hospital room.

"Good afternoon, Mrs. Foxe. I'm Detective Sergeant Mitchell," his hearty voice boomed. He waited in silence until the nurse's footsteps had faded, then closed the door.

"That's better," he said. "Now we can have a nice, cozy chat."

Diana felt her stomach knot. The sergeant suddenly seemed intimidating. "I think you're supposed to leave the door open," she said. "I would prefer that."

"Not a wise move in our case." The man's cheery smile disappeared completely. "I'm Senior Special Agent Bob Heinrichs," he said, abandoning his perfect British accent.

Diana drew in a deep breath of astonishment as she glanced at his Customs Service card. "Good grief, Bob, you had me totally fooled."

Heinrichs perched on the end of the bed. "We may not have much time, so you'd better fill me in as quickly as you can. I've seen the police report and statement, but I need to hear your version."

She grimaced. "There seem to be a couple of disconcerting gaps in my memory."

"We'd better find out how severe they are. Our last phone contact was on Saturday night. I told you that a false entry had been made in the American Consular records, showing your supposed marriage to Peter Foxe. You reported that you'd contacted Raleton to inform him you'd been too overcome by grief to attend Peter's funeral but that you had some important personal things to discuss with him. He invited you to spend a few days at the manor. Carry on from there, please."

Diana did her best to match his brisk professionalism. "Matthew suggested that I drive down Tuesday evening, in time for dinner at eight.''

"You're quite sure he suggested the time?"

"Quite sure." She frowned. "Do you think he planned all along to set me up for an accident?"

"Why do you think you were set up? The police report states that you took a bend in the road too fast and lost control of your car."

"Is that what Matthew Raleton told the police?"

Bob nodded. "It's not true, I take it?"

"No. That part of my memory is perfectly clear. There was a huge patch of oil. When I came around the bend, Raleton's car was heading straight for me. I swerved to avoid him, hit the oil, and..." She closed her eyes. "The doctor says I blacked out. And that Raleton pulled me out of my car just minutes before it exploded."

"Maybe," Bob said grimly.

"But if he didn't drag me clear, who did?"

"Perhaps nobody. It's equally likely that you were thrown clear and the police arrived before Raleton could toss you back into the flames."

"That's another odd coincidence, isn't it? I mean, the police turning up so promptly. That road only leads to Raleton Manor."

"According to their report, they were escorting Raleton's aunt, Emily Carruthers, back home. She fell down outside a local restaurant."

It was a logical enough explanation, although the string of coincidences didn't sit well with Diana's instincts.

"Why didn't the report mention the oil on the road?" she asked finally. "The police must have seen it."

"They did. But they assumed it had leaked from your engine, and Raleton's. His car sideswiped an oak tree, you know."

She gulped. "No, I didn't."

Bob patted her consolingly on the shoulder. "Don't worry about the accident right now. A good night's sleep, and I'm sure you'll feel like a new woman."

"I hope so," she responded wearily. "This operation is much too important to allow room for mistakes."

"Too important and too dangerous," he agreed soberly, hesitating visibly before adding, "I think you ought to know, Diana, that an autopsy done on Peter Foxe, shows he was dead before his car ever caught fire. There's no doubt that he was murdered."

"Poor Peter," she said. "He wasn't a really bad person, you know."

The Customs agent looked at Diana long and hard. "Look," he said at last, "before we send you into Raleton Manor, we need to be absolutely sure you're up to par and haven't forgotten anything crucial in your cover story. Do you feel strong enough to give me a full report on what Peter did during those last few days before he died?"

She rubbed her forehead tiredly. "But I already gave you one. Over the phone, just a few days ago."

"I know," he said, "but your accident changes everything, Diana. If your cover has been blown, we need to know."

"Where do you want me to start?" she asked.

"At the beginning," he replied.

She wrinkled her forehead in an effort to concentrate. "I arrived in London at the beginning of April," she said finally. "A junior diplomat at the American Embassy gave a party two days later. It was arranged for Peter to get an invitation and for me to be there as well. Peter had ditched his girlfriend and was obviously on the prowl." Diana grimaced humorously. "Our eyes met across the crowded room. He took one look at my flat chest and my purple eyeliner and made straight for me. He asked me to dance. He was a wonderful dancer, and we had a good time together. I saw him every night for the next two weeks." She stopped abruptly. "What's the point of going over this again, Bob?"

"Humor me, Diana. Just remember that your life might depend on some half-forgotten detail. If your cover's blown, we have to find out how. If not, and the car accident really was just that, then this is a heaven-sent opportunity to get you inside Raleton Manor—why, you could spin out your convalescence for a couple of weeks there."

Only an agent would view a concussion, a broken rib and several dozen bruises as a heaven-sent opportunity, Diana thought ruefully. But at least her brain no longer felt quite so fuzzy.

"I had the impression Peter was desperately unhappy," she said suddenly. "He drank too much and smoked too much—as if he would do anything to keep himself occupied."

Bob frowned. "You never mentioned this before."

"I know. I'd never realized just how strong my impression was." She smiled apologetically. "I guess there's nothing like a bang on the head for focusing the attention."

Bob didn't smile back. "How about your personal relationship with Peter?"

"Well, I told you I didn't have much difficulty controlling his sexual advances. He invited me into his bed the first couple of dates we had, but once I'd refused, he didn't push for me to change my mind."

"But he invited you to move into his apartment?"

Diana shrugged. "It sounds screwy, but eight days before he died, he drank so much that I persuaded him to take a cab home. I made him a bed on the floor, so he couldn't roll off anything. The next morning over a breakfast of black coffee and aspirins, Peter presented me with an emerald-and-platinum bracelet and asked me to move in. He said he had some important decisions to make. I think he wanted me around as a sort of adult baby-sitter."

"He still didn't ask you to sleep with him?"

"He kind of glossed over the whole subject." She smiled wryly. "Anyway, I moved in, but I didn't learn very much. He told me his older brother, Matthew, was in Austria. He seemed very anxious for him to come home. In fact, he spent the entire week before he died in an advanced state of acute nervous tension. It was a farcical situation in many ways, with the pair of us cooped up, both counting the minutes until Matthew came home, neither willing to tell the other why we were so anxious."

"That brings us up to the night Peter died." Bob now paced restlessly across the room.

"I reported everything I know the last time we spoke. Peter left about seven for a dinner meeting. But he wouldn't come across with any names, although he did say he expected to be seeing his brother soon. He was so emotionally strung out that night, he was barely coherent."

Bob stopped his pacing. "I'm pulling you off this case," he said finally, his words clipped with tension.

She shot up in bed, wincing at her ribs. "You can't do that!"

"Diana, I've been at this game longer than you, and I know the most difficult part is learning when to call it quits. But somebody obviously set you up for a car accident remarkably like Foxe's. We think Raleton forced your car onto a carefully prepared oil slick and then a tree-lined ditch. And you expect me to send you into his *house?*"

"But the evidence against him is all circumstantial!"

"We've traced Raleton's movements on the day his brother was murdered," Bob said abruptly. "It may be circumstantial, but that evidence is very strong."

"He wasn't in Austria?"

"Only in the morning. He and a delightfully stacked countess had spent a week on the ski slopes. But with almost no warning, he flew home. He landed at Heathrow about three that afternoon, but didn't turn up at Raleton Manor until very late that night. He had the motive and the opportunity to kill Peter, and we have to assume he did. Washington would tie my ass in a sling if I allowed you into Raleton's house now."

They both heard the footsteps at the same moment. "I'm an experienced field agent," Diana said urgently, "and I've been in more dangerous situations than this. Please don't take me off the case."

"Finished with your questions, Sergeant?" the nurse asked, poking her head around the door.

Bob Heinrichs put on his raincoat and gave her a reassuring smile. Almost before Diana's eyes, he seemed to become shorter, rounder and altogether more bumbling. "We didn't realize we were holding you up," he said, his voice once again tinged with a hearty west-of-England burr. "Mrs. Foxe has been very helpful, and I'm happy to say that the police are unlikely to make any charges. When will she be ready to go home?"

"Probably not until Saturday." She popped a thermometer into Diana's mouth.

"We'll count on Saturday, then, Mrs. Foxe." Bob flashed a warning glance at Diana. "I'm sure your American friend will be delighted to pick you up. We'll have you on a plane back to the States before you know it." And with that Bob Heinrichs left the room.

*

THURSDAY MORNING dawned pleasantly sunny, and Diana felt a renewed surge of optimism as she lay propped against her pillows. By the time she'd poured her second cup of breakfast tea, she was almost convinced that a few days inside Raleton Manor were all she needed to wrap up the investigation. The only hitch was that, technically, she was required to obey Bob's orders.

A nurse's aide came to take the tray and, to Diana's delight, allowed her to get out of bed and go to the bathroom. Diana even managed to sneak a quick shower and felt so refreshed that she was foolhardy enough to check her appearance in the bathroom mirror.

The gash high on her forehead was painted with orange antiseptic, and her shadowed green eyes stared at her out of a stark white face, liberally decorated with red-and-purple bruises. At least her lips had returned to normal, but the wreckage of her punk hairstyle drooped around her face like wet chicken feathers. All in all, she looked about as appealing as one of Count Dracula's discarded victims.

She got back in bed as the nurse lectured her on the dangers of hot water on concussed heads and fell asleep almost at once.

When she opened her eyes, Matthew Raleton was standing in the doorway, conferring with one of the doctors. His face was in profile, highlighting the arrogant thrust of his jaw and the thin, aristocratic flair of his nostrils. By some mysterious alchemy, the formality of his dark blue pinstripe suit merely emphasized the lithe, muscular sensuality of the body it encased.

Diana recognized the pull of his sheer sexual magnetism and fought against it. Hormones, as her boss liked to say, make a lousy basis for investigative judgments.

Taking leave of the doctor, Matthew walked swiftly into her room.

"Hello, Diana," he said, sitting at her bedside. "You're looking much better. The doctor said you rested well last night."

"I guess so." She kept her voice listless. "But it's boring here. In America, they have televisions in hospital rooms."

"I'm sorry if you've been bored," he replied, his voice patient. "I would have come to visit you last night, but my meetings in London went on longer than I'd expected." He paused for a moment. "Diana, are you aware that my stepbrother died intestate?"

"You mean he didn't leave a will?"

"Yes. To be blunt, Diana, Peter's affairs are in a mess."

"I guess he wasn't the type to think much about the future."

"Unfortunately not, which leaves you in a somewhat difficult position. And I expect you'll want to get back home as soon as you can, to resume your life without worrying about this legal mess."

She fluttered her lashes helplessly. "But I'm Peter's widow. I'll have to take care of it, won't I?"

"Not if you'll give me the power to act for you, Diana."

Don't you wish, buddy, Diana thought, lowering her gaze. Then,

"You're so good to me, Matthew," she murmured. "But I'm not ready to go back to the States." She realized that she was about to disobey Bob Heinrichs's orders, and was swept by a wave of combined nervousness and exhilaration. She disguised both with a bright, artificial laugh. "I want to stay in England, but Peter and I...didn't set up a joint bank account, and my money has run out...."

"I see," he said. "And you were hoping for a gift from me to help you out?"

"I don't exactly need money," she said. "But I did wonder if you'd let me stay at Raleton Manor until Peter's lawyers have a chance to straighten things out for me. I *was* Peter's wife, so I must be entitled to some of his money eventually."

"In theory. But I'm afraid Peter had no money to leave. I'll be very surprised if his estate consists of anything but debts."

"Peter can't have been in debt," she protested. "He was president of his own company, and he told me it was making pots of money."

"My stepbrother didn't own any companies. He founded Business Art five years ago, but he didn't own it when he died."

"Then who did?"

"I did. Or, to be more accurate, I was, and still am, the majority shareholder."

Diana wondered how such a fascinating piece of information had slipped past Customs' financial research team. "But Peter told me he started the company with his inheritance!"

"That's true. Unfortunately, Peter was much better at coming up with bright ideas than he was at running a business. He got himself hopelessly in debt—with the sort of people who break your kneecaps when you don't pay up—and he needed cash fast. So he sold me his shares. Since then, he's been working for a salary, and I'm quite sure he spent every penny."

Diana shut her eyes and summoned up a few of her convenient fake tears.

Matthew's mocking voice froze them in their tracks. "If Peter's 'fortune' was that important to you, you should have checked it out more carefully before you married him. You would have learned that appearances can be very deceptive."

"It isn't the money that bothers me," she murmured. "But unless you let me stay at Raleton Manor, I can't afford to remain in England." Her voice was a sob-choked whisper. "I'm not ready to leave Peter's homeland just yet. I want to at least meet the rest of his family.''

When her tears had stopped, Matthew sat on the edge of her bed and gently pushed back her tangled mess of hair.

"I'm sorry I spoke so harshly, Diana. Peter's death upset me a great deal. And I was hurt that he had married without telling any of us. Forgive me? Please?''

Diana hadn't expected an apology. She put her hand over his. "Peter knew you cared about him. I think he trusted you more than anybody else in the world.''

"That's what I'm afraid of,'' Matthew said. "He phoned me three times during the week before he died, but I was out every time.''

Diana held her breath. "But I thought Peter reached you in the end.''

Matthew looked down at her hand. "Yes. He reached me in the end.'' He stood up and strode briskly across the room. "Anyway, I never intended to imply that you aren't welcome at Raleton Manor, Diana. I'd be delighted to have you as a guest. In fact, the doctor has already suggested that you spend a couple of weeks convalescing there. Starting tomorrow, if you sleep well tonight. Isn't that good news?''

"It sure is!'' Diana smiled with unfeigned delight.

"I have to drive up to London again this afternoon, so I won't see you this evening,'' Matthew said. He paused in the doorway, reaching inside a pocket. "I almost forgot that present I promised you. It's a perfect match for your eyes.'' He tossed a small, silver-wrapped package onto the bed and walked off down the corridor.

Inside the silver paper was a gray leather box. Opening the lid, Diana found a teardrop emerald pendant, surrounded by diamonds and elaborately set in old-fashioned, red-hued gold. She held it up to the light with trembling fingers. It was identical to the pendant Peter had been carrying on the day he died.

A HOSPITAL ORDERLY brought a small suitcase to Diana's room early on Friday morning. "Lord Raleton had this delivered for you,'' he said.

When Diana unpacked it, she found navy-blue shoes with a matching purse, a heather-toned wool skirt and jacket, and a navy-blue silk blouse. Checking the signature labels, she hazarded a wry guess that the outfit had cost slightly more than six weeks of her before-tax income. There was also a slip of delicate mauve satin and a wisp of mauve lace held together by two minuscule strips of ribbon. This, she concluded, must be what Matthew Raleton considered a bra. An almost-invisible lace triangle passed for a pair of panties.

She dressed quickly, reminding herself that looking attractive for Matthew Raleton was not part of her assignment, yet she still wished she looked less like a punk rocker fallen on hard times. As for Bob Heinrichs, she promised herself to call the embassy the next day and leave him a coded message.

She tried to thank Matthew for the gift of new clothes, but he brushed aside her gratitude. "It took twenty minutes in Harrods. One of the nurses checked your sizes for me. My chauffeur will pick up your things at Peter's flat this afternoon."

"How will he get in?" she asked. "My keys were lost when my car burned."

"I have a set of my own," he said.

And just where had he gotten those? Diana wondered.

A Rolls-Royce waited at the curbside, guarded by an elderly man named Tom who bowed as he swung open the door for Diana. Once they'd set off, she took the pendant from her purse and held it out to Matthew.

"I really want to thank you for this beautiful gift," she said. "But Matthew, I'm not sure—"

He covered her hand with his, wrapping her fingers around the pendant. "No buts," he said, smiling. "You're my sister-in-law. And the first woman I've ever met who has truly green eyes. I had fun choosing it."

"Peter bought a necklace just like this as a birthday gift for his mother," she said. "He had it with him the night he died."

Matthew's smile faded. "I'm sorry," he said. "I didn't mean to awaken painful memories."

She drew in a deep breath. "I'd like to know where you got it, Matthew."

"I bought it yesterday at a London showroom," he said in a voice devoid of expression. "Nevil Cranston's—he's a well-known dealer. Also a cousin of Peter's and a business acquaintance of mine." Matthew went on in the same level tone. "Craftsmen have been making duplicates of their favorite designs for generations, Diana. It's an unfortunate coincidence, but that's all it is."

Either he was incredibly quick-thinking, or his explanation was the simple truth. Did she really think Matthew had murdered his stepbrother and pocketed the pendant? And even if he had, would he then give it to the one person who might recognize it?

Diana smothered a sigh as she put the necklace away. She could see no way of pursuing the subject.

Matthew's quiet voice interrupted her uneasy reflections.

"Would you like me to exchange the pendant for something else?"

"No," she said, "but I'm still not sure I should accept something so expensive."

"Cost is often relative, and I owe Peter a lot. After my mother died, he brought laughter and happiness back into our lives. Please keep the necklace, Diana, if it doesn't bring back unhappy memories. I would like to think of you wearing it."

He sounded so *damn* sincere. "Well, thank you—"

ABOUT TWO HOURS LATER, they drove through an imposing pair of wrought-iron gates, which had responded to an electronic command.

"This is it, Diana. Home sweet home," Matthew said.

She swung easily out of the car, then remembered it would be to her advantage to remain convalescent for as long as possible. She adopted a feeble totter, but her heels were higher than she'd thought, and she tripped over a crack in the cobblestones.

He caught her in his arms and she was startled by the muscled hardness of his body. Before she could protest, he had swept her up and now strode effortlessly across the courtyard toward the massive oak doors.

Diana's skin burned with a strange, cold fire. "Please put me down," she said. "I feel as if we're acting in a bad remake of *Gone With the Wind*."

He grinned. "Even if we are, nobody's watching." Without putting her down, he punched a number code into an electronic lock and the heavy doors swung open.

She had a blurred impression of dark paneling, vaulted ceilings and the smell of spring flowers, as he climbed a curving oak staircase and pushed open the double doors at the right of the upstairs hallway.

She found herself in a blue-carpeted, tapestry-hung bedroom. The covers were already turned back invitingly on the massive, carved-oak bed. Matthew walked swiftly across the huge room, setting her down carefully against the plumped-up pillows.

"I'll send the housekeeper to help you undress," he said. "Right now you look as if unzipping your zipper requires more energy than you've got." He smiled faintly, the tiny warm smile that had haunted her ever since she'd first glimpsed it on Ken's videotapes.

"Welcome to Raleton Manor," he said softly. "I hope your stay here will be everything you want it to be."

THAT EVENING, Diana wore a silver-threaded silk dress that clung to the slight swell of her breasts and stretched tautly over her narrow hips before flaring into fullness. She had covered her facial bruises with makeup and scattered glitter over her eyelids. To Matthew, she looked like a clone of all the women Peter had ever dated—except for her eyes. Those damned green eyes of hers were not only fascinating, he decided, but dangerously intelligent. If Diana Mackenzie was taking pains to appear something she wasn't, he was determined to find out why.

"I'm glad to see you found your way downstairs safely," he said with formal courtesy. "May I get you a drink?"

"Thank you, just a soda. I took a couple of painkillers, so I'd better stay away from alcohol."

Handing her the drink he said, "I hope you rested well this afternoon. You certainly look very glamorous."

"Well, thanks for the compliment, Matthew." Her voice rippled with laughter. "But we both know that between the bruises and the Mercurochrome, I look like a holdover from last year's Halloween party."

At that moment, an agitated voice called from the hallway. "Matthew! You must come and talk to Cook right away!" A tiny elderly woman scurried into the drawing room. "Do you know that Mrs. Thanet has used a *pint* of cream to make the pudding, and a *whole* chicken making soup. There's nothing I can say to make her realize what dire straits this country is in. The German U-boats sank another two convoys coming from America only last week!" Her cheeks were scarlet with indignation.

"You're forgetting, Aunt Emily," he said soothingly, "that the Nazis have been defeated and we can eat what we like."

Matthew helped her to a seat on the sofa. Poor Emily, he thought, Peter's death had really upset her. Her mental confusion had never been long-lasting before. He noticed Diana's startled expression as he fetched Emily a sherry.

His stepmother walked into the room. Janet looked as perfectly dressed and made-up as usual.

"This is my stepmother, Lady Raleton," he told Diana. "And my aunt, the Honorable Emily Carruthers, my father's sister. Janet, Aunt Emily, this is Diana Mackenzie Foxe."

"We're so glad you decided to come and stay with us," Janet murmured. She shook hands, taking care to avoid Diana's eyes, then went to pour herself a mammoth shot of vodka with a splash of tonic.

But Aunt Emily got to her feet, her eyes blurred by tears. "My dear, I'm so very sorry," she said, clasping Diana's hands. "Such a tragic loss, and you still so young. Dear Peter! He was the sweetest little boy, you know. So full of fun and mischief."

"I think dinner's ready," Janet interjected, setting her glass down on the bar with a bang. "I'll ask Mrs. Thanet to serve the meal."

Matthew was quite glad of his stepmother's interruption. These days, he never knew what his aunt might say. She could go for half an hour without making a sensible comment. Then, in the next second, she could come up with some pithy observation. Obviously Janet was no more anxious to have Emily get too insightful at tonight's dinner table.

Diana was ill at ease with Janet, but chatted gracefully with Emily, never once losing patience with her. Immediately after dinner, Janet excused herself, complaining of a pounding headache.

"I'm sorry you're not feeling well, Lady Raleton," Diana said. She paused awkwardly. "I hope you don't think that my coming here is an intrusion."

"My dear, you were Peter's wife, and your place is with his family. And please call me Janet."

Diana shifted nervously on her chair. She laced her fingers into a tight knot. "I'm so sorry about what happened to Peter. I wish I could have done something to prevent his...his accident."

Janet's eyes filled with tears. "He made so many foolish choices," she said. "Oh, God, if only he hadn't tried so hard to be something he wasn't." She glanced at Matthew for an instant, a hint of accusation in her gaze, then grabbed a napkin from the table and held it to her face as she hurried from the room.

Painful silence descended upon the dining room until Aunt Emily stood up and patted Diana gently on the shoulder. "Janet blames herself for what happened to Peter. Mothers do, even if they've done everything to bring up their children properly. You two go into the drawing room and enjoy your coffee. I'll see that Janet's comfortable.''

Mrs. Thanet had already set a tray of coffee and liqueurs on a low table close to the fire.

Diana curled up on the hearth rug, her legs tucked under her skirt, back resting against the chair. ''Your aunt is a very kind lady,'' she said.

''Yes. She was also extremely good-looking as a young woman and a leader in the fight to get more women accepted at our universities.'' He hesitated a moment. ''I appreciate your patience with her. Peter's death brought back some bad memories. Her husband was an intelligence officer during World War II. He managed to wangle a twelve-hour pass, and she went up to London to meet him, taking their young son with her. The hotel where they stayed was wiped out in a bombing raid, which killed both him and the boy.''

''Oh God, Matthew, that's an absolutely tragic story! Poor Aunt Emily.''

''She'd tell you to save your sympathy. In fact, she's led an active life since the war. She was one of the first people in England to organize an association that helped put displaced children in touch with missing members of their families.''

''She sounds like a remarkable woman.''

''She is. I'm surprised Peter never talked about her to you. He always had a soft spot for Aunt Emily.''

''Peter and I didn't spend much time talking,'' Diana said, staring into the fire. ''At least, not about family.''

He was suddenly tired of this cat-and-mouse game. ''How did you spend your time?'' he asked with deadly softness. ''In bed, making wild, passionate love?''

She recoiled visibly and jumped to her feet. Her voice shook slightly when she spoke. ''I think we should ignore what you just said. Good night, Matthew.''

He grabbed her arm as she walked past him, forgetting her injuries until she gave a little groan. He relaxed his grip, instantly contrite.

''Oh *damn*. I'm sorry, Diana.''

''It's all right,'' she murmured. ''I think I'll live.''

Her face was in profile to him, clearly displaying the bruise on her cheekbone. Of their own accord, his fingers began to trace the outline of the bruise, then the delicate curve of her jaw.

''Don't,'' she whispered. ''Matthew, please stop.''

"I can't," he said.

She held herself unyielding in his arms, but her green eyes slowly drifted closed, and he felt the faint quiver of her surrender when he captured her mouth beneath his. His hands caressed her back, coming to rest on the soft swell of her hips. She made a sound, somewhere between pain and pleasure, then opened her mouth to accept the urgent thrust of his tongue.

He had forgotten that sexual desire could feel this intense, forgotten that passion could be aroused so quickly. He wanted their kiss to last forever—or end right now, so that he could rip off Diana's clothes and carry her straight to his bed.

Then suddenly he pulled away from Diana as if she had burned him, forced himself to speak coolly and rationally.

"I'm sorry," he said, his voice harsh with the effort of control. "That should never have happened."

"No," she agreed quietly, turning away. "Good night, Matthew."

"Wait! Please, Diana. The doctor gave me some sleeping pills for you."

She still didn't turn around. "Thanks, but I don't like taking pills."

"In this case, you should make an exception. Your body needs sleep and the doctor told me to be sure you took this medication—at least for a couple of nights. Here."

Diana popped the pill into her mouth.

"If you need anything during the night, my bedroom is just next door."

"I don't think I'm likely to disturb you," she replied. "I've taken a sleeping pill, remember?"

AS SOON AS she was safely out of Matthew's sight, Diana spat out the pill. Even if Dr. Jennings had prescribed them, which she doubted, she had no intention of spending her first night at Raleton Manor in a drug-induced stupor. Undercover agents who planned to collect Social Security learned to sleep lightly.

Her suitcase had been brought from Peter's apartment earlier that evening. It sat on a stand in the corner of the room but she was too tired to unpack it. She put on her nightgown and climbed into bed.

Sleep proved elusive, and after thirty minutes of tossing and turning, Diana was reduced to delivering herself a bracing lecture.

You are thirty years old. You are the veteran of five successful undercover operations. You are past the stage when a quick kiss with your chief suspect should throw you into a stage of quivering confusion. But it had.

Diana closed her eyes and began counting sheep, refusing to acknowledge that the imaginary shepherd bore a striking resemblance to Matthew Raleton.

She counted two hundred and ninety-eight sheep before consciousness faded.

When she woke up shortly afterward, she knew she was not alone. Across the room, tissue paper rustled. Somebody was searching her suitcase.

Diana rolled out of bed and snapped on the light.

Aunt Emily blinked, then tucked her hands into the pockets of her dressing gown. "Diana, my dear, I'm so terribly sorry I disturbed you. I was looking for my knitting."

"Aunt Emily," she said, "you really shouldn't go wandering around in the dark. You might fall and hurt yourself."

"You and Matthew are both a pair of fusspots." Emily's face brightened as she glanced toward the door. "Why, and there is the dear boy! Hello, Matthew."

"I came to see what the noise was," he replied, tightening the belt of his scarlet silk dressing gown. From the expanse of darkly tanned chest and muscular legs, Diana concluded that it was all he was wearing. His body looked enticing enough concealed in clothes. Half naked, it was spectacular.

"Everything's fine," Diana said. "Just some mislaid knitting."

"I see you got out of bed in a hurry," he said. "I'm sorry you were disturbed, but with all the commotion, I assume you'd have woken up with or without that sleeping pill."

He tucked Emily's hand under his arm and escorted her to the door. "I saw your knitting on a table in the morning room," he said. "I'll fetch it for you."

They both bade Diana good night.

*

SHE HAD NO IDEA what caused her to wake up the second time since this intruder was making no sound at all.

A ray of gray light crept through a chink in the damask draperies and she had little difficulty in recognizing Matthew as he crossed the room. She watched him lift the lid of her suitcase and riffle quickly through it.

Whatever his task, it was soon accomplished. He left the room noiselessly then paused outside, turning so suddenly that Diana scarcely had time to close her eyes before she sensed he was coming over to the bed.

She felt the faint warmth of his body heat and knew he was staring down at her. She waited several minutes before opening her eyes, then checked the room visually to ensure she was alone before getting out of bed. She went straight to her suitcase, carefully examining the contents, but her search was unproductive.

Totally baffled, Diana clambered back into bed. She would report the incident to Bob Heinrichs as soon as possible, she decided, yawning.

A MAID BROUGHT her breakfast in bed the next morning, a luxury that Diana decided had definite merit. Afterward, she put on sneakers, a pair of jeans and a baggy sweater.

She carried her breakfast tray downstairs.

"I have a message for you, madam," Mrs. Thanet told her. "Lady Raleton had to drive up to London, and she asked me to apologize on her behalf. She'll return in time for dinner."

Diana concealed a sigh of relief. "I quite understand."

"And Lord Raleton is working in his study," she went on primly. "We never disturb His Lordship when he's in his study."

Diana gave the woman her sunniest smile. "Then I think I'll take a stroll."

Once outside, the first person she encountered was Aunt Emily, carrying a basket of freshly gathered herbs. She proceeded to tell Diana about the famous part of the garden, designed in 1750 by Capability Brown.

"And the house has a secret staircase as well, you know," Emily went on. "The entrance is in Matthew's bedroom."

This seemed to be one of her lucid moments, Diana thought.

After lunch, when Aunt Emily was dozing in the conservatory and Matthew was again in his locked study, Diana told Mrs. Thanet that she was going to take an afternoon nap.

Once upstairs, Diana paused outside the entrance to Matthew's room. But the door swung open as soon as she turned the handle.

She wasn't quite sure what she expected to find. And *comfort-*

able seemed to be the best word to describe both room and furniture.

Overcoming her instinctive reluctance to pry, Diana began a quick but methodical search of Matthew's drawers and cupboards, soon discovering that he was extremely tidy and possessed a large wardrobe of expensively tailored clothes. Her search failed to turn up a single personal or business document, so that the obvious conclusion was that he had something to hide and considered his personal papers too dangerous to leave lying around. Which meant that he kept them in his study or perhaps in a hidden wall safe. Such a safe should be easy to find.

She started at the wall by the door and worked her way slowly toward the bed. She was leaning across a nightstand lifting one of the oil paintings to ensure that it didn't conceal anything, when strong, masculine hands grasped her by the shoulders.

Matthew's voice was only a gentle murmur. "May I help you find something?" he asked. "If you tell me what you're looking for, perhaps I can save you some time."

Somehow, she controlled her panic, and replied, "Aunt Emily told me there's a secret staircase in this room, and she seemed okay at the time. I was trying to find it."

Matthew twisted her around and crooked his forefinger under her chin. "How disappointing," he murmured, his thumb brushing lightly across her lips. "You're asking me to reveal my dullest secret."

Diana's lips throbbed where he had touched them. It was the oddest sensation. She felt her cheeks flame. "I thought maybe there was a locking device under the picture...."

"I'm afraid not," he said. "Actually the stairway is concealed in the only piece of sixteenth-century craftsmanship still in the room."

"You mean the, um, fireplace."

"Very good." He strode over to the fireplace and twisted the center of a wild rose, the fifth flower below the family crest. A narrow panel beside the fireplace swung sharply outward, revealing a pitch-black opening. "What bachelor needs etchings when he has a secret staircase?" he asked. "Would you like to take a closer look at my staircase, Diana?"

"Thank you," she said, stepping into the dark opening, breathing in the dank smell of centuries-old dust. The floor was uneven. On one side, bricks had been laid into a long, narrow shelf. A dusty pewter candlestick stood on it, together with a small bronze sculpture and a pile of mildewed comic books. Another sculpture rested on the floor, almost as if it had once been used as a doorstop.

Matthew thumbed through the comic books, smiling. "One day I'm going to remove the evidence of my misspent youth. You've no idea how scary ghost stories seem when you read them by flickering candlelight in a freezing cold priests' hole."

"Priests' hole?" Diana repeated, stepping back into the bedroom. "Is that what the staircase was for?"

"Yes. My ancestors were what's known as recusants, people who remained loyal to the old faith. This stairway led to a system of underground escape tunnels. You never knew when a neighbor or even a servant might betray you if you helped the priests, so you needed an escape route." Matthew grinned. "The outside entrance was boarded up in the late eighteen hundreds, when the irate wife of Baron Raleton found him in bed with two of the village girls."

"Where does the staircase end now?"

"In the wine cellar. And, Diana—" Matthew's hand shot out and clamped around her wrist "—how about trusting me with the truth for once?" he asked quietly. "What were you really looking for?"

"I told you. But I'm sorry I came into your room without asking permission."

His expression was grim. "Diana, don't play games with me. For your own sake, tell me where Peter hid the payoff money for the phony antiques."

Her shock was genuine. "Matthew, I don't know what you're talking about! Peter never told me a thing about phony antiques or payoffs."

The anger in Matthew's eyes was replaced by an impenetrable, Arctic coldness. "On the contrary," he said. "I'm certain you know all about payoffs and buying favors. Just what do you want from me, Diana? You're giving out very confusing signals."

His lean, sardonic features took on a deceiving impression of tenderness as he bent closer. He released her wrist, slowly traced the outline of her mouth. "You're a very desirable woman," he said huskily, then closed the final, tiny gap between their mouths and sealed her lips with a kiss.

A hundred years later, he ended the kiss and Diana returned to earth. Dear God, she thought, thirty-year-old career women didn't hear celestial choruses, or rocket off to distant galaxies just because a man had kissed them.

"I have to g-go," she said, "I, er, I need to call the American Embassy about replacing my passport. The old one got burned, you know."

"You'd better hurry." His voice was totally controlled. "It probably closes to the public at five."

Back in her room, it took Diana at least twenty minutes before she was calm enough to call Bob Heinrichs's unlisted number.

When he answered, she quoted her ID, then made an oblique request for a meeting.

Bob's final words meant that he would meet her at the hospital, immediately after her appointment for a checkup on Tuesday morning.

It would certainly be a relief to make an official report and receive Bob's expert feedback, she reflected. His career with Customs probably spanned a dozen years or more, and his professional judgment would no doubt help her to understand much of what she currently found confusing.

DR. JENNINGS, still looking overworked, pronounced Diana to be healing faster than he would have believed possible. He checked a final CAT scan of her head and told her, "Relax for another week, and you'll have a hard time remembering you were in a car crash. Goodbye, Mrs. Foxe. But next time you're behind the wheel of a car, remember you're holding a lethal weapon."

It was scarcely noon by the time Diana had finished dressing and left the outpatients' reception area. She glanced around carefully, and in a gloomy corner by the telephone, spotted a man who looked like Bob Heinrichs. She was concentrating so hard on him that she walked straight into another man, whose arm was encased in a heavy plaster cast.

"Oh, excuse me!" she apologized. "Are you all right?"

It was Bob. The merest hint of warning flashed in his eyes before he spoke. "Well, now, isn't that a coincidence!" He seized her hand and pumped it up and down. "Bruce Harris, ma'am, at your service. I'm from Washington, D.C., over here enjoying the sights until my car had a little disagreement with a tour bus. How about you?"

"It's the most amazing coincidence," she said, playing along.

"I'm Diana Mackenzie Foxe. I manage a fashion boutique in Washington. I was in a car accident, too."

"It must be fate," Bob declared loudly. "Let me treat you to a cup of tea."

She followed him into the elevator and as he leaned across to press the button for the cafeteria, she caught the faint smell of his aftershave. It was an unusually spicy cologne, sharp but oddly pleasant.

In the cafeteria he spotted a table in the far corner. He gestured with his sling. "I'll requisition that if you'll buy us some tea."

Diana nodded, returning with a cup each and two cellophane-wrapped sticky buns.

"You've done a fabulous job with your disguise," she said softly.

"A good wig and a pair of brown contacts," he said dismissively, then pointed to the buns. "I haven't eaten in a while. Mind if I grab one?"

"Please take both of them. I eat such huge breakfasts at Raleton Manor that I'm never hungry for lunch."

"Speaking of the manor," he said, suddenly stern, "I thought I'd forbidden you to go there."

She felt herself blush. "I know, Bob, and I'm sorry. But the opportunity came up, and it seemed crazy not to take it."

"Okay, but you must keep me informed. I arranged for a CIA guy to pick you up at the hospital on Saturday for a flight home. You can imagine how bad it made Customs look when he reported that my operative had flown the coop. Anyway, what have you discovered at Raleton Manor?"

"More questions than answers," Diana admitted, breathing a sigh of relief that he hadn't chosen to pull rank and send her home for insubordination. "Matthew isn't the only one with secrets. Peter's mother is just about ready to fly apart at the seams, and Matthew's aunt is either crazy, cunning, or both."

She filled him in on most of what had happened, ending apologetically, "I guess you'd hoped for something a bit more definitive."

Bob reached out and touched her hand. "Something's bothering you," he said. "What is it?"

"Nothing. Everything." She pushed back her chair. "Bob, I have this gut feeling there's a giant piece of the puzzle that isn't sitting in its proper place. Things aren't tying together."

"Of course not. It's still too early in the investigation."

"There *is* one strange thing," Diana said suddenly. "Matthew and I were alone a couple of nights ago, and he accused me of knowing where Peter had—quote—hidden the payoff money for the phony antiques—unquote. Do you have any idea what he was talking about?"

Bob pondered her words for a few minutes, a frown creasing his forehead. "Interesting," he muttered. "That might explain why Foxe was murdered."

"I'm sorry, Bob, but you're losing me."

"I called headquarters last night. Ken and Charlie and I discussed Foxe's murder. Our conclusion was that there must have been a falling out among thieves. And thieves usually fall out over money. Maybe this is your missing puzzle piece. What if Foxe siphoned off some of the profits he was supposed to share and the others found out? That would explain why he was so terrified the week before he died, and it sure would explain Raleton's question about a missing payoff."

Diana clasped her hands together under the table. Her fingers were icy cold. The trouble was that the apparent facts were in conflict with her instincts, but Bob didn't seem to be a man who relied much on instinct. Diana was now certain that Matthew would never have murdered his stepbrother, or even agreed to it. She felt equally certain that if they had been working together, Peter wouldn't have gotten away with any illegal profits. He just wasn't clever enough.

"But, Bob, why did Matthew ask me about antiques as if he was really interested in a missing Russian payment for high-tech items?"

Bob pushed his teacup away impatiently. "For heaven's sake, Diana! He's a professional criminal, and he's not going to risk giving you information you don't already have. What do you expect him to say? 'Did Peter mention where he hid the money from the Russians for those smuggled seismometers?'"

"Then why risk mentioning a missing payoff at all?"

"Because he's frantic to find the money, of course! The value of those last three shipments is around two million dollars!"

"But if Peter had absconded with the money, don't you think Matthew would have found out where the loot was hidden *before* he authorized his brother's murder?"

Bob's mouth tightened into a thin line. "You're forgetting that he was frolicking on the ski slopes until the day Peter was killed. Maybe a few wires got crossed in issuing the instructions for

Peter's 'accident.' In my opinion, Diana, this explains why Matthew invited you to stay at his place. He's hoping you're going to lead him to the missing money.''

"Then somebody should tell him he's hoping in vain," Diana said ruefully. "If Peter made off with two million, he sure didn't tell me."

Bob leaned forward, grasping her hand in his eagerness to make his point. "Are you sure, Diana? I'd like you to think back over those last few hours you spent with Peter. Review *everything* he said and did. Are you sure he didn't ask you to take special care of a briefcase, maybe? A package?"

"Bob, you've heard all my reports...but there is one incident I remember," she said finally. "Peter took a heavy carton into the office the day before he died, and he seemed to fuss over it quite a bit."

"You never mentioned this before," Bob said sharply. "How big was it? How heavy?"

"I didn't pay much attention to it. I think Peter told me it was a pair of sculptures intended for a bank somewhere in New Jersey."

"Did he say what sort? Marble? Bronze?"

"No. He seemed kind of nervous that morning, but I didn't connect that with the artwork. As I've told you, he was strung out for the whole week before he died."

"All I have to do now is find out if there was a shipment scheduled for a bank in New Jersey," Bob murmured. Then he smiled. "You told me Raleton's study door is always locked. Well, I've brought you a present."

He slid a small leather case across the table, hiding his action by clasping her hands. "Happy lock picking," he said.

Diana shoved the wallet into her purse, her smile freezing as she saw Matthew Raleton at the entrance, his gaze fixed on their intertwined hands.

She lowered her head, avoiding eye contact. "Matthew's here," she said. "He's coming over."

Bob got to his feet, smiling with a nonchalance Diana could only admire. "It's been great meeting you, Diana," he said loudly. "Gotta run now. See you back in D.C.!"

He wove his way swiftly through the tables, yet avoided any appearance of undue haste. Watching him, Diana reflected that Bob Heinrichs was undoubtedly one of the most skillful operatives she had ever met. When he reached the side entrance safely, she rose, still pretending not to have noticed Matthew. She gave a little jump of shock when he halted in front of her.

"Hello, Diana," he said, his smile hard.

"Why, Matthew, you startled me!"

"I came to see if I could offer you a lift home," he said.

"I was having a cup of tea with—an acquaintance."

"Yes, I saw you both. I hope his hasty departure had nothing to do with my arrival."

"Why should it?" she asked coolly. "I met Bruce for the first time about twenty minutes ago. He fractured his elbow in a car accident. I was happy to spend some time with a fellow American."

"Amazing how casual acquaintances can look like longtime friends, isn't it?"

"Yes," she said shortly. Then, "Would you tell me something, Matthew? Why are you so hostile toward me? Have I somehow offended you?"

His gaze traveled over her face and came to rest on her lips. "You married my brother," he said with lethal quiet.

Anger brought a flush to her cheeks. "Oh, *now* I see! I should have realized that an ordinary American woman wouldn't be good enough for the Raletons!"

"You misunderstood my meaning—although I'm not sure you're so ordinary. Your vibes, as my brother would have said, don't seem to fit your image."

She had known from the first that he was dangerously perceptive. If she wanted to come out of this assignment unscathed, she would have to improve her defenses. Too many of their conversations were becoming personal.

"I'm sorry," she said, "but I've no idea what you're talking about."

His grim expression gradually faded. "Look, it's too sunny a day to be hanging about here. I know a pub with the best meat pasties this side of Cornwall. If you haven't eaten lunch already, will you come and share one with me?"

"Thank you," she said, almost more startled by her response than by his invitation. "I'd enjoy that."

*

OVER THEIR PUB LUNCH, Matthew had asked her to go with him to London the next day, to sort out Peter's belongings at his flat.

Diana spent the entire journey parrying Matthew's questions about her relationship with his brother. She was exhausted by the number of lies she'd had to invent.

They left the Jaguar in the underground parking garage and took the elevator up to Peter's flat. Diana opened the big bay window in the living room and fresh, damp air blew in off the River Thames.

"We'd better get busy," Matthew called. "As Peter's executor I must take care of his outstanding correspondence so I'll get to work on his papers, if you'll deal with his clothes."

Diana had spent the days immediately following Peter's death searching the apartment from top to bottom. Matthew would find only unpaid bills and routine correspondence, plus a few documents she had carefully planted.

"That sounds fine," she said.

She had already filled four plastic sacks for the Salvation Army when Matthew called from the living room.

She went out to him.

"None of these keys seem to work in the center desk drawer, Diana. Do you have any more?"

"The lock often sticks," she said. "Shall I try?"

On her second attempt, she unlocked the drawer. She knew exactly what was inside: Peter's birth certificate, his university record, a few personal letters—and a copy of her fake marriage certificate, which she had put there herself.

Matthew took a long time reading the brief information on the forged certificate. Then he smoothed out the creases and set it on top of the other papers.

Diana had started back to the bedroom, but he caught her wrist and pulled her around to face him. "Why did you marry my stepbrother?" he asked.

"Because we were in love," she said defiantly.

The scratchy sound of a key turning in the front door lock saved her from having to elaborate. Matthew drew her swiftly behind the protection of his body and almost simultaneously, the door swung open and a tall, handsome man of about fifty stepped into the living room.

Matthew released her arm. "Why, hello, Nevil," he said. "What a surprise! It never occurred to me that you would still have a key."

"I was Peter's closest friend right up to the day he died. Naturally I still have a key."

Matthew threw a glance toward Diana. "Nevertheless, perhaps you should hand it over to Peter's wife."

"But of course, old chap, whatever you think proper." He crossed the living room, halting in front of Diana. "My dear, I'm so sorry to intrude. Such a tragic bereavement. Matthew, dear chap, please introduce me to Peter's lovely widow."

Matthew was a model of politeness as he did so, though without mention of the fact that Cranston was the dealer from whom he claimed to have bought the emerald pendant.

"How do you do?" Diana said, shaking hands and making a rapid mental assessment of Peter's cousin. He was well built, superbly dressed, handsome in the English style of blue eyes, light brown hair and ruddy complexion. All in all, impressive.

"My dear Diana," he murmured, enfolding her hand between both of his. "Allow me to express once again my deepest condolences. Peter's death was a tragic loss for you and for us all. Such a delightful young man!"

Matthew swung on his heel and strode over to the window.

"Peter was a lot of fun to be with," Diana agreed. "He told me what very close friends you were. I'm glad to meet you at last."

"I'm thrilled to know that Peter shared the importance of our friendship with you," Nevil responded smoothly. "I often used to boast that I'm the person most responsible for helping him to understand his real goals in life."

Matthew turned suddenly. "Why have you come here?" he demanded harshly.

"Why, it was a matter of business, but I hardly like to intrude…"

"Just explain why you came, please."

"How horribly impatient you are, Matthew!" Nevil's smile was edged with anger. "Diana, come and sit with me on the sofa, where we can be comfortable. Now, since he insists, I'll explain. You may know I've been helping out at Business Art. Well, it seems a consignment of antiques was shipped to New Jersey a couple of days after Peter died. We had word today that one packing crate was incomplete."

"What was missing?"

"Of all things, the bronze head of a Roman emperor. And the president of the bank who ordered it is kicking up the devil of a fuss."

Some vague memory tugged at Diana's mind. "What does the head look like?" she asked. "Although I don't think you'll find any antique sculpture here."

"According to the insurance forms and the bill of loading, it's about eighteen inches high, in excellent condition. It's been identified as a third-century representation of the Emperor Caracalla wearing the laurel wreath of victory."

Diana remembered exactly where she had seen the bust: on the dusty floor of the manor's secret staircase. Instinct, and nine years of professional experience, told her that she must have a chance to examine it—closely.

Opening her eyes very wide, she looked straight at Nevil Cranston. "I'm afraid I don't ever remember seeing Peter with a bronze sculpture of any sort," she said with perfect truth. "Is it very valuable, Nevil?"

"Not particularly," he said, a touch impatiently. "It's valued at nine thousand pounds."

"I guess it wouldn't be very good for the company's image if we just wrote and told the buyer we've lost it?" Diana questioned artlessly.

A slight choking sound from Matthew's corner caused them to look in his direction, but he was merely blowing his nose.

"Why don't you take a good look around the flat?" he suggested politely. "Diana and I will just carry on organizing these papers."

Nevil conducted a thorough search but to no avail.

Once again clasping Diana's hand between his plump palms, he said, "My dear, it's been a joy to make your acquaintance, despite the sad circumstances that brought us together."

Diana wasn't sure if he meant the sad circumstance of the missing head or of his cousin's death.

He turned to say goodbye to Matthew. "No doubt I shall see you some weekend soon, old chap, at the manor."

"I'm planning to be there for the next week or so."

"No business trips scheduled?"

"Not right at the moment—and Nevil!" Matthew's voice halted him on the threshold. "You forgot to give Diana that key. *Old chap.*"

Nevil's smile never faltered, but his blue eyes were ice cold as he handed Diana the key ring.

She watched Matthew lock and bolt the door behind Nevil, then hurried into the kitchen, though she knew there was no escape from confrontation.

He was right behind her.

"All right," he said. "Enough of the fun and games. Why the hell didn't you tell Nevil where the sculpture is? I need the whole truth from you, Diana. Now. You're putting on some sort of an act—that much I'm sure of. The only thing I don't know yet is why."

"You have no reason to make such crazy accusations!"

"No logical reason, perhaps, but plenty of intuitive ones."

"Is your intuition always so reliable?"

"Yes," he said soberly. "I think it is. My father left me a mansion that needed half a million pounds' worth of structural repairs, a widowed aunt, and a stepmother who thought cutting down on household expenses meant buying champagne and caviar in the giant economy sizes. I needed lots of money fast, so I learned to gamble for very high stakes. To gamble successfully, you have to be able to read all the emotions people spend their lives trying to hide. Eventually I'll find out what you're hiding, Diana."

"Are you saying that you're a professional *gambler?*" she exclaimed.

"No. I make my money in the international financial markets, but we're all punters at heart. In the end, the man who blinks first loses. And I can assure you, Diana, that you'd lose your nifty little designer shirt if you tried to play in my league. Your eyes always give you away. There's a split-second flash of emotion in them before you manage to pull down the shutters. Like now," he added softly. "You were angry, then a bit scared and then you carefully blanked out your expression. Why are you scared of me, Diana?"

"Because you're an intimidating man." She moved to the other side of the kitchen. "And while we're on the subject, perhaps *you'd* like to explain why *you* didn't tell Nevil where the bust is."

"Because Peter asked me not to."

"What do you mean?" she snapped. "You told me you hadn't been in touch with Peter!"

"He communicated with me by mail," Matthew replied tightly. "Two parcels arrived for me the day he died. One contained the bronze bust, the other, a bronze statue. Peter had enclosed a letter with each, asking me to hide them in the priests' hole and not to reveal their whereabouts to anybody.''

"So what do you plan to do with the bronzes now?"

"Obviously Peter considered them exceptionally valuable, so I planned to ask somebody I could trust to explain why. However, I haven't had time to go tracking down reputable antiques dealers.''

"Other than Nevil Cranston. You did visit his showroom when you bought that pendant.''

"I had good reason for not asking his opinion. And how about answering my question? Why did you lie to Nevil?''

"Peter asked you not to discuss the sculptures. How do you know he didn't give me the same instructions?''

"I don't,'' Matthew said wearily. "In fact, I wish to God I knew exactly what he *did* tell you.''

"He told me you were the best older brother any man could have,'' Diana said. "Were you?''

His face whitened. "No,'' he replied. "I was a lousy brother.'' He strode out of the kitchen, slamming the door.

MATTHEW TRIED TO LIGHTEN the mood over dinner. He had invited Diana to a favorite restaurant in town. They started to guess the other diners' occupations.

"Okay, if you say that boring-looking couple by the door are having a passionate affair, then I say that man is really a secret agent.'' Matthew tilted his wineglass toward a distant corner of the restaurant, his eyes gleaming with laughter. "He's been lurking behind the menu for the past twenty minutes, but anybody can see he's really trying to watch the door.''

Diana swiveled around to inspect him, then laughed. "You're *hopeless,* Matthew. Obviously that poor guy has been stood up. I've never seen anybody who looks less like a secret agent. He has 'Successful Stockbroker' written all over him.''

"Then why is he keeping his face buried behind the menu?''

"He's probably embarrassed.''

Matthew grinned. "Maybe. But I still say he's a spy.''

She sighed. "And what is he spying on? The veal cutlets? Which are very good, by the way.''

"Oh, damn!'' Matthew looked dejected. "A spiffy-looking redhead just walked in and joined him. I guess he's a stockbroker after all.'' He picked up his wineglass and held it to Diana's lips.

"You've finished your wine," he said softly then. "Drink some of mine."

Mesmerized, she touched her lips to the glass and almost choked on the first sip as a hearty hand thumped her on the back.

"Well, now, if it isn't little Diana Mackenzie, all grown up and purtier than ever!" The cheerful Texas accent boomed across their table. Bob Heinrichs, wearing a gray wig and a mound of stomach padding, pumped Diana's hand enthusiastically. He winked at her, his tanned, pouched face looking every day of sixty.

"Diana, honey, what are you doing over here in London? Last I heard from your folks, you were selling dresses in a fancy store in Washington."

"I'm on vacation. But you must let me introduce my friend. This is Matthew Raleton. Matthew, this is—"

"Bobby Henderson, from Houston, Texas," Bob said, grasping Matthew's hand. "It sure is a real pleasure to meet you, yes sir."

They chatted briefly, then "Bobby" leaned over to give her a farewell hug, and Diana caught that spicy aftershave again. She smiled up at him, almost relieved that something about his disguise wasn't perfect.

"Goodbye," she said. "Take care of yourself, Bobby."

"You too. And say howdy to your folks for me, y'hear?"

"I wonder where he parked his horse," Matthew remarked dryly as Bob returned to his own table. "Good Lord, he's sitting with your stockbroker and his redhead!"

Fortunately Diana had nothing in her mouth, or she would have choked. "I told you he was a stockbroker," she said, smiling weakly. "Bobby must be over here discussing investments."

Bob's intrusion had reminded Diana all too clearly of why she was here. She was on tenterhooks as she drank a creamy Irish coffee, and as soon as the waiter brought the bill, she made an excuse to leave the table.

As she'd expected, Bob was waiting in the narrow hallway. He spoke rapidly.

"I had you followed from Foxe's apartment," he said. "There's been another murder."

She controlled her start of fear. "Who?"

"Remember the Soviet attaché who was seen talking to Foxe in Hyde Park? He was found dead in his apartment but it doesn't look like a KGB killing. I'd say the whole smuggling ring is falling apart—violently."

"Investigations are usually more successful when a criminal organization is breaking up. That's good news for us."

"Maybe. I'd like to order you home, but Ken and Charlie insist the decision is yours."

"I want to stay undercover, Bob. I think I'm getting somewhere. This afternoon, Nevil Cranston came looking for a small bronze bust. I think it's tied in with Peter's smuggling activities, and what's more, I know where it is. Matthew has a secret—"

"So this is where you are!" Matthew's voice broke in right behind her. "Are you ready to start our long trek home?"

"Quite ready," she said with more composure than she felt. "Goodbye again, Bobby. I'll be in touch."

"I'm at the Grosvenor Hotel, don't forget."

It was spitting with rain outside, but Diana was glad of an excuse to avoid speaking as they ran, head bent against the chill, to the car. Once in the Jaguar, she leaned back against the soft leather upholstery, willing herself to relax. She had a long night ahead: even at this hour, London's streets were clogged with traffic, and it was still more than two hours to Raleton Manor.

Fortunately, Matthew seemed no more in the mood for idle chit-chat than she, and she was drifting into a light doze when she realized that the Jaguar had made a sharp turn into an underground garage. She sat up, feeling very wide awake. "What's happened? Where are we going?"

"To my apartment. You look exhausted, and I'm rather tired. It seemed pointless to battle motorway traffic when I have a perfectly good flat in town. I hope you don't mind."

His flat was the penthouse in a new ten-story building near Sloane Square. Diana realized at once that, unlike Raleton Manor, this was very much the luxury home of a swinging bachelor. The living room carpet was silver-gray, the walls pristine white, the furniture opulently down-padded. In front of the fireplace were giant-sized Icelandic fur rugs. Perfect for high-class orgies, Diana reflected with grim humor.

Matthew paused in the doorway to adjust a dimmer beside the light switch. Immediately all the lamps cut their output to half, as simultaneously, seductive music drifted out from a concealed stereo system.

Diana saw, however, that Matthew's mood did not match the languorous setting. His temper was coming to a very rapid boil. "Would you like a brandy?" he asked, still playing the role of polite host. "Or perhaps you'd prefer some more coffee?"

She had no intention of inquiring into the causes of his escalating temper. As a good undercover operative, she knew when it was wise to retreat.

"Nothing for me, thanks," she said. "My bruised rib is reminding me it's past my bedtime."

In two strides, he was at her side. "Very prettily done," he said with deadly quietness. "Now, would you tell me who the buffoon with the Texas accent really is? How did he know you'd be at that restaurant? I only chose it at the last minute. Is he having you followed?"

She was too tired to cope with an interrogation. Too tired and too...something else. "Matthew, what's the matter with you? Bobby is an old friend of my parents'. My father was in the oil business. We met by sheer chance. We told you that."

"Sure. In fact, you've told me a hell of a lot in the brief time we've known each other. Is *any* of it true?"

She brushed past him. "If you'll show me where my room is, I'd like to go to sleep now."

He crossed the room, taking her into his arms and holding her curved tightly to him. His angry grasp ought to have been agony for her bruised ribs. Oddly enough, she scarcely noticed them.

His eyes seemed piercingly gray, threatening her with their powers of perception. "Let's try for at least one honest conversation before you go to bed," he said harshly. "If you don't feel like talking about Bobby the Friendly Oilman, why don't we chat about my brother. I believe we started a conversation like this once before. Tell me, Diana, were you and Peter lovers before your marriage? Better yet, were the two of you ever married at all?"

Her heart leaped. "Matthew, what do you mean?"

"Oh, God, I don't know anymore. Maybe I mean this." His hands cupped her face, holding her captive. Their eyes clashed for only an instant; then, with a low groan, he bent his head and covered her lips with his.

She had been waiting all night for his kiss, although her conscious mind would have denied it. Perhaps he had been waiting, too, for she sensed the frustration seething inside him as he thrust his tongue aggressively against her lips, demanding admission. His mouth tasted hot, angry—and unbearably sweet. She chose to respond only to the sweetness.

"Don't say anything," he murmured finally. "Don't let there be any more lies between us. Not tonight. I want you, Diana. I want to make love to you."

"I want you, too," she whispered. "I tried not to let it happen, but it did." Her voice was husky with emotion, seeming to promise truth, loyalty and a special sort of tenderness. For once, Matthew decided not to question the illusion.

He tilted her face again to receive his kiss. Their mouths touched, lightly at first. His tongue traced the outline of her mouth, and now her lips opened.

He had tasted her mouth a dozen times in his dreams, but the reality far exceeded the fantasy. Her body, slender and unexpectedly strong, curved into his as if it had been sculpted to fit. He buried his face in her hair, more than a little shocked by the intensity and speed of his arousal. As she stroked his back, he felt as if heat, liquid and molten, flowed from her fingers through his clothes.

Her head was nestled against his chest, and her breath began to come in little gasps when he slipped his hands under her sweater and caressed her breasts through the thin lace cups of her bra. Her nipples felt diamond-hard beneath his teasing fingers. He pulled her tightly against him, frustrated beyond bearing by the clothing that lay between them.

She seemed to know what he was feeling, for she moved out of his arms, slowly pulled her sweater over her head and tossed it onto the floor. Her cheeks turned pink, but her eyes never left his face as she unhooked her bra and threw it next to the sweater. Then she spoke.

"Your turn," she said huskily, pointing to his shirt.

His hands were suddenly equipped with ten wooden stubs instead of fingers. It took him at least half a lifetime to unbutton his shirt, with Diana looking at him, her mouth curved into a tiny smile and her half-naked body maddeningly out of reach.

He finally managed to remove his shirt. Then he held out his hand, and she came to him willingly, their fingers lacing together as he led her to the bedroom.

They tumbled haphazardly onto the covers, Diana leaning over him, the tips of her breasts grazing his chest. Desire exploded inside him. Mindlessly he dragged her closer until they were crushed together; then he rolled over, holding her hands high above her head and capturing her hips firmly beneath his. His fingers, miraculously competent again, undid the side zipper of her skirt, pushing it aside. Then her stockings. His own clothes were disposed of even more swiftly. As soon as they were naked, he entered her, clasping her flesh to flesh in the ultimate embrace.

He knew a brief moment of regret when he realized how close they both were to fulfillment. Her face was already dreamy, her body slick with desire. Just the thought of how she would look when he brought her to climax was almost enough to drive him over the edge. His control began to slip. Ruthlessly he dragged it back, forcing himself to wait until he knew she was ready. He felt the need begin to grow within her, cresting to meet the urgent thrusts of his body.

A deep, unaccustomed wave of satisfaction, coupled with an odd sort of tenderness, surged through him as she clutched at his shoulders and tossed her head frantically on the pillow. He held himself back for one minute longer, lifting a damp curl away from her cheek and leaning over to kiss the spot where it had rested. For a split second her entire body was still. Then she reached up and touched him lightly on the mouth, wonder and pleasure reflected in her eyes. Emotion swept through him—unfamiliar, painful and indescribably sweet.

"You're beautiful, Diana," he murmured.

"So are you."

His movements quickened, totally beyond his power of control. Her body tautened beneath his as she cried out the culmination of her passion. He drank the soft sounds into his mouth, absorbing the taste and texture of her.

The universe exploded around him.

He wondered if he would ever be able to pick up the pieces.

*

DIANA WOKE UP EARLY the next morning, but Matthew had already left her room. Discreet of him, she thought cynically, not allowing herself to examine the turmoil of her emotions too closely.

On the carpet outside her door, Diana found a note explaining that he had some business to attend to and would pick her up around noon to drive back to Salisbury.

Perhaps it was just as well, she reflected, soaking in the tub. She wasn't really feeling up to postmortems. Making love with Matthew had been more intense, more poignant, than any other experience she'd ever had, but it was one she couldn't afford to repeat. In a few days she would go back to Washington, and Matthew would go back to flirting with movie stars and princesses. Always provided, of course, that he wasn't in jail.

At that thought, Diana gave a gasp somewhere between despair and laughter. Because she loved him? No, dammit, she didn't love him. She, the respectable American daughter of a Scottish nationalist and an Irish republican, could never have been crazy enough to fall in love with an English aristocrat. Her mother's ancestors would be whirling in their shallow, famine-caused graves.

MRS. THANET HAD a late lunch waiting for them in the dining room. "Would you like me to serve the soufflé?" she asked. "It needs to be eaten while it's hot."

"Thank you," Matthew said. "By the way, Mrs. Thanet, I thought you might like a few hours to yourself this evening, so don't bother about dinner. With Janet away, Mrs. Foxe and I will eat out."

"You know I never mind cooking, my lord. It's no trouble."

"I know, but I thought Diana might like to visit the White Pelican in Sherston village. It's one of the most attractive inns in this part of the country, and they have an excellent new chef." He swiveled around on his chair. "Would you enjoy that, Diana?"

Far too much, she thought ruefully, but aloud she merely said, "That would be fun."

"Then it's all settled," Matthew said.

"There's fresh fruit salad for dessert," the housekeeper said as she left the dining room. "I've put it on the sideboard with a jug of cream."

Diana tasted her soufflé and sighed appreciatively. "Mmm... simply delicious."

Matthew seemed preoccupied. Then, "I didn't plan what happened last night between the two of us," he said abruptly. "Do you want me to apologize?"

Her heart skipped a beat, then raced forward in double time. She suddenly became fascinated by a pile of crumbs on the table. "You don't have to apologize. I understand what happened. We were both a bit uptight. Anyway—" she wanted to change the subject "—have you decided what you're going to do about that bronze? The head of the emperor Caracalla?"

He took a moment to reply. "I'll try to see if I can spot why it was of special interest to Peter and Nevil. After that, I suppose

I'll crate it up and send it off to a friend of mine at Edinburgh University."

He came over to Diana's side then, drawing her to her feet and gathering her into his arms. She knew he was going to kiss her, but she didn't turn away. His mouth was warm and sweet, and common sense flew to the four winds as he parted her lips, his kiss a virtual seduction all by itself. Within seconds, her senses were singing and heat was suffusing her body. Was she crazy? She'd spent all morning telling herself that she simply couldn't afford to let Matthew make love to her again, and here she was, melting into his arms.

She forced herself to retreat from his embrace. "Mrs. Thanet will be coming in to clear the table," she said.

Matthew sighed. "Unfortunately, you're right." He glanced at his watch. "In any case, I have to leave right away. Aunt Emily is at the Ibbotsons' and I must pick her up by three. I'll only just make it."

Diana busied herself with stacking the luncheon plates. "If she's coming home, Mrs. Thanet will have to make dinner, so we might as well eat here."

"My aunt rarely has more than toast and soup in the evening."

"Oh...do you still want me to go out to dinner with you to-night?"

"I want that very much. Could you be ready by six o'clock?"

She smiled. "I think I should probably make it."

His eyes met hers, full of promise. "I'll be waiting," he said.

DIANA WAS EATING DESSERT, a frothy confection of crushed strawberries and whipped cream, when she finally acknowledged that she was longing to make love to Matthew again. He was discussing a movie they had both seen recently, one she hadn't much enjoyed, and after a while, she realized she was no longer listening. She put down her spoon and leaned back in her chair, watching the candlelight flicker across his face. He was wearing his usual conservative dark suit and pristine white shirt, but her mind was filled with erotic images of his naked body, slick with sweat and tense with passion. Heat started in the pit of her stomach and spread out to her fingertips.

He glanced up, asking her a question, and she was very much afraid that her eyes betrayed exactly what she was feeling.

"I'm sorry," she said. "What did you say?"

"It wasn't important." He pushed his half-eaten dessert to one side. "I want to make love to you," he said. "I want to take you into my bed and see your hair spread out on my pillow. I want to feel your heart pound and your body melt into mine. Most of all, I want to hear you cry out my name when I bring you to fulfillment."

His eyes were so alive, so warm with passion, it was difficult to remember that she had once thought they were cold. Diana laced her fingers together, staring down at them intently. She wasn't sure if she was ready to let him discover the truth about her feelings.

He reached across the table and clasped her fingers. His hand was warm and strong. "Are you ready to go home with me?" he asked softly.

Slowly, she lifted her head. "I'm ready."

THEY CAME OUT into the moonlit darkness of the small parking lot, their hands locked together. Matthew reached into his pocket for the keys, opening the door of the Jaguar on the passenger side. Diana started to get in, but he suddenly gave a low groan and pulled her into his arms. He gave her a short, fierce kiss, holding her tight against his body.

"To keep me sane for the next ten miles," he said huskily.

She was burning with desire when she got into the car. Matthew slipped into the driver's seat and touched his fingers lightly to her mouth before turning on the ignition.

"Can you see to reverse?" Diana asked. "The lighting in this parking lot is terrible."

"The outdoor lights must have blown a fuse." Matthew squinted into the rearview mirror. "I think I can make it, though."

She twisted in her seat, looking around. But she didn't have time to cry out before a thin, ski-masked figure unfurled itself from a crouch on the floor and pressed a gun to her head.

"Keep driving, Lord Raleton," the black-clad figure commanded. "And turn left when you leave the lot."

Matthew looked at the gun, then headed out onto the road.

"That was a real smart decision," the man said softly, his voice blurred by the mask. "My finger's already getting kind of itchy on this trigger. Turn right at the next crossroads, please."

"That road is a dead end. It doesn't lead anywhere."

"On the contrary, it leads right where I want to go. Keep driving, Lord Raleton, and take it real easy on the corners. We wouldn't want any accidents.''

The Jaguar was traveling over an extremely narrow, bumpy lane. Probably an old farm track, Diana thought, trying to ignore the gun poking against her skull. She concentrated on breathing steadily, for until she regained some measure of calm, she would have no hope of planning an escape.

The lane ended in a grassy clearing, surrounded by trees. ''Stop the car here,'' the gunman ordered. ''Switch off the headlights. We're meeting an old friend.''

A second figure, almost invisible among the shadows, moved slowly toward the Jaguar. When he reached it, he switched on a powerful flashlight, half-blinding Diana and Matthew.

''Lord Raleton, put your hands on your head and get out,'' the masked gunman ordered. ''My associate will open the door. Don't try anything fancy, or your little playmate here will come to a swift and painful end.''

Matthew shrugged helplessly as he followed their abductor's orders.

''Now you,'' the gunman told Diana. ''And don't bump my hand. This trigger seems to be just about jumping under my finger.''

Sweat trickled down Diana's back. She had the eerie sensation of moving through a nightmare.

They were ordered to stand on either side of the car. Their two captors then joined forces, standing together about six or seven feet away. Close enough to make sure of hitting their targets, Diana thought grimly.

Now the masked gunman gave a quick nod, and the other man switched off the flashlight, tossing it casually into the bushes.

No longer dazzled by the beam of light, Diana could soon see more clearly. She swallowed a horrified gasp at the sound of a familiar voice.

''Matthew, old chap, so glad we managed to find you. And Diana, too, looking prettier than ever!''

''What the hell is this all about?'' Matthew demanded.

Nevil Cranston removed his hand from his jacket pocket. He was carrying a businesslike .38 automatic. Now he walked forward a couple of paces and pointed at Matthew's stomach.

''You're a smart fellow, so I'm sure you already know. My partner and I would like you to tell us what you've done with the two million dollars' worth of diamonds Peter sent you.''

Diamonds? Diana shot a quick glance in Matthew's direction. His face was expressionless.

"I don't know anything about any diamonds," he said. "Neither does Diana, I'm sure."

Nevil sighed. "You have this very annoying tendency to make things difficult, Matthew. And I am slightly more than two million dollars in the hole. I have clients in the States waiting to be paid for the seismometers they shipped to us, for which *we* were paid off in diamonds. They are, quite understandably, very angry clients. I have to pay them soon, Matthew."

"I still have no idea what you're talking about, but even if I knew, I'd be a fool to tell you."

"Have you noticed, old chap, that my colleague and I are the people holding the guns? The way I see it, you'd be incredibly foolish *not* to tell me. A collection of fancy stones won't be much use to either of you if you're dead."

"Just how gullible do you think I am, Nevil? Once you have these diamonds, my life expectancy will be about twenty seconds."

"You wrong me, but then, you never have appreciated the finer points of my character. I abhor violence."

"But how can you avoid killing us? You can't afford to take the risk that one of us won't go to the police."

"Knowing your bourgeois addiction to the forces of law and order, Matthew, I'm *certain* you'll go to the police. However, your actions after tomorrow morning are of little interest to me. As soon as I have the diamonds, I plan to take off for Paraguay—one of those wonderful countries that has no extradition treaties with England—or most other countries. British warrants have no legal authority there. After tomorrow morning, you may tell the police anything you please, but we'll make sure you're in no position to tell them tonight."

"You won't hurt Diana? Do I have your word on that?"

"Certainly, old chap." Nevil smiled. "The last thing in the world we want is for anybody to get hurt."

And if Matthew believes that, I have a nice line in bridges I'd like to sell him, Diana thought acidly.

She wondered if she dared risk faking a faint. She could probably disarm Nevil in the resulting confusion, but what about his colleague? She had an intuitive feeling that he was the man in charge, the cool, professional way he handled his weapon, a lethal .357 magnum.

On balance, Diana decided she had very little to lose by pretending to be on the verge of hysteria. She was fairly certain that neither gunman would try to kill her until they had the diamonds.

She allowed herself to sway, but didn't risk a stumble. "Why are you doing this to me?" she asked in a deliberately shaky voice. "Why have you brought me here? I can't help you. Peter never told me anything about any diamonds. We got married only a few weeks ago—"

Even in the moonlight, she could see the disgust that curled Nevil's lip. "Don't persist in that ridiculous story," he interjected coldly. "Whatever money you're hoping to squeeze out of Matthew is fine by me. But Peter and I have been lovers since he was in my art history class at Cambridge. We might have been having a few problems, but Peter would no more have married you than he would have married my Persian cat."

Diana's stomach took a double backflip dive toward her feet and stayed there. For a few moments she was too stunned to think. Then the significance struck her. No wonder Peter had never tried to make love to her! No wonder he had ditched his girlfriends with such regularity! A dozen minor mysteries suddenly became clear. Now she understood why Matthew had always seemed so suspicious of her marriage.

Diana's thoughts were jolted back to the present when Nevil began to swear violently at Matthew.

"Perhaps my friend can induce you both to be a little more cooperative," Nevil added. He turned. "I'll cover the girl while you tie Matthew's hands."

The masked man tucked his gun into a professional-looking shoulder holster, then unwound a length of thin cord. He walked toward Matthew on incredibly light feet.

Despite the .38 aimed at her heart, Diana's fear was under better control and she was struck by something about the gunman's silent stride. She didn't dare move, but as he crossed in front of her, she drew in a deep breath and smelled the faint but unmistakable tang of Bob Heinrichs's spicy aftershave.

For a few vital seconds, Diana was literally immobilized by disbelief. When her brain finally started functioning again, she realized that her initial shock had prevented her from detecting the scent in the car.

As she watched Bob pull Matthew's hands behind him, Diana suddenly discovered that she was no longer frightened. She was simply angry—furiously angry at the magnitude of Bob's betrayal.

There was no way, she vowed, that she would let him get away with two million dollars' worth of diamonds. He had already done more than enough harm to the United States. He wasn't going to make a massive profit into the bargain.

But in that restaurant in London, *she* had told him that Matthew had the Caracalla bronze. The diamonds must be inside it!

Diana was so overwhelmed with her discovery of Bob's treachery that she almost forgot Nevil and his gun, until he began sliding it gently up and down her throat.

"Your little lady friend is trembling, Matthew." Nevil's voice was soft. "Are you ready to tell us where you've hidden those diamonds?"

"I'll tell you when you let Diana go."

"You seem very concerned for dear little Diana."

"I don't want her to get hurt, that's all."

Nevil forced Diana's face upward and stared at her, coldly assessing. "She's quite ordinary-looking except for those fabulous green eyes. For the life of me, I can't understand what you see in her."

"No," Matthew said dryly, "I'm quite sure you can't."

Nevil's eyes glittered angrily. He yanked Diana around and dragged her over to Matthew.

"My patience just ran out," he said tightly. "You have thirty seconds, and then I shoot one of her kneecaps."

Diana didn't think Nevil was fooling. Matthew seemed to reach the same conclusion. "All right!" he exploded. "The diamonds are in my bedroom. They're inside that bronze you were so anxious to find. But you'll never get at them without me. They're in a safe, and there's a voice control on the lock. You'll have to take me with you."

Diana knew there was no such safe, which meant that he must have some sort of plan for their escape. Her heart squeezed tight with emotion she had no time to analyze.

Unfortunately, their chances of escape were even slimmer than Matthew realized. Nevil Cranston was one thing. Bob Heinrichs was an altogether different proposition. Not only was he a traitor, he also had years of professional training.

And Diana knew she wouldn't live five minutes if he ever realized she had penetrated his disguise.

There was no time to think. "I'll tie the girl's hands," Bob said to Nevil. "You get Raleton into the car. This is taking far too long."

They drove in tension-laden silence along the deserted country lanes until they arrived at the gates of the manor.

"Give the command that opens the gates," Nevil said and Matthew lowered the window to speak the number sequence into an electronic control box.

Bob stirred impatiently. "You're sure the house is empty?" he asked Nevil.

"I'm sure. Janet called me from Lyme Regis. The chauffeur's there, too."

"What about the housekeeper?"

"She has a small flat over one of the garages. The rest of the staff live out."

"What about the old woman?"

"Aunt Emily? Don't worry about her." Nevil laughed. "She's three parts deaf and nuttier than a fruitcake. Besides, her bedroom is way over in the west wing. She'll never know we're inside."

They entered the house without incident, Nevil keeping his gun trained on Matthew, Bob with his on Diana.

"Where's the wall safe?" Bob asked curtly, once they were in the bedroom. He seemed to ignore Nevil now and openly assumed control.

"It's built into a priests' hole by the fireplace."

"Priests' hole?" Bob echoed.

"A hiding place for priests built during the sixteenth century," Nevil explained quickly. "I recall Peter mentioning that this house had one, but I've never actually seen it."

"How do we get access to it?" Bob asked.

"It's controlled by a spring-lock device, hidden in one of those carved flowers. I can give you directions, but it's rather a delicate operation," Matthew replied.

"You can fiddle with the antique rosebuds," Bob told Nevil, a definite edge to his voice.

Matthew instructed Nevil.

"Find the family crest in the top right-hand corner and count six flowers down," said Matthew. "You'll need two hands to work the mechanism."

Nevil hesitated only a second before slipping his gun into his pocket.

"Now press the center of the flower with one hand and with the other, gently rotate the petals of the rose to the left."

Matthew was deliberately giving the wrong directions, Diana realized. She edged closer to the fireplace, keeping her back turned away from Bob. She had been manipulating her wrists so that the thin cord around them was loosening. Soon she would be free.

Nevil swore frustratedly. "I can feel the damn flower moving, but nothing seems to happen!"

"It does have a tendency to jam," Matthew told him. "Try to press and rotate the petals in one movement."

"It's not budging," Nevil said finally.

"I could do it for you," Matthew offered. "But only if you untie my hands."

Bob hesitated, then nodded in agreement, and Nevil hacked through the cord with Matthew's letter opener. He moved aside, allowing Matthew access to the carved pilaster. For a split second, Matthew's gaze locked with Diana's, and she gave a quarter turn so that he could see she had succeeded in freeing her hands.

His expression didn't change by so much as a millimeter, but she felt the warm rush of his approval leap out across the small space that separated them.

"The lock isn't all that difficult once you have the knack," Matthew said, as the secret door swung open and a rush of cool, dank air assailed Diana's nostrils.

Matthew stepped quickly into the priests' hole before either Nevil or Bob could protest. "The safe is in here," he said, "about halfway down these stairs." His foot was poised on the first stone step. "Coming, Nevil?" he called over his shoulder. "We might as well get this over with."

Nevil, alarmed that his quarry might disappear from view, pushed past Diana and rushed into the darkness.

"Get away from that entrance," Bob ordered harshly, moving toward Diana.

She heard a tiny noise at the bedroom's main door just as Bob caught up with her. Aunt Emily stood framed in the doorway.

"Why, hello, Diana, what are you doing in Matthew's room? Have you seen my knitting?"

The old lady peered shortsightedly around as she stepped inside, then gasped with horror at the black ski-masked figure of Bob Heinrichs. "Oh, my goodness! Who is that nasty man? Have the Nazis invaded?"

Bob whirled, squatting to take aim with his .357. Leaping forward, Diana let fly with a double-fisted karate chop to his arm. The gun exploded, its bullet discharging into the carpet as Bob dropped the weapon. Diana managed to snatch it away from his grasping fingers, but he gripped her hand so tightly that she couldn't take proper hold of it. She struggled with him in deadly, silent combat, using every skill she had ever learned. But Bob had received the same training and was physically stronger. Diana wondered desperately if she had any hope of hanging on until Matthew returned.

She should have known better than to allow her concentration to deviate. Bob took advantage of her brief lapse, twisting her arm into a punishing half nelson. The gun fell from her nerveless fingers, but she managed to kick it out of his reach.

It was the last victory Bob seemed likely to allow her. He swung his leg upward, hooking it behind her body and sweeping her to the floor. In a single, skillful maneuver, he retrieved the gun and knelt over her, holding her arms over her head with one hand.

"You know, don't you?" he remarked sadly.

"Yes, I know."

He twirled the gun, still not aiming it at her. "I didn't want this to happen, Diana. I tried to persuade you to go back—"

His words ended in a choked gurgle, and he collapsed in a dead weight on top of her.

"That'll teach him," Aunt Emily panted, brandishing the fireplace poker over Bob's inert body. She sighed regretfully. "I don't think he's dead, my dear. But would you like to crawl out from underneath him and see?"

Diana retrieved the gun, then bent down and felt for a pulse.

"He's alive," she told Emily. "And that's good news. Let's cover him up and call the doctor, because I want to be a witness when he goes on trial for treason."

"What I want is to know where Matthew is. This is his bedroom, so why isn't he here to protect you?"

"Good heavens! Matthew! I'll be back in a minute." Diana dropped a hasty kiss on Aunt Emily's cheek and tore into the priests' hole, only to bump into Matthew, who was ascending the shallow steps three at a time.

"Thank God!" He swept her into his arms.

"What did you do with Nevil?" she asked.

"I ducked into a side passage and bopped his gun hand as he ran past me. Now he's chained to a storage rack, inspecting my wine cellar. Where's the man with the ski mask?"

She grinned. "Out cold. Aunt Emily knocked him out with a poker, but—"

"*Knocked him out with a poker?* My tiny, frail aunt?"

Diana laughed. "Yep, but we'd better not leave her alone with

Bob Heinrichs for long. Knowing his powers of recuperation, he'll be coming around any minute.''

"Bob Heinrichs?"

"The other gunman," she said. "I recognized him. Come on, Matthew."

Emily had covered Bob with a blanket and was standing over her victim, poker at the ready. Matthew gave her a big hug and led her to an armchair, returning the poker to its shiny brass stand. Then he dialed the police.

"I already called Dr. Farrell," Aunt Emily said. "You can tell them he's on his way."

"They'll be here in ten to fifteen minutes," Matthew said.

Diana threw herself onto the rumpled bed, stretching luxuriously. "Now, if we knew where those diamonds were, I'd call this a really successful evening."

Matthew grinned. "Your wish, m'lady, is my command." He strolled over to the priests' hole and returned brandishing a bronze statue of a plump, somewhat matronly Greek goddess with a sleek hunting dog nestled at her feet.

Matthew plunked the statue down on the bed. "Remember this?" he asked Diana. "Peter sent it to me when he sent the Caracalla bust. That's genuine, but I think *this* is a modern reproduction. What do you suppose we'd find if we cut off the head?"

Her tiredness forgotten, Diana sat bolt upright. "Two million dollars' worth of diamonds!" She shot off the bed. "Wait here!" she commanded.

She flew down the stairs and into the small room off the kitchen where the chauffeur kept his tools. She found a small blowtorch and raced back up, thrusting it into Matthew's hands.

"Quick, do it before the police get here."

Matthew set the statue down on his desk and applied the flame to the bronze neck. "Get me a towel, will you?" he asked Diana.

He wrapped it around the metal head, twisting slowly. Trailing strands of molten bronze, it came off in his hand. He held the statue out to Diana, who carried it over to the bed, Matthew and Aunt Emily hard on her heels.

When she upended the statue, a waterfall of glittering diamonds cascaded down, coming to rest in little piles scattered across the bed.

"Oh, my!" Aunt Emily exclaimed. "I haven't seen so many diamonds since I went to the king's coronation!"

Matthew surveyed the gems in silence, his good-humored grin

gradually fading. "I didn't really believe they existed until now,"
he said. "Where the *hell* did Peter get them?"

Diana met his gaze steadily over the twinkling blaze of the
diamonds. "If you'll let me place a phone call to the States," she
said wearily, "I can probably get permission to tell you."

DIANA PICKED UP THE PHONE in her room and dialed.

"Agent Mackenzie?" the duty officer said after a brief delay.
"The deputy director is having dinner with the secretary of the
treasury. Is this call priority one?"

"Yes. This is a major emergency."

"I'm connecting you immediately. Please hold."

She had to fight a crazy impulse to burst into tears of relief
when she heard Charlie's voice. "What's happened, Diana?" he
asked.

"Brace yourself for bad news, Charlie. I've uncovered evidence
that Bob Heinrichs is in charge of Business Art's smuggling ring,
and I'm pretty certain he was also responsible for Peter Foxe's
murder. My best guess is he's a double agent working for the KGB
as a recruiter."

For once it seemed that Charlie was incapable of speech. Then
he cleared his throat and said, "Please explain."

"He tried to kill Matthew Raleton and me. It was a pretty convincing demonstration of guilt." Diana went on to give her boss
a concise account of events.

"Current status of the operation?" Charlie asked.

"The local police are about to move in. Bob is concussed, but
if you want to extradite him, I need a legal expert. And there's
two million dollars' worth of diamonds sitting in Matthew's bedroom. Somebody has to decide who they belong to."

"Give me fifteen minutes to make the necessary calls," Charlie
said grimly. "And, Diana, please make arrangements to fly back
to Washington as soon as possible. We need you for debriefing."

"I'll be on a plane within twelve hours," she promised, ignor-
ing the sudden emotion that welled up, blurring her vision.
"There's something else. I need your permission to tell Matthew
Raleton what's been going on."

"Not a good idea if you can avoid it."

"For God's sake, Charlie, the man was set up by one of our
own agents! He thinks I'm his dead brother's wife, and you're
asking me to leave without giving him any explanations!"

"Well...okay. But keep the revelations minimal. And one more thing," he growled. "You did a great job. Well done, kid."

She smiled, tasting the bitterness of personal defeat in the midst of her professional victory. "Sure," she said.

THANK GOD THE CONCORDE flew directly from London to Washington today, Matthew thought, looking out at a sea of white clouds. Thirty minutes more and they'd be landing. If he was lucky, he should be seeing Diana in a couple of hours.

Just because he now knew he loved Diana, however, Matthew didn't make the mistake of assuming she loved him. Love wasn't always reciprocal, and just because he went dizzy with longing every time he visualized her sparkling green eyes didn't mean she returned his feelings.

He had spent the past ten days "helping the police with their inquiries," and the experience had left him with lingering feelings of guilt. He blamed himself for not having confronted Peter a couple of months ago, when he suspected that he was in trouble again. When Peter's last, desperate message had finally reached Matthew, it had been too late.

Matthew stared ahead, wondering what strange set of personal demons had changed a cheerful, fun-loving twelve-year-old boy into a troubled man who was willing to betray his country for the sake of a few thousand pounds. Nevil Cranston had clearly played a large part in Peter's downfall, but in the last resort, Peter had to be held accountable for his own actions.

DIANA READ THE PARAGRAPH she had just spent fifteen minutes composing and cursed under her breath. Gritting her teeth, she pressed the delete key again. So far, she had wasted two days trying to write up a final report on Operation Temptation.

She stared at the cursor flickering on her screen, wondering where Matthew was right now. Maybe at this very moment he was getting into bed, unbuttoning his formal white shirt, revealing his tanned, muscular body in all its primitive, masculine glory. Naturally, he wasn't alone. A woman was lying on the sheets waiting for him, her body curved into a position of sensuous abandon. Surprisingly, that woman was Diana Mackenzie! And Matthew was responding to her with extremely gratifying ardor.

"Working hard, kid?" Diana jumped guiltily as Charlie Groves's voice boomed behind her. Then, "Forget the report for now," he said. "There's one final debriefing session this evening, so you might as well collect your things. The meeting won't be held in this building."

"Do we have to take a cab?" Diana asked, locking her office door behind them. "You know we'll never get one at this time of day."

"Your transportation is provided," Charlie replied as he showed her into a small public reception room. "I think this is the person you've been hoping to see."

For the first time in her life, Diana understood what it meant to be weak-kneed with happiness. "Hi!" she said, grinning foolishly. "What are you doing here?"

"I came to invite you out to dinner," Matthew said, his mouth curving into the tiny self-mocking smile that turned her bones to water. "If you'd like to suggest a restaurant, I have a cab waiting outside."

Her heart was beating very fast, but her voice sounded surprisingly casual. "We could go to my apartment if you like."

"I'd like that very much," he said simply.

SHE WAS PROUD of her apartment, although she supposed Matthew might find it barely adequate. "It's lovely," he said, walking into her living room. "It's like you—clean lines, soft cushions and unexpected splashes of color."

"I think I'm flattered." She smiled. "Why have you come to the States, Matthew?"

"To see you. To talk to you."

Her heart gave a leap of hope. "I'm glad you came."

He shoved his hands into his pants pockets. "How are things going at work?" he asked.

"Fine, thanks, although writing reports is my least favorite task."

"I'm sure you know that Nevil has decided to cooperate with the police in England. He's spilling the beans."

"That's fortunate, because Heinrichs hasn't said a word so far."

Matthew looked at her a bit sheepishly. "You were right, Diana, about that emerald pendant. Heinrichs retrieved it from Peter and gave it back to Nevil, so that's why he was able to sell me the very same necklace. But Nevil insists he knew nothing about Peter's murder until Heinrichs told him he was dead."

"It could be true. I'm sure Bob made all the decisions."

"I think Heinrichs must have set up your accident, as well. A man called me that night, just before you were due to arrive from London. He claimed to be from the local police and said that my aunt had fallen and hurt herself. He asked me to come right away. I suspect Heinrichs deliberately tripped her. He must have learned from Nevil that she and an old friend have been meeting in the same restaurant every week for the past thirty years."

"So that's why you were driving hell for leather toward town!"

"Yes. It was a miracle we didn't crash into each other head-on."

She shuddered. "I have another question for you. The night Aunt Emily came into my room, why did you come back a couple of hours later to search my suitcase?"

He smiled wryly. "Not to search. I was replacing the underwear Aunt Emily had taken when she was after her knitting. One of the side effects of her conviction that World War II is still raging is that she tends to hoard pretty clothes."

Diana started to giggle. "Matthew! You mean all that stealth was over a pair of panties?"

He laughed. "You should know that the truth often sounds ridiculous. Lies can be made to sound much more elegant."

"Yes," she said, sobering. "I do know that."

Their conversation lapsed until Matthew suddenly muttered, "To hell with this!" and swept her into his arms. "This is the truth, Diana," he said. "Forgive me if it's a little rough around the edges."

His embrace was so tight she could scarcely breathe. His lips moved feverishly against hers, almost desperate in the urgency of his need. His hands roamed her back, touching her with fire, and she pushed her fingers into the springy thickness of his hair, shivering with delight as his tongue thrust deeper into her mouth.

A long time later, he lifted his head. His face was flushed, and Diana could see the pulse throbbing in his throat.

"Come back to England with me," he said huskily. "I'm hoping if I keep you there long enough, you'll eventually agree to marry me."

Her heart was hammering so fiercely she could barely speak. "I love you," she whispered, "but I'm not sure that's enough. Matthew, you're a baron, living on a huge estate that's been in your family for generations. How could I ever hope to make a suitable baroness?"

He smiled tenderly. "Well, I realize our family isn't nearly respectable enough for somebody as upright and law-abiding as you. But with your good example to follow, maybe we can all be trained into better behavior.'' He lowered his voice seductively. ''Now you've said you love me, you know there isn't a chance in the world that I'll let you go.''

She tried to ignore the fact that he was unbuttoning her blouse. ''You haven't even met my family,'' she pointed out. ''Ah, dear God, Matthew, don't!''

''What?'' he inquired innocently. ''Don't meet your family?''

''No,'' she gasped. ''I meant don't kiss my breast like— Oh, God, Matthew! What are you doing?''

''I'm kissing you senseless.'' His mouth ceased its teasing of her nipples and began to trace an erotic path up toward the hollows of her throat. ''It's very enjoyable.''

Love and laughter mingling in his eyes, Matthew swept his hands smoothly over her shoulders and cupped her face, tilting it upward so that his mouth rested only a breath away. His eyes darkened, the laughter dying away, leaving only desire. ''I love you, Diana. Will you marry me? Please.''

Her hands closed over his. ''On one condition.''

''Anything.''

''That you make love to me right now, before I go totally crazy with wanting you.''

''My darling Diana, you make the most wonderful conditions!'' And with the arrogance of six centuries of inherited authority, Lord Matthew Raleton swept his bride-to-be into his arms and carried her into the bedroom.

FREE FALL
Jasmine Cresswell

Liz saw the crowd outside her apartment building as soon as she turned the corner from the bus stop. Her mouth went dry and her stomach lurched in horrified recognition. Her hands cradled her waist.

"Oh no! Please, no!"

She saw the chalk outline on the pavement as soon as she elbowed her way through the crowd. She walked up to the building's entrance.

"Which apartment is yours?" the officers guarding the door asked.

She glanced up, finally allowing herself to look at the open window. It was hers, of course. Hers and Karen Zeit's. She had known all along that it would be.

"I live in 6B," she said flatly.

She felt the policemen exchange glances. She wrapped her arms tightly around her body. She was shivering, she realized, and the little clicking noise resonating inside her head had to be the chattering of her teeth.

"I'm Lieutenant Rodriguez. You'd better come along inside and get warm."

"Karen's dead," Liz said flatly once they were inside. "Isn't she?"

"I'm afraid so. If it's any consolation, Ms. Meacham, I'm sure your roommate died instantly."

"Have you told her parents yet? Their phone number is on the bulletin board in Karen's bedroom."

"We found it, and we're working on notifying the parents. Have you shared an apartment with the deceased for long, Ms. Meacham?"

The deceased. "I moved in with Karen six weeks ago."

"I see. And did you know her before that?"

"No. I only moved to Denver recently."

"Just for the record, would you mind telling me where you lived before you moved in with the deceased?"

Liz cleared her throat. "I lived in Seattle."

"Seattle is a big city, Ms. Meacham. Could I have an address, please? Just for the record, of course."

Of course, she thought with silent irony. Nevertheless, she gave him what he was asking for. "755 West Arbor Avenue. Apartment 14D."

"Do you know where the deceased was employed, Ms. Meacham?"

"She worked for Dexter Rand. She was the senior secretary in his Denver office."

"Dexter Rand? You mean the senator? Was the deceased interested in politics?"

"Not that I know of. I think she just enjoyed the hectic pace of Dexter's office."

Something in her voice must have betrayed her. Or perhaps it was her slip in using Dexter's first name. The lieutenant looked up quickly. "Nothing personal in their relationship?"

"Not that I know of."

"Would you have known?"

The look Liz gave him was cool. "Probably not."

The lieutenant changed the subject. "And you, Ms. Meacham? Where do you work?"

"I'm in charge of market research at Peperito's."

"Peperito's? The Mexican-food company?"

"Yes."

The lieutenant flipped through his notes. "Did the deceased give any indication that she was depressed, Ms. Meacham? Did she have any reason to take her own life? Any arguments with men friends...colleagues...the senator...that sort of thing?"

"I don't know much about Karen's personal life," Liz said.

"I'd like to ask just a few more questions, if I may—"

"No." She shook her head. The police were going to find out about her past sooner or later, but tonight she was too tired and too scared to face up to any more of Lieutenant Rodriguez. "I want to go to a hotel," she said abruptly.

"If you wait another half hour until the technicians have finished upstairs, you can go into your apartment and pack a suitcase."

"I don't want to go into my apartment." Liz fought to keep her voice calm. "I want to get out of here, Lieutenant. Now."

Surprisingly, he didn't protest.

"Do you need a ride, Ms. Meacham?"

"No thanks. My car's right in the parking lot. I took the bus this morning because the roads were so icy, but it's not freezing anymore.''

"Still, you want to drive carefully, Ms. Meacham. We don't need any more accidents tonight.''

She wasn't the one who was accident-prone, she reflected darkly as she drove to Dexter Rand's house. She parked the car against the only free stretch of sidewalk and stared at the high brick wall surrounding Dexter's home.

I'll tell him about Karen before the police get to him. I owe him that much.

"Good evening, ma'am,'' the maid who opened the door greeted her. "May I take your coat?''

Liz blinked and stared at the maid. Her coat. The maid expected her to stay and socialize.

"Er...no, thanks,'' Liz mumbled. "I don't think I'm staying.''

She and the maid saw Dexter at almost the same moment. The maid greeted him with evident relief. Liz stared at him in numb silence. All she could think of was that he looked even better in real life than he did on television. His six-feet-two-inch body was still perfectly proportioned, and his dark, coarse hair remained indecently thick, with no more the occasional thread of gray to mark the passing of the last nine years. On him, even the crow's-feet around his eyes looked good. She wished he'd gone bald or developed a beer belly.

"This young lady was just leaving,'' the maid said.

"But not before I've had a chance to say hello, I hope....'' Dexter's professionally warm voice trailed away into stunned silence. "Liz?'' he asked hoarsely. "Liz, what in the world are you doing here?''

"Karen's dead. They found her on the sidewalk outside her apartment building. The police think she jumped.''

"My secretary Karen...killed herself? Oh, my God!'' Dexter reached out and drew Liz farther into the foyer, away from the front door.

"I'm leaving, Dexter,'' Liz said in a monotone.

"No, you're not. We need to talk.'' He gave a passing guest one of his patented thousand-watt smiles, slipped his arm around Liz's waist, and propelled her with iron force through the foyer, skillfully eluding the half-dozen people who tried to engage him in conversation. He finally stopped at a heavy oak door and punched an electronic key code into the pad above the lock.

"Let's sit down," he said, gesturing toward the sofa once the door had opened. "Damn it, I still can't believe Karen's dead!"

"The police think she threw herself out of the living-room window. I guess she must have...done it...right after she got home from work."

Dexter's eyes were shadowed with pain and a hint of some other emotion Liz couldn't identify. "That's terrible, almost unbelievable. How could she sit and chat about her plans for the weekend, when she intended to do this to herself a couple of hours later? How could I have missed all her signals?"

"Maybe something happened after she got home. A devastating phone call or something."

"I sure would like to think so." Dexter looked up, a new question obviously occurring to him. "How do you know all this, Liz? Come to think of it, how did you know Karen? She never mentioned your name to me."

Liz avoided his eyes. "She was—my roommate."

"You were sharing an apartment with my personal secretary?"

"Yes."

"Did she know about—us?"

"No."

"Odd that she never spoke about you."

"We'd been sharing the apartment less than two months. She probably had no reason to mention me. Why would she?"

He shrugged. "Things like that usually come up in conversation, although Karen never did talk much about her friends."

"I wasn't a friend, only a roommate. We didn't know each other at all well."

Dexter scrutinized her intently for a moment. "What are you doing here in Denver, Liz? When we parted company, I didn't think anything would tear you away from life in the Big Apple."

If only he knew how grateful she'd been five years ago to find an obscure job in an obscure corner of southern Ohio. Better that he should never know. She smiled brightly.

"It was tough leaving New York, but you know what companies are like these days. If you want a promotion, you have to be prepared to relocate."

"Why didn't you go back to skating, not even to teach?"

She pushed her fingers through her hair, her smile brighter than ever. "There's nothing more pathetic than a second-rate athlete trying to eke out a living on the fringes of the sports world."

"You aren't a second-rate athlete, Liz, and we both know it.

You went to pieces during that last championship. I know we were having our problems, and we were young, but I still say your sister made the situation worse.''

"Poor Alison. You never did like her, did you?''

"The fact that she was your twin didn't make her your friend, Liz.''

Liz laughed harshly. "Nine years and nothing changes. Isn't this about where our last conversation ended?''

Dexter looked down. "You're right, and this isn't the moment for hashing over the past. You came here for a reason, Liz, and that must be connected with Karen's death. If you believed she'd committed suicide, you wouldn't have come. Only something really important would reconcile you to seeing me again. We didn't exactly part friends, and I imagine my marriage to Susan only made things worse.''

Liz sprang up from the sofa, turning her back on him. "I'm sorry about your wife,'' she said abruptly. "Nowadays you don't expect a woman as young as Susan to die of heart disease.''

"Statistically it happens, but I guess we never anticipate people we love becoming statistics.'' There was a tiny pause, and Dexter's voice roughened. "Amanda has found it really difficult to accept her mother's death.''

Liz swallowed hard. "How old is Amanda now?''

"She's almost eight, and in my totally unprejudiced opinion, she's gorgeous. But you aren't here to discuss Amanda,'' Dexter said. "What's bothering you so much about Karen Zeit's death that you were prepared to talk to me face-to-face?''

As soon as he asked the question, Liz walked over to the windows, keeping her back toward him when she finally spoke.

"I think Karen was murdered.''

Silence. She was grateful that he didn't protest, or tell her in polite euphemisms that she was crazy. After a second or two, he simply walked over to where she was standing, turned her around and looked at her assessingly with those cool gray eyes of his. He asked only one question. "Why?''

"Karen isn't my first roommate to die. I was working in Seattle until I moved to Denver at the beginning of March. I shared apartments with two other people there, and both of them died almost the same way as Karen. The police are going to arrest me, Dex,'' she said, her voice shaking. "Somebody's going to contact the police in Seattle and then it will all be over. I'm going to be arrested.''

He grasped her hands reassuringly. "Not if I can avoid it. Aside from the fact that you can't believe the coincidence of three room-mates committing suicide within three months, do you have any other reason for thinking Karen and the others might have been murdered?"

She shook her head. "Not a thing, unless you count my feeling that they weren't suicidal people."

"Did you know them well enough to judge?"

"Not Karen, maybe. But the other two. Jill and I had been acquainted for a couple of years. We belonged to the same health club. And Brian...I guess you could say we knew each other pretty well."

"Were you and Brian lovers?" Dexter asked carefully.

"We'd talked about getting engaged. We were living together."

"That doesn't answer my question, Liz."

"I think it does. If it's any of your business."

After an uncomfortable silence, Dexter said, "My feeling is that you should spend the night here so that we can work on our stories while my public relations aide holds the reporters at bay. Then we'll meet the press together tomorrow morning. Is that okay with you?"

It seemed slightly less okay than spending the night in a cage with a hungry tiger. The only thing that might possibly be worse was the prospect of driving to a hotel room and spending the night alone with her imagination and her suddenly overactive memories. "You're right," she said quietly. "I think maybe it would be best if I stayed here."

"Don't worry." For the first time, Liz could hear a note of bitterness in Dexter's voice. "We're experts, remember? We've done all this before."

THE NEXT MORNING, however, Dexter was considerably rattled when he took the podium in the reception room. A Lieutenant Rodriguez had caught and grilled him just before he was due to speak. It was clear Rodriguez thought he was much more than Karen Zeit's boss. Still, Dexter was a professional, and could eas-ily hide his shaken nerves.

"I'm sorry that the occasion for our get-together this morning is such a sad one," he said without preamble. "Karen Zeit was my personal secretary for the past year. She worked long hours with tireless efficiency, and kept my personal and business schedules untangled with almost magical skill. She will be sorely missed in my office, and by her colleagues. I like to think that we had become friends, as well as employer and employee, so that her loss is a double blow for me. I think most of your questions can be answered far better by the police department than they can by me, but I'll do my best to respond to anything relevant.''

A reporter from one of the TV stations spoke up. "I was talking to the superintendent at Karen Zeit's apartment building this morning, and it turns out that she was sharing her apartment with a young woman called Elizabeth Meacham. You were once married to a member of our U.S. Olympic figure skating team, and her name was also Elizabeth Meacham. Is this just a strange coincidence, Senator, or is it possible that your secretary was sharing an apartment with your ex-wife?''

Dexter's grin was a masterpiece of rueful, good-natured resignation. "It's no coincidence, Harry, as I'm sure you realized.'' Dexter turned and smiled toward Liz. "We anticipated that this item of news would set all your journalistic noses twitching, so my former wife very kindly volunteered to join us here this morning. Liz.''

Dexter held out his hand. Liz rose to her feet and slowly walked across the room to Dexter's side. It had been a while since she last faced a roomful of journalists, but not long enough to forget how easily they could savage you.

"Karen and I met at a party a couple of months ago,'' she said. "We talked about sharing an apartment. When I found out who Karen worked for, I explained that Dexter and I had once been married. Neither Karen nor I thought that had any bearing on our decision to share an apartment, so I moved in.''

The journalists all began shouting questions at her. Deafened by the bombardment, she forced herself to maintain her inner calm. A question from one of the TV journalists caught her attention.

"Hard feelings toward the senator?'' she said with a casual smile. "Oh, no. Dexter and I reconciled our differences a long time ago. We're both ten years older now, and events have taken on a whole different perspective.'' If she'd been a kid, she'd have had her hands behind her back crossing her fingers when she uttered that whopper.

The editor from the *Boulder Post* was on his feet. "Senator, I understand that the autopsy results suggest that Karen Zeit didn't commit suicide. As of now, the police are treating this as a case of homicide. Do you have any comment on that?''

Liz plastered the noncommittal look onto her face so firmly that she was afraid it might never come off. Dear heaven, how long had the police suspected Karen had been murdered? She looked up at Dexter, marveling that he could appear so calm. At nineteen, she had never bothered to look below that surface calm. Now—instinctively—she recognized how much effort it was costing him to appear unconcerned.

"If the police autopsy suggests that Karen Zeit was murdered, then I certainly would have no grounds or expertise for disputing their verdict," Dexter said. "If it does turn out that she was murdered, I hope very much that her killer is found quickly and brought to justice."

"So you have no fears, Senator, that this investigation is going to touch close to home?"

"Karen was my personal secretary. Obviously I'm extremely interested in finding out how she died."

"And how about the note she left, Senator?"

"What note?"

"The one claiming you're the father of her baby and that you refused to marry her."

Minutes later, Dexter repeated the words he'd quickly improvised to Liz, and Evan Howard, his public relations aide. "For what it's worth," he said, "I would like you to know there isn't a word of truth in Karen's note. If it isn't a forgery, she was fantasizing."

Evan's head shot up, and Liz thought she saw genuine astonishment in his eyes. "You're sure of that? You didn't get her pregnant? You're saying you two weren't—you know—intimate?"

There was a hint of weariness in Dexter's reply. "No, we weren't intimate. You're taking Lieutenant Rodriguez too seriously, Evan."

"No." Evan's voice was quiet now. "The truth is, Dexter, Karen told me in confidence that the two of you were lovers. You know, after that weekend you went up to Aspen together. She was...um...hoping to marry you. I told her not to count on it." He cast a worried glance in Liz's direction, then plunged ahead. "I warned her that you hadn't been taking your women...um...seriously since Susan..."

When had Dexter ever taken his women seriously? Liz thought cynically. Certainly not during his marriage to her.

"You repeated all this to Lieutenant Rodriguez?" Dexter asked.

Evan hung his head. "I had to. He kept on asking all these questions about Karen and you."

Dexter merely shrugged. "Whatever Karen may have said to you, I wasn't her lover and I didn't get her pregnant."

"Sure, Dexter, if you say so, but remember the police'll probably be able to run paternity tests on the fetus—"

Dexter cast a single, hard glance at his publicist. "That's good news."

Evan reddened. "Yes. Their tests will prove the baby couldn't have been yours, of course."

"Of course." Dexter didn't bother to disguise the heavy irony in his reply. "If the lieutenant asks, tell him I'd be delighted to give a blood sample for comparative testing. Think positively, Evan. Count your blessings that it's two years until I'm up for reelection."

Evan visibly brightened. "That's true. Two and a half years, actually."

Once his aide had left, Dexter said, "He's not usually this upset. He normally panics for ten minutes, then has the whole situation under control ten minutes later."

"Maybe he's thrown because he thinks you killed her."

Her words fell into a little pool of silence. Dexter stopped riffling through the pages of his calendar and looked up at her. "What about you, Liz? Do you think I killed Karen?"

She gave an odd little laugh. "I wish I could say yes."

"Why can't you?"

"Maybe because I can't imagine you ever feeling passionate enough about a woman to kill her."

He looked away. "You're wrong," he said quietly. "I've felt that passionate—and that desperate. But not over Karen."

Susan, Liz thought, and was aware of a sharp little twist of pain in her stomach.

Dexter looked at her closely. "You know who the police are going to suspect if they ever give up on me, don't you?"

"Yes. I know I ought to run to Rodriguez screaming that you did it. Because if you didn't kill Karen, that surely puts me right at the top of the list of likely murderers. Except I know I didn't kill her, or my other two roommates. So maybe you didn't kill her either, despite all the evidence."

"Or get her pregnant?"

She glanced down at her hands. "I—don't know about that."

His voice sounded harsh. "I suppose I should be grateful for small mercies. I guess it's better to have your ex-wife think you're a lecher than a murderer."

Liz dug her nails into her palms. "You...were unfaithful while we were married. How do I know what your sexual morals might be nowadays?"

"I was never unfaithful to you," Dexter said, sounding suddenly tired. "Other people—namely your sister—put ideas into your head. She couldn't stand it when you were happy, Liz. She was insanely jealous of you—of your skating success, of us...." He trailed off. It was all water under the bridge now. Anyway, he'd always been convinced that Alison had serious emotional problems.

"Does it matter if we believe each other?" Liz said, changing the subject.

"I think maybe it does. The police aren't going to look very far for their murderer when they have you and me as convenient suspects, and I'd like to find out what I'm being set up for. Because I sure as hell don't think it's coincidence that my secretary got herself murdered while she just happened to be living with my ex-wife."

"You think I'm setting you up?"

"No, but somebody is." Dexter looked at Liz thoughtfully. "Who first suggested that you should move into Karen's apartment?"

Liz cast her mind back, trying to visualize the crowded room at the party where she had first met Karen. "I did," she said. "I'm almost sure of it. Karen asked me all the usual questions, like how long I had been in Denver, where I was working, that sort of thing. I told her I'd just started a new job at Peperito's, and that I was looking for a roommate. She told me that by coincidence her roommate had just moved out—"

"As far as I know, Karen never had a roommate. The subject came up once, and she specifically told me she lived alone." Dexter must have caught some fleeting change in Liz's expression because his eyes flashed dark with irritation. "We were talking about a spate of burglaries in her neighborhood, Liz."

"Maybe it was the burglaries that changed her mind."

"Could be. Who was giving this party? Whoever it was, must be a friend of Karen's."

"Pieter Ullmann."

"The skater?"

"Yes, he won the gold at the last Olympics."

"I detect a tinge of acid in your voice. Didn't he deserve his gold?"

"Sure he did. He's probably the best male skater since Scott Hamilton. I'm just tired of athletes who think an Olympic gold is the key to every woman's bedroom door."

Dexter laughed. "So why did you go to his party?"

"Mikhail invited me to go with him. Pieter was—is—his star pupil at the moment."

"Of course, I should've remembered from the winter games." Dexter's voice was carefully neutral. "How is Mikhail these days? I haven't seen him since he first arrived in the States after his defection, but I heard lots of good things about his teaching program, even before Pieter carried off the gold."

"Mikhail's the best figure-skating coach in the United States," Liz said, smiling affectionately as she thought of her brother-in-law. Now that Alison was dead, and their mother barely aware of her surroundings, Mikhail was Liz's closest substitute for a family.

"He's never tried to persuade you back onto the ice?"

"We don't have any sort of professional relationship. Mikhail always admired Alison's skating style much more than mine. That's what first attracted him to her."

"Technical perfection over fire and heart?"

"Alison was a magnificent skater!"

"You always said so," Dexter agreed. After an awkward silence, he said, "Tell me about Jill. And Brian."

It was easier to discuss Jill than Brian, so she did that first. "Jill and I knew each other for at least two years, but we weren't close friends. We went to the same health club. I don't think I knew anything more about her than that she had a terrific body, she was around my age, and had a job as a social worker."

"What about her friends?"

"She had lots of them. Male and female. She was out most nights."

"Did you like them?"

Once again, Liz fell silent. "I don't think I ever met any of them," she admitted finally. "Except maybe to say hi at the door."

"In fact, if you added up everything you know about Jill, you just might be able to fill two sides of a small piece of paper."

Liz felt a chill ripple down her spine. "That's an underestimation, but not by much."

"Did you know Brian any better?"

"Of course I did! I was living with him, for heaven's sake!"

"You were living with Jill and Karen, too."

"No, I was sharing an apartment. It's different."

"Is it? Think. Do you really know any more about Brian than you do about Jill and Karen?"

"Yes," she said, through gritted teeth. "Unlike some people, I don't hop into bed with anybody who looks good in a pair of pants. Brian was a professor at the university. He had a doctoral degree in electrical engineering. He was forty-five, and a wonderfully calm, considerate human being. He'd been married once when he was a student, but the marriage only lasted a few months before his wife left him for another man." She smiled grimly. "As you can see, we had a lot in common."

Dexter broke the resulting moment of silence. "Where are you going to stay tonight?"

"I hadn't thought about it," she admitted. "But there are dozens of motels around the airport."

"You could stay here," he said. "We have plenty of room."

"Thank you very much for the offer, but I don't think—"

"Liz, we could help each other, if you'd only spend some time with me. We haven't even started to work out a list of Karen's friends. Please consider it. For both our sakes."

She closed her eyes, cursing silently. "All right," she said, drawing in a deep breath. "If you really think it would be helpful, I'll pack a suitcase after work and join you later on this evening."

"Wonderful." Dexter's smile was warm, happy, intimate—and made her want to scream in protest at its devastating effect on her hormones. She held her body stiff as he gave her a quick, friendly hug.

"See you tonight, Liz. I'll be waiting for you."

WAIT HE DID. Colleagues bludgeoned Liz with questions all day, slowing down her work considerably, and then, when she arrived home, literally shaking with fatigue, she had to deal with none other than Pieter Ullmann, who was lounging in Karen's favorite armchair.

"What the blazes are you doing here?" she demanded. "Who let you in?"

"And I'm thrilled to see you, too, darling." Pieter switched off the television set, jumped gracefully to his feet and bounded across the room to drop a kiss on her cheek. She turned her head just in time, and his kiss landed on her ear.

"Knock it off," she said wearily. "Who let you in, Pieter?"

"Your superintendent's wife," he said cheerily. "I gave her my autograph, and she was thrilled."

"How touching. However, I'd be grateful if you'd leave. I have a bunch of things to do tonight."

"I came to offer you my sympathy," he said, sounding mortally wounded by her curt rejection. "And my help."

"Thanks. The sympathy's accepted, the help isn't needed. Goodbye."

He winced. "Liz, darling, try to show a few social graces."

She threw her coat onto the nearest available chair. "I'm too tired to be socially gracious. Go home, Pieter."

"Being the generous person that I am, I'll ignore your hostility and invite you to come back to my apartment. What do you say? I'll call the caterers and we can have a quiet dinner, just the two of us. Champagne. Lobster. Whatever you want."

"And then a quiet little night in bed? Just the two of us?"

Pieter smiled. "Darling, my bedmates are much too ecstatic to be quiet."

"Pieter, I'm not coming to your apartment."

"Dearest Liz, if you don't want to have the best night of your life, that's your business. My sole purpose at this moment is to make sure you're okay. You're not going to spend the night here alone, are you, Liz?"

"No," she said, a little surprised by his sudden seriousness.

"Pieter, are you the father of Karen's baby?"

"No damn it! The baby wasn't mine! It couldn't have been, because we never slept together."

"Then why are you yelling?"

"Because she came on to me like gangbusters, and a whole bunch of my friends know that."

"I haven't known you to ever turn down a willing female, Pieter."

"You don't know a hell of a lot," Pieter said tightly, "about me, or about your roommate. From the way Karen approached me, I'd guess half the men in Denver could have been the father of her baby. But whoever the father was, it wasn't me."

"The police think Dex—Senator Rand is the father of Karen's child."

"That's their problem. Or his. Anyway, it sure isn't mine."

Pieter zipped up his jacket and strode toward the front door, swinging around and looking at Liz when he got there. His eyes were shadowed. "Have you thought about taking a vacation, Liz? Somewhere a long way away from Denver?"

"I only just moved here, for heaven's sake!"

"Looks like now would be a real good time to move on."

"Pieter, what are you trying to tell me?"

He shrugged, reaching for the door. Liz had the feeling he was regretting having come, regretting even more having spoken so freely. "Nothing, babe. I guess I'm just running off at the mouth. See you around, huh?" He left the apartment, slamming the door loudly behind him.

Liz spent half an hour packing and was almost out the door when the phone rang. Reluctantly she snatched the receiver from the cradle and barked, "Hello!"

"You sound horribly fierce, Lizushka. What is all this that I hear is going on up there in Denver?"

"Mikhail!" With a sigh of relief, she sank into the chair alongside the phone. Mikhail had married Alison just as Liz's own marriage to Dexter was going down in flames. He had defected from the Soviet Union during the world figure-skating championships five years ago, shortly after Alison had died in an Aeroflot plane crash. Drawn together by shared grief, he had been Liz's closest friend and confidant ever since his arrival in America. The warm sound of his accented voice made her smile, and she felt herself relax for the first time in hours.

"I was at the rink all day and I didn't hear the news until I came home and turned on the TV while I cooked supper. Lizushka, this is terrible. Another of your roommates is dead, and you have been seeing Dexter Rand? What in the world have you gotten yourself into?"

"I don't know, Mikhail. I just absolutely and completely have no idea."

"But how did you get mixed up again with that monster Dexter? I know how bitter you felt after your divorce, and rightly so."

"Karen Zeit worked for him."

"And you never knew this? In all the weeks you shared an apartment with her, you never discussed her job?"

Liz felt herself blush. "I knew Karen worked for Dexter," she admitted.

Mikhail said nothing, but she could feel the silence gradually fill with his concern. "I thought we were friends," he said at last. "Good friends. Why didn't you tell me about Karen's job?"

"It...there was nothing to tell."

"Are you sure, *dorogoya?*" He spoke the Russian endearment softly. "I don't want you to get hurt again. Are you quite certain that the smiles you exchanged with the senator on the TV were just for the reporters?"

"I'm a hundred percent positive! That news conference didn't mean a thing in terms of our personal relationship. We just decided that it would look better for both of us if we joined forces to meet the press, that's all."

After reassuring her brother-in-law that she was planning to stay with a friend from work, Liz finally set out for Dexter's.

As it turned out, she missed dinner completely, but made it in time to say good-night to Amanda, an extraordinarily beautiful and polite child. Dexter played a quick game of dominoes with his daughter, then came into the kitchen just as Liz finished pouring out two cups of orange-and-cinnamon tea. Dexter took a long sip of his before speaking. "Today I learned that the police have moved us up from being run-of-the-mill suspicious characters into being prime suspects. The preliminary pathology results show that Karen died around four-thirty. The highly efficient Lieutenant Rodriguez has checked our schedules and determined that neither of us have alibis. He clearly suspects us of working in collusion to do away with poor Karen."

"He thinks we were working together?"

"He's convinced of it. We were planning to marry again, you see, only Karen inconveniently became pregnant and wouldn't have an abortion. Since U.S. senators from Colorado can't hope to get elected with sex scandals featuring prominently in their résumés, you and I hatched this plan to toss Karen from a window and make it look like suicide."

The scenario was so preposterous that she would have laughed if she hadn't been so scared. "That's flat out ridiculous."

"Maybe so, but the fact is, I have no alibi. I left a meeting with the manager of Stapleton Airport at three forty-five. I should have arrived here about twenty minutes later. I actually arrived home at five o'clock."

"What happened?" she asked, returning to her chair.

"I went to the library," he said wryly. "The main one, downtown. The meeting with the airport manager had finished a half hour earlier than we expected, and I've been wanting to double-check some facts in a book on Denver's old neighborhoods. Nobody was waiting for me, so I grabbed the chance.''

"Did you check the book out? There might be a time on the computer.''

"No, the book's for reference only. And before you ask, I didn't speak to any of the librarians. I knew where the book was shelved and I went straight there.''

"It's a lousy alibi, Dex. Don't you have a research staff to double-check facts for you? Important senators don't visit the library unless it's an official visit.''

"Liz, honey, you're singing the lieutenant's song. But you're no better off than I am. Rodriguez claims you left your office at the crucial time without telling anybody where you were going.''

"Of course I didn't say where I was going!" Liz protested. "That was the whole point of the exercise. The darn phone hadn't stopped ringing all day, so I hid in one of the typists' offices, trying to catch up on my paperwork.''

"Where was the typist?''

"Out sick with the flu.''

"Well, good luck telling that one to the lieutenant.''

Several seconds passed. "Pieter Ullmann was at my apartment tonight,'' she said, breaking the momentary silence. "From the remarks he dropped about Karen, I guess several people could have been the father of her baby.''

"He had an affair with her?''

"He said not. But he also claimed she came on to him in a big way.''

Dexter frowned. "I can't even picture Karen as a sexually active woman, let alone a sexually aggressive one. I'm feeling guilty because I spent so little time thinking about her as a person. Once the lieutenant started questioning me, I realized I knew almost nothing about her.''

"Rodriguez thinks you're concealing information.''

"Of course he does. Unfortunately I'm not. I wish I knew something—anything—that would help us unravel what was going on in Karen's life. I suppose you haven't come up with any wonderful new insights since this morning?''

"Nothing wonderful. But I've been thinking a lot about what my roommates may have had in common, something that linked them.''

"And you thought of a link?''

"Well, all three of them worked for the government, although their jobs were so different it almost doesn't coun—"

"Explain their connection to the government," Dexter interrupted, his body radiating a sudden tension.

She was startled by his intensity. "Karen's link is obvious. She was your personal assistant, and you're a U.S. senator."

"Go on. What about Jill?"

"She worked as a civilian employee for the navy."

"And Brian?"

"He was a professor of electrical engineering at the university, but he didn't do much teaching, and I think his recent research was in the field of electronics. Almost all his income came from projects funded by the government, and a lot of his work was secret, I do know that."

"Have you any idea what he was working on when he died?"

"Not specifically. Even if it hadn't been secret, I wouldn't have understood what he was doing. He mentioned once that he was part of the design team for a new fighter jet."

"A new fighter jet," Dexter muttered. He stared abstractedly into the middle distance, then rose to his feet. "I need to make a phone call to Washington," he said. "Come into the study, will you? Liz, I think—just possibly—you may be onto something."

"Mind telling me what? You think it's significant that all my roommates worked for the government?"

"Yes, I do, although at the moment I don't see precisely how. What we need is information, and I should get that from my phone call."

After making his call on a supposedly "safe" phone, Dexter said, "I've asked my contact at the FBI to run a comprehensive check on Brian Jensen. There have been leaks of classified information from my Washington office pertaining to a new fighter jet."

"Could you ask the FBI to run checks on Karen Zeit, as well?"

"The FBI is short of money and staff. I had to beg to get anything done on Brian Jensen. Unless the Colorado law-enforcement authorities ask for FBI assistance, we haven't a hope of persuading the Bureau to run two background checks. Besides, Karen lived with you and worked with me. Between the two of us, surely we ought to be able to come up with some information about her."

"I brought her address book with me." Liz searched in her purse, then produced the slender maroon notebook with a flourish.

"There aren't too many names in it, which should make it easier to track people down."

Dexter took the book and quickly thumbed through the pages. "The lieutenant slipped up, didn't he? Why didn't he take this with him?"

"Karen kept it with her recipe books in the kitchen. I guess he missed it."

"Hmm. Your name's here with a work phone number, so is mine with a D.C. address and number. Here's Evan Howard's home address and phone number." Dexter flicked over the pages. "Home addresses and numbers for all the people in my Colorado office. Phone numbers for the hairdresser, the doctor and the dentist. An address for Pieter Ullmann. No phone number. And there are a dozen names I don't recognize. How about you?"

"Rachel Landers is a woman Karen took gourmet cooking lessons with every Saturday. Bev Dixon and Rita Kominsky are tennis partners. I don't know any of the others. They all seem to be men."

"There's something odd here, isn't there?"

"They're all Denver or Colorado Springs addresses," Liz said. "Is that what you mean?"

"Yes. Karen only came to Colorado from Kansas City two years ago. You'd think she'd have one or two friends from Kansas that she kept in touch with."

"Maybe she filed those addresses somewhere else."

"Maybe." Dexter closed the notebook with a snap and got purposefully to his feet. "It seems to me our Saturday morning is mapped out for us. We have to try to talk to everybody on this list, starting with the people whose names neither of us recognize."

"Sounds good. What about Amanda, though? Won't she resent it if we leave her alone all day?"

"I promised to spend the evening with her."

"That works out well, because I've agreed to have dinner with Mikhail."

Dexter turned away, his movement abrupt. "Would you like a nightcap? A brandy? A diet soda?"

"No thanks. But you're right, we should get to bed."

Her words fell like stones into the sudden silence, weighted with a meaning she had never intended to give them. Dexter shoved his hands into the pockets of his pants, as if he didn't know what else to do with them.

"It's still there, isn't it?" he said quietly. "For both of us."

"I don't know what you me..." The lie died away, unfinished. "Yes," she admitted, meeting Dexter's gaze. "It's still there. But I realize now that people don't have to...to get involved just because they're attracted to each other."

Dexter came and stood in front of her. "You think now we've talked about it, we'll be able to ignore it?"

"We should be able to. We're mature adults."

"How adult?" he murmured, pulling her into his arms. Liz tried to ignore the shiver of delight that coursed through her, but she didn't move away.

His head bent slowly toward her, his breath warm against her skin. Against her will, her eyes drifted closed, so she didn't see the moment when his mouth covered hers, but she felt his touch with every fiber of her being.

"You taste even better now you've grown up," he said.

Liz mumbled something and broke away, babbling about needing sleep.

Thankfully, the next morning Dexter appeared to have forgotten they'd ever kissed.

The first part of the morning taught Liz how frustrating—not to mention exhausting—a supposedly simple investigation could be. She and Dexter called first on Karen's tennis partners. None of them had any idea who her other friends might be, or what she did when she wasn't playing tennis.

Six of the dozen men listed in Karen's notebook weren't home. Another had moved out of state, leaving no forwarding address. Four were at home and willing to answer questions, but had nothing more to say than that they'd met Karen only recently and didn't know her very well.

The last person on their Most Wanted list turned out to be an airline steward, who'd just flown back to Denver from Hong Kong. The news of Karen's death clearly came as a shock to him. His surprise might have contributed to his willingness to talk but he—like all the others—denied being a close friend of the dead woman.

"Karen was just somebody I met at a party, if you know what I mean."

"Yes, I know what you mean," Dexter responded neutrally. "Did she spend more than one night with you?"

"How d'you know she spent the night?" The steward's voice

contained a heavy touch of belligerence. "I never said anything about taking her home, and I sure didn't get her pregnant."

"Karen mentioned something once...." Liz carefully didn't specify what her roommate had mentioned, and the steward jumped in.

"Hey, whatever she said, it wasn't any great love affair between us, you know. She was upset about some guy who'd dumped on her, and I offered her a few hours of fun. To take her mind off things, you know? We only met a couple of times after that first night."

Dexter spoke quickly. "Did she tell you anything about the man who'd been treating her so badly? His name, perhaps, or where he lived?"

The steward gave a reminiscent smile and winked. "Hey, she might have, if you know what I mean. I never paid too much attention to what Karen said. That little lady was some bundle of fire, a regular crackerjack in bed. We were really something together." He caught Liz's eye and saw that his kiss-and-tell boasting wasn't going over too well.

"Maybe I do remember one thing," he amended. "This guy— she mentioned once that she worked for him."

Liz quickly asked another question, but the rest of their conversation revealed little more than that the steward remained very impressed with his own skill in the bedroom.

"He and Pieter Ullmann sound like soul mates," Liz commented as they returned to the car. "We should introduce them to each other."

"He certainly seems like a bad choice of companion, if Karen was feeling unsure of herself," Dexter agreed. He clicked the seat belt closed, not looking at Liz when he spoke again. "Feel free to report what we just learned to Lieutenant Rodriguez. For what it's worth, Liz, I'll repeat that Karen and I were never lovers, so I can't be the father of the child she was carrying. Although, God knows, after what that steward said, there's no reason for you to believe me."

"Actually there is." Liz's thoughts became clearer in her own mind as she spoke. "In the first place, I don't think you'd ever get involved with somebody working in your office. Secondly, I've seen you with Amanda and I'm sure you'd never murder a woman who was carrying your baby. If Karen had been pregnant with your child, you'd have married her—even if only to have a fighting chance of claiming custody.''

''Rodriguez would say Karen might not have told me she was pregnant.''

''He can't have it both ways. If you didn't know she was pregnant, you had no reason to kill her.''

Dexter sent her one of the smiles that always made her heart turn over. Damn him. ''Thanks, Liz,'' he said simply. ''I appreciate the vote of confidence.'' He turned on the ignition. ''Well, if you're not bound and determined to head for the nearest police station, we have an interesting question to resolve. If Karen didn't mean me when she referred to her boss, who did she mean?''

''An old boss from Kansas City?''

''Could be.''

''Why did she leave her last job?''

He frowned in concentration. ''She'd worked on somebody's political campaign, and they'd lost, if I'm remembering correctly.''

''Who checked her references?''

''Evan Howard screens all potential employees in the Colorado office. I'll ask him to check the personnel files and get back to me with some names and addresses.'' He gestured to the notebook lying on Liz's lap. ''Do we have any other hot leads in Denver?''

''Except for the people who are out of town, there are no more men left on our list.''

''Then let's go visit one of the women. Unless you're hungry?''

She shook her head. ''Not at all.''

''Then how about visiting some of the people from my office? Maybe she indulged in heart-to-hearts over the watercooler.''

''We could try them. But Rachel Landers's home is much closer than anybody who works for you. She has an apartment on Havana, and that's only ten minutes from here.''

''Okay.'' Dexter headed the car west. ''Rachel Landers? Wasn't she the woman Karen took cooking classes with?''

''Yes.''

Dexter frowned. ''You know, I could have sworn Karen didn't enjoy cooking, although I can't remember why I have that impression.''

''You must be mistaken. Nobody could prepare food like we ate when she got home from her Saturday classes. Karen was a real expert, Dex." She peered out of the window. "Here's Rachel's building. Her apartment number's 304."

Rachel Landers, a plain woman of about thirty-five, eyes almost invisible behind pebble-lensed glasses, was at home and more than willing to cooperate. Delighted to be entertaining a United States senator and a former world figure-skating champion—even if the morning newspaper had implied they might well be guilty of murder—she insisted on serving them freshly brewed coffee and homemade pastries.

"I can see you put your gourmet cookery classes to wonderful use," Liz said, finishing a mouthful of flaky, raspberry-filled turnover.

"Thank you." A hot red blush crept up Rachel's neck. Not a flush of pleasure, Liz realized, but of acute embarrassment.

"Did you and Karen meet at a cooking class?" she asked, wondering how such an innocuous compliment could possibly have upset Rachel.

"No." The blush receded. "I do a little bit of catering on the side, and a customer recommended me to that nice young man who won the Olympic medal for figure skating. Oh, you probably know him, since you're in that line of work yourself. Pieter Ullmann. He was so young to be hosting a party, but he'd just won his gold medal and he was celebrating."

Liz felt a little leap of excitement. "You met Karen at Pieter's house? That must have been over a year ago."

"Yes, like I said, it was just after Pieter had come back from the Winter Olympics."

Liz wasn't sure whether to be excited or disappointed. On the one hand, it was interesting to learn that Karen's acquaintance with Pieter stretched much farther back than he'd been willing to admit. On the other hand, she'd been half hoping that Rachel would reveal some entirely new name and set of relationships.

Dexter returned his coffee cup to the tray. "How many of Chef Robert's classes did Karen actually attend with you, Miss Landers?"

Again the ugly red flush stained Rachel's neck and pushed into her cheeks. She sat down hard on a nearby chair. "I don't know what to say, Senator," she mumbled. "You see, I read in the papers that she was pregnant."

"What has Karen's pregnancy got to do with her cooking lessons?" Dexter asked. "Was she having an affair with the chef?"

Rachel stared fixedly at her sensible, low-heeled shoes. The flush had now crept up to the tips of her ears. "The cookery classes were just a cover," she whispered. "Karen never attended them. I—I gave her food to bring home."

Later, Liz said to Mikhail, "I had moments today when I wondered if Dexter and I were the only people in Denver who didn't know Karen was having an affair with a married man."

Her brother-in-law smiled sympathetically, wrinkling his nose as he handed Liz her plate of chicken and biscuits. "While we eat, let us talk of more cheerful subjects."

Just then, the doorbell rang, and Mikhail pulled a face as he walked to the door. "Likely an angry mother whose child I refused to take on as a student. I think sometimes to buy a guard dog." He opened the door. "Pieter! I wasn't expecting you tonight. Nothing's wrong, I hope? No pulled muscles or sprained wrists?"

Pieter's voice came low and urgent. "Mikhail, I'm in big trouble. The police came to see me. They found a letter in Karen's papers—"

"You'd better come in and calm down, Pieter. Liz is here."

"Hello, beautiful."

"Hello, Pieter. Forgotten my name?" she queried dryly.

"So tell us what caused this visit from the police," Mikhail said, settling into his own chair.

"They found a letter, shoved inside one of Karen's journals. Man, it's trouble. It reads like I'd been involved in blood doping before the last Olympics, and Karen was trying to blackmail me."

Liz gave an exclamation of concern. "But Pieter, didn't you explain to the police that blood doping's only useful to endurance athletes? There would be no point in you trying to boost your blood supply for a figure-skating competition."

"That is irrelevant," Mikhail said impatiently. "Pieter claims he didn't write the letter, so what we must do is contact our lawyer and insist on having a copy submitted to an independent graphologist."

"We'll have dinner another time, Mikhail. I'll clear up while you phone," Liz offered, carrying the chicken back into the kitchen.

"Thanks," Mikhail responded, his mind clearly with the lawyer.

Liz covered the remains of the chicken with plastic wrap and returned it to the fridge. She was wiping down the counters when Mikhail and Pieter came into the kitchen.

"The lawyer's coming right over," Mikhail said briefly.

"Great. In that case, I'm going to leave you guys to it," she said. "I've been a bit short on sleep these past few days, and an early night would be welcome."

Both Mikhail and Pieter protested that there was no reason for her to go, but she felt their secret relief when she insisted that she needed to get back to Denver. She knew Mikhail well enough to guess that he was a great deal more worried than he cared to admit. Quite apart from any problems Pieter might face, Mikhail could not possibly afford to have the rumor getting around that his athletes indulged in illicit practices in order to win.

She gave Mikhail a hug as he walked her to her car. "Don't worry," she said. "The letter's obviously ridiculous, and anybody who knows anything about figure skating will be able to tell the police that. It must be a forgery."

"You are so swift to rush to everyone's defense," Mikhail said, his smile wistful. "Even Pieter, whom you do not like. *Dorogoya,* did it never cross your mind even for an instant that Pieter is so nervous because the letter is his?"

"And true, you mean?" Liz couldn't disguise her bewilderment. "Are you saying that you suspect Pieter did infuse himself with extra blood?"

Mikhail hesitated. "I...shall be very careful not to ask," he replied slowly.

THE WEEKEND DIDN'T GET any better.

Dexter had a premonition of disaster the next day when he arrived at Evan's house and found the front door unlocked. He took a single step inside, then froze.

Liz, her face and hands smeared with blood, was three feet away from him, crouched over Evan's—obviously dead—body.

For a moment she didn't seem aware of his presence, then her head jerked up, and she stared at him from terrified blue-gray eyes.

"What happened?" he asked.

She didn't say anything, but her eyes widened in panic. Her mouth opened, then closed again, and he realized that she was literally incapable of speech.

He walked to her side.

"What happened?" he asked her again, more gently this time. He knelt down to brush his thumbs swiftly across Evan's eyes, restoring a tiny measure of dignity to the sprawling body. Then he put his arm around Liz and helped her to her feet.

She flinched at his touch, but he was relieved to see some of the wildness leave her eyes. "I didn't do it," she said. "Dexter, I didn't kill him."

"I never thought you did." He spoke the truth. Despite the compromising situation in which he'd found her, he knew Liz hadn't killed Evan. "How did you get in? Was the front door open?"

"Yes. I j-just w-walked in."

"Did you see anything suspicious?"

"No. The house was empty.... Evan was—like that—when I found him."

She had always been a hopeless liar, and he knew at once that she wasn't telling the truth. Evan might have been at the point of death when she entered the living room, but he hadn't been dead. That was why she was covered in blood. She'd tried to save him.

"What did Evan say to you before he died?" Dexter asked quietly.

She looked at him with renewed horror, as if she couldn't bear to hear the question, and he saw full-blown panic return to her face. "The police," she muttered. "Oh God, the police!"

She tore herself out of Dexter's arms and dashed blindly down the hall, bumping into an ornamental stand and sending a china vase crashing to the floor.

He followed her into the kitchen, his most immediate concern to calm her down before he called the police. She rammed the faucet full on and splashed steaming water onto her face, scrubbing with a ferocity that suggested she wanted to wash away not only Evan's blood, but all memory of the scene in the living room.

"Did you call a doctor?" he asked. If she had, they needed to worry about the imminent arrival of somebody who was going to ask a series of very awkward questions.

"No, I didn't call anybody. I've got to get out of here! You should go, too." Liz was clearly hanging on to her self-control by the merest thread. "Did you touch anything?" she demanded. "We have to get rid of our fingerprints." She elbowed past him without waiting for a reply, a roll of paper towels clutched in her hand.

"Liz, stop! Talk to me for God's sake! You can't dash around wiping off fingerprints!"

"Watch me!"

He caught hold of her arm. "Sit down, calm down, and tell me what happened."

"Sit down! Calm down!" She laughed, and began rubbing feverishly at the front door handle. "I'm getting out of here, Dexter, just as soon as I've cleaned off my prints. If the police find me anywhere near Evan's body, they're going to have me handcuffed and in a squad car as soon as they can spit out a Miranda warning. I don't blame them, either. If I were in Lieutenant Rodriguez's shoes, I'd arrest the pair of us."

Despite her panic, Dexter knew she had a point. On the other hand, he and Liz had discovered a crime and had a duty to report it. Sometimes, he thought wryly, duty was a damn nuisance.

"Nothing's going to bring Evan back to life," Liz said, almost as if she had read his thoughts. "And since I can't help him, I don't see any point in getting myself arrested."

She was right, Dexter conceded. Moreover, he suspected he might be playing straight into the murderer's hands if he and Liz were found here, hovering over Evan's body.

"Where do you plan to go?" he asked.

"To the airport. To some place far away."

"Is Boston far enough?" he asked, coming to a decision. "I planned to take Amanda to stay with her grandparents, anyway. If we left this afternoon, I'd just be moving things up a couple of days."

"I couldn't possible impose on your parents—"

"Please come," he said, not even sure himself why her company seemed so important. "We have a lot to discuss, a lot of information to share, and there's no time now."

She was suddenly very still. It occurred to him for the first time that she probably suspected him of being involved in Evan's death. Her question confirmed it.

"Why did you come here?" she asked. "I thought you planned to spend the morning with Amanda."

"I did. Then I learned Karen's personnel file was missing, and after I spoke to Lieutenant Rodriguez, somebody called, claiming to be a police officer. He said Evan had found Karen's file, and he asked me to come over here right away. Since there's no sign of a policeman or a file, I guess we can safely assume the call was a fake. I thought you were at the office, catching up on work. What brought you?''

"A phone call, too. Evan insisted he had something very important to tell me." She looked away. "He also told me it would be dangerous to get in touch with you."

"Dangerous?" Dexter tried without success to fit this piece of information into the puzzle. "Who was it dangerous for? Did he say?''

She hesitated for a second or two. "For me. For Evan. Not for you. At least, I don't think for you.''

"I see." In fact, he saw a lot more than he wanted to. Like the reason for her panic at the sight of him. "Liz, I didn't kill Evan."

The color had once again completely faded from her face. "That's what you said about Karen, too.''

"You're right," he replied quietly. "It looks suspicious, doesn't it?"

"Yes." Her reply was no more than a whisper.

"You told me you didn't murder Karen, though she was your third roommate to die. And you told me you didn't kill Evan, though I found you hunched over his body, covered in blood."

"I was trying to give him mouth-to-mouth resuscitation."

"I believe you."

He let the words fall into the sudden silence of the hallway. He thought she was about to speak, when the blare of a police siren shattered the quiet. Liz tensed, her entire body going ramrod stiff.

"Do you think they're coming here?"

"Doesn't sound like it, the direction's wrong. But we'd better leave, just in case. There's a back entrance. Let's take it.''

"My car's in front," she said, as they emerged into Evan's backyard.

He stopped and listened for a moment before taking her hand. "No police around that I can hear," he said, guiding her down the narrow path to the front of the house. "Drive your car to the airport, then book us three one-way tickets on the next flight to Boston. Do you have money?"

"A credit card."

"Good. I'll meet you at the departures gate."

"My clothes..." she said. "The blood—"

"Stop off at one of the big discount stores on the way to the airport. Change in their ladies' room and throw away the skirt you're wearing. I'll pack a suitcase for you at the house."

The sound of another siren sliced through the air, and this time it didn't conveniently fade into the distance. Dexter sprinted toward his car. "I'll pick up Amanda," he said. "Give me one hour. Get moving, Liz! You don't have time to stand around thinking!"

DEXTER DEVOTED most of the ensuing four-hour flight to entertaining his daughter. Darkness had long since descended when he finally drove the rental car into the maple-lined driveway of the centuries-old Rand family home. Amanda, wedged between Liz and her father on the front seat of the car, fought a valiant battle against dozing off. With a visible effort, she would straighten up and demand attention every time Dexter addressed a remark to Liz.

Strangely enough, Liz found this typical childlike need for attention and reassurance more endearing than the polite self-possession Amanda had displayed on the first occasion they met. A couple of times she had to restrain herself from putting an arm around the child and saying, "It's okay. Relax. I'm not going to take him from you. I couldn't, even if I tried."

Dexter's parents greeted Liz with the polite, formal reserve she expected. By contrast, their welcome to Amanda showed just how far off the mark Liz had always been in assuming that neither Mr. nor Mrs. Rand was capable of deep emotion. While the four Rands were having their happy reunion, Liz slipped away to have a long, hot bath in the guest room ensuite, and then she gratefully slipped into an exhausted slumber.

It was still pitch-dark when she awoke out of her bone-deep sleep. Fear clutched at her throat and chilled her limbs. Whatever caused her to wake had been terrifying. Slowly the realization dawned that it had been her own dreams that had jerked her so abruptly into consciousness. Suddenly, with the brilliance of a spotlight shining behind a flimsy curtain, she realized precisely what it was that had brought her awake. She went to find Dexter, leaned over and shook his shoulder. With the instincts of a long-time combat pilot, he sat up, instantly awake and alert.

"What is it?"

"Evan—when he was dying. He said somebody would have to kill me."

"What? Did he speak to you by name? Give any sign that he'd recognized you?"

"He called me Liz a couple of times. And remember, he'd phoned my office asking me to come around to the house, so he was expecting to see me. Presumably when he went to the door and let in the murderer, he thought it was me. So all in all, it seems like Evan knew exactly who he was speaking to, and tried to warn me."

Dexter took her hands and pulled her against his chest, stroking her hair with gentle fingers. "I won't let it happen, Liz. I swear to you, I won't let it happen. Now that we know you're at risk, there are all sorts of things we can do to protect you."

Rationally she knew that even Dexter couldn't stop a truly determined killer, but the passionate concern in his voice soothed her ache of fear. "Should we call the police?" she asked.

"I have a better idea than that—we can contact the FBI. I'll explain more later. First I need to know what else Evan said before he died."

She looked up at him without moving from the warm circle of his arms. Nestled against his chest, it was difficult to remember that yesterday, however briefly, she had suspected him of murder.

"What else did Evan say?" She organized her thoughts. "Well, he admitted that he'd been in love with Karen."

Dexter didn't seem surprised. "I wondered if the baby was his," he said quietly. "Once or twice, Evan let slip remarks that indicated he cared about Karen."

"Why didn't you say anything to the police?"

He shrugged. "I didn't have anything constructive to say. There were already enough groundless suspicions bubbling in the police cauldron without adding mine to the stew. I did point out to Rodriguez that Evan was responsible for the personnel records in my Colorado office."

"You think Evan deliberately lost Karen's file?"

"I suspected it all along."

"But why?"

"Evan screens every applicant, checks all references. He would be the first person to know if Karen's records didn't quite tie together. Either he recommended her knowing her references didn't check out, or he became suspicious later on, double-checked and then destroyed the file, knowing her records wouldn't stand up to scrutiny.''

"It fits," Liz admitted. "He said that he'd been a fool, and that he'd done it all for her. The odd thing is, Dex, I still don't believe Evan was the father of Karen's baby.''

This time, Dexter appeared startled. "Did he actually say that? For a dying man, he seems to have said an awful lot.''

"He only mumbled a few half sentences. The rest is conjecture on my part. But he did make specific reference to another man. It was almost as if discovering Karen was pregnant had finally made him accept the truth. 'He is so beautiful and so dangerous.' Those were the last words Evan spoke before he died.''

Dexter smiled grimly. "Well, that takes us a giant step farther forward in unraveling the puzzle. Now we know there was a mystery man in Karen's life who exerted a great deal of influence over her. We knew that four days ago.''

"We also know that somebody must have wanted to introduce Karen onto your staff really badly, to go to all the trouble of compromising Evan Howard.''

"You're right. Which makes me more convinced than ever that those security leaks from my Washington office were somehow engineered from Denver by Karen.''

"But she had no clearance to handle secret documents, did she?''

"By the time Karen made her sixth or seventh trip to my D.C. office, she might have been able to gain access to a supposedly off-limits area. She was probably trained to find ways of doing just that.''

Liz shivered, her fear returning with renewed intensity. "But I don't understand what this has to do with me! Why am I going to be killed? Dexter, for heaven's sake, what connection have I got with secret documents missing from your office? I sell *picante* sauce, for heaven's sake!''

"Maybe," he said slowly, "the perpetrators want a specific person to be accused of your murder.''

Liz's head jerked up and she stopped her pacing. "You?''

"Don't you get the feeling that somebody out there is working very hard to set me up?''

Liz gave a small, scared laugh. "I'm real anxious to frustrate them, Dex. Tell me how."

Dexter stared silently into the darkness for several seconds. His decision reached, he flung back the bedclothes and reached for his jeans. "We'll do what I suggested in the first place. We'll get the FBI to take you into protective custody."

"They'll agree to do that?"

"If I tell them they have to," he said. "Whether or not I'm being set up, you seem to be on line as the next victim. I'll contact Harry Cooper at the FBI...." His voice died away. "Damn! We're not at home. I can't contact him from here except by calling the Bureau and leaving a message with the switchboard operator. Maybe I'm becoming paranoid, but I don't want to do that." He pulled on his T-shirt, then resumed. "Would you be willing to come to Washington with me on the early flight? Most of the emergency safe houses are in the D.C. area, so you'd be flying to the right place. If we take the first flight out from Logan, we can be talking to Harry in his office by nine o'clock."

"If I have to fly to Washington in order to stay alive, I vote in favor," Liz said dryly.

DEXTER'S PARENTS accepted their son's departure with the same equanimity with which they had greeted his unexpected arrival the night before. Amanda, however, was hopping mad that her father and Liz were taking off together.

Liz was concerned about Amanda's escalating dislike for her, but she had little time to mull over the problem. Dexter plied her with questions all the way to the airport, making her recount Evan's dying words in painstaking detail, and then analyzing every possibly meaning that they could come up with for the enigmatic phrases. By the time their plane landed in Washington, Liz felt that her brain had been sucked dry, and the only firm conclusion she and Dexter had reached was that some beautiful and dangerous man, clearly not Evan, must be the father of Karen's baby.

"How do we define beautiful and dangerous?" Dexter queried ruefully. "That airline steward we interviewed was damn good-looking in a meaty kind of way, but do you think he could be termed dangerous?"

"Lethally boring," Liz commented. "And the kind of bedmate

who likes to find out if you can do it suspended from the chandelier. But I doubt if that's what Evan meant."

"With all his international travel, an airline steward might be able to set up the contacts to make a sale of stolen documents, though. It's a possibility, however remote."

"He didn't seem bright enough," Liz said.

"How do we know that wasn't a brilliant facade?" Dexter's face showed a hint of weariness. "Damn, but I have the feeling we're running awfully hard just to remain in the same place."

The morning didn't improve. Murphy's Law was in full operation, and when they arrived at the FBI building they learned that Agent Harry Cooper was in Seattle until the next day. "Probably checking on Brian for me," Dexter commented ruefully to Liz. The receptionist suggested that a deputy chief would be able to speak with the senator at three-thirty that afternoon. "He will have to cancel another appointment in order to see you, Senator," she added reprovingly. "A very important appointment."

"My business with the director happens to be a matter of vital national security," Dexter said, his own voice biting.

The receptionist looked offended. "National security is what the Bureau deals in, Senator. All our business is of the highest importance."

"You're losing your touch," Liz said teasingly as they emerged from the FBI building. "A few years ago, she'd have been eating out of your hand."

"A few years ago I wasn't old and impatient—and you weren't in danger of being murdered."

"Where to next? Your office?"

"Would you mind waiting there with me until it's time for our appointment with the deputy director?"

"If you like. Or I could check into a hotel—"

"No hotels," he said flatly. "The best way to protect both of us is to make sure you're always in a group of at least three people. That way I can't be framed, so presumably you won't be killed."

Convinced, Liz accompanied Dex to his suite of offices. He made brief introductions, then took Liz into his private office, asking a secretary and two research assistants to join them. No sooner had he begun working when the phone rang. One of the research assistants picked it up. "A personal call for you on line three, Senator."

Dexter took the phone and listened in silence for about a minute. Without placing his hand over the mouthpiece, he looked at his three staff members and nodded politely toward the door. "I'm sorry, this call may take a few minutes. Would you mind leaving me?"

Liz stepped forward. "Dexter, no! Remember what we agreed."

He looked in her direction, but Liz had the feeling he scarcely knew her. He turned back toward his assistants without acknowledging her in any way. "Would you start work on this amendment, please? Right away."

The young man and the two women trooped obediently from the room. Liz hurried forward and leaned against the desk. "Dexter, for God's sake, what is it?"

He spoke into the phone as if he had no awareness of her existence. "I am alone now."

The voice at the other end of the line echoed in the sudden, suffocating silence of the office. "Amanda has a message for you, Senator. She says please cancel your appointment with the deputy director of the FBI."

A child gave an anguished cry. "Daddy, where are you?"

"Don't leave your office, Senator, and keep Ms. Meacham with you. We'll be in touch."

The line went dead.

Dexter returned the phone to the cradle with infinite care. "I was mad at her," he said. "When we left Boston this morning, Amanda knew I was mad at her."

Liz swallowed hard over the horror that had lodged like a physical object in her throat. She reached out and touched him very gently on the back of his hand. He was ice-cold.

"We have to call your parents, Dex. Maybe...maybe Amanda's at home with them. Maybe the call was just some horrible, sick joke."

"You know it wasn't." He pressed a hand against his eyes, as if willing himself to think rationally. "My parents' number is in the Rolodex," he said, and she realized he couldn't remember his own parents' phone number.

She searched swiftly through the card index, then dialed with shaking hands. It was a personal line, and Mrs. Rand answered the phoned with a bright "Hello."

"This is Liz. Liz Meacham. We've run into a bit of a problem here.'' She refrained from any further explanation, not wanting to worry Dexter's parents, if by any chance the threatening phone call turned out to be a hoax. "Could you please hold on for a moment while I pass you over to Dex?''

She put the phone into Dexter's hand, and he gripped it so tightly that his entire fist went white.

"Where's Amanda?'' he asked without any preliminaries.

"Heavens, you sound fierce,'' Mrs. Rand replied cheerily. "Amanda's on her way. Your secretary didn't expect to be in Washington until five at the earliest.''

"My secretary? My secretary came to your house to collect Amanda? Is that what happened, Mother?''

"But of course it is. You should know, for goodness' sake. Judy was following your instructions. Dexter, dear heaven, has the plane crashed or something?''

After reassuring his mother that nothing had gone wrong, Dexter hung up the phone, his face drained of every trace of color. "I couldn't tell her,'' he said. "She and my father wouldn't understand. They'd think it was just a question of paying the ransom, and I don't believe money is what these kidnappers are after. My parents would want to contact the police, and I know Amanda will die as soon as we do that.''

"Is Judy really your secretary?'' Liz asked.

"Yes, one of them.''

"Is she in the office today?''

Dexter blinked, focusing his thoughts on the mundane question with obvious difficulty. "I believe I saw her as we came in.''

He depressed a button on his intercom and a pleasant voice answered, "Yes, Senator?''

"Judy, have you ever met my mother? In person, I mean?''

"Why no, Senator. Although we've spoken several times over the phone, when she's been trying to track you down.''

"Thank you. And I guess you've never met my father, either?''

"No, Senator. He attended a Christmas party once, but I had the flu and didn't get to meet him.''

"Thanks, Judy. By the way, screen all my calls, will you? I only want to take personal ones.'' Dexter flipped off the intercom and leaned back in his chair. "They knew exactly whose name to use,'' he said bitterly. "I suppose we have Karen to thank for that.''

Dexter's fist crashed onto the desk, sending papers flying. "Damn it, Liz, I can't just sit here waiting! I'll go mad. Why don't they tell me what they want me to do? God knows, I'm willing!"

"Perhaps we should ask one of your secretaries to cancel our appointment with the deputy director of the FBI?"

Dexter closed his eyes for a second. "Thank God you're here, Liz. At least one of us is thinking." He pressed his intercom again. "Judy, please contact the FBI and tell them that I won't be able to keep my appointment with the deputy director at three-thirty this afternoon. Make all the necessary apologies, won't you?"

"Certainly, Senator. Should I give any special reason?"

Dexter's mouth tightened. "You could say an unexpected emergency."

"I'll call right away, Senator."

Liz walked over to the window and stared down at the crowds hurrying toward the Capitol building. She sensed Dexter come up behind her. "Liz, I'm sorry," he said, putting his arms around her waist. "I went to pieces for a while, but I'm back together again now."

"No father could hear that his daughter had been kidnapped and carry on as if nothing had happened," she said. "I understood."

"I've only just realized that it was your safety I put at risk by canceling our appointment with the deputy director. I had absolutely no right to ask you to make that sacrifice."

"You didn't ask," she reminded him. "I suggested that you should make the call."

Dexter picked up a pen and scrawled a series of eleven digits across the back of her hand. "That's what you might call a high-powered emergency number," he said. "Dial it anytime, and you can summon pretty much whatever help you need."

"Why don't you call it now and ask for a commando squad to rescue Amanda?"

"We have no idea where Amanda is. Where would a commando squad start looking?"

The phone rang and Dexter snatched up the receiver.

"A personal call for you on line three, Senator. The caller preferred not to give her name."

"Put her through."

"Good afternoon, Senator." The voice was crisp, businesslike, and strangely flattened, as if it echoed through some sort of synthesizer. "Please depress the red button on the right of your phone, thus scrambling our conversation and making it impossible to trace."

Dexter pressed the button. "I have done what you asked."

"Please wait a moment, Senator, while I check the accuracy of your statement."

The pause lasted about thirty seconds. "I am delighted to see that you are prepared to cooperate, Senator. It bodes well for our future negotiations."

"I want my daughter back. Where is she?"

"Your daughter is well and reasonably happy, although she misses your company. She will continue to be well if you follow some simple instructions. Please listen carefully, Senator, since I don't plan to repeat this information. Within the next half hour, your office will receive a delivery from the Golden Slipper Boutique. The delivery will be made by an employee of the store and will consist of evening clothes and accessories for Elizabeth Meacham. You will pay cash on delivery for these purchases. We know that you, Senator, keep a spare tuxedo in your office. You and Ms. Meacham will dress for the evening in the clothes I have indicated. At six o'clock, having said a cheerful good-night to any of your staffers still lingering in the office, you will summon a cab. You and Ms. Meacham will drive directly to the French Embassy, where a reception for the new ambassador from Chad is being given. Your office, I'm sure, received an invitation. You will be contacted again later this evening...."

But later came and went. Liz and Dexter lingered for hours at the reception. No one approached them with cryptic messages or whispered instructions. The crowd had thinned to a mere handful of guests when Liz and Dexter finally took their leave.

"Your limousine, monsieur?" the doorman asked.

"We'd like a cab, please," Dexter responded.

The doorman whistled one up, accepting Dexter's tip smoothly. "Your destination, monsieur? I will tell the driver."

Dexter and Liz exchanged helpless glances. "To my apartment, I guess," he said. "Tell him The Fountains, in Chevy Chase."

"Certainly, monsieur." The cab door was slammed, and Liz

leaned back against the tattered leather of the seat, trying to think of something she could say that might make Dexter feel better.

"Perhaps they couldn't approach us because there were too many people—" He broke off as the cab swerved violently to the right, cresting the sidewalk but continuing to move.

"What the devil?" Dexter demanded, just as an ambulance with lights flashing and siren howling roared out of the Georgetown hospital driveway and catapulted in front of the cab. The cabdriver braked immediately and swung around in his seat, leveling an extremely menacing gun straight at Liz's head.

"Either of you move and she gets it," he said.

The two doors closest to the sidewalk were wrenched open. "He has a gun!" Liz screamed in warning.

It was all she said. A leather-gloved hand was clamped over her mouth and she was hauled from the cab. For a crucial second she failed to struggle, thinking that her abductor might be intent upon rescuing her from the gun-toting cabbie. In the two seconds it took to realize her mistake, all chance to scream and attract attention had been lost. With one hand still clamped over her mouth, her captor pulled her arms behind her back with brutal efficiency and bundled her face first onto the floor of the ambulance. The driver didn't even wait for the doors to be slammed behind her before he released the brake and set the ambulance shooting forward into the narrow Georgetown street.

The fist pressing her down to the ground relaxed its pressure. "You can sit up now, *dorogoya.*"

She lifted her head, too stunned to move the rest of her body. "Mikhail?" she whispered. *"Mikhail?"*

He smiled the warm, familiar smile she knew so well. "Hello, Lizushka. Welcome to Washington."

HE COULDN'T do a damn thing, because they had him covered by two guns: the cabbie's .45 Magnum and the 9-millimeter Soviet Makarov pistol aimed square between his eyes by the squat, balding man who'd just climbed into the front passenger seat.

Dexter silently cursed his helplessness. Dear God! Now they—whoever they were—had not only Amanda, but Liz, as well! The sick knot of guilt in his guts hardened into a bitter determination to frustrate his opponents or die trying.

The gunman in the passenger seat steadied his aim with brisk professionalism. Not a good sign. "Good evening, Senator Rand. My name is Igor. It is certainly my pleasure to meet you."

"Where's Amanda?" Dexter asked, the words torn from him. "What have you done with my daughter?" With a superhuman effort, he managed to bite back the need to ask anything more about Liz. It might give him some infinitesimal advantage if Igor and his crew thought him indifferent to Liz's fate.

"Amanda is already at home with her grandparents, Senator Rand. We have released her as a gesture of goodwill. We want you to see that cooperating with us is not a difficult business. It was never part of our plan to harm your daughter. We Russians are sentimental about little children."

Dexter leaned back against the seat and stared out of the cab window. He recognized exactly where they were. Ironically, for all the good it would do him, they were driving past CIA headquarters in suburban Virginia. Their journey continued through Reston until, after about an hour, the cab stopped outside a pleasant-looking house in a semirural setting.

Once inside, Igor gestured with his gun to indicate a phone on the glass-topped coffee table. "Please feel free to call your parents' home, Senator."

"I want to check that the phone isn't rigged."

"I repeat, Senator. Feel free."

Dexter called Information in New York, and asked for the number of an old friend from his Air Force academy days. The woman responding sounded bored enough to be the genuine phone-company article. He even heard her gum snap as she connected him to the computer, which provided the correct number. Dexter then dialed his parents' home. His father answered with a crisp "Hello."

"Hi, Dad, this is Dex. Sorry to bother you at this hour, but is Amanda there?"

"Yes, she is, but she's on her way to bed. What in the world's gotten into you, Dexter? Dragging her off to Washington, and then turning around and telling your secretary to bring her back again to us! The poor child's exhausted from all that useless flying."

Dexter gripped the phone and willed himself to stay calm. "Let me talk to Amanda, Dad. And could you save the lectures until tomorrow?"

"Here's Amanda," Mr. Rand said, his tone still disapproving.

"Hi, Daddy! Why didn't you come to see me when I was in your secretary's apartment? Judy was pretty nice, but I didn't like being there with her. She told me you were too busy to come and see me."

Dexter drew in a long, shaky breath. "Hello, sweetheart, it's great to hear your voice. I'm sorry we missed each other today. Was Judy—? What did Judy give you for lunch?"

"Hot dogs, and she let me have two slices of chocolate cake." Amanda sounded less than interested in Judy. "Why didn't you come to see me, Dad?"

"Judy and I had a bit of a mix-up in our communications, sweetheart. I didn't actually know you'd arrived in Washington. In fact, I didn't really want you to leave Grandma and Grandpa's house, so if anyone else comes to get you, anyone at all, you just stay put with Gran and Gramps, okay?"

"Okay. When are you coming to see me?"

"I don't know exactly, sweetheart, but soon, very soon."

"I miss you, Dad." A small pause. "Is Ms. Meacham with you?"

"Not at the moment. Amanda, promise me you'll stick close to your grandparents, will you? That's very important."

"Okay. Grandpa and I are going fishing tomorrow. And Grandma says I have to go to bed now. It's eleven o'clock and a ridic—ridikolus hour for me to be up."

"Yes, it is late." Dexter's voice thickened. "Good night, Amanda. I love you lots and lots."

"I love you, too." She yawned. "Good night, Dad. Take care."

"I will," Dexter said, holding the receiver long after his daughter had hung up.

"Satisfied, Senator?" Igor asked. "Your daughter, as you heard, is well and happy."

Dexter played back the conversation in his mind. Amanda's chatter had been entirely natural.

He shifted his position on the sofa and looked straight into Igor's eyes. "Okay," he said. "What do I have to pay to keep my daughter safe?"

MEANWHILE, LIZ was aware of nothing save an overwhelming sense of betrayal. "Why, Mikhail?" she asked. "Why are you doing this?"

"Doing what, *dorogoya?*"

She shook her head. "Mikhail! You've kidnapped me, for God's sake!"

His eyes twinkled. "God, Lizushka, has nothing at all to do with my actions. I follow the orders of my government."

Bile rose in her throat. "Your defection...it wasn't genuine, was it?"

"Only you Americans, in your arrogance, would believe that I wished to change my nationality. My defection was a carefully planned move, approved by the leaders of the KGB."

"What's going on, Mikhail? Why have I been kidnapped? How are you hoping to set up Dexter?"

"So you did at least work out that much."

"If you're planning to use me as leverage against Dexter, you're wasting your time."

"Lizushka, I never waste my time."

"I would say you've been wasting your time for the past four years. How does it help the Soviet Union to have you train Americans like Pieter Ullmann to become Olympic winners?"

Mikhail was silent, and enlightenment dawned. "That was a mistake, wasn't it?" Liz breathed. "Pieter was never supposed to win! You assumed you'd be able to psych him out, to tempt him into breaking training at some crucial point."

"Pieter's been a womanizing fool since he was sixteen!" Mikhail burst out. "How was I to know that where skating is concerned, he is pure dedication and hard work?"

"Two hours watching him on the ice should have given you a hint," Liz taunted. "Maybe you're not quite such an expert judge of character as you think, Mikhail. Your masters can't have been too pleased with you recently. I doubt if they sprang you from the Soviet Union so that you could produce winners for the United States."

"Whatever my mistakes with Pieter, I have read your character well, Lizushka. You share in abundance the two fatal flaws of all Americans: you believe your friends tell you the truth, and you have hope for the future."

"Those aren't flaws, Mikhail, they're strengths."

"You are naive, *dorogoya.* Perhaps it is better so. Perhaps you will be lucky enough to die without suffering the anguish of knowing your death approaches."

When they let her out of the ambulance, Liz saw that they were in the driveway of a typical two-story, upper-income suburban house. Whether they had driven into Maryland or Virginia, she had no idea. Of Dexter there was no sign.

Mikhail had bound her wrists together with surgical strapping tape, and he held his hand tightly over her mouth as they walked up the gravel path to the house. His gun poked into the small of her back, so she didn't even consider screaming, but some absurd, lingering hope of rescue caused her to sneak surreptitious glances to the left and right as she was propelled toward the back door.

There were other houses in the neighborhood, she saw, although they were relatively far away and screened behind trees and bushes. But even if she could somehow make a break for it, she knew she couldn't assume those houses represented safety. The chances were good that they contained enemies rather than friends. Mikhail said something in Russian to the ambulance driver, a young man shaped like a gorilla, carrying a submachine gun that seemed to grow like an extension from his right arm.

Sandwiched between the two men, Liz was taken in through a back door and conducted down a brightly lighted staircase to the basement. Liz barely had time to register that it was furnished in typical suburban style—complete with a Ping-Pong table in the center of the large room—before Mikhail bent forward and murmured in her ear.

"The moment has arrived," he said softly. "There is somebody who has been waiting most anxiously to see you, *dorogoya*."

Liz clutched at her stomach when a woman walked into the room. "Alison?" she whispered. *"Alison?"*

The woman smiled. "That's who I am, sweetie. Although not for long."

"Wh-what have you done to your hair? And your nose is different." Liz realized belatedly that she was hardly addressing the major issue. "I thought...we all thought you were dead."

"You were intended to, sweetie."

"But how could you let us all believe you'd been killed? Good God, Alison, Mom had a stroke when she heard about the plane crash!"

A faint trace of color stained Alison's cheekbones. "Mother had high blood pressure for years, so she was probably headed for a stroke anyway."

Liz stared at her sister in stupefied silence. Even as a child, Alison had always been capable of twisting the truth to fit her own personal needs. Dex had been right about her—almost. He hadn't pegged her for the complete psychopath she obviously was. Liz clenched her fists in an effort to keep herself from screaming.

"What's going on?" she asked tightly. "Why have you suddenly decided to come back from the dead? And why have you changed your hair and your nose to look like me?"

"That, sweetie, should be obvious even to you. Alison Kerachev isn't coming back from the dead. Elizabeth Meacham is merely going to be played by a different person. God, Liz, I had to spend months on a starvation diet trying to keep pace with your weight loss. Every time Mikhail sent us a new picture and a new set of statistics, you'd lost another couple of pounds and another few inches. What the hell's been going on in your life?"

"My roommates were getting murdered," Liz said dryly. "I have this weird aversion to coming home and finding my friends splattered over the sidewalk. It affects my appetite."

Alison shrugged. "They weren't friends, only acquaintances. Besides, you're so damned stars-and-stripes patriotic, you ought to be glad they're dead. They were all spying for the Soviet Union. Karen didn't even exist except as a creation of the KGB. She was smuggled into the country two years ago, direct from her Siberian training camp."

"I'm a market-research specialist with a medium-sized Mexican-food company," Liz said. "What interest could the Soviet government possibly have in me? Why in the world would they spend all this money to replace a junior manager at Peperito's?"

"Nobody cares about your job at Peperito's," Mikhail said curtly. "We are replacing you in your role as the former wife of Dexter Rand. It is the illustrious senator who interests our government."

"You think Dexter won't notice the substitution?" she asked. "He'll know Alison isn't me the second she walks into the room."

Alison glanced toward her husband. "I do hope she isn't correct, sweetie."

"In the last resort it doesn't matter—provided the realization doesn't come for a week or two. You know as well as I do that the senator will be forced to comply with our wishes, if he wants to remain alive. Our plan is foolproof."

"But you already kidnapped Amanda!" Liz said. "If the KGB want to force Dexter to do something—anything—you have the perfect method of control!"

Alison turned away from a narrow wall mirror where she had been admiring her silhouette. "Taking Amanda was nothing more than a device for getting the two of you to the French Embassy and keeping you away from the FBI."

"Why is Dexter so important to you?" Liz asked Mikhail. "There must be at least twenty or thirty senators with more political clout than him."

Alison smiled pityingly. "Shall I give her a lesson in world politics, Mikhail?"

"If you wish."

"As soon as Dexter became a senator, the KGB started to compile a dossier on him. His expertise in weapons technology was most worrying."

Alison's utter coolness made a shiver run down Liz's back.

"Alison, don't do this," she pleaded. "Don't betray your own country."

Alison didn't reply at once, and Mikhail jumped in. "Russia is Alison's country now."

Alison stubbed out her cigarette. "Your ex-husband is upstairs, sis. Take off your gown."

POSITIVELY EXUDING CORDIALITY, Igor chuckled at Dexter's grim question. "You are required to pay nothing, Senator Rand. We ask merely for a little cooperation."

"Kidnapping Amanda and abducting Elizabeth Meacham at gunpoint isn't likely to inspire me with feelings of goodwill."

"But Senator, how can you be so unreasonable? Amanda is safely at home with her grandparents. And, as a further gesture of our extreme benevolence, I have somebody else waiting to see you. She comes now." Igor clicked his fingers to the cabdriver, who walked over to the door and pulled it open.

"Dexter!"

At the heartrending cry, he stood up and turned around, just in time to see Liz being half dragged, half carried into the living room. Her arms were held by two men: the cabbie, and another man whom Dexter vaguely recognized but couldn't quite place.

"Oh Dex, I'm so frightened!"

With gentle hands he pried her away from his chest, so that he could look at her more closely. "What's happened?" he asked softly. "Are you hurt?"

"They hit me," she whispered.

Alarm prickled down Dexter's spine. The antennae that had so often warned him of danger in his fighter-pilot days quivered into alertness. Why was Igor allowing Liz to sob out her ill-treatment in his arms? Why did he have this odd sensation of breathless expectancy—as if everybody in the room were waiting for him to show some reaction to this encounter with Liz?

To buy himself some time, he drew her back into his arms and dropped a light kiss on her forehead. To his surprise, she wriggled within his clasp and turned up her mouth, asking for a kiss. He responded automatically, his mind reeling, waiting for the flame that always burst into life when he and Liz exchanged kisses. Nothing. His body didn't harden, his pulse didn't quicken. Nothing.

Dexter slowly raised his head from the kiss, breathing deeply, and simultaneously casting a quick, surreptitious glance around the room. He became aware of three things: Liz smelled of cigarette smoke and a heavy, unfamiliar perfume; Igor was looking like a cat who'd swallowed the cream and the canary; and the man who had dragged Liz into the room two minutes earlier was Mikhail Kerachev.

Mikhail Kerachev. Alison's husband. Alison, who was dead. Liz's brother-in-law.

Dexter rapidly concluded that he would stake his life on the fact that the woman in his arms was not Liz.

"Liz, my dear, come and sit on the sofa." Turning to Igor, he spoke stiffly, as he would have done if he'd really felt compelled to ask for a favor on Liz's behalf. "She needs water."

"But certainly. Anything for your ladylove."

"She is not my ladylove," Dexter said swiftly. *Too swiftly?* he wondered. He tried once again to adjust his voice to the controlled, strained tones he would have used if Liz had really been curled at his side, nursing her bruises. "If you think I have any special feelings for Liz, you're wrong. She is merely my former wife. You of all people should know that any relationship between us ceased to exist long ago. We hadn't seen one another in nine years until you precipitated our reunion by killing Karen Zeit."

"The reality of your relationship with Ms. Meacham is of little interest to us, Senator Rand. As is so often the case, truth is irrelevant. The appearance of truth is all that concerns us."

"Is that what this is all about?" Dexter asked. "Is there some specific lie you're expecting me to palm off as truth?"

"So quick," Igor murmured admiringly. "We shall deal well together, Comrade Senator."

"That seems unlikely. And I am not your comrade."

"Not yet, Senator. But wait. You have not heard the terms of my proposition."

"Just tell me," Dexter said wearily.

"You will change your *Yea* vote on the F-19B fighter aircraft to a *Nay*. If you, a respected military expert, switch your vote and speak against the project, the F-19B will not go into production."

"Which will be very convenient for your government," Dexter said softly. "That plane is the best airborne defensive weapon ever to leave the drawing board."

"Indeed. Do you agree to our terms, Senator Rand?"

"Yes," Dexter said instantly. "I agree."

A NOISE OVERHEAD—a sound almost like furniture being moved— caught her guard's attention for a couple of minutes. Liz scooted her chair a vital six inches closer to the wall, the carpet muffling the telltale scraping noises. Her goal was the nail head she had seen sticking out of the paneling. If she could just pierce the surgical tape that kept her hands strapped uselessly behind her back, she would be one step closer to a successful escape.

She poked the nail through the tape and began sawing away, keeping her upper body still so that the guard wouldn't realize what she was doing.

She had a couple of advantages, Liz thought, flexing her wrists within the layers of tape. The guard didn't expect her to try to escape, and he didn't know that she had taken self-defense classes. If she could somehow get him to come up close without arousing his suspicion, Liz thought—hoped—prayed—she would have a chance of overpowering him.

Her hands were free! Now, how the devil was she going to get the guard to come closer? Liz waited until his gaze wandered toward the door, then toppled her chair with as much of a crash as she could muster on the carpeted floor. Blood drumming in her skull, she lay on her side, coiled and ready to spring. She watched the irritated guard stride across the room.

Go for his eyes. The instruction from her defense class remained with her, although Liz wasn't sure she'd be able to carry it out. *Your life depends on it,* she told herself. *No wimping out, kiddo. This isn't a trial run. This is for real.*

Muttering angrily, the guard bent over her. She launched herself upward from the balls of her feet, butting her head into his stomach with the full force of her weight. Before he could catch his breath, she stomped on his instep with the steel-shafted heel of her shoe, simultaneously sticking her fingers straight into his eyes. He screamed in pain even as he raised his gun. He was too late. Liz lowered her fist in a chop that knocked the weapon from his hand. They both dived for it, but she succeeded in grabbing it. She brought the barrel crashing down on his head. It connected with a sickening thud of metal pounding against bone.

HOURS HAD PASSED. Something had gone wrong for the Russians, who were acting odd and distracted. If he was going to make a run for it, the dining room would provide his only possible escape route. Dexter turned unobtrusively to scan the room behind him. A slight movement caught his eyes, and he froze. Someone was crouched there, half-hidden by the bulk of the china cabinet. His heart leaped.

A black-clad man, face masked with greasepaint, rose slowly to his feet, fingers pressed against his mouth in an urgent signal for Dexter to keep quiet.

"What is going on over there?" Igor demanded suddenly. "What are you doing by the door, Senator Rand?"

"Keeping out of your way," Dexter replied easily, shoving his hands into the pockets of his pants and lounging carelessly against the wall.

Mikhail and Yuri had disappeared. Dexter sincerely hoped they had walked straight into the arms of a pair of waiting commandos. He was becoming more and more optimistic that somehow Liz had managed to escape and dial the emergency number he'd made her memorize. How else had the commandos known where to come?

Pretending to refasten the studs on his shirt, he risked another quick look into the dining room. The single black-clad figure had now become four. Dexter let his hand creep up toward the light switch. One of the blackened faces dipped in a brief, authoritative nod of approval.

In a single swift move, Dexter flipped off the overhead switch and leaned forward to grab the table lamp, jerking the cord from the wall socket. In the last moment of light, he took aim at Igor, then threw the lamp with all the force he could muster. He heard the satisfying clunk of lamp hitting flesh, a split second before the four black shadows erupted into the room.

"What the *hell* do you think you're doing?" Alison demanded when one of the commandos walked over and slipped her wrists into a pair of handcuffs.

"Arresting you. I have to warn you that anything you say may be taken down and used in evidence at your trial—"

Panic swept over Alison's lovely features. "I don't know what you're thinking of," she said, her voice husky. She looked with desperate appeal toward Dexter, who was talking softly and animatedly to another of the commandos. "Dexter, darling," she called. "Darling, please tell this silly man he's making a dreadful mistake."

Dexter turned slowly, allowing every ounce of his scorn to show. "Why would I do that, Alison? I hope they lock you in jail and throw away the key."

She paled. "A-Alison? Y-you knew I wasn't Liz? All the time?"

"Not all the time. You had me fooled for about five seconds."

"But we're identical!"

Dexter smiled coldly. "You're nothing like Liz. You never have been and you never will be."

"But you can't let me go to prison!"

"Watch me." Dexter left the room without a backward glance. He saw Liz as soon as he stepped out of the front door.

"Dex!" She ran into his arms, and he held her tight.

"The KGB are such fools," he said, lovingly plucking a dead leaf and a wisp of cobweb from her hair. "Imagine thinking I wouldn't know the difference between you and Alison."

"How could you possible tell us apart?" Liz asked. "They made her look just like me."

"When she kissed me, I felt empty. My heart didn't start pounding, and my skin didn't feel as if it was on fire."

"Is that how you feel when we kiss?" Liz lifted her face, blue-gray eyes dark with wonder. "I thought it was only me who felt like that."

He hadn't realized how much he loved her eyes until he had seen Alison's cold ones. "I think that's how I feel," he said solemnly. "But it's been so damn long I've almost forgotten. Can we test it and see?"

She raised her mouth eagerly to meet his. Their lips joined in an explosion of need and pent-up anxiety.

She put up her hand to touch his cheek. He caught her fingers, and kissed every spot where he could see a cut or a graze. "Did they tell you Amanda is safe?" he asked. "She's been back home with my parents since early this evening."

She nodded. "The commander told me. I'm so glad for you, Dex. My biggest nightmare was that they'd kill her before the Special Forces could get to wherever Mikhail and gang were hiding her."

"We'll fly home tomorrow and see her," he said.

"I'd like that. You won't feel completely secure until you've hugged her."

"Marry me, Liz," he said huskily. "We were so young before. This time we'll get it right, I know we will."

She went very still. She was quiet for so long that he forced a laugh. "I hoped it wouldn't be such a difficult decision."

She looked up, her expression grave. "What about Amanda, Dex? She doesn't like me."

"Darling Liz, I love my daughter to distraction, but that doesn't give her the right to choose my wife. Anyway, I'm confident you can show her that stepmothers are wonderful."

"I'd like to try," Liz whispered. "I love you so much, Dex. I think maybe I never stopped loving you."

"I love you, too. Darling Liz, it's so good to have you back. Promise you'll never leave me again."

"I promise," she whispered, and she sealed that promise with a long, long kiss....

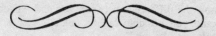

BAYOU MOON

Rebecca York

A sudden cloudburst peppered the dark surface of the bayou like a blast of bird shot. The young woman standing on the bank shivered, but she didn't step back.

For the first time since she'd stumbled off the set of the *Brad Everett Show,* her tortured thoughts cleared. She'd come to the spot she'd been looking for. The ruined icehouse where she and Vance had played twenty years ago. Now the bricks had crumbled even more.

Reaching out, she picked up a chunk and slipped it into the outside pocket of her loose cotton dress. Six, eight, ten others followed.

The bricks were heavy, and she hunkered down on the bank, tucking her skirt around her ankles.

Vance. For a moment her heart squeezed painfully. He'd wanted to help, but the grief on his face had stopped her from telling him any of the details.

Struggling to her feet, she took a decisive step toward the water. She'd made a royal mess of her life.

"Lisa!"

A figure was hurrying down the path.

"Lisa, wait—don't—"

She was more afraid of him than the water. Heart pounding, she launched herself off the bank. The cool water received her. The bricks helped carry her to the bottom.

*

TESS BEAUMONT looked up from the TV monitor and consulted the notebook on her desk. On the screen, Brad Everett continued. "With us are two women who say they lost their jobs because they wouldn't—uh—play ball with the boss."

The camera followed the dramatic sweep of the talk-show host's hand to the front of the studio where three women and a man sat in stylish barrel chairs.

"Let's start with Erica Barry, who claims she was fired from her job at a major New Orleans corporation because she declined to have an affair with her supervisor.''

A slightly chunky but attractive woman in her early thirties, Ms. Barry was wearing a buttoned-up silk shirtwaist set off with a brightly colored scarf. Her blond hair was pulled back in a severe bun. As she told about her frequent out-of-town trips with her boss and unwelcome physical contact, women in the audience began to murmur sympathetically—until Brad flashed a photograph on the screen. In it she was wearing a tight blouse that revealed ripe cleavage.

"But that was a publicity photo for the Miss Sugar Cane Page—''

Brad cut her off with a rapid series of questions about her after-hours relationships with male employees.

Tess suddenly felt very sorry for Erica Barry.

AT THE OTHER END of the hall in the station KEFT executive offices, Desmond LeRoy reached for a cigar.

During most of his adult life, he had felt a great kinship with Prince Charles. It was damn tough waiting for your mom to bow out. Then nine months ago, while she was on a cruise, he'd gotten a frantic call from the ship's doctor saying his mother had died of a massive heart attack.

For the first time in his life, Desmond felt alone—and strangely helpless. Her will had left him set for life. It didn't offer a clue how to cope with KEFT on his own.

Now Larry Melbourne, his station manager, breezed into the office for their ten-thirty meeting. "So what do you think of the new schedule?''

"Expensive.''

"You gotta spend money to make money. See, we needed a big-draw game show for the midmorning slump," Larry continued as he pulled up a chair. "And it will help set us up for when Brad leaves.''

Desmond felt sweat gather under his collar. Brad Everett wasn't going to be a permanent fixture at KEFT because independent stations vied for the honor of his presence. Three or four months in a city, and he moved on. Which meant KEFT in New Orleans had only six to ten more weeks before he jumped ship.

IT HAD BEEN a long day, and Tess was clearing the last folder off her desk when Chris Spencer, the news director, stepped into her doorway.

"I've got a drowning in Savannah Bayou," he said. "If we hustle, we can open the six-o'clock news with a shot of the police pulling the body out."

Tess shivered. The name Savannah Bayou conjured dark water as flat as a windowpane. Gum trees and cypress pushing against each other. Insects choking the air. Snakes and alligators. Quicksand.

Chris must have caught her expression. "Drowning. Yeah. Not exactly a fun gig for a woman. Maybe I can send Roger Dallas." He was another field reporter. Tess loathed his heavy-handed techniques.

"No. I'll take it."

"Good. Ken's got the directions. Can you be ready in fifteen minutes?"

"Yes."

When she climbed into the van, Ken Holloway, the cameraman/sound technician observed, "No rest for the weary."

She hadn't been to this precise spot before, but when the KEFT van pulled onto a narrow byway bordered with bay trees and live oaks, their branches thick with gray-green streamers of Spanish moss, Tess unconsciously edged away from the window.

"Chris shouldn't have sent you to something like this."

"I'm okay." She sat up. "I'm always a little spooked by this part of the world."

Ken nodded. "The way people tell it, there's some bad stuff that goes on in the back country, all right."

"What have you heard, exactly?"

"Well, you know, drug pirates. Swamp rats who'd kill you if they thought you'd found their illegal traps. Cockfights. Voodoo. What about you?"

"The same kind of stories. Nothing anyone can prove."

At the end of the lane, two police cars and an ambulance blocked the way. Two men in wet suits maneuvered a lifeless form toward the side of the bayou.

Ken cut the engine and twisted around to grab his Minicam.

Tess jumped down from the van and started toward the water. Maybe one of the police officers or a bystander could give her some background about the dead woman.

Out of the corner of her eye she saw Ken lift his camera and begin to shoot. Tires squealed in back of the van and Tess whirled around in time to see a tall, rangy man jump out of a red Mustang. His jeans and blue shirt were faded, and his alligator boots were scuffed. But they were expensive.

As he paused for a moment, his deep-set eyes focused on Tess, and her composure evaporated.

She didn't know the man. But she knew the type. Arrogant. Clannish. Dangerous when provoked.

Eternity stretched as he pinned her with his ebony gaze. Then his attention snapped toward the scene at the edge of the water. In the next moment he was striding toward Ken.

"Hé. Hé là-bas!" he snarled. "You there!"

Ken's head jerked up as the stranger grabbed his shoulder. "What the—"

"No pictures."

"Listen, buddy—"

The newcomer's large hand transferred itself to the Minicam and he ripped it from Ken's grasp.

"You can't do that, mister." Ken snatched for the camera, but the stranger shoved him to the ground.

As Tess watched in stunned silence, he swung back his arm and the Minicam arced through the air, hit the water with a loud splash and vanished.

THE PHONE in the van wasn't working, and the only place in town open after eight was the Paradise Café, a bar.

On the other end of the line, Chris Spencer was speaking. "What? I can't hear you."

"Sorry." Tess tried to pitch her voice above the loud talk and the recorded Cajun fiddle music. "It took a football team to subdue the guy. They have him in custody now."

"He sure as hell is going to pay for the camera."

"His name is Vance Gautreau. He's the victim's brother. He's a carpenter—restores old houses. Learned the trade from his uncle."

"Think he'd talk to you?"

"After what happened? I wouldn't count on it. Maybe I could interview some of the local—"

"Forget it. Channel Four did it as a special report fifteen minutes ago—with plenty of speculation from the locals. I don't want to come in with anything second-rate."

"Sorry."

"What if you went over to the jail and bailed Gautreau out? He'd have to be grateful."

"How can I bail him out when he hasn't been before a judge yet?" Tess asked. "And where am I supposed to get the money?"

"The sheriff will take your money. I'll bet Gautreau will give you an interview. And there's an emergency stash in the van. Ken knows where. Tess, if anyone can pull it off, you can."

"Oh, sure."

"Sweetie, this story's bigger than you think. Trust me."

Tess found she was having trouble drawing a steady breath. On some gut level, Vance Gautreau represented a threat. She'd seen his violent streak firsthand.

"Tess—please. Doesn't the name Gautreau ring a bell?" Chris asked.

"No."

"His sister—the dead woman—was Lisa Gautreau. She was the star attraction on the *Brad Everett Show* a couple of weeks ago."

A couple of weeks ago Everett had been going for the sleaze factor. "She a prostitute or something?"

"No. It was the program he did on rape victims."

"Oh, my God. The poor thing. And now she's killed herself."

"We don't know that for sure. Maybe it was murder. Maybe the husband didn't like her spilling her guts on national TV. Or maybe it was the hotheaded brother."

"I see. But you still want me to spring him from jail?"

"Look, I was just thinking out loud, you know," Chris explained hastily. "This guy's our best source of information."

Tess sighed, wishing that she'd turned Chris down in the first place. Ending the call, she went to tell the cameraman they wouldn't be leaving for a while. He brought her the money from the van, then pulled into a spot where he could watch the action.

THE SCARRED NAMEPLATE on the sheriff's desk said Frank Haney. He was a big man in a rumpled uniform decorated with half-moon patches of sweat at the armpits. Tess knew he recognized her, because he'd been there when she'd tended Ken with the first-aid kit from the van. Now he kept her waiting as he turned the pages of a battered issue of *Field & Stream*.

"Ain't had many visitors like you of recent."

"I'd like to post bail for Mr. Gautreau."

"Five hundred bucks."

Tess counted the money into his moist hand, pretty sure this wasn't a legal transaction. Was he going to get her for bribing an officer after he impounded the evidence?

No. Haney slipped the bills into his desk drawer and pushed back his chair. "It's your funeral, lady."

She grappled with her second thoughts and waited for him to reappear through the barred door at the back.

When the door clanked, Tess looked up. The man in custody was somewhat the worse for wear. His dark hair was tousled, his shirt was torn, and his right eye was going to hurt like hell tomorrow.

When the sheriff jerked his thumb in her direction, Gautreau's gaze followed. "This lady's bought and paid for you."

Shrugging, Gautreau opened the door. Tess followed him outside and stopped short. While she'd been in the jail, the moon had come up. It was large and full, hovering over the treetops like a UFO.

As Tess turned toward it, coherent thought was swallowed up by the eerie glow. The moon. It had hung above her like this, out here in the bayou country, once before. She felt the orange light fill her head and had to wrench her gaze away, back to the man she was supposed to interview. His broad shoulders were rapidly receding.

Tess wasn't sure why her heart was pounding. Vance Gautreau was leaving. She was off the hook. But she'd paid KEFT's good money to spring him. And Ken was watching from the van.

"Wait!"

At his car door, Gautreau turned. "What do you want?"

"To talk to you."

His voice was bitter. "You're with that TV station."

"Yes."

"You vultures are all the same. You smell death, and you come circling around."

"The public has the right to know—"

"Why a poor, wounded girl killed herself."

"Did she?"

"What else do you suppose, *chère?*"

"You tell me."

The anguish on his face was suddenly so real that a tender place inside her chest ached painfully. He pivoted to face her fully.

"She was ashamed to talk to me about what happened to her, but when that bastard Brad Everett called, she let him parade her

in front of ten million people. That's how I found out. Some
masked guy grabbed her in the parking lot of the bank where she'd
gone to get some cash from the machine, tied her up, threw her
on the ground and shoved her face in the mud so she could hardly
breathe. Then he beat her up. And then he raped her.''

Tess had gone completely still, her gaze fixed on the man who
stood before her. Without thinking, she reached out and clasped
his hand.

For heartbeats, neither one of them moved. His hand was hard
and rough and warm.

Earlier his violence had been unnerving. Now his calm was
equally disturbing. He didn't stir. Except that his gaze had fixed
on her as if he were really seeing her as a person—as a woman—
for the first time.

Then his lip curled. ''Don't try any more of your reporter's
tricks on me, *chère*. If I haven't satisfied your curiosity, you can
watch her spill her guts on the cursed tape.''

FIFTEEN MINUTES LATER the red Mustang ground to a halt in front
of a flight of white-painted stairs. Vance took the steps to the
second-floor gallery two at a time and unlocked the double front
door.

Five years ago, the riverboat captain's house had been just another nineteenth-century relic rotting in the cotton fields. But
Vance had gotten a crew to truck it overland. Then he'd lovingly
restored the high-ceilinged rooms. Now his Greek Revival home
sat serene and proud on the shores of Savannah Bayou.

As soon as he stepped inside, he became aware of the jailhouse
stench that clung to his clothes and body. With clumsy fingers, he
tore off his clothes and stuffed everything but his boots into the
trash.

He'd vowed he'd never end up in a cell like that again. And
for ten years he'd made it stick. But his anger had driven everything from his mind except the need to keep a stranger from film-
ing his sister's lifeless body. Surely she was entitled to that much
privacy.

The water in the shower was as hot as his skin could stand.
Throwing his head back, he closed his eyes and let the hot spray
beat against his skin. To his surprise, a woman's face flashed into
his vision. It was the cursed TV reporter—all blond and innocent.
He didn't even know her name. But her face wouldn't leave him.

Erica Barry had spent the middle of the day driving aimlessly around the streets thinking about all the men she'd known over the years. Somehow guys always managed to make a fool of her. Talk-show host Brad Everett was only the latest in a long line.

When it started getting dark, she turned back toward her little white shotgun house. On the front porch was a basket of fruit and a card thanking her for being on the *Brad Everett Show*. The gift brought a mirthless laugh to her lips.

The phone was ringing as she inserted the key in the lock. Ignoring the summons, she set the basket on the dining-room table. As she stared at it the laughter changed to tears. The phone rang again. She waited until it stopped before lifting the receiver off the hook.

She cried until the reservoir of tears simply dried up. Then she opened a bottle of cream sherry and put a stack of jazz records on the turntable.

The knock on the door came at eleven-thirty.

Erica kept silent for several moments, but the music had betrayed her presence, and the knock came again.

Finally she tiptoed to the door and called, "Who is it?"

"I'd like to talk to you, Erica."

She was startled. Why was *he* here? Why now?

"I'd like to come in," he repeated. "Please."

She opened the door on the chain. Maybe she wouldn't have let him in if she hadn't killed most of the sherry. It helped her decide she had nothing left to lose—with this man or any other. She unhooked the chain.

They stood looking at each other. "I'm sorry about what happened on the program," he murmured.

"My fault for volunteering."

"Did you and Lisa know each other?" he asked.

"Lisa who?"

"Just another guest who was in the wrong place at the wrong time."

As he followed her toward the couch, she wondered why the conversation wasn't making sense. Probably too much wine.

But even so, there was no way she could have known about the coil of rope wrapped around his waist or the four-inch switchblade knife in his trouser pocket. She found out about the rope first. The knife came later.

*

THE MONSTERS came only when the moon was round and yellow in the midnight sky. They were gray, indistinct shapes—shadows flickering on the wall. But their voices were loud and rough and solid.

The terror started with their voices in the darkness. No, one terrible voice. Whispering. Urging the others on.

Then the front door splintered, and the invaders were in the house. Evil. Come to hurt Momma—and her.

"Momma. I'm frightened, Momma."

The only answer was a woman's scream.

No savior stood between the little girl and the attackers. The window. Momma had told her if the monsters ever came, she might have to get out the window.

It was a long fall.

"Où est l'enfant?"

"Arrêtez-la! Stop her."

Tess shrank into the underbrush until the booted feet had thundered past. Then she pushed herself up.

The moon hung above her, huge and orange. She could make out the shapes of trees in the inky blackness.

Did that mean the monsters could see her? With a little sob, she started to run through the thick, wet underbrush. On and on, in her white nightgown.

Insects buzzed around her face. Night creatures slithered through the rank weeds.

A green tendril curled around her ankle, trapping her. They had her. They would do it to her, too. The terrible thing that started with Momma's scream.

With a shriek of panic, Tess wrenched her foot away and fled on. Into orange light. The moon.

Tess was standing at the window, breathing in quick, shallow gasps. Somehow she'd been back in the past, fleeing from the half-remembered monsters of her childhood. All at once her knees gave way and she sank into the wicker chair by the window.

Outside, the huge orange face mocked her, and she pulled down the shade with a snap.

What in the name of God had just happened to her?

The bayou. Lisa Gautreau's limp body. The moon.

The connection didn't make perfect sense, but it would have to do.

Her fists clenched. She wouldn't allow it after all this time. The monsters in the swamp were not her reality. Reality was her life in New Orleans.

What if she and Aunt Pauline talked about it? No, that was a step neither one of them had ever dared take. They'd keep the conspiracy of silence.

But maybe seeing her aunt would help.

As SOON AS it was light, she called the nursing home and told them she was coming.

The huddled figure in the bed was small and pitifully frail. But the aged eyes brightened when they spotted the early-morning visitor.

"Tess!"

"How are you, Aunt Pauline?"

"I'm just fine, honey," the shrunken old woman quavered. She wore a lace bed jacket over her gown.

Tess leaned over and they embraced.

"I watched you on the evening news the other night. It makes me proud as punch every time I see you."

The old woman groped for the silver locket around her neck. When she saw Tess was watching, her bony hand dropped back to her lap.

"I tried to call him," she murmured.

"Who?"

"I couldn't have any children of my own. Did I ever tell you that?"

"No. Who did you try to call?" Tess prompted gently.

The old woman's hand flew to her mouth. Then her eyes grew shuttered. "Call? I—I—must be confused."

"Aunt Pauline. Is there something you want to tell me?"

"Remember to water the garden and pull the weeds."

"I do."

"Your mother loved plants, too. We had that in common."

"What else do you remember about my mother? We've never talked about what happened before you took me home with you."

The old woman turned her face away. "We will not talk about that," she whispered.

Tess swallowed her frustration. Maybe another time.

She stayed for a few more minutes. But then she thought she'd better get to work before somebody missed her.

"WHERE the hell did you get to?" Larry Melbourne growled as his only female reporter entered the newsroom.

"I was visiting my aunt in the nursing home," she said.

"Well, you picked the wrong day. Chris is breathing fire. And we're up to our ears in murder."

"*Our* ears?"

"Yeah. It was Erica Barry."

Larry caught the shock of recognition on Tess's face. "That's right. Another of Brad's guests. Kind of spooky."

All Tess could do was nod.

"The police are on their way over to talk to LeRoy right now. Only he doesn't know that yet. After I tell LeRoy, I get to interrupt Brad's rehearsal with the news."

Tess asked, "Who've we got covering the murder?"

"George Foster."

He was a recent LSU graduate. "Tell Chris I'm on my way."

Larry reeled off an address on South Rampart.

"Thanks. Call the van and let them know I'm coming."

VANCE GAUTREAU rarely watched television. Especially not KEFT. So he wasn't sure why he switched on the set in the kitchen while he brewed a pot of chicory-laced coffee.

The regular morning's programming had been interrupted by some sort of crime report. The KEFT truck was parked in front of a pretty little shotgun house, marred with yellow police crime-scene tape. A crowd of onlookers milled around.

Vance grimaced. Today *he* was watching somebody else's tragedy. The irony made him reach out to switch off the television set until he saw the pretty blond reporter who'd bought him out of jail.

"This is Tess Beaumont reporting."

The name suited her. Beaumont was elegant and Tess had a homey, reassuring ring.

"New Orleans resident Erica Barry was found stabbed to death early this morning. A friend who stopped by on her way to work discovered the body."

Sacré bleu! Another woman's life snuffed out.

"At this hour, police have no leads," Tess continued, "although they are saying that robbery does not appear to be a motive, and there was a ritualistic quality to the murder. We'll have further information on the noon news.''

TESS STAYED with the van until noon. But when she told Chris they weren't going to get any more information from the police for several days, he suggested that she go back to the stories she was working on.

"Since I'm already out, I thought I might try to get some more information on the Lisa Gautreau case."

Chris hesitated. "You still want to pursue that one?"

It was a chance to change her mind. She didn't take it. "Yes."

Chris began speaking again. "Lisa was married to a man named Glen Devoe. Maybe he's more talkative than the brother. Do you want to go over there?"

"Yes."

He gave her an address on Coliseum Street in the Garden District. The house was one of the antebellum mansions built by the English settlers who came to New Orleans in the early 1800s. It boasted double verandas supported by ornate columns and enough stained glass to outfit a small church. The cast-iron fence enclosed a lush garden.

There was no answer when Tess rang the bell. Strange. In a place like this, there should at least be a servant at home. Maybe someone was around the back.

A brick path led around the side of the house, connecting with a covered walkway between the garage and the back door.

Normal-looking. Natural. Yet Tess was suddenly aware that this spot was completely isolated from the street. Better leave. She had just made an about-face when a muscular arm reached out from the thick foliage along the white-painted wall and grabbed her.

Before she could scream, a man's callused hand clamped over her mouth and she was pulled behind the wild fronds of a banana tree.

Panic rising in her throat, Tess struggled, but her attacker held her fast.

"Shh! Be still! *Pour l'amour de Dieu.* If you don't want to end up as dead as Lisa."

The warning was no louder than a buzz against her ear, but she knew the voice. It was Vance Gautreau.

Before she could ponder that, heavy feet pounded along the

brick pavement, and two rough-looking characters stopped on the sidewalk. They both had guns. Tess's scalp crawled. Involuntarily, she shrank back against the man behind her. His body was tense, as if he were poised to spring.

"Who was that blond broad? You see her face?"

"*Non.*"

"Where'd she go?"

"Around back."

The feet pounded on, and Tess sucked air into her burning lungs.

Gautreau seemed to realize that his palm still covered her mouth, and he cautiously lifted his hand.

The pursuers had disappeared from her line of sight, but he held her back. "*Non.* When they don't find you, they'll come this way again—and they'll start beating the bushes."

Gautreau pulled her toward the house. There was a low door almost hidden by the foundation planting. In the next moment Vance pushed her inside. Following quickly, he pulled the door shut just as the footsteps returned.

Outside, hard-edged hands chopped at the shrubbery. Guttural voices cursed—a bastard combination of Cajun French and English. Inside the basement, they hardly breathed. But she could feel his heart beating rapidly and knew he wasn't as calm as he'd appeared. Her own heart was threatening to pound its way through her chest.

His weight shifted subtly, and she realized he was leaning against the door. Would that be enough to keep it closed?

The doorknob rattled. The pressure of Vance's large body against the barrier held it firm. At the same time, his arms tightened protectively around her.

It took several seconds for her to realize that the footsteps were retreating again. She tried to draw away.

"Wait. They may be out there—hoping to flush you from hiding." The words were low, but she obeyed the command.

Now that the danger was receding, every sense except sight was focused on the man who held her in his embrace. His legs were long, his torso hard, his shoulders a broad ledge where her hands could cling.

She felt another change in the way he was holding her. His head bent, and his cheek pressed against hers.

"You were very brave, *chère.*"

"No. I was very frightened."

"But you didn't give us away." He eased his grasp on her. "I think they're gone. For now."

"Who were they?" Tess whispered.

"We can't talk here. It's not safe."

He opened the door, and Tess followed him into the sunlight, blinking. He gave her only a moment to adjust before he was leading her swiftly across the yard to a side gate. A few moments later they were in the next street. Vance opened the doors of a nondescript black van and almost shoved her inside.

He climbed in after her and closed the door. "What are you doing here?"

"I wanted to talk to Mr. Devoe, to understand about Lisa, if I could."

"What's Lisa to you?"

"A woman. A human being. Maybe if I can figure out why she felt so alone, why life was intolerable, I can keep the same thing from happening to someone else," she said.

"She was alone because she wouldn't let me help her."

"But her husband—"

"Scum! Glen Devoe is a dangerous man," Vance continued. "If you want to do another live remote, you'll stop looking for him."

"Where is he?"

"He doesn't confide in me. Maybe he's hiding from his rivals in town."

"Rivals in what?"

"It's a bad idea to go poking into his business."

"Then I guess it's lucky the door was unlocked."

"It wasn't exactly luck."

"Are you saying you were breaking into your sister's house?"

He shrugged. "You say you want to find out what happened. Not quite so much as I do, I think."

"If you suspect foul play, you can go to the police."

His laugh was harsh.

"Let me help you."

"Not a chance, *chère*. I work better alone."

"I like to pay my debts. Maybe you just saved my life."

"Consider it a fair exchange for getting me out of the sheriff's clutches. Now I'm going to drive you back to your car. And if the coast is clear, that's where we part company, *chère*."

Tess made a colossal effort to gather her scattered wits. "Wait. Where are you going?"

He paused. "You're going to have to take care of yourself, *chère*. I've got other business tonight."

THE WORST TIME at the nursing home was at night, when the hallways and rooms were swathed in shadows and you could hear the inmates tossing and moaning in their sleep.

Living hulks. Old. Infirm. Useless, Pauline Beaumont thought as she tried to find a comfortable position for her bony body in the narrow hospital bed.

She was just like everybody else here—waiting in this twilight way station, praying for the Angel of Death to take her by the hand and lead her out of her misery.

It was strange to end up like this—to think of herself as dried up and useless. But she'd always been a practical woman, and there wasn't much left for her in this world. Just Tess.

She was so proud of that girl. As proud as if she were her own daughter. But there was the guilt, too. Still, she'd done the right thing all those years ago, hadn't she?

Why had Tess been asking questions? Did she know something? No. That was impossible. There was nothing to worry about. You couldn't change the past.

"Pauline."

She remembered that voice. He'd stolen into the room as silent as fog.

"You called me." She tried to hitch herself up in bed.

He put a restraining hand on her shoulder. "You just rest easy now. You were good for the girl. You gave her a chance."

Pauline sighed, contented. It had all been for the best. And if anyone could bring her absolution, this man could.

"You haven't been talking to her, have you? I mean, about what happened twenty years ago?"

"Oh, no! Not ever. Didn't we agree?"

"It's been a hard burden to carry."

"Yes—" The syllable whooshed out of her.

"And you deserve to lay down your burden."

"Oh, yes. Yes."

The man stepped closer to the bed and raised the pillow that had been dangling from one hand.

"Sleep in peace, Pauline." He brought the pillow down over her face, pressing firmly through the feeble spasms. There wouldn't be a mark on her. It would look as if a sick old woman had simply died in her sleep.

When he was sure it was over, the Angel of Death left the room and let himself out through the side door he'd left unlocked.

IT WAS a sunny day. But not too warm. Just the kind of morning Aunt Pauline had loved to putter around her garden. Tess tried to feel her aunt's presence as she walked toward the old family crypt in Metairie Cemetery, but all she felt was alone. Completely alone.

Not many people were gathered at the cemetery to hear the farewell. Some of the staff from the station. Those few of Pauline's friends who were still alive. And one paunchy, middle-aged man Tess didn't know.

Later, after the few guests who'd come back to the house had left, Tess wandered into her aunt's room. On the bed was the suitcase she'd brought home from the hospital. Aunt Pauline's locket was at the bottom, and when her fingers closed around it, Tess felt a profound sense of relief. She clicked it open. Her own confirmation picture was inside. She could see a line around the outside. Was something underneath? She tried to pry up the silver backing and broke a fingernail. *Sorry, Aunt Pauline. I'd better stop fooling with it.* After putting the picture back, she fastened the chain around her neck.

BY FRIDAY afternoon, when Chris came into her office and asked, "How are you doing?" Tess answered, "Better than I expected."

They talked about her aunt for a few minutes, although Tess was aware that this wasn't just a social call.

The news director looked apologetic. "I know you're supposed to be off this evening, but I need someone to cover the final round of that computer marathon this evening."

"Sorry, but I'm meeting with Lisa Gautreau's aunt. Ernestine Achord."

Chris rocked back on his heels. "I'm impressed. How did you manage that?"

"I tracked her down through the funeral home that handled the arrangements. I was all ready for another slap in the face, but the aunt's willing to give me some background—if I come this evening. I'm driving out there later."

"To Savannah Bayou? It's rough country out there. I don't exactly love the idea of your driving out that way at night."

"How come you weren't so solicitous the last time you arranged to have me hang around Savannah Bayou at night—and spring a miscreant from jail?"

He looked sheepish. "Tess, you know how I get in the heat of battle."

While they had been talking, people had been passing in the hall. Now, although Chris was blocking her view of the corridor, Tess had the sudden uneasy feeling that someone was quietly listening to their conversation.

Chris misinterpreted her doubtful look.

"Besides, you had Ken with you. And a KEFT van. Tonight you're on your own."

She lifted her gaze to his. "Chris, I'm all right. You don't have to worry about me."

Chris grinned. "So what time are you leaving for your Cajun dinner?"

"In a couple of hours."

ON THE CROWDED ROAD, drivers on their way home were jockeying for position. And some nut kept riding her bumper. Glancing in the rearview mirror, Tess tried to see his face, but a baseball hat shielded his eyes. She had no trouble seeing his vehicle, however. His big blue pickup was in danger of pushing her right off the road.

To add to her problems, her own car's steering seemed sluggish. If the appointment hadn't been important, she would have turned around and gone home.

Tess let out a long sigh when she reached the exit. She was out of the worst of the traffic. But her relief was short-lived.

Coming back so soon to this flat, brooding country was like taking another expedition into her own psyche. Cursing herself for being so late, she switched on her brights. They illuminated the narrow road, but there were no lights in the distance. No houses. And once or twice she caught a glimpse of the bayou—a ribbon of polished onyx in the dim light. Was there swamp beyond it?

Tess kept her eyes glued to the center of the headlight beam. Yet the foliage on either side of the road remained a dark blue that seemed to press closer.

Then there were headlights, high and painfully bright in her rearview mirror—coming fast. The other vehicle was crowding her toward the side of the road. It was big, like the pickup on the highway.

Yanking on the wheel, she tried to swerve out of the way. It took a tremendous effort to make the Oldsmobile respond, and her whole body was trembling violently.

Tess slowed to a crawl, then stopped and turned on the hazard lights. Someone had come within a hairsbreadth of rear-ending her. And even though her car had been serviced in the past month, there was obviously something wrong with the steering.

Another car passed, honking, and Tess jumped. Whatever her options, she couldn't simply sit here half on and half off the road. She was sure to get hit.

Well, she was only about five miles from Savannah Bayou. She would drive very slowly into town and call Mrs. Achord.

Turning on the radio, she found a station playing a cheerful mix of golden oldies and light rock.

Hazard lights still blinking, she began to make her slow way into town—dismayed that in five minutes since the near miss, the steering had deteriorated even more.

At least the country was more open now, and she didn't feel quite so hemmed in. When she came to a straight stretch, she increased her speed a bit.

In the distance she could see another set of headlights coming toward her. Fast and blinding.

Tess's pulse began to pound wildly. She was sure that the pickup truck had circled around and was coming back!

Pulling on the rigid wheel, she tried to edge over, but her right tire sank into mud. And the headlights were coming at her like a train.

She could see nothing but the blazing headlights. Hear nothing but the squeal of rubber. Then a quick, sideswiping blow sent her car off the shoulder.

As her temple banged against the mirror, Tess screamed. The pain and ringing in her ears were followed by the sickening sensation of free fall. All at once there was nothing below but the slick black surface of the bayou.

The car broke through with a muffled splash. Then it rocked and sank lower. The mud below it made an eager sucking noise, then there was a dull thump as the car came to rest against some submerged obstacle.

But Tess wasn't safe yet.

The car was filling with water.

With a little sob, she scrambled over the seat and yanked at the back door handle. It didn't move.

*

THE WATER WAS in the back seat now, lapping at her feet, blocking the bottom of the door so it wouldn't open.

With clumsy fingers Tess grasped the window crank, and as the glass started to roll down, she gave a little sob of relief. She managed to wiggle through—and plunged into water over her head. The bayou seemed to draw her down, but when her feet hit the muddy bottom, she thrust upward. Clearing the surface, she began to thrash her way toward the shoreline.

Somewhere in the darkness Tess heard an ominous splash. Teeth gritted, she redoubled her efforts and finally reached the bank, to lie panting in the coarse weeds.

Unconsciously, her fingers went to her aunt's locket as if it were a talisman. Whether or not it was the source of her survival, she was grateful.

Standing, she realized that she'd lost her shoes in the bayou. Her purse was probably still on the car's front seat, and that made her feel all the more defenseless.

She was still holding on to a tree for support when another pair of headlights cut through the darkness. Turning, she began to stagger in the opposite direction. But she was trapped by the bayou on her right. And she couldn't cross the pavement.

The vehicle skidded to a stop. Then heavy footsteps were pounding toward her.

"*Que de diable?* What the devil?"

She was terrified of the inky water. Yet its unknown dangers were better than the known horror. Desperately she struggled toward the bank, but firm hands caught her and pulled her back.

"Tess. It's Vance Gautreau. I'm not going to hurt you."

"What—what are you doing here?" But relief flooded through her. Terror had given her strength. Now she slumped against him and he held her against his hard length, his fingers touching her shoulders, her back.

"I was looking for you, *chère*. You were late, and Tante Ernestine was worried. What happened?"

"Someone in a truck ran me off the road—my car—"

"*Sacré bleu!* You could have been killed. How did you get out?"

"I—I—opened the back window—before the water..."

"I knew you were brave. Yes. And cool." His fingers traced over her cheeks, her lips. Then he lifted her face toward his and held her, not just with his light touch but with the intensity of his dark gaze. "I don't know what's happening between us. But it seems I can't get you out of my mind."

She felt his breath fan her cheek, then he lowered his head, and his lips were on hers.

She forgot the car in the bayou. The sounds of the night around them. Everything except the way it felt to have Vance making love to her.

They swayed together, clinging, kissing, touching each other. He pulled her closer, his hands sliding down her back to her hips, anchoring her to him.

He pulled himself together first and swung her up into his arms. Striding to his red Mustang, he settled her in the passenger seat and went around to the driver's side.

"I'm getting your car wet."

"The devil take the car."

As he started the engine she began to shiver, and he turned on the heat. "It's not far. We'll get you warm."

"I'm not cold. I'm—"

"Reacting to what happened."

To her brush with death? Or the passion that had flared between them?

A few minutes later he turned off onto a rutted road that crossed the bayou on a narrow wooden bridge. Soon he pulled up in front of a one-story house.

"I'm not sure I would have found this place in the dark."

"I know. That's why I was searching for you. Tante Ernestine called me the other day. I said if she was meeting with you, I'd be there."

Tess glanced over at Vance. She was darned if she was going to let him carry her in. Before he could come around to her side, she had opened the door and stepped out. Gravel dug into her stocking feet as Vance moved ahead of her, knocked twice and opened the door.

As she stepped onto the porch, an elusive memory flickered as flimsy as mist.

Vance put a hand on her shoulder, urging her forward before

she could reel in the recollection. She was enveloped by mouth-watering aromas. Black-eyed peas. Gumbo. Shrimp or crayfish simmering in a rich, spicy sauce.

The room was neatly but sparsely furnished. Simple wood furniture brightened by calico pillows and rag rugs. Everything precisely placed.

The tiny, white-haired woman sitting in a rocking chair near the window had a lacy pink shawl draped over her shoulders. Her face was deeply lined. Wide-set, doelike eyes faltered and then honed in on Tess.

"Where are your shoes, *ma chère?*"

Vance answered for her. "There's been an accident. That's why she's late. Her car went into the bayou, *Tante*. She needs a bath and a change of clothes."

"*Ça c'est une affaire, oui!* How did this happen?"

"An accident," Tess repeated. "My steering wasn't right. Then a truck swerved across the road."

Vance looked at her questioningly, but Tess stared down at the old woman, realizing for the first time that the liquid brown eyes were sightless.

Vance was beside his aunt, touching her shoulder. "You rest yourself. I'll get Tess what she needs."

Still not herself, she let him lead her toward the back of the house.

"How does she manage?" she whispered.

"She knows the inside of this house as well as the lines in her own face." Vance ushered her into a small bathroom and turned on the taps in an old-fashioned claw-footed tub. "I'll be right back."

Tess was standing in the middle of the room when he reappeared. A large fluffy towel and several items of women's clothing were piled in his arms.

Tess picked up a softly flowered cotton dress and unfolded it. "This doesn't look much like your aunt's."

"It's Lisa's. She didn't take her old things when she moved to the city. You don't mind wearing it, do you?"

"No. Thanks for offering it."

Tess's eyes went to his chest. She could see the imprint of her body clearly against the fabric of his shirt.

He followed her gaze. "There's a clean shirt in my old bedroom."

"You lived here?"

"Both of us did. Me and Lisa. After our mother died. And you're staying here for the night."

"What do you mean? I have to get home."

"No, you don't. It's Friday night. Besides, you can't go anywhere unless I drive you. And at the moment, this is the safest place for you."

"Why?"

"Because whoever forced your car into the bayou thinks you're dead. I presume you noticed they didn't stop to help."

The remark sent a shudder up Tess's spine.

He grasped her shoulders. "We have to talk about what happened. When you're feeling better."

"What do you mean? We have to call the police."

He snorted. "The police out here are Frank Haney or his deputy. If you want to report this, forget about the bath. You can say a passing motorist picked you up, and I'll drop you at the jail, because if Haney sees you with me, he's likely to decide I'm the one who ran you off the road."

"You can't be serious."

"*Oui.* You already know how he deals with scum like me."

"Vance, you're not—"

"Okay. Forget his opinion of me. The point is that all he's going to do is tell you there's nothing to investigate. Unless you happened to get the license of the pickup."

"No. Of course I didn't. But doesn't Haney care about the law?"

"Only when it suits him. He cares more about the money he's getting from Glen Devoe."

"How do you know?"

Vance slipped his hands into his back pockets. "I'll drive you down there if that's what you want."

Tess shook her head. "No."

"Then I'll be out in the front room if you need anything," he said quietly, and left her alone.

TESS CAME BACK to find Vance closing the front door after himself. He'd changed into a white shirt that set off his dark good looks. He moved to the kitchen and spoke in a low voice to his aunt. She nodded.

He set a steaming platter on the table. Ernestine was spooning rice into another dish. Taking it in her hands, she turned toward the table.

"Is the path clear?"

"Yes," Tess answered, and the old woman carried it through the door.

"Where have you been?" Tess asked Vance.

"Arranging to have your car towed. A friend of mind will take care of it in the morning."

"Thank you."

Ernestine had seated herself. Vance took the chair opposite and gestured for Tess to sit between them.

"You didn't have to fix all this for me," Tess protested, serving herself some gumbo.

"Vance made that gumbo. He thinks I'll starve if he doesn't bring me dinner once a week. But I can cook for myself." She sat up straighter. "When I started losin' my sight ten years ago, Alphonse, my husband, God rest his soul, he says he isn't goin' to lose out on the best food along the bayou. So he fixed the kitchen up—with everything in its place. You do what you have to, *chère*."

"Alphonse and Ernestine took care of me and Lisa when nobody else gave a damn," Vance said. "Alphonse taught me my trade."

"This is almost like the dinners we used to have with you and Lisa," Ernestine said.

Tess could see that Vance didn't like the comparison.

"Tess isn't Lisa. She doesn't look anything like her."

"What does Tess look like?"

His eyes swept over their guest. "Blue eyes. Dark blond hair. I think she's missing her hot rollers right now."

"Is that the best you can do, boy?"

Vance's gaze came back to her and held. "She's very pretty, even when her hair isn't curled. Her eyes are big, with thick lashes. Her face is delicate. Her nose is small. Her lips are soft."

"Soft?"

Tess saw a flush creep up his neck.

"That's how they look."

"Umm. Is she a small woman?"

"I'm five-five. I weigh 120 pounds."

Ernestine laughed. "I know she's pretty. I know she makes your blood run hot—even though you're suspicious of her city ways."

Tess flushed scarlet. But to her surprise, Vance joined in the laughter. "We walked right into your line of fire, *Tante*."

"We all know one another better, eh?" she asked.

"Yes," Tess agreed.

Ernestine cleared her throat. "I like you, Tess Beaumont. But I'm sorry. When I ask you out here, I don't know it will put you in danger."

Tess leaned toward her. "I don't think it has anything to do with you. On the highway a man in a blue truck kept honking and trying to push me faster. I think he was the type who'll go out of his way to teach an annoying woman driver a lesson."

Vance gave Tess an incredulous stare. She shook her head. Why let his aunt think that this was all her fault?

To Ernestine, she said, "You've known men like that, haven't you?"

"*Oui, ma chère*. But you may need to look further. You come out here to talk to me about Lisa. Don't you know her husband guards his business closely? Others who get in his way end up in the bayou."

"But he doesn't know I'm poking into his business," Tess argued. "Did anyone else know I was coming here?"

"Only Vance."

"You say nobody knows about your investigation," Vance cut in. "Are you doing it on your own?"

"No. It's an assignment."

"So your boss knows about it."

"And everybody else at the last senior staff planning meeting, but none of them—" She stopped abruptly.

"Which one wants you out of the picture?" Vance asked quietly.

"I wouldn't put it like that, but there's another field reporter I've had some friction with. He's angry about a woman getting the good assignments."

"His name?" Vance prompted.

"Roger Dallas. In his mind, he's set up a competition between the two of us. He wants the weekend anchor job."

"How dangerous is he?"

"I didn't think he'd try anything—physical. And there's no proof it was him."

"Maybe we can get some proof. Starting in the morning when Lonnie hauls your car out of the bayou."

Tess nodded, unsure what to say.

"Drop the investigation," Vance said.

"Is that why you wanted to be here? To persuade me to forget about it?"

"I'm here to find out what Ernestine thinks she knows—and how much trouble it's going to get her into."

"I learned how to stay out of trouble years ago. Not like some." Ernestine stopped abruptly, and a chill moved over Tess's skin.

"What is it?" she asked.

"Nothing. Something from long ago just touched me. Before Lisa. It's of no importance now. But Lisa's story is—" She fumbled for the right word. "Complicated. She was fragile. And she remade the world to suit herself."

"How do you mean?" Tess asked.

"She told herself stories. About how she wished her life was. And when she met Glen Devoe, she was living in the city—pretending that Vance and Alphonse and her mother and me were no more real than swamp mist. She spun him a bunch of fairy stories about where she came from. She was so pretty. And a good talker."

"Lisa hurt both of you terribly. But you both loved her," Tess said.

"Then somebody ripped the fairy story to shreds. At least for her," Vance grated.

Ernestine shook her head. "There's so much we don't understand. All she had to do to get our help was ask, but she was too proud to let us share the burden."

"Or too frightened," Vance interjected. "Or maybe she thought we wouldn't stand by her anymore."

None of them had any real answers. Finally the old woman scraped back her chair. "I *am* tired. If you want to know more, we can talk again in the morning."

TESS AWOKE to sun streaming in the window, birds warbling in the swamp, and the aroma of something delicious coming from the kitchen. Chicory-laced coffee dominated. But she also caught the subtle scent of orange water and brandy and suspected that someone was frying *pain perdu,* the bayou's special French toast.

Fifteen minutes later she joined them in the kitchen. Ernestine was sitting at the table, a mug of coffee in her hands. Vance was frying the bread.

"Did you sleep well, *chère?*" the old woman asked.

"Fine. Thank you. And you?"

"As well as can be expected at my age."

Tess joined her hostess at the table and then said, "I—is there anything I can do?"

"*Non.* Just relax," Vance answered. As he poured her a mug of the aromatic coffee and set it before her on the table, she was aware of the intimacy of eating breakfast together.

Vance brought a platter of the *pain perdu* to the table and slipped into the seat opposite his aunt. Vance and Tess poured maple syrup on their French toast. Ernestine used honey.

"It's wonderful," Tess said approvingly after her first forkful. It was tempting to simply appreciate the food and the relaxed atmosphere. But whatever had happened in the past twelve hours, she had come here on business. Although she hadn't achieved much, perhaps there was something personal she could accomplish. She inclined her head toward Ernestine. "I guess you've lived around here for a long time."

"Seventy-five years, me. And my family, two hundred years."

"So you must know a lot about the area?"

"Oh my, yes. I have cousins and friends all along the bayou."

"Maybe I can do a story on the local customs," Tess suggested. "Umm, do people still go out in the swamp foraging for plants and—uh—herbs?"

"Some do."

"Did you ever hear about a local woman who—"

But Vance had reached across the table. *"Non,"* he mouthed.

"A woman who what?" Ernestine asked.

"I think Tess needs to get her car," Vance broke in as he pushed back his chair. "Lonnie called this morning. Perhaps we'd better go and see about it."

The statement was couched politely, but Tess knew it was an order. She stood up. "I'm grateful for your hospitality, Mrs. Achord."

"I enjoyed the visit. I'm sorry you have to leave so soon. I hope there isn't too much trouble with the car."

"We'll get things straightened out," Vance told her, and marched Tess out the door and toward the car. Not until he'd started down the narrow dirt road did he speak.

"If you want to get yourself in trouble, that's one thing. But don't pretend to be interested in a story on the local customs so you can pump Ernestine for information. Don't try to get her involved."

HE'D WANTED everyone to think he was out here lounging on his houseboat. But driving into town every time he had personal business was getting old, Glen Devoe thought as he climbed into his Mercedes. It was time to open up the house again. Reaching for his car phone, he dialed the sous-chef he'd stolen from Commander's Palace.

"Henri, I'm coming back to town. So you'll have to stop lounging around in your lover's bed. I want crayfish bisque and tournedos with béarnaise sauce for lunch. And bananas Foster for dessert."

"Yes, sir." The answer came back loud and clear, for Glen Devoe was used to having his wishes carried out.

Which was why he needed to lean on his contact at KEFT. Things weren't going so well there. But they would. Was it harder to control men or women? he wondered.

There were lots of women you could stop dead in their tracks with a little intimidation. Lisa hadn't been one of them. Neither was this Tess Beaumont.

With men, now, you almost always had to get tough. But his motto had always been Whatever It Takes.

LONNIE AND VANCE were standing on either side of the opened hood of Tess's Oldsmobile, conferring like shamans.

"Are you going to let me in on the bad news?" she asked.

"Right here, see?" Lonnie reached into the guts of the vehicle. "This doohickey, he's supposed to be attached to this here hose. Only he's been worked loose."

Not so much the words but how he said them and twirled the metal made Tess's chest suddenly constrict.

Vance put an arm over her shoulder. "Either the guy who usually works on this thing is a damn fool, or someone did a nice job of sabotage."

"I know as much about cars as you do about applying eye shadow," she muttered.

"I guess you'll have to take my word for it. And Lonnie's."

Tess had heard the note of desperation in her own voice. She was silent for several moments, then she nodded. "I didn't want to hear it."

"Who would?"

She pressed more firmly against Vance's chest, glad of the stability of his body. From those first panicked moments last night

when she'd felt the dark water rising, she'd known that someone
had run her off the road and left her to drown. But it was worse
than that. They'd tampered with the line of her steering fluid first.
Suddenly she felt as if she were standing at the edge of a dark,
bottomless pit.

"Lonnie will get back to you with an estimate," Vance told
her. "And the work will be done well."

"Yes. Thank you. How long will it take?"

"A day or two," Vance answered.

He kept a tight grip on her as they made their way back to his
car. For a while Tess slumped in her seat and watched live oaks,
cypress and tung trees speed past.

"Is this the way back to town?" she asked vaguely.

"No. We're not going back to the city."

"What do you mean? I have work to do."

Vance pulled into a half-circle driveway in front of an elegant
little Greek Revival house. A moment later he had come around
to Tess's side. "*Chère,* someone tried to kill you. You're not going
home where they can try again."

"But—"

He began to propel her up the wide wooden steps toward the
covered gallery. At the top he turned to face her.

"Don't tell me you're not frightened. What exactly were you
planning to do?"

She asked a question of her own. "Where are we?"

"My house."

"You're taking a lot for granted."

"I'm taking nothing for granted, *chère.*"

She shook her head. "I've never met a man like you before.
I've never met anyone who was so absolutely sure of himself—
except when it comes to us."

He acknowledged the observation with a tight nod.

"Vance, I think you set a lot of store by bravery. Well, don't
try to make me into the one who's a coward."

She had his full attention now. "You can't turn off feelings.
Neither can I. I don't pretend to understand what's happening between us, but I don't want to toss it away before it has a chance
to bloom."

She didn't catch what he said then. But when his mouth came
down hard over hers, the little gasp trapped in her throat had nothing to do with protest.

*

SHE KNEW Vance was a man of strong passions. Yet always before there'd been an edge of restraint in their dealings. Suddenly all the civilized barriers fell as his lips moved over hers with a savage desire.

If you counted the hours they'd been together, she barely knew him. But she'd spent twenty-four years with Tess Beaumont, and she was discovering she barely knew herself. She *would* know him. And herself. Her lips opened for the invasion of his tongue. Her fingers dug into the corded muscles of his back. Her hips swayed against his.

"Tess. *Mon Dieu.* Tess."

He fumbled behind her, and the door eased open. Then they were inside in the cool, darkened hall, and the door slammed behind them, shutting out the world.

"Chère?"

She cupped his face in her trembling hands. He turned his head, catching and caressing her fingertips with his lips and teeth.

"You're afraid." His tone was low and gritty.

"Yes."

"Then we'd better stop." His voice turned raw.

"No. I don't want to stop. It's not you I'm afraid of. It's the feeling of being out of control."

"Ah, Tess. Then we're on equal footing, after all." He took her hands in his, to kiss her knuckles. When his lips finally came back to her mouth, they were gentle and persuasive. The tenderness brought a new, different wave of heat shimmering through her.

She knew he had felt it, too, as he tipped her face up to his.

"Will you come up to my bedroom, then?"

"Oh, yes."

He took her arm and led her to the broad flight of stairs. Only fifteen steps. But it was a long, erotic climb as he kept stopping to turn her to him for lingering kisses and touches interspersed with endearments murmured in French.

He wouldn't be hurried. Near the top of the flight, he paused on the stair below her, trapping her between the banister and his supple body as he turned her in his arms. Her face was even with his. Her sensitized breasts against his chest. Her aching feminine softness cradling the hard shaft of his arousal.

Suddenly the time for slow dancing was over.

"I need you."

"Je te désire."

The words were punctuated by hot, hungry kisses.

Impatient now, Vance swung Tess into his arms, carried her the rest of the way up the stairs, and strode down the hall to his bedroom. Standing her on her swaying legs, he pulled the cotton shift off and tossed it out of the way. His own clothes rained to the floor.

Then they were both naked and vulnerable and wanting. Vance pulled her back into his arms. Flesh against flesh at last as he dragged her down to the bed with him.

Dimly, through her own pleasure, she marveled at the tension she'd roused in his body—and how he held back, waiting until her craving matched his.

Her fingers dug into the muscles of his arms. "Vance. Now, please. Now."

"Oui, bien-aimée. Oui."

He moved above her then, filling her body, filling her senses, filling her heart. It was like a gift. A gift she could return in kind, in this private world that the two of them had made.

He took her up, over the horizon, into a world she'd only dimly imagined. And then she was clinging to him, crying out at the unbelievable joy of her fulfillment.

She felt him follow her over the edge, heard his hoarse exclamation of satisfaction, and pressed her lips to his cheek.

They were both too stunned to move. Finally, he lifted his head and looked down into her half-closed eyes. Smiling up at him, she touched her finger to his lips and felt him smile back.

When his body no longer covered hers, the air-conditioned air seemed cold, and she shivered.

He reached around her and began to pull the spread down. "You only have to lift your hips—now."

She complied. Then they were under the covers snuggling close together. After a few minutes she felt him drag in a long breath and expel it slowly.

"I know there's something you're keeping back," she murmured. "Don't make me worry about what it is."

"I want to hold you and keep you safe. Last night after your car went into the bayou, I was pretty sure it was a deliberate attack. Now there's no other way to interpret the facts. So I'm going to ask you a very important question. Are there any other stories you're working on or is the Lisa Gautreau case the only one that's likely to get you in trouble?''

"I—no. There's nothing else."

"Then it looks as if you don't have much choice. Monday morning you go in to the news director and tell him you're withdrawing from the story."

"No!"

"Who do you think you are, *chère,* the heroine of some action-adventure movie where the bullets miraculously keep missing their mark? This is real life. Someone's afraid you're going to find out what happened to Lisa. And when you do, it will lead back to them."

"But she killed herself. I'm trying to understand why."

His eyebrow arched. "Did she? We don't know that for sure. I don't want anything to happen to you because of Lisa."

"I—I don't want that, either."

"You're staying with me for the rest of the weekend so I'll know you're safe. On Monday we'll go into the studio, and you'll let everybody know you're off the story."

"But if you're planning to keep on with your own private investigation, let me help you. No one has to know," Tess said.

"You are the most stubborn woman I've ever met."

She relaxed against him, letting the tension seep out of her body. "I don't know if I can stay all weekend. I'm supposed to be on call. I should phone and let Chris Spencer, the news director, know where I am."

"That defeats the purpose of hiding out."

"Telling Chris is okay. I can trust him."

"Can you?" He turned to her, his face hard. "Tell me about the staff. I already know something about Roger Dallas."

For the next forty-five minutes Tess gave Vance a rundown of the men at KEFT, from the team she saw most often—Roger, Chris, Larry—to Brad Everett and owner Desmond LeRoy.

"On balance, not a very nice bunch of co-workers," he observed. "Any one of those men could have gotten to your car yesterday and started that leak in the steering fluid. Any one of them could have run you off the road."

"I won't argue anymore."

"You can call Chris from here."

"Should I tell him what happened?"

"No. And don't even hint about needing to talk to him Monday. You want to be able to watch his face."

Luckily, no problems requiring her presence had developed. But Chris was glad she was back in touch.

"We'd better stop by your house and get you some clothes," Vance said when she'd hung up. "Where do you live?"

She gave him the address. "It's Aunt Pauline's house. My house now, I guess."

VANCE APPROACHED her abode with the wariness he'd used the day they'd both shown up at Glen Devoe's.

When they finally drove by, Tess peered at the facade. As far as she could tell, everything was exactly as she'd left it.

"How many rooms?"

"Living room, dining room, kitchen, three bedrooms—I use one for an office—and one bathroom."

"The entrance is on the side?" Vance asked.

"Yes."

"Too bad. That means anybody could be hiding back there in the shadows." He pulled up down the block. "You sit tight. I'm going to check things out."

"I'm coming with you."

He shot her an exasperated look and got out of the car, but she followed him.

The wind whipped at her hair as a few fat drops of rain fell. Thunder rumbled in the distance.

"Wait," Tess called as Vance disappeared into the shadows.

To her relief, he reappeared a moment later, a pistol in his hand.

"Give me your key," he demanded.

Tess stood outside with her heart thumping while he turned on lights and inspected every room.

"I think you're okay. I guess whoever tried to get you wants to go the accident route."

His casual words were far from comforting, and she was glad she didn't have to stand there looking alarmed, since her answering machine was beeping.

Vance gave it the once-over before pressing the button.

"Tess, this is Ken Holloway. I have some information you'll want to hear about Lisa Gautreau."

Tess's eyes shot to Vance's.

"Who the hell is this guy?"

"He's the guy whose camera you pitched into the bayou."

"Wonderful. He's going to be thrilled when you show up with me."

A smile touched her lips. "I can explain that you make a better second impression." She dialed his number.

"Hi. This is Ken," his cheerful voice began. "Sorry we didn't connect, but I'm out doing the town. If you'll leave your name and number, I'll get back to you."

Vance uttered a Cajun expletive.

Tess's answering machine was still beeping. "Let me see what else I have. Then I can try to find out where Ken went." She pressed the button again.

"Ms. Beaumont, if I were you, I'd drop the Lisa Gautreau story." The voice was low and whispery—obviously disguised. Yet it tugged at Tess's subconscious.

"I—I—know that man," she gasped.

"Who is it? Somebody at the station?"

Tess tried vainly to bring the insubstantial memory into focus.

The light was still blinking. She felt her throat tighten, but she hit the Play button once more.

"Tess. Where are you?" It was Ken again, his voice urgent. "It's Saturday, noon. I'm getting out of town for a few days. But I need to talk to you first. Alone. If you come home this afternoon, I'm at Legacy Cemetery Number Three. About two hundred yards straight back from the main gate, there's a double crypt with two vases of stone flowers in front. Meet me—" The message clicked off before he'd finished.

Vance's face was hard. "I don't like any of this. First someone warns you off. Then your friend sets up a meeting in a cemetery, of all places. You realize this might be a trap."

Tess shook her head. "Ken is my friend. He probably wants to meet some place where we won't run into anyone we know. He isn't one of the bad guys."

"Then *I'll* meet him."

"You can't, remember. He'd run the other way."

They stared at each other, both aware that somewhere along the line, priorities had changed.

They had come to pick up extra clothes for Tess. Now they were in a hurry, so she only grabbed a sweater and pulled it on. As they stepped outside, purple clouds hovered like a dark shroud, and the wind had risen.

The rain was still holding off as they made a quick pass by the cemetery entrance, but Tess expected the heavens to open any time.

"I can't take you up to the gate, in case somebody's watching," Vance said.

"I know."

As he pulled in around the corner, he said, "Wait a couple of minutes before you go searching for that tomb. I'll be where I can see you."

"All right."

By the time Tess reached the archway, raindrops were thudding around her.

Ahead of her were rows of shadowy little buildings—a city of the dead. Peering into the murky atmosphere, she tried to locate the crypt Ken had specified, but the stone flower baskets were nowhere in sight.

Tess shivered as rain began to pelt her hair and shoulders. Ahead of her was a green canvas tent beside one of the crypts. Sprinting, she made it to the shelter as the heavens opened up.

Tess jumped as lightning lanced the sky and thunder rumbled over the necropolis.

"Tess...Tess..."

Was her overactive imagination playing tricks on her?

"Ken? Vance?" No one answered, but as the rain let up a bit, she thought she saw a flash of white. A man in a white shirt beckoning to her?

"Tess. Oh, God, Tess..."

She was sure she heard her name again.

"Ken?" she called out. When he didn't answer, she headed for the spot where she thought she'd seen the shirt.

Ahead, to her profound relief, the stone baskets appeared.

"Ken?" she called again, but he still didn't answer. Then she saw the white shirt again.

Ken was standing, awkward as a scarecrow, in the shadow of a sepulchre. His clothes were dripping, his face was drained of all color—except for the little round red hole in the middle of his forehead.

"Ken. Oh, no. Oh, please, no." She stretched upward and plucked at his stiffened arm. His sightless eyes didn't change direction, but he swayed toward her, and it was then that she saw the rope around his chest—the rope that must be holding him erect.

The sight of it freed the scream that had been frozen in her throat. It ripped from her lungs just as thunder cracked again.

Vaguely she realized that she hadn't seen any lightning first. She felt the heat flash past her face.

The crack came again, this time with a searing pain across the top of her head.

"Get down, *chère*. For God's sake, get down." Vance was lunging toward her from out of the rain, shielding her body.

"Someone's shooting at you," he clipped out as he dragged her around the side of the sepulchre. When she was behind the brick wall, he rolled over and freed the gun from his waistband.

There was another loud report. At the front of the building a patch of brick and mortar crumbled. Seconds later Vance returned the fire, shooting into the mist and darkness at an enemy he couldn't see.

But no more volleys came from the shadows. Dazed, Tess pushed herself erect and pressed her hand to her head where it throbbed. Her palm came away wet and sticky.

"*Mon Dieu.* You're hit," Vance growled.

"No, I...must have...have...bumped..."

He was beside her in an instant, bending her head forward. "It just creased your scalp, thank God. But head wounds can bleed a lot. Come on, we're getting out of here."

"What about Ken? Shouldn't we wait for the police?"

"There's nothing you can do for him now, *chère*. We'll call the police as soon as we get to a phone. It's better not to stay, because they're going to ask questions you can't answer. We don't know what happened here."

Vance was right, she supposed. "What about...I mean, maybe there's some clue. Don't we have to look?"

He swore under his breath. "Unfortunately, you're right. Stay here."

Tess wasn't about to stay there by herself. When she reached the front of the crypt, she found Vance going through the dead man's pockets. Then he reached for Ken's left hand.

She couldn't see what he was doing. "Did you find something?"

He made a negative sound before beginning to search around the steps. "If there were any footprints, they've probably been washed away or trampled on by us. Come on. We've pressed our luck long enough. Let's go."

Adrenaline had been keeping her upright. All at once Tess wondered if she had the strength to make it to the car.

Vance must have seen the fatigue sweep over her face. "Come on, *chère*." Swinging her up into his arms, he started for the gate.

When they reached the car, Vance got out a blanket, wrapped it around Tess and lowered her to the seat.

Eyes closed, she leaned back and drew her knees up, hugging them tightly against her chest.

A few blocks from the cemetery, Vance pulled into a gas station with a pay phone. Tess looked up in alarm. "I'm going to call the police," he explained as he exited the car.

Tess nodded slightly. As the door closed, tears began to leak from behind her closed eyelids.

As he walked he reached into the pocket of his jeans and pulled out the shiny silver object he'd found in the graveyard and hidden before Tess had had a chance to see it.

For long moments, he stood looking at the metal disk in his hand. It might very well be a clue to the identity of the man who had killed Ken Holloway. The man who was after Tess.

AFTER GLANCING briefly at Tess, Vance didn't try to engage her in conversation as they sped toward Savannah Bayou. She was grateful. With the rhythm of the car rocking her, she could feel her mind closing down.

"We're here."

Tess's lids fluttered open. Startled, she looked around. They were at Ernestine's little house.

"What are we doing here?" The rain had stopped and mist was rising.

"It's safer."

Safer than what?

As they stepped onto the porch, she glanced at him. "Where's Ernestine?"

"One of her friends takes her shopping. Come on inside." His voice was low. "You need to crawl into bed and sleep."

"Umm." He was right about that.

He led her to the bedroom where she'd spent Friday night and pressed his lips against her cheek. "I'll be back by the time you wake up."

"What about Ernestine? You can't leave her a note."

"Actually, I can. There's a magnetic board we use. With big plastic letters."

Some of the fog had lifted from her brain. "Where are you going?"

"I need to take care of a little business," he answered.

"Does this have something to do with Lisa?"

"It could."

"You never did intend to let me help you, did you?"

"*Chère*, stop asking me questions. You have to let me handle things my way." With that he stalked out of the little room.

Tess lay staring at the empty doorway. Thoroughly exhausted, she finally slept. At first she dreamed about Vance. Yet even her subconscious was unable to conjure up a happy ending for the two of them. Instead she fled back in time. She was a little girl again. With Momma. In the house near the bayou.

Memories that had been buried rose to the surface. She was playing with fragrant dried leaves while Momma crumbled a basket of them and put them into waxed paper packets. A woman came to the door and said her little boy was sick with the flux. Momma gave her a little box of white powder. The woman thanked her, paid her and went away.

Then the woman was there again, crying and yelling at Momma. And Momma kept shaking her head and saying she didn't understand what had happened.

Suddenly everything changed, and Tess was standing in the middle of the swamp bewildered, terrified and crying.

Aunt Pauline came gliding toward her across the dark water, the silver locket clasped in her hands. She gestured with it toward Tess.

"Aunt Pauline, where's Momma?" she wailed.

"Look in the locket, child. Look—"

Her aunt's voice was drowned out by the sound of voices. Confused, frightened, Tess tried to hold on to the dream. Aunt Pauline was trying to tell her something important.

No, it wasn't Aunt Pauline, she realized. She could hear someone else talking. Tess opened her eyes and blinked.

A stooped figure filled the doorway.

"Ernestine?"

"You're awake, *hein?*" the old woman said.

"Yes."

"Lonnie was just here. He brought your car."

"It's fixed, then."

Ernestine nodded. "*Chère*, I've been waiting for you to wake up. I want to ask you a question."

"About Vance?"

"*Non,* about Otelie Hugo."

"My mother!" She felt an eerie sensation as the afternoon's dream snapped back into her consciousness. For a moment she was almost ill.

"So the name was right, for truth." Ernestine looked pleased. "I've put some clean clothes on the end of the bed. Come and let me get you something to eat."

"I—I'm not hungry."

"Then we'll just talk." The old woman shuffled off.

A few minutes later, Tess found her stirring a pot of soup. "That does smell good," she said.

"Eat a little bit. It will make you feel better."

Pulling out a chair, Tess sat down. But she was too excited to touch the soup. "My mother. How do you know her name? Did you know her?"

Ernestine shook her head. "*Non.* Only her reputation as a botanist."

"Then..."

"First a woman's odd name popped into my mind and I remembered she lived near here long ago. It stayed with me. Then...I started thinking about the questions you asked the other morning before Vance took you to see your car...and I wondered. But I wasn't sure they were connected."

Tess dug her fingers into a fold of clothes. "What can you tell me?"

"Not too much. But I know where Otelie Hugo lived."

"Where?"

"The other side of Antonville. About fifteen miles up the bayou. I have family there. And I recollect the talk about her—and her husband. He was from the back country, but he had a scholarship to the university. They came out here to study the plants. He was killed in a boating accident. She stayed on with the little girl, her."

Tess jumped up and began to pace back and forth.

"People didn't like them at first. I think they tried too hard to be part of the community. But after he passed on, she changed. She knew about tonics and remedies for sore throat and skin rashes. People came to her for advice."

"Yes!" Like the dream. "Do you know what happened to her?"

Ernestine shook her head. "*Non,* I'm sorry."

Tess knelt beside her. "Tell me about the house."

"It still belongs to the university, I think."

Tess felt her excitement mount. "I have to see it. Maybe there's even some clue about what happened. Can you give me directions?"

"Don't you think it would be better to wait for Vance, *chère?* Didn't he—didn't he say someone was after you?"

"I don't have to ask Vance's permission." Tess took the old woman's wrinkled hands between her own. "Don't you understand what this means to me? You're dangling a key in front of me. A key to the part of my life that's been hidden all these years."

Ernestine squeezed her hand. "*Bien.* If you must go now, take the road along the bayou to Antonville. Go through town. On the other side, look for the university name on a mailbox."

"Thank you." Tess started for the door. Then she turned. "Will you be all right?"

"*Bien sûr.* I'll wait for Vance. And I'll tell him where you've gone."

It was several frustrating miles beyond Antonville before she spotted a mailbox with Charter University on it. Behind it was a post with a No Trespassing sign. Her hands gripped the wheel as she turned in. The one-lane road was rutted, and scraggly trees, dripping with Spanish moss, seemed to press in against the car.

She came upon the bungalow suddenly. It was low and weathered and—as she'd suspected—a lot like Ernestine's. She sat for several minutes, simply staring at the front windows. But there was no sudden rush of memory. Disappointed, she got out and wandered around the back.

Two poles still stood about ten feet apart, but the line on which her mother had hung the laundry was missing. Tess could imagine white sheets and cotton underwear flapping in the breeze. Walking over to one of the posts, she ran her fingers along the wood, and the scene around her seemed to blur. Once again she was a little girl watching Momma hang out the wash.

"Aunt Pauline says bleach won't get the dirt out of my white pinafore."

Momma pulled the pinafore out of the laundry basket. "Well, it did. It worked like a charm. See how white it is?"

"Why did Aunt Pauline yell at you? Doesn't she love you?"

"She doesn't understand why I want to live out here." She knelt down and took Tess's hands. "Honey, if something happened to me, would you mind going to live with Aunt Pauline?"

"Nothing's gonna happen to you, Momma!"

"Shh, baby. It's all right."

The long-ago scene shattered as a man's voice said, "Careful, you don't want to get splinters from that old wood."

Tess's whole body jerked and she found herself looking into a round face with a double chin and bushy brows. Perhaps he was in his early fifties. He was the observer at her aunt's graveside service. Today he wore a white cotton shirt over baggy trousers.

"Who—who are you?" she asked.

"Glen Devoe."

*

"LISA'S HUSBAND," Tess breathed. "Have I met you before?"

He smiled engagingly. "Haven't had the pleasure."

"What are you doing here?" she demanded. "And why were you at the cemetery?"

"I wanted to explain to you about Lisa. Then I decided not to intrude on your grief."

"How did you know I was here?"

"Folks along the bayou tell me things."

He went on. "Please. I want to explain about Lisa. I was at the bayou the afternoon she went into the water. I tried to stop her, but it was too late."

He looked distressed. He sounded convincing. Yet she found it difficult to trust him. "Why did she do it?"

"She was never quite right in the head. After she was raped, I kept trying to help her, but she kind of closed up."

Was that the truth? Usually Tess was good at analyzing people's subtle cues. But this man's voice kept getting in the way.

Devoe sighed. "Lisa was always a mystery to me. I'd appreciate anything you could tell me. Do you know if—uh—she told her aunt about anything else besides the rape?"

"I'm afraid my conversation with Lisa's aunt was confidential."

"You're not being very helpful. I thought we could do this the easy way." Pulling out a gun, he leveled it at her chest.

A wispy breath trickled from Tess's lungs. When Devoe took a step forward, she took two back.

"No use tryin' to split," he said. His speech was more colloquial now. "I made sure your car ain't gonna start."

He ignored her gasp and kept talking.

"What do you care about Lisa? She was *my* wife."

Tess continued to stare at him, hardly able to get past the awful sound of his voice. She knew it now. It was the voice from that terrible night long ago.

"You brought the men to my mother's house," she breathed.

"Yeah. They're simple people. Superstitious, too. It was easy to stir them up. I just made sure a few of the folks who got herbs and stuff from your ma died."

Tess was speechless.

"You can bring in a ton of drugs from the gulf—and stash 'em where nobody'll bother 'em. 'Less some nosy bitch starts poking around," he growled.

Tess fought the nausea rising in her throat.

"Your aunt and I had a deal, you know. I'd get rid of your mother, and she'd get you."

Tess's hand jerked to the locket. "You're lying. She wouldn't have done that."

He tipped his head to one side. "Guess you'll have to take my word for it. What I say around here goes."

"What happened to my mother?" she managed.

"She's in the quicksand."

"Oh, God." Tess covered her mouth with her hands.

"Where you shoulda been," Devoe continued. "'Cause now here we are—again. You meddlin' in my business—just like your mother. And Lisa."

He didn't seem to want a response.

"Lisa. Now, that wasn't so simple. She fooled me. I didn't know she used to be the skinny little girl living with the Achords. All grown up, she was so pretty, so sexy. So willing to please. That girl could—" He stopped abruptly.

"But a man's wife shouldn't try to blackmail him. So I hired someone to teach her a lesson."

Tess gagged. "You had someone rape—"

He cut her off. "Then she turns up on TV, and now the whole thing's too public. I can't kill her, but I can take her medicine away and replace it with something else. So she's guaranteed to self-destruct."

"You monster."

VANCE HELD the button up against the large-size navy sports jacket. The circle of brass with the crest in the center was a perfect match to the one still attached to the expensive fabric.

Cursing under his breath, he stepped out of the closet and glanced quickly around the well-appointed bedroom. Rosewood furniture. A brocade spread. Silver-handled brushes on the dressing table. Only the best for the man who lived here.

Vance's ebony eyes narrowed. A button torn off a sports jacket. That still wasn't going to be enough for the police. He could have torn it off himself and said he found it at the cemetery. But it proved that Tess was still in danger.

Mon Dieu. He'd better get back to Ernestine's on the double.

TESS STARED at Glen Devoe's beefy face. She recognized the look in his eyes. She'd seen it before when she'd interviewed public officials convicted of corruption. Like him, they tended to be out of touch with reality. Now she was pretty sure that for a moment he wasn't really seeing her.

She had a split second in which to go with her gut reaction. With a silent prayer that she was right, she ducked behind a tree.

The shot came—too late to stop her.

Hidden by the foliage, Tess turned and sprinted into the twilight shadows of the swamp. It had been her nightmare for years. Now it was her only refuge.

Tess heard the crack of gunfire behind her.

"Stop, damn you!" Devoe screamed.

She ignored the frantic order and kept running—from her terror, from the man behind her.

Another shot rang out. This time it was wider. How many were left?

A canebrake blocked her path. Tess began to claw her way through, but the stiff stems slowed her down. When she broke out onto the other side, she found herself facing a broad ribbon of mud.

Panting, desperate, she tried to think of what to do. She couldn't leap across. And there was no way to know how deep it went.

There was a sudden rustle behind her as her pursuer staggered out of the foliage. "End of the line, honey. It's either me or the quicksand now."

Quicksand. Tess shuddered. Was he telling the truth?

"You're going to tell me what that bastard brother of Lisa's found out about her death—and about my private business,'' Devoe growled.

Tess slowly shook her head. ''I'm not going to tell you anything,'' she said.

He kept the gun trained on her, but when Tess heard the crack of the revolver, to her astonishment it was Devoe who grabbed his shoulder and screamed.

''Drop the gun,'' a voice behind him growled.

When she peered through the cane, she saw Desmond LeRoy coming toward them, a cigar clamped in his teeth. He was a very strange kind of savior.

''Drop the gun, you son of a bitch,'' he repeated.

Devoe's face drained of color. Tossing the weapon to the ground, he sank to his knees. ''Please—''

''Shut up.'' LeRoy spat the cigar into the mud. With a savage kick, he sent Devoe's weapon spinning off in the same direction. It sank below the surface.

Tess edged toward her boss. ''Mr. LeRoy,'' she gasped. ''Thank the Lord. How did you know where to find me?''

LeRoy's gaze didn't leave the other man. ''The aunt. Mrs. Achord.''

Tess nodded. They could turn Lisa's husband over to the police. She could tell them about what had happened to her mother.

LeRoy took a step toward the man on the ground. ''You bastard. First you tried to make me your messenger boy. Then you tried to ruin me, didn't you?''

''No. Please. It wasn't me.''

''Yeah. Explain why Brad Everett broke his contract. Explain why my station manager is missing.'' LeRoy's voice rose. ''Explain how I'm going to attract viewers now. You can't deliver the viewers, you don't get the advertisers. And if you don't get the advertisers, you go down the tubes.'' With the last word, he aimed a savage kick at Devoe's chest. On a piercing scream, he tumbled backward into the muck.

The scream changed from pain to terror as the drug lord began to sink into the goop. It really was quicksand.

Tess stared in horror as Devoe began to thrash wildly with his good arm.

''We can't— We've got to help him.'' Kneeling, Tess stretched out her hand toward the struggling man. But with the flat of his palm, LeRoy slammed Tess backward. He was stronger than he looked. She tumbled to the ground, gasping.

"Stay where you are," he growled.

Eyes bulging, arms lashing, Devoe struggled. "Help me. Help!" he gasped.

"Please—" Tess whispered. "You can't just let him drown. We can turn him over to the police. He'll be punished for what he's done. Not just to you. To my mother."

"Punished! Fat chance. Half the police force is on his payroll. In town. Out here where he picks up his drug shipments. So stay where you are."

It was all over quickly. One last scream, and Lisa's husband sank below the glistening surface.

Tess had seen LeRoy's face turn evil as he watched a man die. He was looking at her with the same expression.

"Ernestine knows you came after me," she managed to say.

"But she doesn't know what happened when I got here. Actually, I was too late to save you. Devoe had already shot you. Then he attacked me, and it was self-defense."

"You can't say Devoe shot me. His gun's at the bottom of the bog. They'll know the bullet didn't come from it."

LeRoy's face had set itself into grim lines. "This gun isn't registered to me. It could be Devoe's." He looked from Tess to the swamp. "And they're not going to find either one of you."

As LeRoy took a step toward Tess, he didn't see the patch of mud lurking under a covering of leaves. When his foot connected, his leg shot out from under him.

Seizing the desperate advantage, Tess went for the gun. Her hand connected and the weapon sailed onto the quicksand.

"You bitch."

In the next moment LeRoy had hooked his fingers into the hem of Tess's dress. The fabric tore as she tried to twist out of his grasp.

She could feel them both sliding over the edge of the firm ground. "No—please. Stop. We're going in—"

But he was beyond hearing.

He snapped back to reality as he hit the muck and made a wild grab for a root. He missed.

Tess followed him into the slime, but landed several feet away. A scream broke from her lips. It was answered by an echoing wail of panic from LeRoy.

She could see him beating at the brown surface with his arms.

"You can float," she called to LeRoy. "If you stop struggling like that, you'll stop sinking."

"Noooooo!"

He paid no heed. Unable to watch him go down, Tess closed her eyes and tried to imagine that she was floating far away in a beautiful pool of warm water. Perhaps if she held absolutely still, she could stay like this for hours.

But LeRoy's ripples were sucking her down, too. The muck pressed painfully against her chest, making it hard to breathe.

"Stop," she gasped. "Hold still. Please."

He didn't answer. But he did slow his thrashing movements. Perhaps he was simply too tired to struggle.

Tess felt the quicksand squeezing the breath from her body. All her anguish came out in a strangled cry for help.

To her astonishment, the plea was answered. "Tess. For the love of God, where are you, Tess?"

"Vance!" she called out.

"*Chère.* Keep talking to me."

"Over here," she puffed. "I—we—"

And a haggard-looking Vance came crashing through the cane-brake.

LeRoy reached out toward him. "Help," he gasped.

Vance didn't answer. Instead he pulled out a knife and began to hack at several of the canes. When they came free, he slid them to Tess.

In the background, LeRoy was screaming at Vance. Tess tried to concentrate on getting free.

"I can't go in there after you. Can you hold on?" Vance's voice was edged with anguish.

"I think so."

"I'll pull you out. You don't have to do any of the work," he promised.

Tess gritted her teeth and clamped her hands on the roughened canes. For long, terrible moments, she felt the quicksand hold her fast. Then she was coming up. Slowly at first and then faster, collapsing onto the bank beside Vance.

"Tess, *mon Dieu,* Tess," he breathed, crushing her against his chest. She held on to him just as tightly.

"Let me see your hands." They were red and gouged from the cane. "I'm sorry. I didn't have any other way."

"I know. I know. It's all right." She pressed her face against his chest. LeRoy was still screaming at them.

Vance continued to ignore him. "How did you end up in there?"

"He pulled me with him. He shot Devoe and tossed him in—and watched him drown. He was going to kill me, too. But we have to get him out."

The look on his face was harsh. "Perhaps." Standing up, he took one of the canes and slipped it to LeRoy. He watched while LeRoy took hold of the shaft, but didn't begin to pull.

"Get me out of here," LeRoy whimpered.

Vance kept a grip on his end of the cane, and reached into his pocket. "This button came off your navy sports coat."

"Yeah, so what? Where the hell did you get it?"

"I found it in the cemetery. In Ken Holloway's hand."

Tess gasped. LeRoy's face hardened.

"Suppose you tell me what happened. Or Tess and I will walk away from here."

"No. You can't— Please—" the little man blubbered. "Get me out of here. I—I—can't breathe."

"Put the pieces of the puzzle together for me. Did you kill my sister?"

"Hell, no. The only other one I had to get besides Ken was Erica Barry."

Tess gasped. "You? But why?"

"She could tie me to Devoe. Please—get me out of here—"

Vance shook his head curtly. "Talk."

For a moment LeRoy's eyes rolled madly and Tess was afraid he would lose his slender grip on sanity. Then he clutched the cane and lifted his chin. "Erica was one of Devoe's honeys back in the good old days. She recognized me when she came to the studio. I had to take care of her.

"You gotta understand," LeRoy pleaded. "You gotta know what it's like to be there on the edge of success. That station was finally paying off for me. Then of all the damn, stinking, rotten luck, *she* turns up. She didn't say anything. But I could tell she remembered me. So I went to her house that night. I thought if I made it look like a ritual murder, the police would think it was some nut."

"My sister—" Vance growled. "Why did she end up in Savannah Bayou?"

LeRoy had begun to blubber. "Not me. Not me."

"Devoe drove her to it," Tess answered. "He switched her medication. He said she was poking into his drug business. Just like my mother."

"What?"

"Later, Vance. Later." She gestured toward the man in the quicksand. His face was crimson now. "Please— Get him out of there. Before it's too late."

"Hang on," Vance growled, hauling back on the pole.

Tess held her breath, but finally, with agonizing slowness, the station owner's pudgy body began to emerge from the quicksand. Then he was flopping onto the ground beside them.

Vance stared down at him. "We'd better call the sheriff."

"He's right here," said a gruff voice behind them.

Vance and Tess whirled to find themselves facing Frank Haney, who looked much as he had that night at the jail.

Vance's whole body tensed when he saw the beefy man.

"Ernestine Achord called me," the sheriff explained. "I guess she figured you were gonna need some help. I got here a few minutes ago and decided to see what developed."

Tess moved closer to Vance.

"Glen Devoe is in there." He gestured toward the quicksand, his eyes never leaving the sheriff.

"Yeah. I heard." He crossed to LeRoy and pulled him to his feet. "Come on. You have the right to remain silent, of course. Except that these folks have already heard your confession. And Ms. Beaumont saw you kill Devoe. Which don't put you in a very good position."

LeRoy's head was bowed, his lips pressed together.

"I'll need a statement from you," Haney said, addressing both Vance and Tess.

Vance nodded almost imperceptibly. When he saw Tess staring at him, he cleared his throat. "I'm glad you showed up when you did."

"Yeah, well, it's going to be a lot easier to enforce the law around here with Devoe gone," Haney said.

Probably the first civil words the two of them had exchanged, Tess thought.

Vance and Tess were silent as Haney hustled LeRoy toward the road.

"Something's bothering you," Vance said finally as they reached his car.

Tess nodded. A lot was bothering her.

Perhaps Vance felt the same way. He started to open the door. Then he turned and his gaze honed in on the locket clasped between her fingers.

"Why do you wear that?"

"It was my aunt's. I put it on after she died. To feel close to
her. Now...Devoe made it sound as if she knew he was going to
kill my mother...was in on it." Tess gulped. "When I went to
sleep in Lisa's bed this afternoon, I dreamed Aunt Pauline came
to rescue me. She was holding out the locket."

"Can I see it?"

Tess nodded. He found the catch and snapped the locket open.
Inside was Tess's confirmation picture. "Do you mind if I take it
out?"

"Go ahead."

Underneath was a flat silver plate.

"Right after her funeral, I tried to get it up. I couldn't," Tess
told him.

Vance inserted a penknife carefully under the edge. The plate
popped up. Inside was a folded yellow piece of onionskin paper.

Handing the locket back to Tess, Vance waited while she removed the paper, spread it open and stared at the lines of tiny
script. "It's addressed to me. Aunt Pauline wrote it."

My dearest Tess,
I believe Mr. Devoe killed your mother. The only way I could
take you home was to swear that I would never speak of her
again. Forgive me.

"Oh, my God," Tess breathed. "She..."

"She had a terrible decision to make," Vance said.

Tess wanted to believe it. But it was a lot to take in.

Vance shifted his weight uneasily. "Ernestine is waiting to find
out what happened to you."

"Yes, she must be terribly worried. We'd better tell her we're
all right."

Tess felt a cord of tension pulling her shoulders back against
the car seat as they rode back to Savannah Bayou. As they approached the house, Tess could see Ernestine on the front porch.

Vance bolted out of the car and hurried to her side.

"Did you bring her back?" she asked.

"*Oui.*"

"*Chère,* are you all right?" she called out to Tess.

"Yes. Thanks to Vance."

"Come in and tell me what happened."

"She's a mess, *Tante.* She was in the swamp."

"Then I can wait until you both bathe and change."

It was good to wash the mud off, Tess thought as she swiftly bathed. "I'm using up your supply of spare dresses," she told Ernestine when she returned to the living room.

"You're welcome to them." The old woman looked uncomfortable. "I'm sorry. That man. Desmond LeRoy. He said he had to get in touch with you. But as soon as I told him where you were, I wondered if I'd made a mistake."

"He fooled a lot of people," Vance said from the doorway. He was wearing fresh jeans and a clean white shirt.

They gave Ernestine a brief account of what had happened after Tess had left for her mother's house. Then Vance stood up and paced to the door. "We should go."

"Yes," Tess whispered. She knew they had both been putting off whatever it was they were going to say to each other.

"Do you want me to take you home?" Vance asked as he started the engine.

Tess's fingers dug into the edge of the seat. "No. Your house is closer. We need to talk."

Tess saw the look of relief flash across Vance's features.

Ten minutes later they were standing uncertainly in front of the steps that led to the gallery.

Vance closed the car door very deliberately. Then he turned to her. "*Chère*, don't torture me any longer. If it's all over between us, tell me now. I've got to know."

Hope unfurled in her chest. "I don't want it to be over."

With a low curse, he crossed the few feet between them and pulled her into his embrace. Her arms went around him and they held each other.

Then they climbed the steps to the gallery.

Once they were in the living room, his expression grew serious. "*Chère*, do you forgive your aunt for what she did to you?" he finally asked.

It was the last thing she'd expected him to ask. "I—I—yes." She raised her face, her eyes searching his.

"Then perhaps you can forgive me, too."

She looked at him questioningly.

"I did the same thing, you know. I made decisions about what was best for you without letting you have any say in the matter."

"You understand that?"

"*Oui.*"

"You understand that a man and woman have to trust and rely

on each other if they're going to make anything important work between them?'' she asked.

"I'm starting to understand. But I'm so used to taking responsibility only for myself. I thought that if I got into trouble, I'd be the one who had to suffer the consequences. Instead, you were almost killed because I wasn't there when you needed me."

"You came back in time."

"Thank the good God."

She knew how hard it had been for him to admit those things. "Still, it must be part of the reason you've kept telling yourself that a woman like me—whatever that is—couldn't love a man like you."

She felt him go very still.

"It's not true, you know," she continued. "If I hadn't been falling in love with you, I wouldn't have gone to your bed. Vance Gautreau, I love you *because* of your background."

"How could you?" he asked in a fierce voice.

"I love you because of what you've been able to make of yourself despite a rotten start in life. Because you're intelligent and creative. Because you have so much strength. And so much tenderness. And because you'd take any risk for the people you care about. I love you."

He cupped her face in his hands and gazed down at her. "Don't put me on some kind of pedestal—or you'll be disappointed."

"Don't worry. I'm a realist. I also know you have a hot temper. And you're impulsive. And *tête dur*—hardheaded."

He nodded. "All of those, *oui*. But I'm beginning to think the luckiest day of my life was the day you walked into that jail. *Je t'aime*," he whispered softly. Then louder, "I love you, Tess."

All at once she was seeing him through a film of tears. Then he was kissing the corners of her eyes, kissing her mouth, holding her as if he would never let her go.

"We'll work it out. I promise," she managed.

"*Oui*. We have to."

"Take me upstairs. Very slowly. The way you did the first time."

"The famous stairs." He laughed softly. Then he swung her into his arms and carried her toward the front hall.

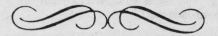

TRIAL BY FIRE
Rebecca York

In the dim light of the garage across from 43 Light Street, Sabrina Barkley folded her hands on the steering wheel. Although she usually arrived at work full of energy, for the past few days she'd awakened feeling as if she'd spent the night running from an unseen pursuer.

Straightening her shoulders, Sabrina strode across the street to Sabrina's Fancy, the lobby shop she'd opened a few years ago.

As she walked in the door, her assistant, Erin Morgan, gave her an appraising look. "Hmm. Which is it? Good news or bad?"

Sabrina forced a laugh. "Both. The hospitality manager at the Harbor Court called yesterday afternoon. They're featuring local crafts people in some of their promotions, and they've ordered two hundred and fifty of my bath-herb-and-soap baskets to put in their suites."

"Way to go!"

"Now all I have to do is find the time to make them up."

As Sabrina crossed to her office, she gave silent thanks once more for Erin Morgan's quiet strength.

After squaring off at the desk, she picked up a pen and began to scribble on a white pad of paper. Color schemes. Scents. Textures. Herbs. Dried flowers. Unusual? Rosemary. Angelica. Lace. Satin ribbons.

Sabrina tried to focus on what she'd written, but as she bent over the paper, the lines of script blurred. Alarm settled like a lead weight on her chest.

The sensation became more acute as the whole room wavered. For an awful moment, currents of heat seemed to ripple through her head, playing over the surface of her brain like static electricity. Frantically her fingers gripped the shaft of the pen she was holding. Then her hand began to move across the page again. But this time the writing instrument took control—as if it were a magic wand and she were under some strange spell. Words and sentences flowed from the tip of the pen. Against her will, they dragged her away with them. Away to another time and another place.

...at the very moment Sara stepped out the door, a screeching raven dived toward the roof of the little cottage.

"No! Get ye gone." Dropping her basket, she rushed at the creature, flapping her apron. But to no avail. The bird circled the chimney before flying off toward the pines at the edge of the clearing.

Heart blocking her windpipe, Sara stood trembling in the little farmyard.

A raven so close to the house. A bad omen.

She started toward the craggy mountains. Yet once she was out in the heather with the wind picking up her red hair and the sun warming her lightly freckled face, she acknowledged how sick she was of the dank stone cottage after a week of rain.

First she gathered wintergreen. Then she picked some of the other plants she'd learned to make into healing potions or use to flavor their simple food. She knew all the best places to look, and her basket was quickly full. Then above her on the side of the cliff, she spied a patch of rock speedwell. Gran was partial to the deep blue flowers, each petal with a crimson line at the base.

She was twenty yards from the valley floor when she heard hooves pounding across the rocky ground. The animal was dark and magnificent—a destrier, one of the highly trained battle horses. The rider must be a laird from the castle, judging from his rich cloak and fine leather boots. He was having trouble with the mount.

"Beware," she cried out.

Too late.

Sara saw the rider tossed into the air, his fall broken by a clump of gorse.

The horse galloped on. The man lay motionless.

Dead.

He lay sprawled on his stomach. Kneeling, she grasped him by the shoulders and rolled him over. His eyes were closed, and gold-tipped lashes lay softly against his tanned cheeks. When she touched his face to brush away the dirt, she sensed the first hint of the man's beard that hadn't fully grown in. His age couldn't be much more than her own fifteen years.

As her fingers touched his skin, he groaned.

He was alive!

With the skills Gran had taught her, she began to assess the damage. His white lawn shirt was covered with dirt. Of more concern was the torn leg of his britches. It was soaked with blood above the knee. Her hands were tearing at the fabric when strong fingers locked around her wrist.

"A wood sprite." His eyes were open now—and as blue as the stained glass in the window of the cathedral. With a shaky hand, he reached out and touched her fiery tresses.

"Be still," she ordered. "You've been hurt. I'm a skilled healer," she said, overstating her abilities a bit. "Let me help you."

Although she saw him clench his teeth as she picked gravel from his flesh, he didn't cry out.

"You're from the castle?" she asked to distract him from the pain.

"I—"

"SABRINA! Sabrina!" His hand was on her arm. Shaking her. But he was hurt. Where did he get the strength? She stared at the hand in utter confusion. Too small. Too feminine.

"Sabrina. What's wrong?"

The familiar voice and the urgent question were like a lifeline, and she clutched at them with all her strength. Inch by inch, she pulled herself to firmer ground.

"Jo?" she finally managed, her voice high and reedy as she stared at private detective Jo O'Malley. Her friend.

"You looked like you were in a trance."

"No. Really." Sabrina sat up straighter and cleared her throat, even as she wondered exactly what she was going to say. "I was, uh, using a brainstorming technique I picked up at a seminar." To her surprise, she sounded almost coherent. Encouraged, she continued, "I guess I just got carried away."

She was still congratulating herself on her quick recovery when her eyes flicked back to the pen clutched in her hand and the lines of script slanting across the page in front of her.

The handwriting was familiar, but the words seemed to have sprung from nowhere.

"Sure. I understand." Jo pursed her lips, stood, and leaned on the edge of the worktable. "I was going to ask you a favor. I wish I hadn't barged in like this."

"Jo. It's okay. Honestly."

"Well, a friend needs a special favor."

"Dried bouquets?"

"No, he needs to borrow some of your expertise."

"With growing herbs?"

Jo sighed. "I guess there's just no good way to introduce the subject. It's got to do with the Graveyard Murders. You've heard of Dan Cassidy, haven't you?"

"I've read about him. He's supposed to be tough. So what exactly does he need from me?"

"Dan's looking for an expert opinion."

"On what? I don't know anything about drugs. Except for some of the herbal compounds. And they aren't going to command big bucks on the street."

"It's better if *he* tells you what he wants," Jo hurried on. "He's springing for lunch at Sabatino's."

WHILE DAN CASSIDY studied his menu, Sabrina studied him, scanning his face, trying for the quick insights she often gleaned.

He glanced up suddenly, discovered her watching him and gave her a piercing look.

"Jo says you're in the herb business," Dan said.

"Yes. I started growing them and researching old uses."

"So how did you get from herbs to the arcane?"

"I'm not exactly into the arcane. I hope that's not what Jo told you."

"She said you have a lot of talents. And now you have your own business?"

"Yes."

"What do you sell?"

"Herb products. Some jewelry. Dried flowers." She gestured with her hands. "So what makes you think I can help you?"

Dan didn't answer. He was staring at the double gold ess charm dangling from her bracelet. "You sell those?"

"It's my logo. I put a foil one in with each purchase as a personalized touch."

"Why a double ess?"

"I got to playing with my name and liked this design."

"The charms must be expensive."

"Not really. I get thousands at a time."

"So your business must be doing pretty well."

His rapid-fire questions went beyond casual interest. In fact, they made her feel as if she were on the witness stand.

Cassidy cleared his throat. "Sorry. This case is putting a lot of pressure on me. I shouldn't be so abrupt."

"Want to tell me something about it?"

"Yes. Do the names Ian Alastair or Bette Kronstat mean anything to you?"

"No. I don't think so."

"They're the two victims of the Graveyard Murders. We didn't know their names initially, because neither one was found with any identification." He looked around the room. "I'm sure you've read something about it. Kronstat was found first. Then Alastair. In different graveyards."

Sabrina's fingers wadded the napkin in her lap. "Wasn't there supposed to be a ritual aspect to the murders?"

"Yes. And we've got a confession from a guy who says he did it. The problem is, I'm not sure I believe him." Reaching down beside his chair, he brought out a glossy photograph. "Would you mind taking a look at this?"

In the dim light, Sabrina couldn't see any details. "It's not a body or anything, is it?"

"No. Just a strange symbol."

"The evil eye," Sabrina offered, almost immediately.

"What?"

"The evil eye," Sabrina repeated. "It's an almost universal symbol. Every culture has it. The idea is that certain men and women have the power to kill or make you sick or give you bad luck just by looking at you."

Dan gave her a sharp look. "What does that have to do with a murder in Baltimore in the twenty-first century?"

"There are plenty of superstitious people who believe in hexes and curses. Even in this country, there are modern witches and devil worshipers."

"I'd like to take you over and show you where the most recent body was found and where this eye was in relationship to it."

"You mean if I don't have anything more pressing this afternoon, you'd like to take me to visit a cemetery where someone didn't bother to bury the latest corpse?" she inquired.

"You could put it that way."

SABRINA WAS making headway on the Harbor Court Hotel plans when there was a knock on the door. Erin leaned into her office. "Is it all right to tell Hilda and Gwynn you're here?"

"Of course. I'll be right out."

Hilda Ahern had been a customer of Sabrina's since she'd sold homemade vinegars and jellies at her Howard County house, and she'd introduced her friend Gwynn Frontenac to the joys of herb teas and exotic spices.

The two ladies were both wealthy widows in their sixties who filled their days with a never-ending stream of harmless enthusiasms.

Sabrina greeted the two customers with a smile.

"I stopped in for some of your tarragon vinegar and that divine lavender soap," Hilda began.

"Of course."

"By the way, what herbs would you recommend for the heart? I've been having some palpitations at night," Gwynn inquired.

Sabrina paused with her hand on the vinegar bottle. "You really should ask your doctor about that," she murmured.

"Oh, *doctors*, what do they know? My internist's just going to give me another one of those stress tests and charge me five hundred dollars for the torture."

"Perhaps you should try Dr. Davenport. He's much more sympathetic to sensibilities of refined women like us," Hilda put in. "I've got some free tickets for his lecture tomorrow. You should come too, hon. He's so knowledgeable about the mind-body connection. I know you'd pick up some pointers."

"How thoughtful of you, Hilda," Sabrina said, taking a ticket from Hilda. "I've heard interesting things about him. I will try to make it."

Before they left, Gwynn leaned toward Sabrina. "It's a long ride back to Ruxton. Can I borrow your little girls' room while you ring up the sale?" she asked, laying her credit card on the antique oak counter.

"Of course. And be sure to try the new hand cream I've put out."

*

WHEN THE CEMETERY GATE clanked behind them, Sabrina felt as if she'd just been shut into a coffin. The road winding between the rows of graves contributed to the claustrophobic effect. It had probably been built in horse-and-buggy days.

"Let's circle around the back of the site," Dan suggested. "That way we won't have to back up to get out."

Poised for a quick getaway, she thought. "Fine," was all she said.

"If we leave the windows open, it won't get so hot in here."

"Okay."

When Dan opened his door, Sabrina remained seated. She didn't usually wait for someone else to escort her out. Now she was in no hurry. As Dan helped her from the car and she stepped onto the dried grass, she felt a wave of heat and humidity wrap around her like a suffocating blanket, making her feel as if the air were too heavy to drag into her lungs. Yet she really didn't want to breathe this atmosphere at all.

"The site's over there." Dan pointed down the hill.

If Dan hadn't held her firmly by the arm, she would have hung back as they headed down the slope toward the murder scene.

"It's one of the oldest grave sites in the cemetery," Dan explained.

Trying to come up with a rational explanation for the odd way she was feeling, Sabrina peered at the time-worn surface of the marker. Carved across the front, the name Ridley was barely visible. And the date. 1820? 1828?

"The victim was lying down, with his head facing in the direction of the stone. His arms were folded across his chest," Dan told her.

Despite the heat and humidity, Sabrina moved closer to Dan. The part of her mind that was still functioning knew it was in danger of shutting down.

"Bad vibrations?"

Sabrina was far beyond putting up any kind of front. "Yes." Unconsciously she took several steps back. As she did, the heel of her shoe came down on something hard nestled in the grass. A bolt of electricity seemed to shoot through her. She felt it all the way to her fingertips. All the way to the tips of her red hair, which stood on end around her face.

"What the hell—" Dan grabbed Sabrina's arm before she toppled over and eased her down to the ground.

She sat there in the weeds, looking around in a daze. The breath that hissed in and out of her lungs burned.

"Are you all right?"

"...hurts..."

"What?"

"My chest...hurts to breathe."

Dan was on his knees beside her, watching her face. The worry in his eyes made her struggle to relax her contorted features. After a moment, she could speak more easily. "It's getting better."

"Thank God." He stroked her arms and shoulders, smoothing down the strands of hair that floated around her face. Her eyes drifted closed, and her head flopped forward against his chest.

"Are you sure you're okay?" he asked.

"I think so," Sabrina whispered.

"I want to find out what you stepped on."

Fear leaped inside her chest, and she grabbed his arm. "Be careful!"

"Don't worry."

Her pounding heart added to the pain in her chest as she watched him searching in the grass around the area where she'd been standing. He poked cautiously at the ground.

"Don't."

"It's okay." When he turned back to her he was holding a perfectly rounded white stone. It was smooth, except for the faint image of a star scratched into the top surface.

He peered at it doubtfully. "Maybe it had some kind of electrical charge. It's gone now."

Sabrina looked at the oval nestled innocently in Dan's hand.

Teeth clenched, she reached out and lightly touched a finger to the star. All that was left was a faint buzzing sensation like insect wings vibrating against a windowpane.

"You don't feel anything?" she whispered.

"What?"

"Tingling."

He shook his head, then looked from her to the stone.

"I'm not making the whole thing up."

"Of course not. I saw your hair standing on end like you'd stuck your finger into an electric socket, and I saw the way it hurt you to breathe." Dan turned the orb in his hand, looking at it from all angles.

Sabrina shuddered. "Put it down."

"What is it?"

"Something bad. Something that's been cursed."

By MUTUAL AGREEMENT, they had started back in the direction of the car. As they climbed the hill and left the immediate area of the grave, Sabrina felt a profound sense of relief. She glanced at Dan, and he smiled.

She smiled back.

When they came abreast of the car, she stopped and wrinkled her nose. "Do you smell something funny?"

"Rotting flowers?"

"No, cherries, I think." The odor was quite unpleasant.

Dan turned on the ignition and closed the windows. The air-conditioning whooshed as it sprang to life. It should have cleared out the smell, but after several moments, Sabrina realized that the aroma was even stronger and somehow very compelling.

Dan gunned the engine. With a jerk, the car shot forward.

The road was narrow and twisting. As the vehicle picked up speed, Dan spun the wheel wildly, somehow keeping the car on the blacktop.

Then a tree seemed to jump in front of them.

"Watch out!" Sabrina shouted.

This time Dan couldn't move fast enough. The car slammed into the obstacle and came to rest with a jarring thunk. They both pitched forward. Sabrina's head hit the mirror. She cried out in pain. Then she was being snapped back by the seat belt.

A loud blaring noise filled the car. The horn. It wouldn't stop. Dan swore.

Sabrina looked up. The scene around them blurred and then bounced into focus. She sucked in a terrified breath. The car was surrounded by a wall of flames.

"Fire!" she screamed above the blaring noise. "Fire!"

"What?"

Her hand swung in an arc.

When Dan didn't respond, Sabrina shrank down, pulling at the seat belt, trying to fold her body under the dashboard. She didn't even consider that she might have conjured it up from her imagination. It was too real, too daunting.

Unhooking the seat belt, Sabrina reached for the door handle and bolted from the car.

The evil-smelling flames licked at her hair, seared her skin, whooshed after her. They gained on her as she ran in a zigzag line; she wove unsteadily across the grass, the sound of the crowd speeding her legs.

Footsteps echoed behind her.

"Sabrina. Damn you. Wait!"

"No! Duncan. Save me. Save me."

Then, magically, as if her deep need had conjured up a savior, he was there, swinging her up into his arms.

He turned around, and all at once she knew that he didn't mean to rescue her at all. "No! No! Not the fire. Don't take me back to the fire." With a scream of terror that ended in a spasm of choking, she began to fight him as if all the demons of hell were dragging her into the inferno.

He was trying to hold her arms, trying to restrain her without hurting her. Still she fought against him, her mind spinning, caught between one illusion and the next, unable to find any reality besides the man who held her. She could hear him gasping in lungfuls of air, feel his fingers digging into her ribs, her shoulders, her hips.

"Stop. I won't hurt you, Sara. Never."

Yet even as they struggled, as their bodies brushed and collided in opposition, another stronger, more elemental force came into play.

Male and female—searching, seeking. And all the usual inhibitions had been stripped away by the drugging vapor that still enveloped them—still held them in its grasp.

The contact of man to woman generated sparks like flint striking steel. All at once the fire was no longer around Sabrina. It was in her.

Dan must have felt the change. "That's it. Don't fight me." His voice was thick. His grasp shifted from force to persuasion. Fingers pressed, kneaded, and began to roam in wide circles across her back and shoulders. Moments—or was it centuries—ago, he'd been trying to carry her to safety. Or into the flames.

Sabrina felt light-headed. Then she looked up at him, focused on the blue of his eyes, and gave a little sob of joy. She was in his arms again, after so many lonely years.

"WHERE THE HELL is everybody?" a voice called.

Illusion had vanished.

With a little cry of loss, Sabrina's eyes snapped open. She swayed, grabbed for something solid, and found herself clinging to muscular forearms.

It took several seconds for her to realize she was holding on to Dan.

A moment later an old man came dodging and puffing through the forest of grave markers.

The caretaker. What was he doing here?

His eyes were wide. "Lord 'a mercy. Heard the horn. Thought you wanted me. Bad like. Then I saw the car plowed into a tree."

Dan shook his head. With fingers that weren't quite steady, he reached up and touched Sabrina's forehead. She winced.

"You hit your head," he mumbled.

He helped her sit, and she leaned back against a stone marker. Her thoughts were still spinning. When she closed her eyes, she saw flames dancing behind her closed lids.

Heart pounding, she opened her eyes again, and the fire disappeared.

"What happened?" she moaned.

Dan didn't answer. Instead he looked uncertainly back at the car.

So did Sabrina. "The rotten cherry smell..."

"When I started the engine."

"Then everything went fuzzy," she said uncertainly.

"Some kind of gas, do you think?"

It was hard to make sense of what he was saying.

"*Something* knocked us silly," Dan continued.

Sabrina nodded slowly, remembering the unpleasant odor and how spacy she'd started feeling right after she'd first smelled it.

"I'd like to know who the hell cherry-bombed an official government vehicle." He started to laugh and sat weakly beside her. "Damn. My head hurts," he muttered after a few minutes. Then he looked at the caretaker. "Better call the police. And an ambulance."

"Already did."

SABRINA, Dan and a couple of officers went back to Sabrina's home. The old farmhouse in Ilchester was situated on twenty acres.

"Did you see anybody approach Mr. Cassidy's car while you were at the cemetery?" Ritz, one of the officers, asked.

"No. But I wasn't looking that way."

"Nobody else was in the vicinity? People visiting graves or anything like that?"

Sabrina hesitated. "Earlier, I thought maybe I saw something in the shadows. Then the caretaker came running when he realized what was going on," Sabrina recounted, vaguely surprised that she sounded so coherent.

"When did the effects of the gas commence?"

Sabrina thought back. "Pretty soon after Mr. Cassidy started the engine."

"What happened?"

"At first everything seemed funny, and distorted. It looked as if the driver's seat had moved far away from me. Then the car started going fast."

"Is there anything else you think is relevant?"

"The rotten-cherry smell, I guess." Sabrina replied. "That was the first thing I noticed."

"You smelled it, too?" Ritz asked Dan.

"Yes. What about the trigger mechanism? Was it the starter?"

"Yes. It was wired like a bomb."

"A bomb!" Sabrina glanced from Dan to Ritz. They both looked impassive.

"Whoever it was didn't want to blow up the car," Dan said. "Maybe they were hoping I'd make it to the highway."

Sabrina went rigid, suddenly understanding the implications. They might have been both killed.

"You think we can get this wrapped up?" Dan said.

"Just a few more questions." The officer turned back to Sabrina. "How long did the experience last?"

The tightness in Dan's voice had made Sabrina's pulse start to pound. She tried to focus on the question. "I guess not more than fifteen minutes."

"Short-term effect," Ritz remarked as he wrote. "Besides the laughing, what else happened to you?"

Sabrina swallowed and glanced quickly at Dan. "A couple of different things. After the car hit the tree, I thought we were surrounded by fire. Then for a few minutes I hallucinated. I felt as if I were somebody else, in a different place."

"Somebody else?" Dan asked, his expression odd as he studied her face.

"In the Middle Ages or something. There was a crowd around us, jeering and shouting. They wanted me dead." She looked pleadingly at Dan. "I was confused. I wasn't sure whether you were there to save me or—"

"Or what?"

She shrugged. "Well, it was just, you know, a fantasy. I was feeling as if I were a peasant girl and you were the lord of the manor."

Ritz was taking it all down.

"LET'S STOP fencing with each other and get to the point," Dan said once they were alone. "I don't particularly want to talk about what happened, but I've got to understand it—for this investigation, if nothing else. We're two adults and we're alone. Anything we say right now is strictly between the two of us."

"You really want to pursue this?"

"No. But we can't just let it go. How about starting with the murder case?"

"Someone tried to kill *you*," Sabrina whispered.

"Or scare me off. Or maybe they didn't know it was me. They could have been after whoever came out to have another look at the murder site."

"Do you believe that?"

"Let's say I'll watch my back from now on."

Sabrina shivered.

Dan leaned forward. "I want to understand what happened after we hit the tree."

She felt heat creep into her face again.

"You thought we were surrounded by fire," he prompted.

"Yes," she whispered.

"Where do you think the image came from?"

She didn't answer, and he sat down on the couch next to her. His nearness made her pulse race. Slowly he leaned toward her, giving her a chance to pull away. She didn't.

His lips hovered questioningly over hers. She tensed, wondering whether she was afraid of him or herself. Or was it the memory of being out of control? She was still frightened by that. Yet she yearned to know how much had been from the drug and how much had been from the man himself.

His lips touched hers.

This kiss was slow, delicious. Not what she would have expected from Dan Cassidy.

He didn't rush her, but when she slid her hands around his waist, she felt him smile. Then slowly, very slowly, he deepened the kiss. His tongue skimmed over the sensitive tissue of her mouth, creating new sensations—sensations they controlled, not ones that controlled them.

There was a thrill of discovery, and for long moments they both enjoyed the exploration. Yet the longer it continued the more she realized that the deeper awareness hadn't gone away. On some subliminal level, the pleasure was tinged with danger.

His fingers played with her unruly curls. Then he smoothed them back from her face.

"I'm confused," she whispered.

"Are you?"

She flushed.

"I think we're both embarrassed about your little fantasy."

She nodded.

His fingers moved from her hair to stroke down the side of her face.

"What do you want?" Sabrina held her breath.

He laughed. "To spend the night with you."

A man could admit that. A woman couldn't—shouldn't.

"But I'll settle for dinner tomorrow," he added.

"I can't."

"Oh?"

"I promised two ladies I know that I'd go to a lecture with them."

"Is that what you usually do for excitement?"

"No. But it will probably be an interesting experience. Besides, they'll be disappointed if I don't show up."

He looked as if he wasn't sure she was being straight with him. "You could tell me about it at lunch on Thursday."

*

SABRINA WAS tense all the next morning. Two or three times during the day, she almost decided to call Hilda to say she wasn't feeling well and couldn't attend the lecture after all. But each time she changed her mind.

At seven, Sabrina drove to the Andromeda Institute, a renovated house not far from the Johns Hopkins campus. After stepping through the entrance, she stood looking around at the well-dressed crowd, feeling a bit apprehensive and out of place.

Hilda tugged on Sabrina's arm. "I want to look at the product displays before the lecture. Afterward, the tables are always so crowded."

Gwynn Frontenac was talking with a slender man. A good six inches taller than her companion, she leaned down to catch what he was saying.

Spotting the newcomers, Gwynn waved and gestured. "Sabrina

Barkley,'' she called across the room, ''come over here this minute.''

As scores of heads turned in Sabrina's direction, she kept a smile plastered on her face.

''Professor Ashford is very anxious to meet you,'' Gwynn explained as Sabrina joined the twosome.

She inclined her head toward the man.

''I'm doing an article on alternative medicine, and Gwynn has been telling me about your shop. Perhaps we could get together for an interview,'' he suggested.

Sabrina glanced quickly at Gwynn, trying not to show her annoyance.

SABRINA TOOK a seat near the middle of the auditorium. No one was talking. Rather, they were sitting in expectant silence, as if the light classical music playing in the background had put them under some kind of spell.

The peaceful feeling was dispelled when a man in a cowboy outfit plopped into the aisle chair in front of her. As he turned his head, Sabrina saw his skin was unusually pale. However, her scrutiny was cut off as the lights dimmed and a swell of music heightened the feeling of expectation.

''Friends,'' Luther Davenport began. ''I have gone to the source of wisdom. Once a week I leave civilization behind and commune with nature. In the woods. In the mountains. In the hidden cave only I have ever entered.''

That sounded nice. Then Sabrina gave herself a mental shake and sat up straighter. Nice? More like hogwash.

It was a relief when Sabrina was distracted by an abrupt movement in front of her, until she realized that the man in Western garb had doubled over and was sitting with his head cradled in his hands.

''Hoarding wisdom is as unconscionable as hoarding money,'' Davenport was saying. ''Through booklets published by the Andromeda Institute, I—''

His words were interrupted by a groan. As Sabrina watched in horror, the cowboy pitched forward, hit the floor and lay sprawled in the aisle—white-faced and unmoving.

Dr. Davenport's voice ceased in the middle of a sentence. And the house lights came up.

''What's happened?''

"What is it?"

Sabrina knelt beside the prostrate figure. The man was shaking violently and struggling for breath. As she leaned toward him, his face contorted as if he were in terrible pain. She grasped the man's hand. "What is it? What's wrong?"

His eyes focused on her. Something in their murky depths made her shudder. Then his jaw clenched, and his body convulsed. With a final shudder, he went perfectly still.

"Get an ambulance," Sabrina shouted. "Hurry."

She had no idea whether anyone responded. She was too busy trying to remember the CPR techniques she'd learned a year ago.

"Can anybody help?" she begged.

When no one came forward, she began the procedure, concentrating on the victim until large hands gripped her by the shoulders.

"Thank you, Ms. Barkley. I'll take over."

It was Dr. Davenport. Sabrina moved aside as he leaned over the unconscious man. But instead of continuing the standard procedure, Davenport lifted a lid and looked into a dilated pupil. Then he stroked his hands across the clammy skin of the slack jaw.

"What—what are you doing? He needs CPR until the rescue squad—"

"I think I can judge the situation better than you," the doctor murmured.

They had been joined by the woman who'd introduced Dr. Davenport. He barked at her, "Quickly. Get me—"

Sabrina didn't hear the last part of the sentence, because it was spoken into the assistant's ear.

The woman rushed away. Sabrina was left staring across a lifeless body into Davenport's deep-set eyes. They were challenging and commanding at the same time. She felt as if she'd been thrust into some kind of contest. And the loser was going to be the man on the floor.

A HUSH HAD fallen over the room. With a flourish that managed to be both calm and theatrical, Davenport pulled the stopper from a small glass vial. Prying the cowboy's jaw open, he poured a white powder into his mouth.

Sabrina could feel her own heart thumping like a kettledrum. For several seconds nothing happened. Then the prostrate figure began to cough.

The breath hissed out of her own lungs. She heard the same sigh repeated many times around her.

The coughing on the floor became louder. The cowboy's jaw muscles twitched. His eyes fluttered open, and he looked around, as if wondering where he was and what had happened.

"The light...the shining light," he whispered.

"My God. Would you look at that," somebody marveled.

There were murmurs of agreement, followed by a babble of excited voices. Sabrina was no less astounded as she stared at the man on the floor who was now struggling to sit up.

Davenport restrained him gently. "Just relax, my friend," he said.

PEOPLE WERE milling around, still talking excitedly about the unexpected drama. Sabrina tensed as she realized she was looking at the stopper to the vial Davenport had been holding. It must have gone flying.

Pretending to check through her purse, she pulled out a tissue and dropped it on the floor over the stopper. Then she quickly folded the prize into the tissue and tucked it into her bag.

HALF AN HOUR later, Sabrina turned into the long driveway that led to her house. When she rounded the last curve, her foot lifted with a jerk from the accelerator. Another car was occupying her usual parking space beside the porch.

When the visitor stepped into the glare of her headlights, Sabrina saw it was Dan Cassidy, dressed casually in jeans and a striped pullover. He stood with his hands thrust into his pockets, and she couldn't help wondering if she'd conjured up his image.

Then he called out to her, and she knew it was no illusion. "I wasn't expecting company," she tossed out as she exited the car.

"I thought you might want someone around," he said.

"Why?"

"After what happened this evening."

"You mean at the Institute?"

He nodded.

"Are they broadcasting it on the radio or something?" Sabrina snapped.

"No. Of course not."

"Then what's it got to do with you?"

Dan hesitated. "If I tell you how I found out, you've got to treat it as strictly confidential."

"Yes?"

"Someone at the lecture tonight is under investigation. I had a man in the audience. He called me from his car phone right after the excitement was over."

"AREN'T YOU going to tell me if anything's developed on the other case?" Sabrina asked after they had gone inside.

Dan looked surprised, as if he'd forgotten all about the original reason why they'd gotten together.

"There's nothing new on that front," he said.

The phone rang, and Dan's gaze shot to the clock on the wall. It was almost twelve. "Expecting someone?" he asked sharply.

Sabrina shook her head. There was an odd feeling in her chest as she crossed to the side table and picked up the phone. It came as much from Dan's wary expression as her own puzzlement over the late call.

After one more ring, she lifted the receiver. "Hello?"

"Ms. Barkley?" The voice was low and whispery and obviously disguised. "I was beginning to think you weren't home."

"Who is this?"

There was no answer. If she'd been alone, she would have hung up.

Dan had come over and put his hand on her shoulder.

"Who is this?" she repeated.

"A friend."

"What do you want?"

"I saw you tonight at the lecture."

Sabrina felt the hair on the top of her scalp prickle.

Dan gestured and she lifted the receiver slightly away from her head. Bending, he brought his ear close so that he could listen in.

"You saw what happened at the Institute?" Sabrina asked.

"With the man. Yes." There was a long pause.

"Are you still there?"

"I'm not calling about that. I'm calling because you're in danger," the voice whispered.

The prickles traveled from Sabrina's scalp down her spine all the way to her toes. "How?"

"Don't you realize how you figure into all this?"

Sabrina's anxious gaze shot to Dan. "No!"

"Somebody's trying to put you out of business—for good."

Beside her, Dan was standing rigidly, his hand covering hers as she clutched the receiver. She felt cold all over. "Wh-who? Dr. Davenport?"

There was an indrawn breath on the other end of the line. "It's dangerous to talk on the phone."

"Then why are you calling?"

"I couldn't just stand by and let it happen."

"Will you meet me?" Dan mouthed.

"Will you meet me?" Sabrina asked.

There was another hesitation on the other end of the wire.

"Please. You can't just tell me I'm in danger. You have to give me more information," Sabrina pleaded.

After several agonizing seconds, she could hear a breath being expelled. "All right. I shouldn't. But I'll meet you at Penn Station. Downstairs where the trains come in."

"When?"

"In an hour."

As A PUBLIC transportation facility, Penn Station was open twenty-four hours a day. Dan and several officers had arrived earlier. Sabrina didn't know where they were. She wasn't supposed to know.

She had left the main area and was approaching the boundary of the walkway. As she turned to go back, she thought she saw a flicker of movement near a column.

"Who's there?" Sabrina called out.

Sabrina's next step drew a sharp warning. "Don't come any closer!"

"All right. Anything you want. Why did you contact me?" Sabrina asked.

"The Servant of Darkness is hurting too many people."

Sabrina drew in a quick breath.

"The Servant is afraid of...you..."

"Why is this servant afraid of me?" Sabrina pressed.

"You don't know? You really don't know?" The speaker gave a strange imitation of mirth before stopping abruptly and gasping for breath. The raspy, labored sound raised goose bumps on Sabrina's arms.

"No. Please. Tell me."

"You fool. Don't...you...remember what happened...all those years ago? In the fire?"

"What fire?"

"The Burning." The voice gasped with pain, and Sabrina saw a figure slump to the floor, a figure wearing an oversize raincoat and a hat pulled low over the face. She rushed forward to help.

"Are you sick?"

"What's happening to me? Ahhh..."

"Let me help you."

"Oh, Satan! Oh, Saraaa..." The exclamation ended in a groan of pain and terror.

"Help. I need help," Sabrina cried out, but she didn't need to shout to get action.

Seconds later she heard footsteps pounding down the platform. Then Dan was beside her, his face pale and strained in the dim light.

She stared up at him in confusion as two other men rushed past. He slung a protective arm over her shoulder.

"Get an ambulance," one of the policemen ordered into his walkie-talkie.

SABRINA WAS vaguely aware that a couple of uniformed policemen were holding the small crowd of curious passengers back at the end of the platform, but her attention was focused closer by. The rescue team had started CPR, fighting for a life that was inexorably slipping away.

"Do you know her?" Dan asked urgently.

"Yes. She used to be a customer of mine." Sabrina struggled to keep her voice steady.

"Her name?"

"June Garrison."

The ambulance attendants had brought one of those portable electric units used to restart the heart. After ripping away the bodice of the woman's dress, one of them pressed the paddles against her skin.

"I think we've lost her," the medic said eventually.

Sabrina felt her heart sink.

Dan's fingers gently rubbed her arms, bringing a warmth that felt like a heat lamp on a January evening. "It's over now. All over," he soothed as he led her to one of the wooden benches.

Gratefully Sabrina slid down onto the firm surface. She could feel herself drawing inward, her mind shutting down.

A voice brought her back. "I've had a quick look at the personal effects," said one of the officers. "There's not much there. June L. Garrison. Age forty-five."

"Can I see the purse?" Dan asked.

Lowell handed him the black leather bag, and he began to riffle through the inside pockets. Moments later he pulled out a folded pink slip. "Looks like she withdrew ten thousand dollars from New Court Savings and Loan just this afternoon."

"Ten thousand dollars?" Sabrina repeated. "How much did she have in her wallet?"

"Ten dollars and change," Lowell answered. "Wonder what she did with all that cash."

"She was at the Andromeda Institute earlier in the evening. My...my assistant said that people sometimes make sizable donations to Dr. Davenport."

"I was wondering about that myself," Dan said. "Is there anything else you can tell us about her?"

"When she used to come into my shop, she was on the quiet side. She was always looking for something to ease her rheumatism."

"A chronic illness would make her an easy mark for a con man like Davenport," Dan pointed out.

"The Servant of Darkness. Do you know what that means?" Lowell broke in.

"Sounds like someone who serves the devil," she guessed.

THE SERVANT of Darkness. The Burning. Satan. Saraaa.

Sabrina jerked erect as she sat in the police car. In the exigency of the moment, when she'd been worried about so many other things, it had simply been a strangled sound trickling from the lips of a dying woman. In the silence of the car, it took on meaning.

It wasn't just a sound. It was a name. Sara. The name of the woman in her story.

A bead of perspiration formed at Sabrina's hairline and slid down the back of her neck.

Was she really getting this right? Or had her mind conjured up the connection?

Her story. Reality. She'd convinced herself they were like two sets of train tracks running beside each other. But she could feel them converging. Her story. The fire she'd imagined at the cemetery. The Servant of Darkness. June Garrison. In some mysterious way, they were connected.

THE STORY she was writing. It was her only clue to what was going on. Sabrina had to go back to it. Before it was too late.

Later that night, she settled herself on the sofa and took her pen in hand. Then, swiftly and surely, the pen began to move across the page.

When Duncan turned her in his arms, Sara could only stare up at him, her eyes heavy-lidded. Then reason stabbed at her sharply like a knife in her breast.

This was wrong. It could lead nowhere. Not between a girl from the village and a laird.

"Duncan. Nay."

He ignored her plea as his lips descended to hers. Her hands pushed against his chest. Her body tried to twist out of his arms. But he held her tight—tight. And there was only one place she could escape....

SABRINA GASPED air into her lungs with the desperation of a drowning swimmer who finally breaks the surface of the water. The room had no reality. It was too warm. Too comfortable. Too modern.

Sabrina pressed her palms against her forehead, feeling as if she were wandering in a cruel maze where every path led to disaster. Was there nowhere she could find refuge from danger? She'd taken up pen and paper to find out what June Garrison had been trying to tell her when she'd died. Fleeing to her Scottish story hadn't given her any answers.

SABRINA CHECKED the cash register to make sure there was enough change, as she did every morning, but she was thinking about Luther Davenport. If he saw her as a business rival and wanted to discredit her, he'd gotten a wonderful start last night.

Sabrina pulled a phone book from under the counter and found Hilda's number. Might Hilda know something? When she picked up the receiver, she realized Erin was on the phone, talking to someone in a low voice.

"Oh, sorry."

"Sabrina? I'll be off in a jiffy."

Her assistant came out of the back room a few minutes later carrying a box full of decorative metal tea canisters. Sabrina tried Hilda again. But there was no answer.

Sabrina was conscious that Erin was hovering around her. "Are you sure you don't want to sit down for a cup of tea and a chat?" her assistant finally asked.

"No. I need to work. Why don't we change the window display. Let's use those canisters, and some of our silver jewelry, too."

"Yes. Maybe that's what we both need," Erin agreed.

At twelve-thirty Dan found Sabrina in the lobby staring at the shop window. Turning to Dan, she felt a rush of pleasure.

"Hi" was all she said.

"Hi, yourself."

She'd thought he'd be dressed for the office. Instead he was wearing jeans and a turquoise knit top that was wonderful with his blond hair and tanned complexion.

"Where are we going?" she blurted.

"I'm planning to kidnap you."

As SABRINA BUCKLED her seat belt, she slid Dan a quick glance. His expression was grim.

"You didn't have to take me to lunch."

"I wanted to."

"Are you going to tell me what's making you so uptight?" she asked.

He didn't answer.

"Is it about the case? Has something happened that I should know about?"

"It's my problem, not yours," he said cryptically as he started the car.

Dan kept his eyes glued to the noontime traffic. He had a lot to worry about, starting with the June Garrison preliminary autopsy report and how it affected the Graveyard Murder case.

The chief of police had had something to say about that one, and it hadn't been a very enjoyable conversation. Dan had been angry and frustrated.

He'd come away from the meeting needing to feel that there was *something* effective he could do. Getting Sabrina out of the city had been the most constructive alternative he could conjure up. He hadn't even let himself think about how much he simply wanted to be with her.

So he'd called up her assistant and made the arrangements.

His jaw clenched, and the cords of his neck tightened. He didn't want to start a conversation about the police report on June Garrison. Or about the way he'd brought Sabrina into the Graveyard Murder case in the first place. From a personal point of view, that was the worst part of all.

However, sooner or later he'd have to come clean with her. But please, God, not yet.

DAN HEADED toward the Science Center, and Sabrina guessed they were going to eat at the Rusty Scupper, several blocks farther on. Instead he pulled up at the entrance to the marina. After cutting the engine, he got out and unlocked the trunk. Inside was a plastic cooler, a shopping bag and a wicker hamper.

"What's all that?"

"Lunch. If you take the hamper, I'll take the rest."

She tested the weight of the basket. "You must have an enormous appetite."

"Yeah." He led her toward one of the small piers. She followed him to a tidy cabin cruiser named *Legal Eagles*.

AS THE BOAT reached open water, the scarf Sabrina was wearing began to blow around her face. Taking it off, she wound it around the handle of the wicker hamper. Then, curious about what Dan had brought, she began poking through the contents of the ice chest. He had obviously gone overboard at the Harborplace food stalls.

"I repeat, this is *lunch?*" she asked as she set out containers on the table in the cockpit.

Dan anchored the boat and sat down in one of the low chairs. "I was working off nervous energy shopping."

Sabrina took a sip of soda. "I'd feel more comfortable if I told you something," she said before she lost her nerve.

"Oh?"

"It has to do with what happened last night at the Institute."

"About Davenport? Something you've remembered?"

"It's about the stuff Davenport gave Edward, the cowboy. He had it in a little bottle. And when Edward lurched against him, the stopper must have gone flying. I found it and picked it up."

"That's withholding evidence. You had an obligation to turn it over to me. Why the hell didn't you?" The question exploded out of him, belying the relaxed pose he'd been cultivating.

Sabrina shrank back. "Did I?"

"It could be important. If we can get an analysis."

Sabrina knit her fingers together in her lap.

Dan stared at her. Then he climbed out of his seat and came over beside her, reaching for her. She held herself stiffly as she felt his hands on her shoulders. "Sabrina, I'm sorry," he muttered. "You didn't deserve that."

His hands tightened on her shoulders. Then they dropped to his sides, and he returned to his chair. "I've been trying to keep my problems to myself. Maybe that was a stupid idea."

"I think that's true for both of us."

"You know, I've had a man in custody for the Graveyard Murders. Raul Simmons. I never thought the case against him was very strong. It was blown to hell in a hand bucket this morning."

"Why is that?"

"Because the graveyard victims died of exactly the same poison that killed June Garrison."

Sabrina felt a wave of cold sweep across her body.

"The stopper should go to the police lab," Dan said after a moment.

"I already gave it to a friend who's in the medical research business."

He looked as if he were mentally counting to ten. "You're sure you can trust her?"

"Of course. She's very reliable. And she knows how to keep things confidential."

Dan seemed somewhat mollified. "When are you supposed to get the results?"

"Later today."

"I hope you're planning to share them with me."

"At this point, it would be stupid not to. And...and...there's something else I have from the Institute."

"What?"

Sabrina pulled her purse over, retrieved two cassettes and handed them to Dan. He read the titles.

"'Tapping Every One of Your Inner Resources' and 'The Uses of Imagination.' You bought these? What's he asking for them, ten dollars apiece?"

"No. That's the funny part. Everything else is for sale at inflated prices. These are free."

Dan turned the boxes over in his hand. "One's got a little silver dot in the corner. I wonder what that means."

Sabrina shrugged.

Dan stood up. "I'd like to have a listen. I've got a recorder in the cabin."

"I wish you had a phone so I could call my friend and see if she's got that lab report," Sabrina mused.

"Actually, I do. A portable. It and the recorder are both stored where the salt air won't ruin the electronics." Dan descended the short flight of steps to the boat's interior. Sabrina followed.

"You'll probably get better reception up on the deck," Dan said as he set the recorder and the phone on the table.

"Before I call, could I ask what you found out about June Garrison?"

Dan sighed. "I've brought you a summary of the report. You can look over it later and see if anything strikes you."

Dan searched through one of the bags he'd brought and handed Sabrina several sheets of paper, which she tucked into her purse.

He slipped his arm across her shoulders. "It's going to take some more digging to figure out her role."

"So I'm supposed to go back to my herbs and pretend that everything is peachy?"

"The police will find out more."

"But I'm just small potatoes. What do they care about unsubstantiated threats?"

"I care." Dan's hand shot out and covered hers. "And I can't take any more of this."

"Any more of what?" she whispered.

"Pretending this conversation is only business."

"You're saying it isn't?"

"It would be, if you were simply another witness."

"What am I?" Sabrina whispered.

He still couldn't spell it out any clearer in words. Sabrina had half turned, ready to take the phone up on deck. He pulled her against him, her back to his front. His hands went to her shoulders, kneading and stroking as if he were starving for the contact. And he was. Greedily his fingers tangled in her hair. When he lifted the heavy tresses to stroke her neck, he felt a shiver go through her body. "Duncan did that to Sara," she murmured.

"Who the hell is Duncan? And Sara?" Even as he said the

names, he felt a dangerous ripple of sensation sweep over his body. Then he turned her to face him, searching her eyes as if they held the answers to all the questions he didn't want to ask.

"I'm not going to let you go," he muttered. Then he pulled her tightly into his embrace, unable to hold back the surge of emotion that swept over him.

Dan could feel her surprise, and then her panic as his lips moved urgently, potently over hers, demanding a response.

He deepened the kiss with deliberate ruthlessness. He knew the instant that she surrendered. Relief and triumph took him as he felt a shudder sweep over her.

"Hold on to me," he growled against her mouth.

Her hands climbed his arm, anchored to his shoulders and stayed put.

"Yes," he grated as his mouth took deeper, fuller possession of hers.

His fingers stroked up and down her arms, then found the sides of her breasts. The tiny moan of surrender was like a shock wave zinging through him.

Deep inside, Sabrina knew she'd been waiting for something like this since he'd walked through the door of her shop.

She was his.

One of his muscular hands tangled urgently in her hair, angling her head so that he could plunder her mouth from a new angle. The other hand slid to the swell of her breast. When his fingers found the hard point of her nipple, pleasure shot downward through her body.

She knew he felt her response as he shifted her in his arms, pulling her more tightly into his heat and hardness. He held her close, close for several moments longer. Then he eased his body away from hers.

She heard him cursing softly. "I had to do that," he murmured. "I'm sorry."

She'd been lost in a world where only two of them existed. Her eyes blinked open. Light-headed, she tried to get a grip on reality.

"I'm taking advantage of you again," he confessed.

"Are you?"

"You may think so later."

"Dan?"

"Go make that call," he said thickly. "Before I forget we *do* have business to take care of."

AT THE GUNWALE Sabrina stood for a moment looking out at the water and taking in large drafts of the salt air. After a moment's hesitation, she began to dial. The switchboard put her right through to her friend, Katie.

"I've got the information you want."

"Great."

Downstairs in the cabin, Sabrina thought she heard Dan make some kind of exclamation above the sound of Davenport's voice. Glancing in his direction, she saw his back was turned to her, making it impossible to catch his eye.

"I'm sorry we took so long," Katie said. "We were looking for something beyond the obvious. But as far as we can tell, there's nothing very startling about this sample. It's a very common stimulant." She named a compound that Sabrina had heard of.

"Um."

"Is that what you expected?"

"I don't know. So it's not a specific antidote for any poison," Sabrina mused. Probably they'd hit another dead end. She looked at Dan again. He stood up quickly and walked toward the counter in the galley area. Was he getting something to eat while he listened to the tape?

"Is the use of the stimulant consistent with the kind of dramatic revival I described?" she asked Katie.

"It could be. Depending on what caused the man's problem in the first place."

"Which we don't know." Sabrina's mind was only half on the conversation now. A wisp of odor drifted toward her. Fruit.

"I've got a written analysis for you," Katie said. "Should I mail it?"

"Umm...hold it at the lab, and I'll pick it up later."

Sabrina was barely paying attention to her friend as she replaced the receiver. With a strange sense of urgency, she set the phone down on the padded bench along the gunwale. As she started toward the stairway to the cabin, the aroma she'd noticed a few moments ago became stronger, and she realized what she was smelling.

The frighteningly familiar odor of rotten cherries.

Oh God, the drug that had hit them in the car. Somehow, here it was on the boat.

Pulse pounding, Sabrina peered into the cabin. Dan was still standing with his back toward her at the galley counter. She heard him curse, saw him bang his fist against the table.

"Dan?"

He didn't answer, didn't react as if he'd heard her at all.

"Dan?" Sabrina called again.

He turned and took a deliberate step toward her. The spark of madness gleamed in the blue depths of his eyes as he advanced, breathing heavily.

"Old witch. What have ye done, old witch?" Dan cried out.

"What?"

"Witch!"

He was advancing purposefully on her now, his right hand raised. Something metallic glinted in the afternoon sunlight, and she saw an eight-inch-long knife that must have come from the galley.

"Dan, what are you doing? It's me, Sabrina."

"No more of your tricks!"

His face a mask of hatred, he kept advancing on her, still swaying slightly so that she alternated between fear of what he might do to her and fear that he would be the one to get hurt.

"Dan," she tried again, her voice rising unsteadily. "I'm not the witch. I'm Sabrina."

"Ye lie," he shouted as he lunged toward her. The knife swung down in an arc. Sabrina dodged aside.

"Dan. It's Sabrina. Dan!" she shouted again, praying that the drug was wearing off, praying that she could get through to him.

MINUTES LATER, Sabrina reached the top of the ladder and scrambled across the flying bridge. Then she was sliding down the windshield at the front of the boat. She landed unevenly on the foredeck, twisting her ankle.

Dan leaped to the deck right behind her. As Sabrina tried to dodge away, he caught her legs and brought her down in a flying tackle that knocked the breath out of her chest in a painful blow.

Half gasping, half sobbing, she fought to wriggle out of Dan's clutches. They rolled together on the deck, both breathing heavily.

Sabrina tried to pull away. When that didn't work, she beat at him with her fists.

"Dan! No!"

"Gotta kill ya. Gotta kill the old witch," he muttered. "Gotta kill ya. Gotta do it for Sara."

AND THEN, suddenly, it was over. Dan's head snapped up. Dull blue eyes blinked and finally focused.

"Dan, it's me. It's Sabrina," she said. He didn't move. He didn't breathe.

"The drug. Like in the car," Dan finally whispered.

"Yes."

"How?"

Sabrina's features contorted. "The tape I gave you," she said in a low voice. "Somehow the cassette must have been fixed to give off the vapor when it was played."

"Davenport," Dan muttered, his eyes still closed.

*

"SABRINA," Dan said gently. "You're a very giving, very caring person. But you've got to take care of yourself. Do you know how to pilot this launch?"

"Yes."

"Good. Because the best thing for you to do right now is to take this boat back to Baltimore so you can get off and walk away from me."

It took a moment for Sabrina to realize what she was hearing. "Dan, don't you understand? What happened a few minutes ago isn't your fault."

He gave her a considering look. As the silence stretched, she felt her nerves grow taut.

"Sabrina," he said at length, "what if I tell you I've been lying to you since you walked into our luncheon appointment?"

"What are you talking about?"

"I didn't ask to meet you because I wanted your help. I asked because I thought you might be a murderer."

Unable to move, Sabrina stared at Dan.

"What? What are you talking about?" she finally managed.

He swallowed sharply. "The police found one of the charms from your shop in the victim's pocket. The ones you put in with packages. That's why I was interested in them."

Sabrina could literally feel the blood draining from her face as she pushed herself away and stared into Dan's piercing blue eyes.

"You're making this up," she gasped. But even as she cried out the denial, there was a ringing in her ears, and for a moment the scene around them wavered and flickered as if it might slip out of existence and replace itself with something that had happened a long time ago. Yet the past was too dangerous a place for her to flee.

"I'm not making it up. It's the truth." His voice was flat and dead. Dan's face was as pale as hers. "I didn't know how you fit in. You could have been the technical adviser, supplying the witchcraft know-how."

Bits and pieces of the previous few days came flying back at her, each one as sharp and piercing as a broken shard of glass. Finally the one that stuck painfully in her psyche was the evening she'd come home from the Andromeda Institute and seen Dan spotlighted in the headlights of her car. "That night, after Davenport suckered me into trying to help Edward... My God, you weren't at my house waiting to comfort me. You were there to pump me for information."

"Yes."

"No wonder you didn't want to tell me who was under investigation." She gave a harsh little laugh. "You thought I was working for Davenport. Didn't you?"

"Yes. That night I did. Until you got that phone call from June Garrison. Then—"

He didn't finish the sentence. But it didn't matter. Sickness swept over Sabrina.

Savagely she twisted the key in the ignition. The engine sprang to life. Dan hadn't taken the boat very far from the mouth of the Patapsco. It wasn't going to be all that difficult to get back to Baltimore. The minute her feet touched the pier, she could walk away from everything she'd dared to hope for with him and never look back.

Or could she?

Sabrina stopped short.

WHAT *exactly* had Dan just said? Nothing at all about his feelings for her. In fact, now that she thought about it, she realized that he'd focused on the one thing that he knew would cut her to the very soul. His duplicity. He knew it was the only thing that would drive her away.

Why? To protect her? Sabrina closed her eyes, trying to come to grips with what she'd been feeling for days. Since the moment she and Dan Cassidy had set eyes on each other in Sabatino's dining room, there'd been something strange going on below the surface of reality. The feeling of disorientation. The feeling that she knew him well. The feeling that her destiny was wound up with his. She couldn't explain any of that, and she'd been afraid to probe too deeply.

Moving with deliberate swiftness, Sabrina cut the engine. As the motor sputtered and then stopped, Dan's head jerked up, and he stared at her.

"What are you doing?"

Without answering, she descended the ladder, walked to the anchor and sent it splashing into the water. For several seconds, she stood with her back to Dan, gathering her courage together.

Then she turned. "All right, Cassidy, I was going to run away just like you wanted. But I've changed my mind. I think you owe me the truth."

"I've told you the truth."

"Part of it. The part you wanted me to know. But you've left something out. You were trying to kill the witch. Is it because of the Graveyard Murders?"

"No."

"Then what?"

His expression was closed.

"All right, don't tell me about the witch. Tell me about Sara. Who is she?"

He slapped a fist against the deck and winced. "Dammit. All right. She...she looks something like you. But that's not so surprising. She lives in a little cottage near the mountains. She cures people with her herbs. The doctor doesn't like it. Neither does the witch. It's not too hard to figure out where I got any of that, either."

The hair on the back of Sabrina's neck felt as if someone had touched them with an electric cattle prod. "And what did the witch do to Sara?"

"There was a trial. The old woman tried to save herself by giving evidence against Sabrina—" He stopped abruptly. "I mean Sara. She told the judges that Sara was in league with the devil."

Sabrina sucked in a piercing breath. So that was where the story was leading. She opened her purse and pulled out several sheets of folded paper. "Maybe you'd better read this," she said.

Reluctantly Dan took the offered pages. Sabrina submitted no explanation. So, after one more questioning glance, he began to read.

Sabrina wasn't able to wrench her gaze away from his face. She was absorbed by the changing panorama of emotions as his eyes moved down the page.

"Where in the hell did you get this?'' he asked, his voice gritty.

"At first I thought I made it up. I used to tell myself tales about another time and another place when I was a kid. But this experience is different.'' Sabrina gestured toward the pages.

With a dark look, Dan crumpled the pages in his fist. Afraid he was going to toss the balled-up mass into the water, Sabrina scrambled up, rushed across the deck and pried his fingers open. "I'd like to keep the evidence, if you don't mind.''

"What evidence? I don't know what you think this proves. Under the influence of drugs, sometimes two people share an experience.''

"How can they, unless they plan it first, or agreed beforehand to communicate the images of whatever it is they're experiencing?''

Dan shrugged again, his expression closed.

"Besides, I started writing this before either one of us got cherry-bombed. Before we'd even met, for that matter.''

"So what conclusions do you draw?''

He didn't sound as if he particularly wanted to hear the answer. Sabrina laced her fingers together.

"What if you could talk to Sara, ask her some questions?''

"Oh, come on.''

"Dan, when I start writing the story, I...I sort of turn into her. I mean when I come out of it, I feel like her.''

His arms were folded tightly across his chest, and his shoulders were hunched. "Okay, Sabrina. If you want to try the experiment, I guess I owe you that much,'' he said in a low voice.

HE GAVE HER a little time to get started. As he peered down into the cabin, he could see her sitting at the table writing.

Duncan. Just thinking about him made her heart skip. She reached down and picked a handful of wintergreen and brought the leaves to her nose. There was something about the fresh minty scent that reminded her of Duncan. He'd been away for over a fortnight on business for his father, and she'd missed him with an ache that told her she cared too deeply. He'd come to her almost a dozen times since she'd returned from the castle last winter, all on the pretense of buying remedies for members of his family. After the purchases were made, he always lingered, wanting to talk and touch, and bring a blush of rose to her cheeks with his stirring kisses.

Sara sighed. She knew where things were leading, and it wasn't to the church. Duncan, Duncan, what am I gonna do with ye, lad?

She rounded the path to the mountain pass where she'd first met him. As if by some magic summons, there he was riding through the clearing on a spirited black horse. Sara blinked, sure she'd conjured up the image. But it was really him.

Soon, Duncan sat her on a flat rock. He removed a pouch from his horse and pulled a fine gold necklace from its depths.

"A trinket for a kiss." He opened her hand and placed the gift in her palm.

"Oh, Duncan. It's beautiful." Sara's fingers brushed over the intricate sunburst design on the gold medallion. "It's the prettiest thing I've ever had."

"Then wear it next to your heart and think kindly of the lad who brought it, will ye?"

"Aye."

Duncan took the necklace from her hands and slipped it over Sara's curly red hair. And soon she was letting him do more. Letting his hands mold and shape her breasts. Letting his fingers pull open the laces that held her bodice.

HE DIDN'T KNOW when he'd stopped reading, or when she'd stopped writing. When it had simply started happening. To both of them.

"Duncan. Dan. Don't stop. Not this time. Oh, please, don't stop."

The frantic entreaty came from the woman he held in his arms. The woman whose body moved and twisted against his with the same urgency he felt.

Present and past merged, wavered, tried to stabilize, and finally came to an uneasy accord.

But time and place were of little importance now. Not when this man and woman were finally in each other's arms, bound together by ties stronger than the forces that would tear them apart.

She had been born for him. Reborn for him.

A muffled sound of craving came from her throat. He drank it in like a man who'd somehow survived a long, parched season of need. In that instant, the terrible years of waiting were swept away. Banished.

"Duncan. Dan."

At the words she'd spoken, her eyes blinked open, colliding with his, held and locked. There was a new light—a new understanding—shining in their blue depths.

"Sara. I lost you once," he rasped. "I won't lose you again, Sabrina."

"You didn't believe me."

"Shh—I can't explain it. I only know I can't let you go." His voice was deep, urgent, persuasive.

The confusion of place and time persisted, tantalized, made them both dizzy. All the more reason to cling to the one solid reference point in the universe—each other.

Slowly the confusion gave way to abiding certainty as hands touched and lips brushed, giving and taking pleasure. Time was precious. And they had squandered far too much of it already.

They lay on their sides, facing each other on the narrow bunk. Touching. Kissing. Loving.

Neither one of them wanted to hurry. They drew out the pleasure, letting the power of their feelings build slowly, beautifully, until it was impossible to postpone the joining a moment longer.

He was inside her, then. Hard and deep and throbbing.

She looked up into his face, touched his cheek, murmured wordless syllables that both welcomed him and proclaimed her pleasure at their joining.

The slow pace was over almost as soon as he began to move, and her hips answered his. Now it was all blinding heat and urgency.

Climax took her, spreading out from the point of greatest pleasure in a series of shock waves that brought a cry of ecstasy to her lips. Then she felt him follow her into euphoria and her own rapture was complete.

It had begun slowly. It ended slowly.

"Perfect. That was so perfect."

"Yes."

Sabrina snuggled closer, wishing that nothing would intrude. But now that her body was returning to normal, her mind struggled to make sense of what had happened. "The witch tried to keep it from happening. This time, we won." Sabrina didn't know she'd spoken aloud until she felt Dan's body stiffen. Raising her head, she saw the shock of recognition in his eyes.

He nodded slowly, as though trying to deal with a totally alien concept that had come to hold the ring of undeniable truth.

"Dan, what's going on?"

"I don't know."

"But you believe me? That it was us, all those years ago? That we've come back to finish something?" she asked, holding her breath as she waited for his answer.

"Making love with you was like the fulfillment of a promise someone made a long time ago."

"Yes," she breathed.

Their eyes locked and held for wild heartbeats.

"Making love to you isn't going to keep you safe," Dan said as he got up and opened the drawers under the bunk. When they'd both gotten dressed, he pointed toward the ice chest and hamper they'd stowed in the galley. "I can offer you dinner, though."

She nodded, remembering the quantity of food he'd brought. "Was dinner part of your plans?"

"I guess it was in the back of my mind."

It was almost dark when they came back up on deck. Dan turned on the running lights, and they pulled their chairs close to each other, getting out food and drinks in the semidarkness.

After a few minutes, Dan reached for her hand. "Tell me about your story. The parts I haven't read."

Sabrina began to fill in details, knitting her fingers through his as she spoke. There'd been no one she thought would understand. It was a wonderful relief to simply let the tale pour out.

When there was nothing more to tell, they sat in silence, hands clasped.

"The thing I'm thinking," she whispered, "is that we came back to stop some evil that's survived the centuries."

"The witch's evil," Dan muttered.

SABRINA SAT forward in her seat. "Dan, we have to know more. Would you mind...what about if I try writing it again?"

"So you can find out if Duncan betrayed Sara?"

Sabrina took her bottom lip between her teeth. "If he did, we need that information," she said in a voice that was barely above a whisper.

Neither one of them spoke as they stored the food and went back into the cabin. Trying to look purposeful, Sabrina set the pad of paper and the pen on the table. She was about to sit when she felt Dan's hands on her shoulders.

"Not yet." Turning her quickly, he brought her body tightly against his. "It was getting cold in Scotland the last time you were there. I want you to take something with you to keep you warm."

His lips molded themselves to hers. His fingers combed through her wild red hair.

Her wordless little murmurs were lost in his kiss as her hands slid up and down his strong arms.

When he finally lifted his head, they were both trembling.

"I'd better start," Sabrina whispered.

...Bam. Bam. Bam! The pounding on the door was loud enough to wake the dead. But it was more fear than aggravation that captured Sara Campbell as she moved away from the warmth of the fire and went to answer the urgent call.

"Who is it and what do ye want?"

"Murray Frye to see the healer."

She opened the door a bit and held the candle up to illuminate Frye's face.

"Mistress Campbell. The lass Megan has taken a turn for the worse. We dinna think she'll make it through till morning. I've come to fetch you to town."

"Let's go."

The ride into town was cold and dark.

The family's greeting was tense as they ushered her into their small stone abode. A crackling fire burned in the hearth. Megan lay moaning on her cot.

Sara dropped to her side and laid a hand on her forehead. The child's skin was cold and clammy. Her pupils were dilated, and from her tortured utterings, a wild dream must be haunting her sleep. "I dinna think she has the fever. It must be something else. Help me loosen her dress."

The light wool slid from the girl's shoulders, revealing a series of ugly red patches. Behind her, family members gasped in horror.

"The mark of a witch!" Murray exclaimed.

"No. No. The work of poison, I think," Sara said as she straightened and turned toward the family.

Sara's palms were clammy cold as the men pushed her outside into the bitter cold. After her hands were securely tied with coarse rope, they left her under Murray's guard. "Please let me go. I'll do you no harm."

"Too late for that now. I was at the castle today and heard there will be a reward out for your capture by tomorrow morning. I've got you now, and I'm meaning to collect the gold," the young man sneered.

"Reward? I've done nothing wrong. There must be some mistake. Duncan McReynolds will vouch for me."

"He's not here to vouch for you, my girl. You'll have to tell it to the judges at your trial, now won't you? But when they find the evil-eye symbol under your bed, that will clinch it."

SHE WAS COLD, so cold. As if icy fingers had wrapped themselves around her very bones. She tried to speak. All she could manage was a shaky exclamation.

"Sabrina. Come back. It's all right."

"Dan. Oh, Dan." All she wanted to do was cling to his strength, burrow into his warmth. He held her, rocked her, murmured reassuring words.

"It's like...at the Institute." Sabrina groped for words. "She was tricked into treating someone...."

"It was the other way around at the Institute," Dan said, the grating sound of his voice telling her how much he'd just been shaken.

Sabrina tipped her face toward his. "It's all right. It's going to be all right."

"I don't think so. I didn't keep you warm, did I? He wasn't there to help her when she needed him either."

"Dan, you don't know. Maybe Duncan came back."

"I wouldn't count on it."

THE LIGHTS of the city twinkled in the distance, beckoning them closer. It should have been beautiful sailing into the harbor. Yet Sabrina felt her stomach tightening.

For a summer evening, the pier area looked strangely deserted, Sabrina thought as she climbed out and began to secure the mooring line. As soon as she'd finished, she was surrounded by several men who had come rushing out of the shadows. Two wore business suits. Two were uniformed police officers.

Sabrina took a step back.

"Don't move. Raise your hands above your head," one of the men shouted.

It was then Sabrina saw they all had guns drawn. And they were all pointed at her.

She couldn't have moved if her life had depended on it. All at once she realized the speaker was Brian Lowell, the man who had directed the operation at the train station.

"Ms. Sabrina Barkley?"

"Yes. Of course. We...we...know each other."

"I said raise your hands above your head."

"Wh-what?" Sabrina stammered through her confusion, making an effort to comply.

Behind her she heard a curse, just before Dan's feet hit the deck.

"Stay where you are, Cassidy," Lowell called out.

"What the hell's going on?" Dan demanded, his chin raised in anger toward the man in charge. Both detectives boarded the boat.

"Ms. Barkley is under arrest for the murder of Luther Davenport."

SABRINA WAS allowed to make a phone call. It was to Laura Roswell, the only lawyer she knew. Laura and her assistant, Noel Emery, arrived at the station in less than half an hour. Noel came right in to see Sabrina. Laura went to find out what she could about the case.

"I was able to find out some things upstairs," Laura said, when she returned. "Davenport died very early Friday morning. But since he was supposed to be on a trip, his assistant didn't find him until just before lunch. A ten-thousand-dollar donation from June Garrison is also reported missing."

"But how could they think I was responsible for any of that?" Sabrina asked.

"There's a lot of circumstantial evidence. Last night at the Andromeda Institute, several witnesses saw Davenport humiliate you during the medical emergency."

Sabrina felt the ball of tension in her stomach start to grow. "I felt like he did it on purpose. But surely that's not a motive for murder and robbery."

"They also found another one of your gold charms in Davenport's office."

"And they think I'm stupid enough to commit a bunch of murders and leave such an obvious calling card?" Sabrina asked

through gritted teeth. "Are they charging me with the Graveyard
Murders, too?"

"For the time being, it's just this one." Laura pressed her hand
again. "But you've got to hear the rest of it before we can start
to put together your case," Laura said.

Sabrina braced for more bad news. "Okay. What else do they
have?"

"The police got a search warrant for your house."

"But they couldn't possibly find anything there," she exclaimed
in disbelief.

"They did. Ten thousand dollars in cash in June Garrison's
original bank envelope stuffed into the back of your desk drawer."

"But I don't know anything about the money."

"Someone obviously planted it there," Noel put in. "I guess it
was whoever really killed Davenport."

"Is there anything else?" Sabrina asked.

Laura sighed. "After they found the money, they went tramping
around your property and discovered a stand of lily of the valley
growing out back."

"Since when is it against the law to grow them?" Sabrina
asked.

"The preliminary results are in from Davenport's autopsy. Lily
of the valley poisoning was the cause of death."

"As soon as you get some rest, we're going to start working on
the case," Laura said after Sabrina had been released on five-
hundred-thousand-dollar bond guaranteed by Cameron Randolph,
the husband of her friend Jo. "I know a very sought-after criminal
lawyer who has agreed to be part of the defense team."

"Yes. Thanks. Have you found out anything we can use? What
about Davenport's tapes?"

"The police lab has checked several of them. They do have
subliminal messages. But none of them is drugged."

Sabrina had hoped for more.

"I also talked to Dan Cassidy's office."

Sabrina flinched.

"He's been ordered off the case. And ordered to stay away from
you. Apparently the department is furious about the way he handled things."

AFTER WASHING off the jailhouse stench under an almost scalding
hot shower, Sabrina came downstairs. Physically she felt better.

But she was still all torn up inside. When she thought about Dan, tears gathered in her eyes.

As she sat at the table, she felt as if the kitchen walls were closing in around her. It was all coming together again. She'd assumed that this time around Davenport and the witch were one and the same. Now the only conclusion she could come to was that the witch was alive and well and had set her up again. She had no idea how she was going to confront the overwhelming evidence in the present case. But she still had another avenue of attack. She could try to find out what had happened before.

Hope leaped in her breast as she ran to get a pad of paper from her desk. She didn't know how the story ended. Maybe Duncan had come back in time to save Sara. Maybe that meant Dan was...was...

Sabrina closed her eyes for a moment, willing herself not to hope for anything from Dan. It was better not to think about the man and his motives.

Taking a pad of paper from her desk, she grabbed a pen and sat at the kitchen table.

In the days before her trial Sara had undergone the humiliation of being stripped and examined by several clergymen for a witch's mark. The brown mole she'd had on her bottom since she was born was judged to be conclusive. Even after that terrible experience, she'd clung to the hope that Duncan would come back and pluck her from the mess she was in.

There'd been witnesses against Lillias Weir, too, with plenty of ghastly tales to tell. In the end, Sara suspected, nothing she nor Lillias said or did would have made any difference. After less than an hour of deliberation, the court had found them both guilty and sentenced them to a public burning in seven days.

At noon on the seventh day, they came for her. As she was hustled toward the town square, flanked by guards on either side, she held her head up high. She had done nothing wrong. Let them remember later that she'd gone to her death with dignity.

The crowd was large and jeering. Their cruel shouts echoed in her ears as the burly men led her to the stake. Then Lillias was brought forward. This was the first time Sara had seen her since the trial. The woman appeared to have aged ten years.

Sara couldn't hold back a frightened cry as the men with the torches came forward and the acrid smoke drifted toward her. The evil smell grew worse as they touched the burning tips to the tinder-dry straw.

She screamed in terror and then in pain, twisting against her bonds, trying with all her strength to get away from the flames licking at her clothes and her skin. The crackling sound surrounded her.

Then the only thing she could hear above the roar of the fire was Lillias's shrill voice. It seemed to build in power. Like the flames.

"I curse the lot of ye in this foul town. This is not the end. It is but a pause. The circle will not be complete until the Servant of Darkness prevails."

HARRY ROSENBERG, the attorney who'd agreed to help with Sabrina's case, had a defense strategy that seemed to revolve around finding who had framed Sabrina.

Good luck, Sabrina thought as Erin drove her home from his office. Tired and dispirited by the four-hour meeting, she flaked out on the couch. Since there was hardly anything to eat in the refrigerator, Erin volunteered to go out and get some groceries.

A while later, Sabrina's eyes blinked open. She'd hardly slept the night before, but under the circumstances, she hadn't expected to fall asleep.

"Feeling better?" Erin asked in a voice that sounded artificially chipper as she set down several plastic bags on the kitchen counter.

"A little." Sabrina glanced at her watch. Had Erin really been gone almost two hours? It couldn't have taken that long to get the groceries.

Erin was putting the milk in the refrigerator when the phone rang. "I'll get it."

"Who is it?" Sabrina asked as she came into the kitchen.

Erin jumped. "Oh, I didn't know you were standing there. It's...it's Gwynn Frontenac."

Sabrina sighed and reached for the phone. Erin handed her the receiver and then busied herself with putting groceries away. "Yes?"

"Oh, Sabrina, I read about you in the papers. I want to tell you how sorry I was to hear that you'd been falsely accused."

"Yes, well, thanks..."

"My dear, I know you must be trying to marshal your defenses," Gwynn intoned.

"Yes."

There was a pause during which Sabrina felt her fingers tighten painfully on the receiver.

"I think I might have some information that would be helpful."

"About what?"

"The Servant of Darkness."

THE SKY WAS overcast, and a few raindrops were just starting to sprinkle across Sabrina's windshield as she turned onto the long, tree-lined drive that led to Gwynn Frontenac's house.

Sabrina, who had never been before, stared in fascination at the structure. It was one of those monstrosities the newly rich sometimes built in order to make a statement.

Although the house was ugly, that didn't make it sinister. Still, she was glad she wasn't going in there alone. While she'd gotten ready, Erin had called Noel, who had agreed to meet her. But she hadn't shown up yet. Sabrina tapped her fingers nervously on the steering wheel as she waited for her friend. A curtain stirred at one of the windows. Was Gwynn looking out, wondering why she was sitting in her car? Sighing, Sabrina got out and rang the bell. Gwynn, who opened the door herself, was dressed in a bright orange-and-green-silk dress accented with heavy gold jewelry.

A mixture of relief and anticipation flashed across her features. "Sabrina, I'm so glad you could make it."

"I'm anxious to hear whatever you know that might help my case."

"Yes. I'm sure you are. Come inside and we'll have a nice cup of your herb tea while I tell you all about it."

"Noel Emery is supposed to be meeting me here," Sabrina said uncertainly as she turned and looked back down the driveway.

"Yes. She just phoned. She's running a bit late and said for us to go ahead and get started."

With a grimace, Sabrina stepped across the threshold.

Gwynn locked the door and pocketed the key before leading the way down a hall into a formal living room.

Soon, Gwynn was handing her a cup. "I need to give you some background, Sabrina. You know Hilda was the one who got me interested in Dr. Davenport."

"Yes." Sabrina took a sip from her cup.

Gwynn looked uncomfortable. "I don't want to tell tales about a friend. But I think she was somehow emotionally involved with the man."

Earlier, the chill of the house had enfolded Sabrina. As she sipped her tea, she realized she was starting to feel warm and a little light-headed. She loosened the button at her neck.

"Are you okay?" Gwynn asked.

"Yes. I think so. What do you mean by 'emotionally involved'?"

"I'm afraid Hilda might have developed a romantic interest in the doctor. She hung on to everything he said, wrote him letters, even asked my opinion about some of the notes he sent her."

"He wrote her letters?"

Gwynn nodded. "But I could tell he was leading her on. I suspect he was only interested in getting her to make a big contribution to the Andromeda Institute. Perhaps she found out."

"You're not trying to say you think she killed him, are you?"

"Well, he may have been playing this game with other women, too. But when you finish your tea you ought to take a look at some of the letters she sent him. They're upstairs in my workroom."

SABRINA LET herself be guided to the stairs, and began to climb with Gwynn at her elbow. Her legs felt heavy as if she were wearing lead boots. They gained the second floor and walked down another hall. It was dark with a slight sickly sweet smell.

Gwynn's fingers dug into her arm.

"The letters are in here," Gwynn said, stepping aside so that Sabrina could precede her into a room a little farther down the hall.

It was a workroom, the source of the sickly-sweet odor in the hall. As Sabrina stepped inside, she could see the walls were lined with shelves of glass jars. Some contained familiar leaves. Others held molds and fungi and things she didn't want to examine too closely.

Suddenly Sabrina felt a web of power stronger than any mortal hands grip her, hold her.

"There are a lot of advantages to being a rich widow," Gwynn murmured. "I'm not an ignorant country bumpkin this time. So I have more weapons at my disposal to defeat those who defy me. Now, turn around and submit to me."

In slow motion, every movement a terrible effort as her muscles fought the command, Sabrina turned to face the large woman.

Gwynn looked completely transformed. The slightly dotty widow had vanished. In her place was someone who knew she wielded power. She was holding up a wide velvet cord emblazoned with the evil-eye symbol.

"Don't move. I have you now. Soon we will be going upstairs to complete the ceremony," Gwynn ordered, her voice high and piercing.

Fear welled up from deep in Sabrina's soul. *Run.*

WHATEVER WAS in the tea had fogged her brain, making it difficult to reason, difficult to make her limbs work.

Somehow Sabrina kept herself focused as she staggered down the hall.

At the stairs, she hesitated. Instead of going down, Sabrina began to climb. On the third floor, she began to try doors again. Finally she found one that was unlocked.

She entered the room. It took a moment for her to remember that she'd have to secure the lock so that Gwynn couldn't follow. When she turned back to face the room, she tried to stifle a gasp of shock. Even under ordinary circumstances, the place would have been frightening.

The walls were shrouded by midnight curtains, except for the strange symbols that broke the surface on either side of the door. The only illumination came from the candelabra fitted with tall white tapers placed at intervals around the room.

Sabrina wanted to back out of the door. She'd made a terrible mistake, but now there was no place else to go. She pressed her shoulders against the stout wood as she waited for her eyes to adjust to the eerie, flickering light.

She had run up here and trapped herself. This was what Gwynn had wanted all along.

The sudden knowledge that she wasn't alone was an icy breeze blowing across Sabrina's skin. Paralyzed, unable to breathe, she watched as a figure shouldered itself partway out of the concealing drapery and stood in stark relief against the black background.

Gwynn. Somehow the witch had gotten in here. Through another entrance.

Sabrina fumbled for the lock.

But the tall masculine figure wasn't Gwynn in her blaze of bright silk. Instead Sabrina found she was staring at a disheveled Dan Cassidy. His white shirt hung open where buttons had been pulled off. His blond hair dangled in his face. And as he tried to thrust farther forward, Sabrina saw that his hands were pulled in back of him and fastened to a stout wooden post.

When she took a step toward him, he began to shake his head and twist his body furiously against the post. But there was no hesitation on Sabrina's part. He needed her, and she went to him. Then she saw the ugly red gash partially hidden by the hair that had fallen across his forehead.

"Dan. My God, Dan." With fingers that felt insensitive as metal prongs, she clawed at the scarf that served as a gag. Finally she dragged it down so that it fell around his neck.

"Get out of here," he rasped as soon as he could speak.

"What?"

"Sabrina, it's a setup."

She blinked, trying to take the words in. "I'm not leaving you here." She dropped to her knees and began to inspect the coarse hemp that bound his wrists. It was wound securely around the wooden post.

As she worked at his bonds, Dan talked to her in a low, urgent voice. "Sabrina, she told me a lot of stuff after she tied me up. She's Lillias come back. She's got a whole group of people so frightened and captive to her persuasive techniques that they'll do anything she says. Sign over their insurance to her. Steal from their employers. If you try to cross her, you end up dead. Like the graveyard victims. She killed them as a warning."

"And June Garrison?"

"She was working for her. She figured out some of what was going on and tried to get Gwynn to take her on as an equal partner. Gwynn drugged her and used her to spy on you and Davenport—and to set you up for his murder. She's absolutely ruthless. She's already killed four times that we know of and maybe a lot more. Now, get out of here. Save yourself."

Sabrina ignored the advice. If Gwynn had told Dan that much, she didn't expect that he was going to be able to pass the information on. But why had he fallen into her trap? "How did she get you?" she panted without pausing in her task.

"She said she had information that would save you." His voice was raw.

Sabrina's eyes shot to Dan's. They locked and held as her fingers gripped his.

The door rattled. Sabrina's heart leaped into her throat. Dan swore vehemently. The clatter continued as Sabrina's fingers began to work more frantically at his bonds. He gave a mighty jerk, and the left hand came away with the rope dangling.

"Sabrina." He pulled her into his arms, clamping her tightly against him so that the medallion around her neck was squeezed between them.

For a burning moment, neither one of them moved. Then Dan tore his eyes away from Sabrina's face. "We've got to get out of here," he grated. "Before it's too late."

All at once, a sickeningly familiar smell drifted toward them. Rotten cherries. Lord, no.

Holding her breath, Sabrina dashed toward the door and tried to twist the lock. To her horror she found that it no longer turned. She'd thought Gwynn was trying to get in. Instead she'd locked the door from the outside.

Dan picked up a candlestick and raised it like a club.

"Drop it," Gwynn ordered, stepping into view. "Or I'll shoot your girlfriend." She must have come in through a door that was hidden by the draperies.

There was no escape. It was only a matter of time until Gwynn could do anything she wanted with them. Make them think anything she wanted.

As she looked toward the end of the room where the hallucinogen was pouring in, Sabrina saw their captor standing still as a statue watching them.

"Erin didn't call anyone except me. I have control of her mind."

"H-how?" Sabrina choked out, clinging by her fingernails to sanity.

"Subliminal messages on the music tapes I gave her. A little trick I picked up from my late friend Dr. Davenport. Isn't it wonderful how many more tools there are nowadays?"

Sabrina flinched, knowing this was a woman sure of her power, sure of her control.

Gwynn laughed. "And now I must insist you stay for the excitement of the ceremony. It just wouldn't be the same without the two of you."

Sabrina looked wildly around. Nowhere to turn.

"Sara," she called. "Sara, help me. Don't let it happen again."

"Stop! No!" the witch commanded. "Yield to my power over your mind."

Sabrina ignored the command. "Sara. Please, Sara. Come to me."

The air seemed to tremble. In the flickering light, the focus shifted. Back, back to another time. Before the scene could slip past, she reached out and clutched on to it, the way she'd clutched the pen when the writing had carried her back.

"No! Stop!" the witch cried out.

Sara ignored her. "Duncan, I need you, Duncan," she called. For an agonizing moment, she thought he wasn't going to come to her. Then he was beside her, grasping her shoulder. "Sara. It's not too late then, lass?"

"I won't let it be too late."

'Damn ye, Sara Campbell," the witch shrieked, her voice rising in a desperate wail. "Yield to me. Stop."

Duncan grasped her hand. With an urgent tug, he pulled her down behind the heavy table in the center of the room.

A crack of thunder sounded just as something hot and dangerous shot past Sara's head. Swearing, Duncan thrust her closer to the floor. "Give me the medal ye wear," he grated. "Be quick."

Thunder boomed again as Sara reached around her neck and pulled the medallion free. When she gave it to Duncan, he pressed her hand. Then he moved away from her so that he could swing the large metal pendant in a circle. Standing, he gave a bloodcurdling shout and let the missile fly, just as the thunder cracked again.

The metal disk crashed into one of the candelabra, tipping the brass fixture on its side. The candles hit the curtains, and the dry black fabric instantly blazed up.

"No. Duncan. What have ye done? What have ye done?" Sara cried out.

The witch shrieked.

With a shout of raw anger, Duncan lunged at the witch, knocking savagely at her hand. Then something heavy clunked to the floor. Somehow, Sara knew that Duncan had knocked a terrible weapon from the witch's grasp. In the next moment, he caught the large woman by the shoulders. With the victory cry of a Scottish warlord, he spun her around and sent her hurtling toward the burning draperies.

Sara was transfixed in horror. Wasting no time, Duncan caught her up in his arms and began to stumble toward the door Gwynn had used. A line of fire raced from the wall and tried to snare them. He leaped out of its path and stumbled toward the door. They were both choking and gasping in the smoky haze, and

Sara pressed her face into his shoulders and squeezed her eyes shut.

He surged across the threshold into blessedly cool air, and they both dragged oxygen into their burning lungs.

Duncan started toward the stairs. Sara gripped his shoulder. "Wait."

He looked at her questioningly.

Twisting back toward the burning room, Sara raised her head and began to speak in low, measured tones. "I call on the powers of good in the universe to put a final end to the Servant of Darkness. Lillias will not return to this earth. Her second chance is spent. She is vanquished, now and for all eternity."

A terrible scream of defeat and pain came from within the burning chamber. Then the flames were leaping from the doorway, and a thundering crash shook the floor. That was the last Sara saw before the world went black.

SABRINA'S EYES blinked open. She lay on the grass under the shelter of a tree, a coat blanketing her. For a frightened moment, she tried to remember where she was and how she'd gotten there. Then her gaze took in the ugly stone castle several hundred yards away. Flames flickered behind the windows and shot through the roof, sending a column of black smoke into the air.

All at once she remembered being in the middle of the fire. And the witch. She cringed in horror, until she felt a gentle hand on her shoulder.

"Easy, honey. You're safe. You just fainted, that's all."

"Duncan?"

"It's Dan."

Sabrina stared up at him. Duncan had come to her when she called him.

"It's all over." Dan's voice was edged with relief—and regret.

Sabrina's heart leaped into her throat. "What's all over?" she croaked.

"The horror. The murder case against you. Gwynn didn't plan on my leaving that room alive. So she told me a hell of a lot before you got there. About how she'd set up the Graveyard Murders so I'd suspect you," he grated. "And how she trumped up the Davenport case against you. I could have sent her to the electric chair—if she wasn't dead already." Dan's face had gone tight with strain. "I want you to know you're safe. From the witch. And from the district attorney's office."

"Yes. Thank you."

"If you'd rather not have anything more to do with me, I'll understand."

Suddenly it was almost impossible to draw air into her lungs. "Do—do you want me to have anything more to do with you?"

He swallowed hard. "Yes."

She reached out toward him. It was all the invitation he needed. Leaning down, he gently pulled Sabrina into his embrace. Her arm came up to circle his back. Her face pressed into his shoulder as she absorbed his scent, his strength, his essence. They clung to each other tightly.

"Oh, Dan, I was so scared. The fire. I'm so afraid of fire." She lifted her gaze from his face and stared at the burning building.

Dan found her hand and held it tightly.

"I love you, Sabrina. I have for a long, long time." He traced his fingers over her lips and stared at her as if he hardly believed his good fortune. He kissed her tenderly, lovingly, and then with more passion. And she returned the passion, murmuring her love for him against his lips.

Sabrina touched Dan's lips. "There's something else I want to do. Besides make love to you."

"Get married?"

"Are you proposing?" she asked, a smile dancing on her lips.

"It's about time, don't you think?"

She giggled, then turned serious again. "I want to go back to Scotland with you."

"It won't bring back bad memories?"

"Some. But I can cope with them now. They're not going to interfere with the good stuff." She caressed his cheek with her palm. "I'd like to see if we can find the place where they met."

"If that's what you want."

"Only if you're with me."

He pulled her into his arms, arms that had finally led her to safety, to love. "Sabrina, I'll always be with you."

DREAMSCAPES™
WHISPERS OF LOVE

Save $1.00 off the purchase of any 2 Silhouette® Dreamscapes™ titles.

$1.00 OFF!

any 2 Silhouette® Dreamscapes™ titles.

5 65373 00076 2   (8100) 0 10818

Where love comes alive™

SILHOUETTE® DREAMSCAPES™
WHISPERS OF LOVE

Save $1.00 off the purchase of any 2
Silhouette® Dreamscapes™ titles.

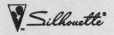

INTIMATE MOMENTS™
Romance, Adventure—Excitement!

Save $2.00 off the purchase of any 3
Silhouette Intimate Moments™ titles.

$2.00 OFF!
any 3 Silhouette Intimate Moments™ titles.

5 65373 00082 3 (8100)0 10819

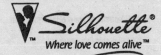

Where love comes alive™

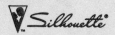

INTIMATE MOMENTS™
Romance, Adventure—Excitement!

Save $2.00 off the purchase of any 3
Silhouette Intimate Moments™ titles.

$2.00 OFF!

any 3 Silhouette Intimate Moments™ titles.

52603600

Where love comes alive™

HARLEQUIN®
INTRIGUE®
BREATHTAKING, ROMANTIC SUSPENSE

Save $1.00 off the purchase of any 2 Harlequin Intrigue® titles.

Visit us at www.eHarlequin.com
T5V8CHIUS
© 2001 Harlequin Enterprises Ltd.

HARLEQUIN®
Makes any time special ®

HARLEQUIN®
INTRIGUE®
BREATHTAKING, ROMANTIC SUSPENSE

Save $1.00 off the purchase of any 2 Harlequin Intrigue® titles.

Visit us at www.eHarlequin.com
T5V8CHICAN
© 2001 Harlequin Enterprises Ltd.

Harlequin Historicals®
Historical Romantic Adventure!

Save $1.00 off the purchase of any 2
Harlequin Historicals® titles.

Visit Harlequin at www.eHarlequin.com
T5V8CHHUS
© 2001 Harlequin Enterprises Ltd.

HARLEQUIN®
Makes any time special ®

Harlequin Historicals®
Historical Romantic Adventure!

Save $1.00 off the purchase of any 2 Harlequin Historicals® titles.

$1.00 OFF!
any 2 Harlequin Historicals® titles.

RETAILER: Harlequin Enterprises Ltd. will pay the face value of this coupon plus 10.25¢ if submitted by customer for this product only. Any other use constitutes fraud. Coupon is nonassignable. Void if taxed, prohibited or restricted by law. Consumer must pay any government taxes. Nielson Clearing House customers submit coupons and proof of sales to: Harlequin Enterprises Ltd., 661 Millidge Avenue, P.O. Box 639, Saint John, N.B. E2L 4A5. Non NCH retailer—for reimbursement submit coupons and proof of sales directly to: Harlequin Enterprises Ltd., Retail Marketing Department, 225 Duncan Mill Rd., Don Mills, Ontario M3B 3K9, Canada. Valid in Canada only.

**Coupon valid until June 30, 2002.
Redeemable at participating retail outlets in Canada only.
Limit one coupon per purchase.**

52604166

 HARLEQUIN®
Makes any time special®